JUSTIN RISHEL

Hollow Resolve

Book 3 of the Martin Aubrey Series

ROWDY DOG PRESS

For Dad. My hero.

Contents

Prologue

Neuros
Sci-World Productions, LTD.
Season 4, Episode 9, *Oh, AIME, You Are My Everything*
Postproduction Script. Director's notes in [brackets].

Camera shot rides on the back of a high speed microdrone, buzzing through the concrete, glass, and steel canyons of the high-tech metropolis of New Aberdeen, Maryland.

Narrator: At the time of its founding, New Aberdeen boasted one of the world's most advanced artificial intelligences at the helm of its traffic coordination system.

The camera drone banks a hard ninety-degree turn to the right, cars below moving as one. The camera dips low, skirting the tops of vehicles only inches below.

Narrator: What began as a quest for simply improving the flow of traffic in the new city evolved into the eventual integration and coordination of nearly every moving thing in the city. Water, power, waste, medical services, fire, police ... all controlled and dispatched by the humbly named Metropolitan Traffic System, or MTS.

Camera slows, tilts, and begins traveling over the heads of pedestrians on the sidewalk. A man and a woman stand on an empty corner near the entrance to a subterranean crosswalk. City noise filters out, and we hear the voices of the host, Nasim Fuurad, and her guest for Episode 9, William Bentson.

Nasim: You have a pet name for the AI, don't you?

William: I do, well, those of us in my line of work do. We call her Amy, spelled A-I-M-E, which stands for Artificial Intelligent Management Entity.

Nasim: AIME, okay. What line of work would you be in?

William: No one really knows, I'm afraid.

(Both laugh)

William: Actually, I'm a special kind of hybrid. A historian and philosopher, I guess you could say. I study the development of specific types of technologies. Chiefly, my work deals with artificial intelligences like AIME here in New Aberdeen.

Nasim: So, I get the historian part of it. You're sort of documenting and exploring the development and evolution of a specific technology. But where does the philosopher part come in? I suppose you look at the effect of tech on society?

William: Yes, I guess that's where it gets a bit weird. As a philosopher, I do examine the impact of the tech on society, sure, but primarily, I try to dive deep into how it changes the human psyche on a moralistic and ethical basis.

[Animation: Cut to a nanocamera footage from inside an advanced server. The camera sores through loops of nanofiber optic cables, over pools of reflective hardened bio gel cells, lights winking from within their navy-blue masses.]

Narrator: Tonight on Neuros, we take a stroll through a brain the size of four coach buses. A brain that controls nearly every aspect of city life in the ultramodern New Aberdeen. Our host, Nasim Fuurad, is with historian and philosopher, William Bentson, who has been studying the evolution of artificial intelligences, their benefits to humankind, and the cost to morality for decades.

Cut to a subterranean server facility in a vast, brightly lit room. Nasim and William stand at the intersection of a narrow aisle and a wide central corridor among server stacks.

[Editing: I want vastness of the space to be felt here. Pauses are a good thing.]

Nasim: Quite cold, isn't it? I feel like a popsicle.

William: Indeed, it is very cold, but we are inside the brain of the beast, so to speak. AIME requires an intense amount of energy to run the software processes that manage everything in the city from where your car goes in the morning on your way to work to where your biowaste goes when it gets flushed out of your house. All that energy and all those processors create a lot of heat.

Nasim: Even with the bio gel core processors?

[Animation: Need intense zoom of bio gel cores. Start from inside server above the boards, then down into the gel all the way to the molecular level.]

William: (Nods vigorously) Yes, even with bio gel cores. To put it in perspective, if AIME used silicon-based processors or even the more advanced bismuth-graphene processors, she'd melt them down in a matter of hours. The energy required to keep older servers cool would be grossly cost prohibitive.

Nasim: Not to mention the size of the space required if AIME used older tech.

William: Of course, we'd be talking about a server room the size of a building, or multiple buildings even.

Nasim: So we could easily get lost in the weeds talking about how AIME works, and I'm not even sure I would totally understand it ...

William: I don't think I would either.

(Both laugh)

Nasim: Right, yeah, so let's instead talk about AIME and her story, if you will. When AIME first came online, what was her immediate impact on the city?

William: She was intended to be a traffic coordination system, hence, her official title—the Metropolitan Traffic System. The city's founders had the goal of making traffic jams and traffic delays a thing of the past. At the same time, self-driving cars were just becoming mainstream. Autopilot cars entered our culture so quickly that people soon forgot what it was like to drive without them. I mean, within a few years, turning a key and using a steering wheel seemed like some pastime our grandparents mused about over hot chocolate.

Nasim: I remember. It seemed like, overnight, driving by humans was history.

William: Exactly. And the founders of New Aberdeen had their sights set on integrating that technology into AIME. Soon after they made their intentions known, every—and I mean every—self-driving car maker was on board. In fact, unless your car's OS is able and willing to turn over control to the Metro Traffic System, or AIME, you can't enter the city in your car. And if AIME senses your car trying to tear control away before she's ready to give it back, she'll shut it down.

Nasim: New Aberdeen is definitely known for its traffic, or lack thereof. Commute times are incredibly short. Traffic accidents are almost nonexistent. Response times for police, fire, and ambulance are fractions of what they are for neighboring cities. What were some unforeseen benefits or drawbacks of an AIME-run traffic system?

William: You've named many yourself. City administrators soon realized that AIME could do much more than speed up commuting times. She can divert car traffic to allow first responders quicker access to emergencies. Hospitals integrated drone technology and allowed MTS to be their air traffic controller. In fact, airspace around the city is just as locked down as the streets in terms of MTS control. Nothing flies in or out without AIME's say-so. And no one flies manually.

Nasim: Those all seem like benefits, William.

William: They are. Yes, they are.

[Animation: Enhance opacity of breath clouds.]

Nasim: What about the downside, Mr. Philosopher? What are the philosophical drawbacks?

[Editing: Pause on William. Find a shot of him being pensive.]

William: (Shrugs) As you are no doubt aware, every positive advance comes with its fair share of side effects, or drawbacks as you call them. I must say that something like AIME has very, very few. But the potential drawbacks, the few she has, are quite huge.

Nasim: Okay, I'm sufficiently horrified. What are the drawbacks?

William: From a moralistic perspective, I've long posited that the general population, on the whole, and individual persons become accustomed to a certain degree of say in their lives. We've evolved in recent generations as a global people that feel we can, on some level, not just participate in life like a scripted actor but engage with it more like an improvisational player. Much of life is beyond that improvisational behavior, but the little that is within our sphere of influence is where we find some of our greatest achievements—scientific exploration, artistic expression, free thought. You get the idea.

Nasim: What we're talking about is control.

William: Yes, it's about control. The philosophy of stoicism teaches us that there are things we can control and things we cannot, and we must accept both as they are. See, humans don't really care about *what* they control, no matter what they might say. They care about *how much* they control, no matter what they're controlling. A person's dominance over aspects of their life is essential to the human condition. It's like a tube of toothpaste with the cap screwed on. Squeeze one end and the other bulges. Squeeze control from one area of life, and people find a way to exercise it somewhere else.

Nasim: I see. But what does all that have to do with AIME?

William: If I'm right, and I think I am, a huge amount of control has been squeezed from the lives of people within this city and others like it. Where is it going to pop up? What are people going to grab onto looking for control? Where are they going to squeeze?

Fade to break.

1

The Bridge

November 10, 2043—3:35 a.m.

"You are approaching New Aberdeen city limits. All vehicles are required to relinquish control to the Metropolitan Traffic System. To proceed, enter your destination." The familiar soft male voice came from the car's speakers.

Sterling Tinsel glanced up from his tablet. "At the bridge already?"

Ahead, the bridge's massive stanchions towered over the five lanes of northbound traffic flowing into New Aberdeen. Driving into the city through the south side was not what he'd call a highlight of his day. The unattractive government-subsidized housing sprawl, the blighted neighborhoods, the homeless. He never looked around while his car traveled through these areas, preferring more to go over the work he had in store for him that day. Why ruin a good mood with seeing those people and how they lived?

He did, however, always glance up for a few moments as the bridge came into view. The stanchions, two white spires that rose from the waters of the Bush River, tapered smoothly from a wide base to sharp points. Their midsections curved outward like two great scythes whose tips hovered a few feet apart some forty stories above the roadway, which itself stood twenty-three stories over the river. From the spires stretched dozens of impossibly thin alloy cables down to anchors spaced along the middle third of the bridge. The roadway was comprised of two decks: northbound traffic into the city rode on the top deck, while southbound lanes rode on the bottom deck.

If the nighttime lights were angled just right, as they were at that moment, Sterling lost sight of the cables completely, allowing him to marvel at the spires themselves standing like two naked appendages warmly welcoming that day's travelers.

Seconds later, the light shifted and the cables reappeared. The bridge was now, to Sterling, just a bridge again.

His eyes fell back to his tablet. As per usual, his car automatically and silently communicated his destination to the Metropolitan Traffic System. The quiet Romantic era opera music dimmed once more as the voice of the MTS came through the speakers. "Destination confirmed. Estimated time to arrival is seventeen minutes."

He scanned the financial reports in his lap, scrolling through the pages with the speed and adeptness that his thirty-five years in finance afforded him. The chief financial officer of his company would want his full analysis at the morning's meeting, which started promptly at 4:00 a.m.

"Erica, what is the time?" he asked aloud.

"The time is 3:40 a.m., sir," the car's operating system, Erica, replied in a smooth female voice.

Plenty of time.

"Autonomous control deactivated. You are now in the

Metropolitan Traffic System."

He felt the slightest shift under him as the car's speed was increased briefly in order to further close the already small gap between him and the car in front of him. Behind, the MTS would be repeating the measure. To each side of his navy-blue SUV, vehicles converged to fill all available daylight between lanes until each car was mere inches apart. The Metropolitan Traffic System was controlled by one of the world's most powerful artificial intelligence computers. Linked with each car's autodriving operating system, it calculated the best route to each destination and adjusted the movement of traffic to create the most efficient means of travel possible for every car.

Sterling knew that his car would enter the bridge in the middle lane and stay there for several minutes until he was shifted, a lane at a time, to the right. Gaps would open next to him as one car was slowed or diverted, and his would magically slide over to fill the space. The void left by his lane shift would be filled immediately by the next car needing to move over. When his office building's street approached, he would find himself in the far-right lane, making the turn quickly but smoothly. If he kept his head down for the entire trip, Sterling would never notice any of these maneuvers as the MTS adjusted the silent electric vehicles with a total absence of abrupt movements. Sometimes, Sterling forgot he was in a car at all.

He loved the MTS.

Sterling finished scanning the final page of the financial report and tapped the screen to flip back to the first page. His left hand drifted down to a fresh black coffee in the cup holder next to him as his right hand scrolled on the tablet.

"Notes," he said loud and clear to the car's computer, which was synced with his personal cloud drive. "EBITDA is ten basis points below plan for the month and projected one basis point below plan for the quarter. Year over year remains strong. Unforeseen seasonal anomalies in South America negatively affected conductor raw materials production and increased expenditures. Organic growth in Asia remains strong at four percent year over year hedging losses—"

A change in the car's motion broke his concentration. He looked up at the line of vehicles ahead.

"What the…"

The interminable river of cars had ceased to flow, frozen in place by an unseen dam. Out the side windows, the massive white spires stood proud, curving around and over him. Their near invisible cables hanging taut as ever.

"Why are we stopped?"

Erica replied immediately. "It appears the MTS is having technical difficulties. We should be on our way momentarily, sir."

"Hmm," Sterling grunted. "Whatever. Send Hannelyn a message letting him know what's going on. Tell him I might be late for our meeting."

"Certainly, sir."

From the speakers, a baritone opera singer belted away in Italian just loud enough for Sterling to hear. Just loud enough to help him concentrate.

"Resume notes," Sterling said. "Strong growth in Asia hedges losses elsewhere. Additionally, acquisitions domestically have set projections ahead of …"

The singer cut off mid aria. The soft trim lighting in the floor boards flickered, then went out, and the car's console touchscreen went black. Once again, the car had stopped dead.

"Erica?"

No response.

He peered through the windows at the cars around him. Through the deeply tinted glass, he saw the expressions of confusion on the other driver's faces.

"Erica?"

No response. The car's OS had never failed to respond. Even in low-power mode, the car always had enough reserve power for Erica to function. If the car ever failed, Erica should immediately move to the next device in the hierarchy, in this case Sterling's tablet, then his phone, followed by his watch. Erica didn't register his commands on any of them.

He tried to lower the windows, as if the darkened glass somehow obstructed the truth. He touched the control switch on the door. Nothing happened. He reached for the manual door handle and pulled. It flapped limply in his fingers, not engaging the latch.

He was stuck.

"Son of a bitch," he shouted and slammed his palm on the leather dashboard. Reaching into his jacket pocket, he extracted his mobile phone and was about to dial his office when the soft aria returned. The baritone resumed his lament over some star-crossed lovers. The lights at his feet came to life, and the console touchscreen blazed back to its former glory. The familiar vibration beneath his feet told him they were beginning to move again.

"Erica, you back?" he asked.

No response.

"Erica?"

No response.

He sighed. "At least we're moving." He made a mental note to get Erica looked at later that day. His gaze fell back to the tablet. "Resume notes."

"Destination confirmed. Estimated time to arrival is seventy-one seconds." The male-voiced MTS artificial intelligence had returned.

Sterling's head shot up. "What the fuck?"

Again, he searched the faces of the cars next to him. On the right, all seemed normal. A truck driver puffed a long-filtered cigarette. A woman in a red coupe laughed into her phone. A van full of uniformed kids stared intently at the screen hanging from the ceiling. On his left, the story seemed different. The driver next to him banged on his car's console. In front of that car, a young woman craned her neck around at the other drivers, her hands up in a gesture of confusion. In the cab of a dump truck, about six cars ahead, he could see the driver tapping his truck's console, apparently to no avail. Sterling spun around. Behind him, the driver slept, slouched back with his mouth hanging agape, but the drivers further back had similar looks of confusion and anger.

"What the fuck is going on?" he whispered. "Erica?" Still no response from his car. "MTS?" No response.

He assumed it had to be a glitch. Nothing to worry about. The cars were still moving. What was the worst that could happen? Probably just something to do with the bridge. Once they were off the bridge, he reasoned, everything would go back to normal.

Soon, the cars resumed their normal speed; the cables passed on either side in a translucent blur. To his astonishment, however, the cars in the right-hand lanes fell back, apparently slowing down. His lane and the two to his left were passing those on the right. The right-hand lanes were slowing down. Why? This had never happened before.

No, Sterling realized after glancing at his speedometer, they weren't slowing down. His car was speeding up. The needle pushed past forty-five miles per hour, then fifty, then sixty.

"Twenty seconds to destination. Please prepare to exit your vehicle."

A second later, the speedometer read seventy-five and climbing.

He spun in his seat. Every car within his eye line that occupied the left three lanes were moving at the exact same speed—as one unit.

Then he noticed something that stopped his heart. Ahead of him, in front of the dump truck, were open lanes of traffic. The entire remaining length of the bridge, approximately one mile, had turned into a runway. More than a dozen other cars sped along it.

The speedometer's needle crested eighty-five miles per hour.

"Ten seconds to destination. Remember to be safe when exiting your vehicle."

"What destination? What the fuck is happening?" he shouted.

The last support cable whipped past his window in a blur.

The dump truck and the other cars in the lead jolted left. A fraction of a second later, the big truck and the other cars smashed into the guardrails. The front ends of the cars shot skyward as they ramped the curb at eighty miles per hour. The truck cut right through the metal barrier like it wasn't there, taking flight into open air for a heartbeat before teetering downward out of sight.

Sterling frantically grabbed for the door handle. It flailed helplessly. His fingers searched for the window switch again, but his brain barely registered its stubborn unresponsiveness. His eyes were glued to the five cars in front of him in his lane that followed the path of the dump truck … through the newly created hole in the barrier. The cars in the other lanes crashed and flipped at the safety rail. Somewhere in his mind, he knew that some went over, some didn't.

The delivery van behind the dump truck was gone. The next two cars jumped the curb and threaded the gap in the barrier, then they were gone too. The sedan in front of him turned on a hairpin, hit the curb, and bounced but didn't go over the edge.

His body felt the g-force of the turn; he slid across the seat and slammed into the passenger door. Everything slowed around him. His shoulders crushed into the ceiling as the SUV's wheels met the concrete curb.

He hung weightless as the car fell and gravity undid itself.

The fall was long. And silent. Sterling closed his eyes. Refused to watch his own end.

Through the speakers came the voice. "You have reached your destination. Have a nice day."

2

The Body

November 10, 2043 — 3:00 a.m.
The water lapped against the rocks in gentle waves with a rhythm that had the power to put Liz Reynolds to sleep if she wasn't careful. In the dark, the brackish mouth of the Bush River was inky black. The lights of the Towers Bridge and the city on the far shore shone on its surface to give the impression of a floating galaxy undulating and breaking with the passing wakes of slow-moving barges and fishing boats. The Towers themselves stood over the mouth of the river like two crescent moons, one a reflection of the other.

The wind off the head of Chesapeake Bay cut through Liz's thick wool peacoat and tossed her hair across her face.

Liz thumbed the top of her penlight, its beam cutting through the dark to land on a pale naked body floating face down a dozen feet away from the rocky shore. The obese corpse bobbed slowly with the motions in the water. Her light passed over the body. Purple and black striations down the back, many small puckered red wounds on the shoulders and upper back.

"Drones coming up, boss." Detective Nathan Winchum, her junior partner, got a kick out of referring to her as boss.

"Hurry up before we lose this guy to the sea life."

The drones would not only provide much needed light but would also scan the water, the riverbed, and the body itself for anything and everything that might be evidence. "Have them scan a fifty-foot radius around the body. And figure out which way the tide was running tonight, would you?"

She turned to be sure he heard her. Winchum was in conversation with a technician, both of them standing over a large plastic case. The technician held a drone the size of a hat box in each hand. Winchum pointed toward Liz and the water beyond. Behind him and the technician, there stirred an increasing amount of activity as the forensics team, more technicians, and uniformed officers worked to secure and investigate the scene.

"Winchum, did you get that?" Liz called out to him. She stood perched atop a small boulder, the largest among the narrow field of rocks giving her the best possible view of the body.

"The tide? Yeah, what about it, boss?" Winchum was now backlit by a half dozen drones hovering fifteen feet off the ground behind him.

"So we can backtrack and figure out where the body went in, Winchum. Jesus, this is basic detective stuff."

"Oh, right. Got it." He ran toward their car to figure out what the tides had been up to … she hoped.

Liz stared down at the barnacle-covered boulder, scraping several off with the toe of her white rubber boots. Water swirled around the base of the rock. The dark line of wet left by each soft wave was slightly lower each time, marking the bay's gradual but unstoppable descent. The tide was going out.

A buzzing overhead signaled the drones getting to work. They blasted the scene with cool white light, and technicians gathered near her, each with a tablet to control one or more of the drones. Tiny multicolored lights on the flying robots signaled that the scanning arrays were working their magic.

She turned toward the small team. "Let me know when you're done collecting all the data so we can bring the body in. Make sure you map everything."

Liz stuffed her hands inside her coat pockets, jumped from the rock, and climbed the small rise toward the line of cars parked in the grass twenty feet away, nodding to other officers and forensics specialists as she passed.

Winchum sat in the front seat of their unmarked cruiser with one leg out the open passenger side door, his fingers tapping and scrolling away on a laptop. The lights inside the car illuminated a face set in deep concentration. If his brow got any more furrowed, Liz thought, the folds would start to stick together. She climbed in the driver's door and slid onto the seat next to him, and he looked up from the tablet.

"Hey, boss. The tide is—"

"On its way out. Yeah, I know," she interrupted.

He squinted at her. "How did you know that? One of those techs look it up for you?"

She cocked her head toward him. "I'm a detective, Winchum. I detect things."

"Then why did you make me look it up?"

"So you'd know it's important, and there is the off chance that I could have made a mistake." She smiled wryly. "Albeit a very small chance."

He turned away to watch the technicians operating the drones. Their lights danced in the sky just a dozen feet over the water. Some flew in a tight formation over the body while others circled in a concentric pattern around it.

"What do you think we got?" he said without turning toward her.

"Well," she said reaching for her cup of coffee on the dash, "my ultrasensitive detecting skills would lead me to believe that we have ourselves a dead man." She sipped her coffee. It was ice cold. "Shit. All this goddamn tech in these cars, and they can't put in a cup warmer? How hard would that be?"

"Lowest bidder, boss." Winchum continued to stare out toward the activity along the shore. "Think he's a jumper?"

Liz shot a glance at the Towers Bridge, its origin a half mile away from where they sat. "No, he's no jumper."

"What makes you say that?" he said. "Oh, right, you're detecting." He turned back toward her.

She chuckled. "Wounds on the visible parts of his body. Entry wounds of some kind and scratch marks or claw marks lead me to believe this man was tortured and killed. Then dumped in the river upstream. The tide is on its way out, remember? If he'd jumped from the bridge behind us, downstream, he'd have been carried out to the bay by the current."

He nodded in apparent comprehension. "And he's naked." Winchum shrugged.

"Look at you, Detective. You're detecting. Kudos to you." He laughed and Liz pointed over his shoulder. "Either way, we'll know soon enough."

A drone technician stood a few feet away from the passenger side of their car. "We're good ma'am. Forensics is going to pull him in now."

She leaned over the front seat, nearly on top of Winchum. "Did you get underneath him?"

"Yes, ma'am," the technician said. "We got a good side scan and we put a micro sub in the water to do the riverbed underneath him."

Minutes later, Liz and Detective Winchum were kneeling beside the ghostly white body of a man lying on his back. His black hair graying at the temples. Forensic specialists revolved around them working. Drones overhead photographed every square inch of the corpse.

"Tell me what you see, Winchum," Liz said.

"White male, early forties, moderately obese," Winchum used a gloved hand to lift the appendages and look underneath them. "Five ten, around two-sixty." He felt the man's fingers, which looked clean despite being bloated and wrinkled. "Hands are stiff with rigor mortis, but"—he flexed the man's arm—"elbows and shoulders are pliant. I'd put time of death about three to four hours ago."

"Cause of death?" Liz asked her protégé.

He pointed to a dark purple line that stretched across the man's throat and around two-thirds of his neck. "Strangulation. Ligature marks indicate it was done with a thin wire of some kind. Some bruising around the ligature marks and petechiae in the eye."

Liz nodded her approval. "What do you make of these wounds?" She pointed to the small volcano-like pucker wounds on the shoulders.

"Puncture wounds, like you said, with some cratering." He pulled a small caliper out of his pocket. "Small ones. Around five-sixteenths of an inch. Too big for a syringe. Maybe a screwdriver?" He turned to her with a questioning expression.

"Look closer. Look at the rims of the crater and the inside of it. What do you see?"

He bent closer to a wound on the man's nearest shoulder, pulled at it with a gloved finger. "They're cauterized. Jesus. A hot poker?"

She raised an eyebrow. "Maybe." She gestured to a forensics tech nearby, holding a tubular device. "Do we have ID yet?"

"Getting it now," the woman said. She bent over the man's outstretched arm and pressed the end of the device to the inside of his elbow. After a second, she pulled it away and touched it to a reader on a tablet hanging around her neck. After a moment of staring blankly at the tablet, a look of satisfaction crossed her face. "Got him. Drew Ziggler. Has a record too." She read from the tablet. "All cyber crimes. Some kind of hacker I guess."

"Okay," Liz said. "Roll him over and let's take a look at those wounds on his back."

A crash behind her made her jump to her feet. The sound was from somewhere in the distance. She spun toward the bridge lit in cold blue light. It reflected off the water below. At first, she thought she must be hearing things, then toward the far end of the bridge, she saw it. A shape falling toward the water. It was clear, even from miles away, a dump truck had crashed through the barrier and now fell toward the water. Another shape, a car right behind it. Another one quickly after. Soon, a dozen cars and vehicles poured from the bridge like water from a spigot. More kept coming. The first hit the water with a near silent crunch. The rest into those that preceded them, collecting briefly before sinking as one into the frigid black water.

3

Comeuppance

Three Weeks Ago
Gilda Elmyr woke up shivering despite the thick quilt covering her. She blinked slowly in the darkness, pulled the top of the covers to her chin, and let out a deep sigh. On her bedside table, a small clock displayed the time—5:30 a.m. Almost time to wake up, but as she got on in years, it seemed like each night of sleep was never enough. Every day she woke more tired than the last, her body slightly weaker than the day before. Her mind, however, was sharp as ever. Her intellect and cunning had afforded her a long and easy life after retirement. While she was a workaday civilian, life was anything but easy. In spite of considerable odds stacked against her, she'd managed to carve out a happy existence. She only had one regret—she had no one to share it with. The thought stung sometimes, but only briefly. She knew, on every level, no one would enjoy her company as much as she did herself.

The room was completely dark. Expensive blackout and sound absorbent windows kept the city's artificial light and street noise from disrupting her preferred sleeping

15

conditions—total darkness and complete quiet. In her days at the orphanage, both when she was running it and as a peon worker, she'd resorted to eye masks and earmuffs. Now, in her comfortable retirement years, she could afford to install fancy windows along with many other comforts, some she needed, like added security, some she merely desired, like a smart shower that came on when her feet hit the tile and adjusted the heat based on her internal temperature.

With two hands, she yanked on the edge of the thick blanket and tucked it ever tighter around her neck. The chill seemed to penetrate her to the bone; she shivered with one intense bodily vibration, then a second later, another one. She knew the heating system was top of the line and would sense her comfort level remotely and adjust itself. She decided to wait a moment before calling building maintenance.

She'd always coveted sleep. She looked at is as a partner, something she could always count on to heal her body and mind. The high-tech pill, Zentransa, that eliminated the need for sleep, the one heralded by so many as the most important invention ever, was something she herself never considered taking, not for a moment. When she was a low-level administrator at the orphanage and even later as she worked her way up the ladder of Child Residential Services to become director of an orphanage, she would have been unable to afford the Z pill. Although her off-the-books income—her well-deserved unofficial personal revenue—gave her enough to afford the Z pill, that money was set aside for her future, which was now her present.

No, she'd decided many years ago, a natural sleep cycle was the only way for her, then and now.

Another chill, this one shocking her from toe to nose,

rippled through her like an electric eel had taken up residence in her spinal cord. A verbal command to the home's operating system confirmed the HVAC was working properly; the temperature was right where it was supposed to be.

Illness, she decided. It was the only explanation. Not one to get sick often, this worried her, but only a little bit. She'd call the doctor later, and he'd come to her house to give her a once-over. She could afford to have doctors make house calls now also. Just another reminder that all the rules she bent, massaged, and twisted from her past had been well worth it.

She breathed through another cold tremor, sweat dripped from the corner of one temple, and stung her half-open eye. In her mind, gratitude bled through the cloud of discomfort. She was thankful to still have it all when, only a few months ago, she almost lost it. All of it. That silly investigation started by God knows who for God knows what reason. It was all just meddling, she'd told the investigators. People trying to ruin other people's lives. It was so long ago and times were different then. She'd done what she'd done—sure, she'd admit that much—but she was only a small part of it. The system was to blame, really.

In the end, a deal was struck. Deals were her specialty. Probation and house arrest were no big deal for her. And all she had to do to keep the life she'd worked so hard to get was name names. Easy enough, as most of them were already dead, but some weren't. So she gave them a list of names long enough to satisfy them. She left a few people off the list, not because she had a soft spot for them but as a sort of insurance should the police or FBI come calling again. She'd suddenly remember a few very important people with whom the investigators would probably like to talk to.

Her teeth chattered, and as she rolled to her left side, she felt the sweat-soaked pillow cold against her cheek, and the shock of it forced her eyes open in a snap. Staring into the darkness beyond her bed, she could sense something was there. Something that wasn't supposed to be.

Her heart, already racing from the chills, pounded with more ferocity. The cold sweat beaded on her lip, but all thoughts of discomfort or possible illness emptied from her mind. She'd lived in fear of moments like these, when someone would come for her, some sicko out for their perverted version of justice.

Another shiver, the most intense so far, dominated her nervous system, tensing her entire body, forcing her to curl into a fetal position, her eyes shut like clams. Nausea filled her gut like ice water, and she had to exert enormous will to keep the contents of her stomach from rushing out.

After a moment, the cramps and chills passed, but the nausea remained. She opened her eyes, could still sense something was there with her, could sense the wrongness of the air, the presence of someone dangerous. Muscles still quivering from the last attack, Gilda pulled the quilt down past her neck and propped herself up.

"Is someone …"

A flash. Blinding light filled her already aching head, forcing her to clamp her eyes shut and turn away.

"Who's there?" she demanded.

"Calm yourself, Ms. Elmyr." The voice spoke from the darkness near the lamp on the bedside table. It was a woman. "This will get much worse if you don't stay calm."

Blinking back tears from the sudden, impossibly bright flash of light, Gilda turned toward the voice. The lamp was on, she realized, and must have been the source of light. Even a moment later, it pained her to look directly at it. The voice came from behind the lamp; the intruder sat in the tufted wingback chair, Gilda's favorite reading spot. Gilda couldn't make out the face blanketed in shadow, but she could tell the woman was tall and slender, legs crossed and wearing an ankle-length black dress.

Gilda was so weak that she could barely manage to sit upright, so she lay back down. Fighting, at her age and in her current state, was out of the question. Whoever this was, she knew they wanted something, or she'd be dead. She could bargain, strike a deal like she always did in hairy situations.

"What is it you want?" Gilda croaked from a sore throat. "What? What do you want? You must want something. I can pay you. I have money and valuables. Please just leave me alone." She laid on the desperation in her voice, wanting to appear weak, which was easy in her current state. She'd never felt worse.

"I want to talk, for now. We still have time to get to the other reasons I'm here if you stay calm."

Gilda's chest tightened, a clamping pressure inside her, pressing down on her organs. She closed her eyes and breathed deep, willing away the fear.

"Very good. The calmer you are, the longer we have together." The woman spoke as if she were a professor and Gilda the student of her life's lessons.

Gilda did not respond, wouldn't give this thug the satisfaction.

"I'm not going to show you my face because you wouldn't recognize me anyway. But I will tell you my story; maybe you'll recognize that."

Instantly, Gilda knew what this was about. The infinitesimal amount of calm she mustered began to wane.

"About nineteen years ago," the faceless woman began, "a young girl and her infant brother came to the orphanage where you held the title 'Director.' The parents of those children were dead and, having no other family to care for them, such was their fate. They weren't there long, however. Families showed interest in the siblings, but no one would commit to taking both of them. One day representatives from a mysterious school came to talk to the girl. She was exactly what they were looking for, exactly the kind of child they wanted, but they only wanted her. The girl told them, and you, that she wouldn't leave without her brother."

Memories came back to Gilda. The Order, those Tappers, the brutal killers. Always so picky about which children they preferred. The children had to be just so. And if they were going to be so insistent, so could Gilda. They'd get what they wanted in the end, if not from her then from someone else. If someone was going to benefit, it might as well be her. Why not her? But it had happened so many times, so many demands, so many children. So many it was impossible to recall exactly to which one this woman was referring. Was this woman a distant relative, a forgotten sibling, or—god forbid—one of the children all grown up? If she was one of the children, that must mean ...

"I ... I ..." Gilda stammered. Her fear rose like a violent volcano.

"Don't bother, Ms. Elmyr." The woman stood and entered the ring of light spilling out from the lamp.

Gilda's aching eyes strained to take in the woman's tall form. Slender with long blonde hair tied in a single braid slung over her shoulder. With a shock, her fear solidified. This woman was one of *them*—one of the children she sold to the Order. One of the children who'd gone on to become a Tapper, a legally sanctioned killer. From neck to foot, the woman wore a form-fitting, black cloak. A *cossack*, Gilda remembered they were called. The Members of the Order had worn them when they visited her orphanage to evaluate and, ultimately, take those children.

Automatically, Gilda's eyes drifted to the woman's hands. She only wore one black glove, her uncovered hand a stark contrast to the other as she clasped them in front of her.

"If you were going to apologize, it doesn't matter anymore. If you weren't, then whatever you were going to say matters even less." The Tapper squinted.

Gilda swallowed what felt like a brick lodged in her throat, a profound heaviness settled on her sternum. She continued staring at the woman's hands, and even in her heightened state of shock and fear, she could see something was off about those hands.

"The girl's name was Francesca, but everyone called her Frannie," the Tapper said. "The boy's name was Hank. Do you remember them, Ms. Elmyr? Francesca and Hank Green?"

Icey stabs of pain jabbed into Gilda's feet. Looking down in surprise, she half expected to see someone jamming blades into her flesh. She saw no one. The stabbing pain traveled up her body up from her feet. She gasped from the pain and issued an inhuman groan.

"I …" Gilda tried to swallow but failed. Her throat was full of sand. "I … too many children. I can't remember."

The woman sighed deeply. "I thought not. But I still think you can help me." She scanned the room with a robotic glare, then stared down at Gilda once more. "I'm looking for information, Ms. Elmyr. Information about the orphan theft perpetrated by you, your peers, and your superiors."

A coughing fit overtook Gilda and, for a moment, an overwhelming urge to vomit, which eventually subsided. "I told the police," she paused for a breath, "everything. They have all my files. Ask them."

The woman shrugged her shoulders, hands still joined in front of her. "I've been through all the police files and every bit of evidence they have." A pause. "I'm not convinced everything has surfaced."

"Are …" Gilda's jaw clinched, cutting off the words for a moment. "Are you here to execute me?" Her eyes shakily took in her own weak form under the blanket. "Has it already started?"

"Can you help me?" The question, to Gilda, was an answer in itself. "It's my theory that you held back when you informed on your colleagues in order to keep yourself out of prison. Call me obsessed, others certainly have, but I just have to see this through. I've committed myself to right this wrong, this enormously heinous wrong. So I'll ask again. Ms. Elmyr, can you help me?"

"You … you don't"—a violent cramp twisted her abdominal muscles, and she fought to get the words out—"don't have authority outside your p-p-prison." She'd lost feeling in most of her legs and had only just noticed the torrential sweat coating the sheets under her and the slick coating on her tight fists.

"Authority isn't quite the word I'd use, Ms. Elmyr." The woman still spoke in that unnervingly even tone, like a doctor giving a routine diagnosis. "I think of it as a charter. That is if you're looking for a definition for what it is I and my order do. And that charter is ill-defined by those who wrote it; therefore, I believe it is up for interpretation."

"Please make it stop. Please." Gilda had to shut her eyes while she pleaded to divert her strength.

"My role requires me to perform my duties without passion or malice aforethought. I am a pig sniffing out truffles. I am a robot, a program, coldly obeying code to execute what it is I must do. And this, Ms. Elmyr, must be done. I will find everyone involved in your crime, the child theft, and I will … process them."

The woman's eyes were dark glass spheres, like a shark's, and Gilda was a wounded tuna listing helplessly toward the ocean floor.

"Can you help me?" the Tapper said again in her deathly still voice.

Gilda once again found herself gazing at the Tapper's hands. It was then she realized the Tapper wore no gloves at all. One hand, which Gilda had previously thought was gloved, was partly stained a deep purple-black from the fingertips to a few inches below the wrist. The rumors were true. The stain existed, a result of so many lives taken. Seeing death, literally, on the woman's hand, made Gilda's decision that much easier. She unclenched her left hand and pointed a trembling bony finger at the egg-shaped finial atop the corner post of her four-poster bed.

The Tapper followed her finger, placed a hand on top of the finial, and gave Gilda a questioning look. Gilda nodded, and the woman snapped the finial off the post with uncommon strength. After examining the underside of the egg, the woman stood on tip toes and peered down into the hollow post. From it, she withdrew a small roll of paper, which she promptly unfurled and read. Looking satisfied, the Tapper stepped closer to the bed, her cossack pressing against the edge of Gilda's quilt.

"These names will be helpful, I'm sure. Thank you, Ms. Elmyr." An audible sigh from the Tapper, then she continued. "Now for a selfish request, not related to our other business. If you hadn't figured it out yet, I am Francesca Green. Hank is my brother and I'm looking for him. The record simply shows that he was adopted shortly after I left the orphanage but not by whom or where he went. How can I find him, Ms. Elmyr?"

She knew it. This woman was one of those children. "Sealed. Those records are sealed, but …" Gilda moaned and stretched out an arm, that barely obeyed her will, to point at a name on the list in the Tapper's hand. A high-ranking man's name. "H-he will know."

The woman turned toward Gilda, a glint of something in her eyes. Sincerity? "Thank you, Ms. Elmyr. Now, we must move on to the last bit of our business together tonight."

Ice blades entered Gilda's groin area, pierced her lower abdomen. Something was tearing her apart from the inside. Involuntarily, and though she lacked feeling in them, Gilda was aware that her legs had contracted upward, her back spasmed for several seconds.

"I've observed you, Ms. Elmyr. I've judged you irredeemable and incorrigible."

Now the ice was accompanied by fire; Gilda's skin pulsated with heat. She would push the blanket off, but her limbs would not function.

"I've selected you, Ms. Elmyr, to receive the Sacred Task."

Gilda's knees were fully to her chest now, her teeth chattering uncontrollably, sweat and tears flooding her eyes, her throat a desert, every nerve ending in her body a conflagration.

"You said you'd make it stop. I … I helped you." Convulsions assaulted Gilda's body for several seconds. "You said …" More untamed coughing interrupted Gilda.

The woman's voice cut through the fog of Gilda's darkening mind. "I said nothing. You assumed by helping me you would be set free, absolved of your transgressions. That is a by-product of your own bias."

"This … you … did this to me?" Gilda wheezed.

The woman nodded. "Yes. I did this. And you are dying." The Tapper sat on the edge of the bed. Gilda felt herself slide a few inches toward her. "I applied the Solution to your neck as you slept. Usually, it works in mere seconds, but I used a modified version, one that works a little slower. I wanted it that way, so we could talk."

Gilda was vaguely aware of the woman's hand on hers.

The Tapper spoke again, her voice piercing the pain and confusion like a sword. "I may be dispassionate about my role, but it doesn't mean I don't have regrets. For instance, I regret this hurts you so much, I really do. No part of me seeks revenge. It was out of necessity that it happened this way. If I could have extracted the information from you and also felt sure I'd be able to administer the Solution, full strength, afterward," she sighed, "then trust me, I would have done just that."

The pain began to recede from Gilda's body. The icy fingers no longer stabbed her extremities. Instead, she lost feeling in them altogether. Her eyes stared through a gray gel. The weight on her sternum now entwined her lungs and heart and neck.

A voice from miles away spoke to her.

"Everything will be over very soon, Ms. Elmyr. Goodbye."

It ended six seconds later as Gilda Elmyr's lungs emptied themselves of air and did not have the strength to refill. Gilda's heart functioned for a moment longer, then it too stopped.

* * *

On the street outside Gilda Elmyr's apartment, Francesca unrolled the yellow slip of paper and read the list of names for the fifth time since pulling it from the hollowed-out bedpost.

Four names scribbled in black ink in Gilda's tight sloping handwriting. Four names Francesca had seen in official government papers but not in the indictments and arrests that rained down on the city government after the child theft ring had been made public.

These four names Gilda had saved for herself as insurance against future charges, no doubt. If the police or federal agents came calling, she'd throw down the list Francesca now held and use it as leverage to extricate herself, once again, from punishment.

Kyle Gardeaux, Miles Armistead, Padmani Brar, and Yunni Tigunder.

The fourth name, the one Gilda had pointed to as the one who would know where to find Hank, called out to her especially loud. Yunni Tigunder. A man she knew to be connected to every important city and state official going back generations. Tigunder allegedly had the sealed documents that would lead her to Hank, the brother she left behind nearly two decades ago. Tigunder's was the last name on the list, however. By sheer luck of Gilda's random order in which she'd placed these names on this paper, Francesca was now forced to wait even longer to find Hank. Forced by the nature of the objectivity required in her role and her own desire to prove to herself that she sought justice, not revenge, she'd follow the list in the order it appeared to her now. Skipping to Yunni's name, visiting him first, would show her bias, her personal stakes over societal needs.

Three names.

Three people.

Three visits.

Then Hank.

4

Martin Aubrey

November 10, 2043—8:00 a.m.
Martin Aubrey scanned the news feed on his tablet while his newly purchased Lincoln XKZ sedan piloted him deftly through the midmorning traffic. The car was new to him, a civilian model available to the general public at any car dealership and a far cry from his previous vehicle—a company car provided by his former employer, OWG Insurance, Inc., which came with upgrades to the carbon fiber shell and glass, making it virtually bullet- and bombproof, an advanced operating system equipped with artificial intelligence, a high-end tracking system, and a multitude of reconnaissance capabilities. This car, the run of the mill Lincoln four door, boasted temperature-controlled seats and self-tinting windows and not much else.

Malina Maddox, Aubrey's cyberwarrior partner, had given the car as many enhancements as she could conjure and, in many respects, outstripped his old OWG car in terms of its operating speed, onboard AI, and smoother ride. Nothing Malina did to improve the car's computer hardware and software, however, could replace the protection provided by the enhanced armor of the vehicle he used to drive.

"Four minutes to your destination," said a soft, androgynous voice from the car's speakers.

Aubrey glanced up from the tablet to see a neighborhood he recognized. He was in an uptown neighborhood of New Aberdeen in the northern reaches of the old Proving Grounds on which the city was built. This area, with streets lined with bars, restaurants, and retail shops, was popular with the twenty-something crowd. As he stared absentmindedly at the passing scenery, gaps formed in the flow of cars ahead and to his left. The Metro Traffic System was at work, and he knew the cars pushed up and back to accommodate his lane change would not feel the tiniest change in their time to destination.

His gaze fell back to the tablet, and he finished reading the article that had kept him occupied for most of the trip uptown. Titled "Breakthrough in Search for BSS Cure," the headline was blazoned in huge red block letters across the top of Global News Sentry's website. According to GNS, scientists were now saying they could reverse engineer the cause of Boarding School Syndrome, the sleep sickness attacking children all over the world. As the illnesses epicenter, New Aberdeen had a front-row seat in its development over the past eleven months.

Aubrey and Malina had been at the center of the investigation that uncovered the disturbing truth—that the hugely popular and society-shifting drug Zentransa was the cause of a disorder that rendered the children of those who took Z unable to wake from a seemingly never-ending sleep. Now called Preadolescent Chronic Somnolent Disorder after public outcry over its more commonly known name of

Boarding School Syndrome, the disorder took seven to ten years to manifest itself in children and only after being born to parents who'd used Z for five to fifteen years. Because it affected nearly ten percent of children in the vulnerable population, combined with the natural slow burn of the disorder, it made for a terrifying experience for parents. Men and women in the city, then the country, then the world, lived in fear of walking into their son or daughter's room only to find them unwakeable.

The thought always gave Aubrey pause. Having no children himself, he could barely fathom what that level of terror must be like.

Naturally, the drug's manufacturer, Ventana, Inc., claimed they'd fixed the problem and the drug was now safe. This came after their deceased CEO, James Sarazin, had been re-placed and most of the board of directors fired. The company had suffered enormously. Ventana shares plummeted nearly ninety-seven percent in the days after Aubrey and Malina leaked the damning information to the press. Ventana had recovered since then, but not by much. The revolutionary drug maker was still on financial life support.

The GNS article detailed promising results researchers had experienced in their tests on lab mice. Apparently, a lab in Hamburg had been able to infect mice with a faster-acting version of the genetic disorder to reproduce PCSD in the animals and pinpoint exactly which genes in their DNA strands were responsible. It wasn't a cure, but it gave hope to the roughly one thousand impacted families around the globe and hundreds of thousands more fearful moms and dads.

"You have arrived at your planned destination. Please exit via the curbside door. Traffic side doors have been locked for your safety."

Aubrey's head snapped up. He'd been in a deep reverie while reading the article and had barely registered the car's stopping, soft as it was. He opened the door and stepped out onto the sidewalk. His car would loiter for a few moments before it would automatically merge back into traffic to circle the block awaiting his beckon.

Flanked by two darkened pubs, the alley he'd come to inspect was in front of him. He'd received a tip from a friend in the police department about a murder that happened here a few nights ago. No leads. No suspects. And although he wasn't asked to look into it, his curiosity got the better of him. He entered the dank alley and took in the scene ten yards ahead.

The good thing about murder in an alley in winter was that no one was in a big hurry to clean up the mess.

Aubrey stood in a spot a dozen steps from the sidewalk behind him, scanning the scene. A large blue dumpster against the right wall of the alley filled most of the space between the two buildings. Another one, identical in all but color, sat fifteen feet further into the alley against the opposite wall. Gray water streamed down the middle of the pavement in a shallow valley toward the street. More dripped from unseen places. He turned his eyes skyward and scanned the roof ledges overhead and the corners of the building's street side. The only cameras he saw were positioned over the sidewalk, which was thirty feet from where he stood and some fifty to sixty feet from the crime scene.

He examined the crime scene again. In the corner where the dumpster met the exterior wall of the pub, out of sight from the street, dark—nearly black—crimson arced in a narrow splatter across the dumpster, roughly five feet high. It made sense. The victim's throat had been slashed left to right as he stood. More dark spots in smaller spray patterns appeared where the victim crumpled to the ground and fell back.

Then the death spot. A mass of blackish-red dry blood in a round pool where the man lay until he bled out.

Aubrey already knew the basics from his connections on the police force. The victim was a young white male, recent college graduate, out with his friends the night he was murdered. His friends said he met a young woman at the bar who seemed quite enamored with him. Around midnight, he left the bar with the woman, and they never saw him again. Cameras above the bar's exterior confirmed he left with the woman. They also showed the couple enter the alley. The woman leading him enthusiastically by the hand. Neither emerged from the alley.

Aubrey looked down the narrow canyon between the buildings. It stretched for blocks, providing rear egress and access for every building down the long avenue. At least a dozen more alleyways branched from the main trunk, each one leading to the street.

The police didn't have a positive facial ID on the woman. Just to be sure, Aubrey had Malina use her exceptional skills to double-check the police tech's work. She too was unable to find a facial match for the woman in any law enforcement database in the country. They were also unable to spot her entering the street via any of the other numerous alleyways, which wasn't saying much. There were hundreds of people coming and going that night.

Aubrey pulled out his phone and dialed Malina.

"Yeah?" she said after one ring.

"You know, I really think you should refer to me as boss or sir or something more fitting of my authority." He smiled.

"Tough shit, Martin. What do you want?" she said with a contained chuckle.

"We need to speak to our friend Jacira Barretto."

She groaned in his ear. "Why? I prefer not to associate with known assassins."

"I'm down at the crime scene from the other night and—"

"Wait." She cut him off. "You know that's not a paying job, right? What are you doing down there?"

"I was curious. Anyway, about Jacira …"

"What about her? You think she's working again?"

"No, I don't think so. But she may know of others operating in the city." A pause. "Can you find her?" If anyone could find an assassin who didn't want to be found, Malina could.

She sighed through the receiver. "I'll try."

"Do or do not. There is no try."

She groaned louder this time. "Okay, I have to go." She hung up.

Aubrey surveyed the bloody scene before him one more time. He wasn't sure what he was looking for, but he was certain he'd know it when he saw it.

A buzzing in his pocket broke his focus. Expecting the caller to be Malina, he pulled out his phone. It wasn't Malina's name on the screen, but he knew the caller well.

"Senior Inspector Liz Reynolds, to what do I owe the pleasure?" he said.

"Hi, Aubrey," Liz Reynolds replied. "Can we talk in person? I need to see you and Malina ASAP. We had a murder victim wash up this morning, and I need to ask you two some questions."

5

The Gray Hat

Closed captioning appeared on the TV below a reporter standing on one end of Towers Bridge at the city's south end. "City officials are asking citizens to remain calm and are saying that they are one hundred percent confident in the Metropolitan Traffic System's artificial intelligence." Behind the woman, crews worked to repair a breach in the bridge's safety rails.

"Can you believe this?" Malina asked. She and Aubrey read the words as they scrawled across the screen.

"Have you ever seen an AI do something like that?" Aubrey glanced across the table at his partner, whose eyes fixated on the screen behind the bar.

The rest of the gastropub was empty, save for one regular who was belly-up and head down in his liquid lunch at the bar. The tall, grizzled bartender wiped the wood around the man's head and elbows. This looked to be a regular occurrence. The seating area was filled with high-top round tables and narrow counter spaces between columns.

"You okay?" said Aubrey.

Malina's eyes jerked away from the TV toward Aubrey. "Yeah, I'm fine. Why?" Her lips curled subtly downward. Her usual soft mousy face appeared more drawn.

"You seem really bothered by this," said Aubrey.

"People died, Martin. Of course it bothers me." She looked away, her eyes bouncing around the empty restaurant. Her hand casually brushed back her spiky black hair. There was something she wasn't telling him. Her feigned indifference was an easy tell, but Aubrey didn't pursue it. "When is she supposed to be here?"

As if in response to her question, a form darkened the door, and Aubrey stood to welcome Liz Reynolds.

After a few moments of pleasantries, Liz hefted her shoulder bag onto the table and removed three flat, rectangular objects. Placing her bag on the floor, she unfolded the tablets and handed one each to Aubrey and Malina.

Aubrey watched as the tablet came to life. Liz controlled what they saw, using her own tablet to command the others. She pulled up a folder that contained hundreds of photos laid out in a mosaic of tiny thumbnails.

"This morning, a body washed up on the south shore of the Bush River." The image of a pale nude body filled Aubrey's tablet. The man was slightly discolored from hours in the water. "We believe cause of death to be strangulation with a cord or wire."

As Liz scrolled through images showing different angles of the body, Malina caught Aubrey's attention. He looked up to see her grimacing and averting her eyes from the screen. Liz didn't seem to notice. Aubrey continued watching the images shoot past.

"Stop." Aubrey leaned into a photo of the man's back. He

zoomed in tight on a small puncture wound in the mottled flesh. "What made those?"

"Not sure, some kind of pointed metal object, like a sharpened screw driver or …"

"Are those scorch marks?"

"Yes. Whatever it was had been heated up."

The pictures continued to fly past.

Aubrey leaned back further from the tablet. "The wounds are only on his back and shoulders."

"Yes."

"He was tortured," said Aubrey. "But only from behind, and he was probably seated while it happened."

"Yes."

"Who is he?" Aubrey asked.

Liz folded her arms and sat back in her chair. "His name is Drew Ziggler."

Aubrey nodded. "Do you know anything about him?"

"A little bit, but not much," said Liz. "I was hoping Malina could help me with that."

Liz and Aubrey turned their attention to Malina, whose eyes had wandered back to the television still covering the accident on the bridge. Floating barge cranes lifted cars from the water to be lowered onto waiting ships.

"What?" Malina said as she turned back to Aubrey and Liz. "What can Malina help you do?"

On the tablet, the image of the man's naked back disappeared to be replaced a second later by a close-up of his face. Malina moved closer to the device and squinted. To Aubrey, the man looked rather plain—black hair, streaks of white over his ears, pudgy cheeks, a large pocked nose.

Malina sat up straight, her brow creased. "His face is

familiar, but I can't quite place it."

"The water can distort things over time. The flesh swells. Maybe a different angle will help."

Liz swiped on her screen a few times, showing numerous views of the head and face. Malina shook her head until one photo slid past showing the back of the man's left shoulder.

"Wait." Malina used her fingers to zoom in to view a tattoo just over the left shoulder blade.

Aubrey did the same and was soon looking at an image of a white rabbit inked into the man's skin. Outlined in black, the cartoonish creature was hunched over as if ready to hop right off the man's cold flesh. "I know him. His name is Drillard."

"Dree-yard?" Aubrey asked.

She spelled it for him.

"Sorry, Malina," Liz said, "we have a DNA match on him. His name is Drew Ziggler."

Malina looked up from the tablet and shook her head defiantly. "No, I mean that was his handle. I never knew his actual name. He's a gray hat from Philadelphia. Moved here a few years ago. Drillard is a play on some author's name whose book showed up in a popular movie from the late twentieth century. The white rabbit tattoo is from the same movie."

"What's a gray hat?" Aubrey asked.

Malina sighed slightly and looked at the ceiling as if deciding on how to explain the term. She turned her attention back to the pair of them. "It's a name for a type of programming systems specialist who tends to work in the murky waters of cracking."

Aubrey glanced at Liz, whose expression appeared as confused as Aubrey felt.

Malina continued, "It's like what you would call hacking, but specifically to find ways around or through systems and cybersecurity. Like cracking a safe but on a computer."

Aubrey nodded. "So, he's a cyber criminal."

Malina frowned and shrugged her shoulders a bit. "Yes and no. A black hat is your true cyber criminal. They're crackers with only nefarious intents. They want to steal, subvert, or cause chaos for their own gain or just because they're bored. A white hat is the opposite. They work to find holes in security to help companies and governments fix them and be better prepared for an attack. A gray hat is in between. Sometimes they work both sides for their own gain. Others, like Drillard, play the Robin Hood type. Stealing from the rich and giving to the poor. Taking down bad actors in society and outing them to the public while protecting others."

Aubrey squinted knowingly at her. "I may know someone like that."

Malina's eyelids half closed, and she gave him the smallest of smiles.

Liz pushed her chair back and began to stand. "I have to get going, but this was good. Listen"—she focused on Malina—"can you send me the names of some of the people he ran with. I need to start talking to them."

"The cracker community is pretty insulated," Malina shook her head. "Most meetups and such are done in back rooms on the dark web. I do know some of them, but I can guarantee they won't talk to you."

"Can you talk to them for me? See what Drillard was up to? Ask if he was in any kind of trouble or if someone was looking for him. I just need to get pointed in the right direction, and I can take it from there." Liz retrieved the tablets from the table.

Malina nodded her consent and got to her feet as Aubrey stood. The three of them walked toward the exit.

"How is Lewis doing? Haven't talked to the new Chief Inspector since his promotion." Aubrey squinted at the daylight as they reached the sidewalk outside.

They continued chatting about Aaron Lewis, Aubrey's old friend at the Metropolitan Police Department, and when he looked back, he noticed Malina was not behind him or anywhere nearby. Parting ways with Liz and promising to get back to her on the Drillard case, he reentered the bar in search of his partner.

Malina stood near the corner of the bar top, staring up at the television.

Aubrey approached her. "Hey, let's get going."

She pointed silently at the screen. He followed her gaze.

The news station was replaying footage from a camera high atop one of the bridge's cables. Five lanes of cars on the bridge had stalled, unmoving. The apparent cause somewhere off-screen. Suddenly, a section of the left three lanes moved ahead out of the camera shot, leaving open lanes ahead of the cars left behind. After a moment, all lanes resumed moving, but it was clear that the left three lanes were speeding rapidly, much faster than the right lanes. In seconds, the cars in the left lanes were whipping past the other cars. When they reached a point almost at the edge of the screen, the lead vehicles turned left at a sharp angle toward the guardrail.

The huge dump truck in the center of the bridge cut through the metal barrier like it was made of paper, the vehicles lined up behind it, following their leader like dutiful lemmings. The other two lead cars slammed into the rail, their front end shooting skyward for a second before the cars behind them impacted a heartbeat later with such force that it looked like the lead cars were catapulted off the bridge. When the third and fourth cars reached the edge, the guardrail was nearly flattened, providing nothing more than a launchpad for the rest of the vehicles.

One after another, they fell from the high bridge like drops of wax from a fiercely burning candle until, finally, the cars stopped falling after more than a dozen from each of the three lanes had hit the water.

The news station had the decency not to show the cars and their passengers hitting the water, but Aubrey could imagine what the scene must have been like. The cars landing with the force that 220 feet of open air provided a one-ton object. Colliding with the water as if it were concrete. The impact killing most of the drivers. After hitting the water, the cars would remain buoyant for a split second until the next vehicle impacted it, forcing it underwater. The effect would be a very temporary collection of cars, trucks, and vans, forming an ill-fated island with cars above and below the surface until they were all gently taken under by the force of gravity. The black water swallowing them into its folds like a pit of tar engulfing an ancient beast.

"The cars on the bridge turned after the last cable," Malina said, her eyes still glued to the television.

"I know. Bad luck. If they would have hit the cables, they probably wouldn't have gone over," Aubrey said. "Still would have been bad, but the loss of life would have been a lot lower."

"Bad luck," Malina repeated. She grunted something unintelligible and turned to Aubrey. "Come on, I've got some work to do."

6

An Unnamed Investigative Firm

Malina tapped Send on her tablet screen to fire off the last of the messages she'd been sending to some of her old acquaintances. She'd mostly been a solo operator since she became a hacker/activist, or hacktivist, but she'd spent a significant amount of time working with small teams made up of kindred spirits. They'd spread the work around, making hacks go much quicker but also allowing them to specialize in certain tasks. Although she prided herself as a jack of all trades, Malina's mastery was in digging. She had always been the best and fastest at searching out needed information from all the darkest corners of the web. This necessitated a degree of detective work and skills in picking her way through security measures, but she merely thought of it as knowing where to look.

Two hours ago, since leaving the meeting with Reynolds, Malina and Aubrey had returned to his apartment-turned-makeshift-headquarters. She'd immediately begun reaching out to fellow hackers, crackers, and downright cyber crimi-nals—anyone who might have information on what Drillard had been up to or what might have happened to him.

She didn't expect to hear much from the dozen people she contacted, knowing that people who lived their lives online were generally more paranoid than most, and she knew that if they sniffed out the fact that she was working for the cops, she'd get nowhere very fast. If word got around she was helping the authorities, she'd be immediately blackballed from any future collaborations. Her messages, therefore, had been carefully crafted. She made sure to stress that she was looking for information on Drillard out of concern for him.

There were a few more rocks she could turn over if her initial inquiries came up empty, but for now, she'd wait. She let the tablet fall to the tabletop and turned to look out the window. Sunlight blazed in through the tall glass. It was that bright winter sun, the juxtaposition of the yellow orb seemingly at its brightest and most intense as a precursor to the harsh cold of winter. Compared to her place, an extralong storage unit she'd turned into a quasi-suitable dwelling, Aubrey's apartment was a palace, complete with natural light, fresh water always on tap, food in the refrigerator, more than one room, and an actual bed.

She stood and crossed the living room, passed the leather couch and television, skirted the small kitchen and its spotless synth-granite counters, and stopped in the threshold of Aubrey's bedroom. He worked from the home office he'd set up when they first became partners in their still unnamed investigative firm. He sat in the far corner in front of three large monitors, which displayed 2D and 3D photographs from a grisly crime scene.

"Jesus, Marty, what are you looking at?"

His fingers moved across a touchpad on the desk in front

of him, rotating the central 3D image, showing him every possible angle of an angular blue object. "A dumpster. That murder from a couple nights ago. Look at the pattern of the castoff from the blood spatter."

He pointed at the screen, and Malina saw an arc of reddish-black spray across the blue side of the dumpster, wide on one end, tapering down to a sharp point. To her, it looked like fire spouting from a dragon's mouth. That dried blood had very recently swam through the veins of a living, warm-bodied person, and now it looked like some macabre modern art masterpiece. The thought made her stomach turn.

"Yeah, looks awesome. Not nightmare-inducing what-soever." She didn't bother containing her sarcasm these days. Their working relationship had reached a point where derision and mockery were to be expected if not encouraged.

He spun in his chair to face her, a Cheshire grin plastered on his face. "I have more like it if you want me to put together a photo album that you could peruse on a lazy Sunday."

"As lovely as that would be, I'll pass." She pressed her back against the doorframe. "I've put out my initial round of feelers for info on Drillard. Like I told Liz, don't expect much in return. Most of these people are either reclusive and just want to be left alone or, as is usually the case, totally hostile toward authorities." She jutted her chin toward Aubrey. "What are you working on? Besides your little murder scene there."

Aubrey turned toward the 3D image still hovering on the screen, the blood spatter enlarged to stretch from edge to edge.

"Just this for now." He shrugged. " I'm hoping that if we can give Homicide a little help on this one, they'll ask us to help on other cases." He lifted his hands. "Call it an investment in the future of our firm."

Malina groaned. "Freebies don't pay the bills. Liz said they'd actually pay us for the Drillard case if we make any headway."

He faced her with another, broader smile. "Hey, if we don't make any money soon, that just means we both get to move into your storage hovel."

She raised an eyebrow. "Only room for one there. It's a studio storage hovel." She left Aubrey to his work and moved to the kitchen to refill her coffee.

At the moment, they had nothing to keep them busy. They delivered on their promise to find Gilda Elmyr for Francesca, their only client up until that morning. And weeks ago, Malina found the whereabouts of the four names on the list Francesca brought to them after her...visit with Gilda. Until Malina and Aubrey had anything to go on regarding the Drillard case, she didn't have anything to do.

Standing in the kitchen, she heard typing from Aubrey's bedroom. Her eyes caught sight of a yellow square of paper on the dining table. She moved toward Francesca's list and picked it up, rubbing the paper between her thumb and forefinger. It was old. It had that rough, dry feeling that paper only gets after many years. The four names on it were written in bold black ink, still crisp after such a long time. Next to each name was a red check mark made by Malina every time she found one of them. Her mind filled with an image of four corpses, one for each name. She didn't have the stomach to find out what happened to the people she located for Francesca. Naturally, she assumed the worst and it made her skin go cold.

A chiming sound caught her ear, and her eyes shot to the

desk where she had been working. A box flashed in the corner of one monitor. She knew immediately what it was—a chat window.

Stepping closer to the desk, she bent to read the screen name of the sender. Champion. She couldn't stop the grin that formed on her lips.

His note was short.

I might be able to help. Come see me.

7

Praeceptists

November 10, 2043—12:00 p.m.
Aubrey had always felt a soft but steady buzz when he started a fresh case. For him, it was like unearthing a fossil. At first, it was just a tiny piece of whitish rock poking through the soil. It could belong to any animal that's ever lived, so you make no guesses, initially. Then, as you clear away more dirt, wipe away the dust, and uncover more of the fossil, the story starts to unfold before you, preserved in time as the truth always is.

What has been can never be completely undone.

The streets were quiet around Aubrey and his partner. The pair walked the two miles from Aubrey's apartment to the home of Malina's contact, Champion. Aubrey had insisted the time and exertion would be good for them, that it would help them think over the problems ahead and those likely to come up in the near future.

The noise of the cars passing by them was, as usual, nearly silent. The people within the vehicles conducted their private affairs behind darkened glass, paying no mind to the world outside. Foot traffic was light under the bright early afternoon sun.

"This Champion is someone from your hacker days?" Aubrey shoved his hands deeper into the pockets of his coat. The air was biting cold in spite of clear skies and the powerful sun.

"He's a contact," Malina replied.

Aubrey angled his shoulders toward her as he walked against the wind. "I need to know more about him than that. Who is he? Why would he have information on Drillard? Can we trust him?"

Malina pulled her hood over her head and sighed loud enough that Aubrey heard it over the wind buffeting them. "Champion and I were part of a group. We called ourselves the Colektive." She gestured with one hand toward a department store they passed. "We were just a group of do-good hackers trying to keep corporations and people in power honest."

"What color hats did you all wear? White, gray, or black?" Aubrey took mental notes as they talked. Any information was good information.

"We were definitely gray hats, all of us." She dipped her head lower and said, "Some of the others probably did some black hat stuff on the side. Our de facto leaders decided what projects we'd work on, each of us getting our assignments without knowing what anyone else was doing, without always knowing the full picture."

"So even if you're caught, you can't turn on the others because you don't really know what they're up to." Aubrey thought it sounded like the Colektive operated like most drug cartels. By keeping members ignorant, they mitigated the damage one person could do to the organization as a whole.

"Right. But sometimes we had to work together on things."

She shrugged deeply. "Champion and I worked on a few ... things together. And we became sort of friendly."

"Friendly?" Aubrey asked.

"The Colektive hasn't operated in years," Malina said, obviously ignoring Aubrey's question. "Currently, I work mostly on exposing assholes to the light of day, so I don't mix with people like Drillard and those crowds anymore. Champ, however, still has his fingers in a little bit of everything, so his intel is probably pretty solid."

"How would Champ know Drillard in the first place?" Aubrey asked. "Even if they practiced the same type of gray hat hacking or cracking, you said yourself that these folks keep to themselves."

"Drillard was ..." Malina drew an audible breath. "He was one of the leaders of the Colektive."

Aubrey froze on the spot. He felt his own eyes go wide and had to blink away the tears the wind induced. Malina continued for a few paces, then stopped and turned.

"You were friends with the murder victim?" His breath came out in a white cloud.

She threw her hands up in supplication. "More like coworkers, but yeah, I knew him."

"Why didn't you mention that fact to Liz?"

A passerby brushed against his shoulder, which broke his momentary shock over this revelation, and he resumed walking.

"Martin," Malina said, giving the area around them a sweeping glance, "the things we did could get me in a lot of trouble. The people we targeted were very powerful, and if they ever found out ..."

"Okay. Okay." Aubrey understood, but his mind spun with

questions about this woman he'd gone into business with. How much was there that he didn't know about her?

Two blocks from Champion's building, a man and woman across the street caught his attention. They stood shoulder to shoulder. The man was black with a full head of gray hair and wore a light-blue suit, patchy in places. The woman had on a long wool dress and cardigan; her blonde hair hung straight down over her ears. She stood stock still, clutching a book against her chest. Her eyes were closed, but her lips moved in what Aubrey could only guess was silent prayer. The man raised a cardboard sign over his head that read, *Technology will be your end. Beware God's judgment.*

Under the handwritten message, there appeared a symbol Aubrey hadn't seen in years—a narrow cross with three concentric circles around the center.

The cross also hung from a cord around the woman's neck.

"Praeceptists," Aubrey said.

Malina stopped. "Where?"

He pointed across the street.

"Jesus," she said. "Haven't seen any of them in a while."

Aubrey shook his head. "Not much these days, but they're around." The man with the sign spun in place. The reverse side read, *His wrath is upon you. Abandon the darkness and embrace the light.* "When I was still patrolling, we'd get calls about people harassing them every now and then. You think hackers are insular; those people keep to themselves like no one I've ever seen."

"If your religion shuns technology, why live in a city built around it?"

Aubrey didn't fault anyone for their belief systems, far from it. Each to their own as long as they didn't cause any trouble. And the Praeceptists had never been known to cause anyone any real harm.

"Their flavor of faith is nothing new. I don't know much about them, but I do know they're harmless."

He and Malina continued staring at the two street preachers like they were a sideshow. Unease began to seep into Aubrey's bones.

"Probably out because of the bridge disaster," he said.

As if she heard Aubrey and Malina talking about her from across the street, the Praeceptist woman's eyes shot open and looked directly at them. Her eyes bored into Aubrey's. Not with anger or fear, just awareness. Awareness of Aubrey's presence.

Malina pulled on his shirt sleeve. "Let's go before you make any more friends."

He took three steps and froze. The low omnipresent hum of car traffic had vanished. He turned toward the street. Every vehicle in the road had stopped. Frustrated drivers and passengers could be seen looking around quizzically, punching buttons on their consoles, talking to the air, banging on dashboards. They were growing angrier by the second.

"What the hell?" Aubrey whispered.

Malina didn't respond. She scanned the lanes of stalled cars along with Aubrey.

A buzzing sound pierced the silence. He pivoted toward it. In the near distance, a few blocks away, a drone flew low between the buildings like a small plane seeking an emergency landing on the road. The sofa sized robot skirted the roofs of the cars, mere feet above them, traveling at what Aubrey figured was around sixty miles per hour.

Aubrey and Malina stood rooted to the sidewalk watching the drone soar in their direction. Instinctively, without looking away from the drone, Aubrey reached out a hand and found Malina's shoulder.

Fifty feet from them, the yellow drone banked hard toward the opposite sidewalk. It glanced off the top of a delivery truck, pinwheeled through the air, and crashed into the glass facade of a tall commercial building ten feet above the sidewalk. The impact shattered the windows on the first floor and sent shards of glass raining down on the pedestrians below. The drone appeared mostly shredded from where Aubrey stood, it's rear third protruding from the building like shrapnel from a wounded body. The rear panel of the yellow flying box was stamped with its owner's emblem—a silver and gold shield with the words Metropolitan Police Department in blue letters over the spread wings of an eagle.

"Let's go," Aubrey said, stepping into the street. "Someone might need help."

The cars in the road were still frozen in place, making for an easy crossing. In ten seconds, they reached the other sidewalk. Pieces of glass, metal, and plastic littered the ground. Every pedestrian stood in shock, hands covering their heads, jogging away from the crash site.

A quick scan of the crowd told Aubrey that no one was seriously injured. While Aubrey was looking over the cuts in an elderly woman's scalp, someone screamed.

"Another one."

Looking up, Aubrey caught sight of it. Another drone

moving toward them from the opposite end of the street than the last. He straightened and took a good look at it. This one moved slower, not at full tilt like the last one. Ten yards from the scene, it stopped and rotated. The side of this drone, roughly the size of a toaster oven, was emblazoned with a red cross on a white background. The drone moved slowly in a strafing pattern across the crowd. A green light flashed from an eye on its underbelly.

"It's okay," Aubrey said. "It's just a medical drone assessing the scene and calling back for help."

The tension in the crowd seemed to fade as people around him settled themselves to await the first responders.

Aubrey finished up with the old woman, reassuring her that she'd be fine, nothing to worry about and to just have a seat on the bench until help came. After searching for a moment, he found Malina kneeling next to a couple near the edge of the road.

It was the Praeceptists. Both were cowering under the man's sign, visibly shaking. Malina had a hand on the woman's back and turned toward him as he approached. Her eyes were sad, her face doleful.

"It's him. It's his wrath," the Praeceptist woman said. She sobbed into her hands while she spoke. "Lord the Father sent it."

The man next to her stood slowly; his clothes were disheveled. The sign fell to his side.

"Yes," he said. "Yes, it was from him." His voice grew steadily louder with each word. "This is his wrath, citizens." He pointed at the drone buried in the structure above them. He shouted now, spittle flying from his mouth, his entire body vibrating with what could only be rage. "This is your doom!

Abandon your ways now or suffer his mighty vengeance!" His eyes searched the crowd, bulging from their sockets. "Live by heresy … and you shall die by heresy!"

As the last syllable left the man's lips, the cars on the street resumed their quiet advance to their destinations.

* * *

"Thanks, Jim. I'm here at the scene of the incident." Eula Fromer spoke directly into the camera drone hovering two feet from her face. The robot's operator stood behind it, staring down at the touchscreen hanging from a lanyard around his neck. "Behind me you'll see what the police are calling a technically faulty drone that witnesses are saying sped very low, mere inches from the tops of the cars on the road, just before it slammed into the front of this building, which houses corporate offices for the First Bank of Aberdeen."

She turned to allow the camera to view the scene. The drone's lenses whirred as they zoomed and panned. Beneath the impact crater in the building, police had cordoned off the area, and work crews swept up broken glass. A flatbed truck with a crane attached to its rear had been parked along the curb, and an operator reached its long arm with an attached grasping tool to extract the rogue drone. A dozen people were gathered around the police barrier watching.

Just as she was about to turn back to the camera to continue her segment, a man with wild hair and wearing a loose blue puffer jacket stepped into frame.

"I have a message for the folks at home. I was here." He pointed to the street corner nearest the crash site. "I was standing right there. I saw it all."

Eula tried to make the most of the interruption. "Can you tell us what you saw, sir?" She moved in close. The directional mics on the drone pointed at the man.

"I'll tell you what I saw. I saw a robot with a mind of its own trying to kill people." He pointed back at the scene without turning his head from the camera or Eula. "That thing was on a mission. It was deliberate, I tell you." He threw his hands in the air. "It was going right for 'em!"

The producer's voice in her earpiece told her to stay with the man, to goad him.

"You're telling me, and the people watching at home, that the drone meant to crash and was trying to hurt the people on the sidewalk?"

"Damn right," he said. "After the bridge thing. I'm telling you and all you," he pointed at the camera, "the AI has lost its marbles. Can't trust it no more."

Eula edged the witness out of frame and squared her shoulders to the camera. "As you can see, people down here are concerned about the recent incidents. Can authorities take appropriate measures to keep us safe? I'm Eula Fromer."

The red light on top of the camera drone's central lens winked out. The wild-haired witness wandered off muttering to himself, and Eula watched Carl the operator land the camera and start packing it away. She reached into her coat pocket for a cigarette when an enormous crunching and grinding sound made her recoil and duck. After searching the vicinity, she realized the danger wasn't close by. To her, it sounded like cars crashing. Normally, she would think it unlikely, as traffic accidents just didn't happen in the city. Lately, however, she'd begun to question that truth.

"Where did that come from?" Carl asked, stock still over the camera's case.

She turned on the spot. More crashing sounds, metal on metal. Glass shattering. Horns blaring. She saw the six police officers around the drone crash notice it too. They were talking into their handsets and pointing, running toward her one second, then past her the next.

"Follow them," she said and began jogging behind the cops. They turned the corner and sprinted toward the next block, the location of a major intersection.

A second later, the camera was in the air, hovering over her and keeping pace for several of her strides until it sped away ahead of her and the cops. As they neared the intersection, she watched the drone bank right. She followed it. Cresting the edge of the corner building, she saw it. A traffic pileup like she'd never seen in the age of AI control over the city.

Cars herringboned off the road into adjacent buildings. Some flipped on their sides; others turned completely around. A hundred vehicles for at least two blocks packed and crushed into the short span. At least four she could see had been pushed up and over the cars in front of them. The lead vehicle, and the main culprit for the massive collision, was a heavy garbage truck lying on its side across all lanes of traffic on the one-way street. It acted like a dam for the river of cars behind it.

Walking nearer to the wreckage, sounds of suffering reached her—moans, screams, cries for help. The smells of hot coolant, burnt rubber, and melting plastic filled the air.

Eula stopped thirty feet short of the first vehicle. The cops ran ahead and began pulling people from their cars and applying first aid. Over it all, in the twisting streams of smoke, the camera drone circled, it's blinking red light breaking through the haze with each flash.

57

8

The Colektive

Aubrey walked the long narrow hallway with Malina at his side. The walls were a neutral beige and bore the signs of the years since the last fresh coat. Bulbs overhead burned a dull yellow in their fixtures. Each door they passed issued forth signs of life—babies crying, music blaring, couples fighting.

Coming abreast of the second to last apartment on their right, the door burst open. A man in a white T-shirt bearing a week's worth of stains stood in the doorway. His jeans hung low and loose with holes at the knees.

"You work for the landlord?" He spoke in a raised voice, but before Aubrey or Malina could answer, the man continued. "The wireless is shit in this building, and that asshole next door won't keep those goddamn dogs quiet. He ain't even supposed to have dogs. I had to get rid of my cat before I moved into this shit heap, and you lettin' him have dogs." He raised his arms and cocked his head. "What the fuck, man?"

Aubrey looked at Malina then back at the man. He opened his mouth to respond, but she beat him to it. "We'll look into it, sir. Very sorry for your trouble." She smiled brightly and pulled Aubrey by the arm. After a moment, the door slammed shut.

He gave Malina a confused look.

"Don't engage with crazy or stupid." She shrugged her bag a little higher on her shoulder. "Sort of my motto."

"Good advice. Is this it?" He pointed to the last door on the right side of the hallway, the number 2A nailed to it. As they came nearer the door, the sound of dogs barking echoed from within the apartment.

"Yeah, that's it," she replied. She looked down at his side and poked at the pistol secured in its holster. "Think you're going to need that?"

He patted the sidearm. "Never know."

Aubrey raised his hand to knock, and Malina said, "No need. He knows we're here."

The barking grew louder, the dogs were just on the other side of the door with deep, resonant voices. Aubrey turned to Malina with his eyebrows stitched together in a questioning glare, to which she replied with a knowing smile. He felt as if he were in the midst of some inside joke. His watch vibrated, and looking down, he saw the various widgets and notifications on its screen going haywire—flashing and scrambling numbers and letters like an old-timey television set losing its signal.

"What the hell?" he said. Malina didn't respond, but he could see her watch behaving the same way.

They both stared at the door. The dogs continued barking in that desperate way, like when a squirrel is just on the other side of a chain-link fence. The urge to reach out and bang on the door was overwhelming, and he shook his head with impatience.

"Don't worry, he's coming," Malina said.

"How do you even know he's here?" Aubrey asked.

"He's always here. He's a recluse."

"Identify yourself," said an electronic voice from somewhere in the vicinity of the peephole.

"Champ, it's Malrey," she said in a clear, loud voice.

Aubrey whispered, "Malrey?"

She shook her head. "Later."

He looked back toward the door, which had begun to click in places along its edges. A soft thunk, and it swung open to reveal a man Aubrey had not expected.

When Malina told him they were going to visit an old friend from the Colektive, he'd expected to meet a stereotypical hacker—an obese male with bad skin and bad hair. A socially awkward introvert. The man he met at the door of apartment 2A was the furthest thing from that.

Champ was a stout six feet three inches tall, built like a rugby player with muscles bulging under ebony skin. Standing in nothing but gray sweatpants in the open doorway, his shoulders nearly touched both sides of the frame. His bald head reflected the low light from inside the apartment, and his clean shave accentuated a sculpted chin.

"Holy cow," he said with a smile that produced dimples like tiny bottomless craters. "It is you. Mal in the flesh." He stretched out to hug Malina, whose tiny frame got lost in the man's arms. Three massive German shepherds sat on their haunches just behind him, obediently waiting for their master's command.

A slightly red-in-the-face Malina pointed to Aubrey, "This is my business partner, Martin Aubrey."

He and Champ shook hands, and Aubrey noticed himself

squeezing a little harder than usual.

Once inside, Champ was quite hospitable, offering them tea and coffee after they sat down on his tufted leather sofa. The living room was neatly done in a modernist style with a nod to pop culture. Posters of famous movies made over to look like oil paintings in wooden frames adorned the walls. Bookshelves were lined with real books and comics. A huge colorful rug dominated the floor. A massive computer workstation sat in the corner. Its screens were dark, but lights on the monitors and a number of small black boxes whirred with LEDs blinking on their surfaces.

"I've actually been meaning to get ahold of you, Mal," Champ said, sitting on a chair made of curved wood.

"Why is that?" she said, sipping from a ceramic mug.

"Rumors. I heard a few that said you were behind that whole Zentransa thing. The leak. That you were the one who took down Sarazin and Ventana."

Aubrey tried to hide the shock building inside him. They'd kept quiet about their investigation into the revolutionary pill and its equally important founder. They had been the ones to take down Zentransa, Ventana, and Sarazin and had nearly lost their lives too many times in the process, but they'd been very careful not to take credit or share their involvement.

Malina gave Champ a confused grimace. "I don't know what you're talking about. That would have been too big for one person anyway."

Champ held up his enormous hands, palms out. "Okay, okay. Keep it to yourself. Why you wouldn't want the world to know you did that, I don't have a clue. Hell of a flex if it was you." He continued smiling and nodding at Malina.

Moments of pleasantries passed, in which it became clear to

Aubrey that the two hackers used to be more than just friends. Aubrey's ire for the shirtless maladroit only grew the longer they sat and talked.

"Let's get to why we're here," Aubrey said, interrupting the reminiscing. "We don't want to waste any more of your time."

Malina drew a breath and said, "Right. Like I said when I contacted you, we wanted to ask you some questions about one of our old friends, Drillard." She reached into her shoulder bag and pulled out a scroll tablet. Unrolling it flat on the coffee table, she tapped it. The screen was scrambled, just as Aubrey's watch had been in the hallway.

"Oh, let me get that." Champ pulled a phone from a hip pocket and tapped it a few times. A second later, the scrambling ceased.

On Malina's tablet, an image of the ghostly face of Drillard appeared, lying on his side with an eye half open, mouth agape, motes of debris pressed into the dead man's cheek. Champ recoiled at the sight, his visage turning a noticeable green.

"Yeah, sorry," she said. "I didn't want to tell you online." She paused. "He was killed."

"I ..." Champ stammered, still avoiding the picture on Malina's scroll tablet, "How do you even know it's him? I've never seen him in person. Have you?"

Aubrey watched her zoom out on the image, showing the dead man's upper half. She then repositioned the picture and zoomed in on the tattoo of the white rabbit on Drillard's back.

"No, but we all knew about his famous tattoo." She slid the tablet toward Champ. "He bragged when he got it and used it as his damn avatar for years."

Champ nodded grimly and turned his head to stare into space.

"You said you had some info. What has he been up to?" Aubrey asked.

Champ shook his head. "I don't have the stomach for this kind of thing, Malina. I never thought you would be looking for his fucking killer." He chanced a peek at the tablet again and immediately shut his eyes.

"Was he working with anyone else from the Colektive?" Malina asked.

"No. I don't know …" He squeezed his eyes tighter, creases stretching across his temples. His abdomen spasmed as if he were about to vomit and doing his best to suppress it.

Aubrey reached out and turned off the tablet that was clearly distracting the man. "What were you going to tell Malina about Drillard?"

Opening one eye and seeming grateful the tablet was off, Champ relaxed. After a deep breath, he said, "I'm sorry. I mostly just wanted to see you." He eyed Malina as if Aubrey was invisible. "It's been a while, you know."

From the corner of his eye, Aubrey watched Malina glance down at her empty hands.

"Do you have any information on him at all?" Aubrey pressed.

Champ shifted his gaze to Aubrey. "I've heard a little bit but nothing really believable."

"Can you elaborate?" Aubrey asked.

"I don't know. Somebody saying something about Drillard and a few others working together." He paused. "On some big job." Champ threw up his hands in desperation. "Look, I wouldn't say anything to you at all if I hadn't just seen Drillard's corpse. And nobody will ever know I told you any of this. Right?"

"Of course," Malina said.

Aubrey took a few notes on his phone before proceeding. "Who was saying this about Drillard?"

Champ shrugged. "Friends of friends of friends. You know how rumor mills are."

"Why do these friends of friends of friends believe Drillard and these others were working on something?" Aubrey asked.

Champ rubbed his shoulder with a meaty hand and rolled his head from side to side on his thick neck. "He and a couple of guys dropped off the grid. Just disappeared. No trace of them in chat rooms, forums, their own websites. No traffic whatsoever bearing their monikers. When that happens, generally people think it's because they're up to something. And when a few people disappear at the same time, it's only natural to think they've teamed up."

Aubrey took a moment to record the information, then continued his questions. "You said it was unbelievable. Why is that?"

Champ leaned back into his chair and focused on Malina. "You remember Ambrosia?"

"Of course," she replied.

"Supposedly, he and Drillard are working together."

A knowing look passed between the two hackers.

"No way," she said.

"I don't get it." Aubrey's eyes bounced between the two of them for a second.

Champ filled in the gaps. "Drillard and Ambrosia were the unofficial leaders of the Colektive. And they hated each other. Always disagreeing on strategies and how to approach things. But mostly, they fought about targets." Champ crossed his arms and sunk deeper in his chair. "Ambrosia always wanted to make a splash, go after the biggest targets. 'Collateral damage be damned,' he'd always say."

Next to Aubrey, Malina adjusted herself. "They had a huge falling out, and that was the end of the Colektive. The two of them working together would be hard to believe," she said.

"Who else is Drillard rumored to be working with?" Aubrey asked.

"A guy named Elton," Champ replied.

Aubrey took down the name. "Another alias?"

"Drillard, Ambrosia, Elton. Those are handles. I don't know their real names." Champ ran a hand over his scalp.

Aubrey shot an eye toward Malina.

"I'll find out," she said. At this, Champ scowled, to which Malina replied, "It's for their own good, Champ. They may be in trouble."

Moments later, having wrapped up their questions, they stood at the open door to leave. The tall, half-naked hacker leaned in for a long hug with Malina. Aubrey was tempted to pull out the picture of Drillard's dead body again but resisted the urge.

Five steps into the hallway, Malina stopped and looked back at Champ leaning against the doorjamb.

"One more question," she said.

Puzzled, Aubrey backtracked to stand next to her. Champ raised an eyebrow, and his grin faded. "Okay. Whatcha got?"

Malina hiked her bag up higher on her shoulder. "Have you been watching the news?"

Champ's face relaxed and his grin reappeared. "The bridge?"

She nodded. "Thoughts?"

Champ shrugged, drawing out the gesture for a long second. "No. No thoughts. All I know is it wasn't me."

This grabbed Aubrey's attention. "Wait." He gripped Malina's elbow. "Are you saying …" He didn't have to finish the sentence.

Malina cocked her head and inhaled deeply. "It's possible. Unlikely but possible."

They were on their way back to the elevator when Aubrey's pocket buzzed. He pulled out his phone. The screen displayed a headline from the *Sentinel Sun News* titled "Deadly Traffic Pileup in the City—Another Glitch or Something Worse?"

He showed Malina the phone as a pool of icy water settled in his gut.

9

The Coppice

Three Weeks Ago

Francesca had to crane her neck in order to take in the tall apartment building she had just exited. From the sidewalk, the structure appeared to go on forever, piercing the clouds high above to continue beyond into the stratosphere. Not even when she was a child, before her long isolation at the Pupil's School of the Order, had she seen a building this size, let alone so many clumped together. The city was uncharted territory for her, and perhaps, it always would be. Her exposure to the urban landscape was, naturally, limited after being raised as a child in the countryside until her father, her last surviving parent, perished in a flash mudslide. After a short spell at an orphanage, she was taken in by the Pupil's School, which was buried deep in the great pine forests near the Coppice. That monolithic, featureless tower known to many as the Keep—as the Coppice to her and her kind, and officially as the Maryland Regional Corrections Center—was the prison that housed the convicted while their fate was decided by the Order of the Coppice.

The Coppice was where Francesca should be at the moment, assigned to a ward of four hundred men or women for whom she was charged with observing, judging, and sentencing. If deemed incorrigible or otherwise irredeemable, Francesca could, as was her right, select the inmate in question for a swift death. Tapper, the derogatory nickname given to Members of the Order of the Coppice, had its roots in the means by which a Member dispatched an inmate; a special Solution applied to the base of a person's neck via a Member's bare forefinger. Thus, it was said, they killed with a tap, although few inmates knew about the Solution or the rituals performed before and after the Task was administered. Francesca was nonetheless amazed, on occasion, at how close to reality the rumors came.

The Coppice was where Francesca belonged. Instead, she found herself outside Martin Aubrey's apartment building having just asked him and Malina Maddox for help…again. They'd found Gilda Elmyr for her, and though she loathed to ask it of them again, she had neither the means nor the expertise to find the four more names she'd uncovered at Gilda's home. She didn't have to simply find them, she reminded herself, but she must prove their guilt in connection to the child theft crimes perpetrated by agents of Maryland's Child Residential Services.

She and her former mentor had discovered the child theft scheme that went back for decades, almost to the founding of the Order itself. Orphans were the lifeblood of the Order of the Coppice, providing the only allowable source for new Members. They were adopted, housed, and educated at the Pupil's School of the Order from a young age, usually preadolescent, to ultimately become full Sisters and Brothers of the Order. The law allowed the Order to adopt only the children who were seen as having little to no hope of being taken in by a welcoming family. Soon after its founding, it became clear to the leaders of the Order that unwanted orphans would only provide a small fraction of the number of Members needed to properly control the prison population.

Francesca didn't know exactly when it began, but at some point, the highest-ranking Member of the Order, known as the Member Principal, began bribing orphanages for their most desirable children. Children that would, more than likely, have found a home with a loving family. Children like seven-year-old Francesca, who was told that there was no hope anyone would adopt her. She was too old. Babies had the best chance at adoption by a good family. Babies like her brother Hank. Hank was just over one year old when the two of them were placed in the orphanage. Gilda Elmyr, the orphanage's director at the time, told her that no one would adopt her and Hank together. Hank had a better shot at being placed with a nice family if he were alone. And the longer she stayed, the less hope there was for baby Hank. If she left with those strange people from the Order and went to live at their school, baby Hank would have a chance at life.

She left to live with the teachers and students at the Pupil's School. She left her brother behind because she was lied to. She left her brother behind because others were greedy and selfish, and they deserved whatever happened to them…

She stopped herself. Revenge was not what she, as a Member, practiced. Malice and passion were for everyone else. She observed, she assessed, she judged. She selected people for the Sacred Task with careful calculus—for who they were, not what they had done.

Francesca opened her eyes, only just realizing that her brief brush with an emotional response had forced them closed. A cold breeze crossed her face, and she blinked back the tears forming. Beyond the glass facade of the building, the doorman stood like a statue, staring at her with an expression of horror mixed with confusion. She had assumed that, it being winter, her long black cassock wouldn't stand out as much as it usually did. She had hoped she could move about the city without eliciting the terrified response that her kind always did. Now, she concluded that from afar, perhaps, she could fool people, but up close, there was no mistaking a Tapper for what they were.

She brushed the light dusting of snow from her shoulders and walked away from Martin Aubrey's apartment building. Half an hour later, she arrived at the train station to depart for the Coppice.

* * *

The train hummed noiselessly along the high monorail, maglev track above the forest of evergreens reaching up from the earth in neat rows. Francesca had a row to herself in the back of the mostly empty first car. As she watched the tall trees blur past, she replayed in her head the conversation she had with Aubrey and Malina earlier that morning.

The last time she had seen either of them was when she requested the whereabouts of Gilda. The time before that had been when she met them for the first time—before the riot at the Coppice. The three of them and Rudolfo had bonded quickly during the ensuing violent chaos, each saving one or more of the others lives a handful of times throughout the day.

Before the crisis at the Coppice, she knew Aubrey had abhorred Members of the Order. He'd been outspoken about his disdain for their unquestioned authority to select inmates for death and the way in which they did so. Rudolfo, she learned, had actually appeared in a courtroom during a trial in which Aubrey, as the lead detective, was a key witness. Rudolfo had entered the courtroom and parted the crowd there as if he were covered in plague-filled pustules, the room going cold as the death dealer sat among them.

Aubrey confessed to them that the feeling of dread he felt around Members would not leave him until, several months ago, he received a call from Rudolfo himself stating that he had information that might help Aubrey in his investigation of the Boarding School Syndrome and the OFP bombings. That phone call was the impetus which forced Aubrey to visit the Keep with his new and very reluctant partner, Malina, and which resulted in the ensuing prison riot and battle for their lives within. It also led to Francesca becoming the first client of Aubrey and Malina's infant investigative firm.

Francesca had no real friends in the way most people would define the term, but she warmly considered her relationship with the two of them to be friendly, if not a true friendship.

Over steaming cups of coffee and tea, they sat at Aubrey's dining table exchanging pleasantries. Moving onto business, Francesca had thought it prudent to update them on the status of Gilda Elmyr.

"Please don't," Aubrey said. "We…um…saw the news stories about her mysterious…about the strange circumstances of her death."

Sensing their unease, Francesca tried to reassure them. "Martin, if the police want to know who ended her life, all they have to do is ask. I was completely within my rights to select her for the Sacred Task." She paused to be sure they understood. "I explained this to Gilda as well on the night she expired."

"Yes," Aubrey held up a hand, "I know, but—"

"And since it cannot be called murder," Francesca cut him off, "you and Malina cannot be arrested as accessories. Therefore, you and Ms. Maddox have nothing to worry about."

Aubrey's eyes fell to the table, and he nodded slowly. "It's not the legal ramifications that are particularly concerning to me, although"—he looked up at the her—"they do concern me. It's more the questions of…distaste we have for the outcome of the work we do for you."

"Death. You have a distaste for death." She stated this as a matter of fact, not a question, and Aubrey nodded his agreement. "Martin, I take for granted you understand I treated Gilda no differently than I would an inmate under my charge."

"I do," Aubrey replied, crossing his arms.

Francesca sincerely wanted them to feel no guilt whatsoever for helping her find Gilda. "I observed her for quite some time before selecting her. I observed her and judged her as being incorrigible and irredeemable. Her past crimes elicited no reconciliatory actions by her in her present life, and her conduct on the day she died was no different than the day she lied to me and the times she lied to so many others about prospective families." Francesca attempted to come across as something akin to a judge, devoid of passion but filled with conviction. "She trafficked in the lives of stolen children. That is a fact, and she would, in my judgment, continue committing those atrocities had she not aged out of the enterprise. It was not remorse but necessity that stopped her crimes."

"Martin and I agree." Malina had been quiet since they sat down. "The world is better off without Gilda Elmyr."

Aubrey nodded.

"And we were willing to deliver Gilda's whereabouts to you, even though we knew what might happen to her." Malina spread her hands in front of her. "But you must see how all the killing stuff feels a little…shitty for us. Right?"

The word "shitty" caught Francesca off guard, but, after a pause, she spoke again. "Yes. I do frequently forget that those who do not serve in my line find death in any form as abhorrent, no matter the circumstances. I know, Martin, that you have been exposed to death and killing by others…and yourself"—she eyed him for two seconds before continuing—"but death and killing in the heat of combat is quite different, isn't it?"

Aubrey raised his chin slightly. "It is. Very different."

Francesca, needing their help, chose her next words carefully. "I am here for more information. The whereabouts of four more individuals involved in the child trafficking crimes with Gilda Elmyr." She paused. "I can promise you that if I judge any of these four people to be reformed, I will not select them for the Sacred Task."

Aubrey swung his gaze to Malina for a moment, then turned back to Francesca and said, "We'll help you. We'll always help you. If there was ever a wise killer at the Keep, it's you. I just wanted you to know how we feel about it."

Leaving the apartment minutes later, grateful that her two associates had agreed to help, she was stopped by Malina.

"Any more luck with finding your brother?" Malina asked.

Francesca felt her lips press together into a tiny frown. "No. Maybe one of the four names on the list I gave you has more information, but I'm attempting to temper my optimism with reality. In all likelihood, I will not find Hank for a very long time and only after an exhaustive search."

Malina shrugged. "I've been looking, as you know, but all the records are sealed and probably only in hard copies anyway. But I'll keep searching, and if you find anything, let me know." Malina then pressed a small tablet and a phone into Francesca's hand. "Take these. They'll help you. The phone has all Martin's and my contact info and some other people who might be able to help. Just in case we aren't available."

Francesca laid a hand on the devices now tucked into the front pocket of her cassock. Feeling the train begin its long, soft turn to the left signifying the ride was nearly over and the prison would soon come into view, she began to reconsider the status of her relationship with Aubrey and Malina. Perhaps the word "friends" was an apt description.

* * *

Francesca leered down through the glass floor, down into the hollow void they called the Great Atrium, the open-air column of space that ran the full height of the Coppice, from the basement level to the forty-eighth floor, where she stood. The atrium was designed to help with air flow throughout the cylindrical monolithic prison complex and to allow natural light to pour in from above; the glass floor beneath her feet and the glass ceiling over her head facilitated this. The topmost floor, the forty-eighth, was the only level not pierced through by the Great Atrium, enabling her to stand in its very center with nothing between her and oblivion but several panes of thick glass.

The forty-seven levels of the prison beneath her resembled an ant farm. Small spots of white jittered around as prisoners milled about here and there on the catwalk that surrounded the atrium on each floor. A wire cage being the only thing that kept them from falling in. Some inmates chatted away in pairs—unheard by her—to exchange information, conversation, or contraband. Some of the bald, tattooed heads stayed low, hoping to go unnoticed, while others were bolder and strutted around like arrogant cocks.

Intermingled among the white inmate uniforms that ebbed and flowed in Francesca's field of vision were the black shapes of the Members of the Order, or Tappers as the inmates called them. Unlike the prisoners, the Members were as still as statues, easy to miss among the comings and goings of a prisoner's daily life. Anywhere they stood, however, an invisible halo formed around them free of prisoners. Such was their mystique and power that inmates, no matter their crimes or prowess, gave them a wide berth.

According to most prisoners, all Members were one in the same—Tappers, Grim Reapers, Death Bringers. One would kill you just as quick and cold as the next. But there was one Member who had developed a reputation that warranted a special level of fear and awe—something bordering on respect.

"That one. With the hair." Francesca heard them whispering about her one day. "The ghost. White hair, white skin. Killed three-hundred in one drop. In the mess hall during the riots. She came in with some magic shit, man. Wiped 'em out."

The rumors about her were only partially true. She had

indeed attacked a large gang of prisoners holding her friends Martin and Malina hostage in one of the mess halls. She wasn't certain how many actually died from the attack, if any. And she didn't use magic. She used chemistry. She and her old Mentor, Rudolfo, mixed buckets of bleach and ammonia to create chloramine, a highly noxious gas, and used it to clear the mess hall of inmates and rescue their friends.

The fact that she'd been away from the Coppice recently and hadn't been given her own ward to watch over only added to the intensity of the gossip about her. She was being punished. She was training other Tappers to be as deadly as her. She was taking over the Order, working from the outside to usurp the Head Tapper. She'd be back soon to kill anyone that had ever looked at her cross-eyed.

"Sister Francesca," called a deep but soft voice behind her.

Francesca raised her head and turned toward a small plump black man sporting a stringy beard and dressed in a Member's cassock. He stood on the outer edge of the round glass floor, and his hands were steepled in front of his chest. As they locked eyes, he warmly bowed his head, which was covered in close-cropped gray hair.

Two elder Members of the Order, Brother Charles and Sister Whitney, who had just taken over as overseers at the Pupil's School of the Order of the Coppice, walked away from Member Principal Cormac by using the walking path that circumvented the glass floor. They didn't greet or acknowledge Francesca. She wondered to herself whether this was due to the rumors circulating about her or some other reason entirely.

She shook off the thought and lowered her head in reply to Cormac's bow. He waved her over, opening a door on the outer wall and standing aside to let her pass. She crossed to the door and squinted against the powerful reflection of the midday sun that assailed her from the glossy white surface that covered the walls of the round room. Every photon of light seemed to be focused on her retinas, the force of which compounded by her staring down into the dark bowels of the prison for several minutes before.

She entered an antechamber and seated herself at a small round table. Soon Francesca was followed by the Member Principal, who planted himself across from her. The room was just as white as the space she'd left a moment ago, but there were no windows here, no violent rays of sunlight aiming to blind her.

Cormac lifted a tablet from the table and scrolled through it for a moment while Francesca sat patiently, her hands clasped across her lap.

Several minutes passed in silence until Member Principal Cormac set the tablet down and leaned back against his chair, taking Francesca in.

"Thank you for coming, Sister," he said.

"My pleasure to serve."

"I trust you've been"—his eyes searched the air—"keeping yourself productive during your convalescence."

"I have." She knew he couldn't say what he wanted to say any more than she could. Her missions in the city couldn't be sanctioned by the Order itself. Were she caught and detained by authorities and, albeit unlikely, found guilty of murder for the lives she'd taken, she'd subsequently be deemed a rogue Member—after which she'd necessarily have to be disavowed and defrocked. Her time away was being officially referred to as "mental fitness recovery" due to the trauma she suffered during the riots.

Soon after the riots were put down, Brother Cormac was appointed to be Member Principal of the Order of the Coppice. Almost immediately, he summoned Francesca to his quarters, where he informed her that she was being granted an undetermined amount of time to recover. However much time she needed, it was hers. When he told her she'd need to keep herself busy to ensure swift healing, he handed her a picture of a woman. The woman she recognized quite well as Gilda Elmyr. Francesca needed no other instructions. She understood her task perfectly—perform her function as a Member of the Order. There was a known criminal who needed judging, needed sentencing. And it would be her prerogative to decide the woman's fate.

Francesca scratched an itch on the back of her left hand, then lifted the edge of her glove to examine the spot. "I thought I was nearly finished, ready to return, but I determined there were four more distinct phases of my recovery."

Member Principal Cormac lifted his chin slowly. "I see." He rested an elbow on the edge of the table. "And have you begun these four phases?"

Francesca continued eying her hand and the skin around her wrist. "I have but only just. I'm confident I can complete the phases in the coming weeks."

"Ah." Cormac rubbed his beard and stared blankly across the room. "Well, we look forward to having you back here. Or you could go back to the Pupil's School for a short time before returning here. Whichever you prefer."

She liked the new Member Principal. He was a gentle soul, seemingly not suited for the life of a Member, but it was well known that efficiencies on his ward were high and he was well respected among the Order.

"Thank you." Her eyes wandered the room and eventually landed on the door to her left. Through it was the previous Member Principal's library, housing thousands of books all ordered by color so that the walls of the room undulated in vivid waves from brown and orange to yellow and red and blue.

As if sensing her question, Cormac said, "I've not redecorated yet. But the books are gone. Well, not gone, just down at the Pupil's School."

"What will it be?" She faced him again.

He frowned. "I'm not certain. Maybe a gym? I do like to exercise."

She couldn't stop her eyes from veering down to the man's well-rounded belly.

"I said I like to exercise, not that I actually do it very often." He patted his stomach and chuckled heartily.

Francesca allowed herself a rare smile at the Member Principal's joke.

* * *

Three more names. Three more judgments to deliver and then she'd give Yunni Tigunder his sentence. Before she did that, however, Francesca would make certain to extract whatever information he had on her brother Hank.

Then … she didn't know what she'd do. Find Hank? Meet him? Tell him everything she knew about their parents? Tell him everything about herself and her life? That she was a life taker?

Her reflection in the polished steel elevator doors suddenly came into sharp focus. Less than a year had passed since she became a full Member of the Order, and yet here she stared into a face that bore a lifetime of wear—the corners of her eyes appeared more creased, her hair lacked its previous sheen, her lips seemed paler and sadder.

The elevator slowed and gave an uncharacteristic jolt as it halted on the ground floor. The doors opened, and the reflection in front of her split in two, then disappeared. A gray lifeless hallway lay ahead.

Minutes later, she stood on the edge of the train platform with dozens of workers milling about around her, awaiting the monorail prison transport. Everyone kept a comfortable distance from Francesca. The train only made two stops on its route—its origin at the New Aberdeen Station and its terminus at the Coppice. It picked up and dropped off workers on each trip, but the bulk of its passengers only ever rode the train one way. Prisoners didn't arrive on every trip to the Coppice, it being necessary to clean and sanitize between cohorts of soon-to-be inmates and the justice system's preference to send a full train rather than a handful at a time. When the convicted were on board, there was room enough to accommodate a full nine cars worth of them. Sometimes new cohorts of prisoners would arrive daily, while sometimes they only came once a week or once month. Regardless of the influx of inmates into the general population of the prison, Members were expected to be efficient in their performing of the Sacred Task on the inmates of their ward, but quotas were never given by the Member Principal. The lack of quotas was designed to help maintain objectivity in the selections Members made. Additionally, a natural counter to any lazy random selections or cluster selections to reduce the numbers in a Member's ward was the means itself by which the Order dispatched inmates.

Known as the Solution, the inky black liquid poison was applied with a Member's finger to a selected person's neck. It was a Member's solemn duty to perform the Sacred Task, and it was done with a bare hand. No gloves could ever be used. The only protection Members had from the Solution was a thin film of oil applied to the finger just before the poison was used. The oil allowed some of the poison to enter their system, enough to make them ill for a short time after each Sacred Task but not enough to kill them … right away. Over time, a Member's body accumulated higher and higher concentrations of the Solution and, eventually, they would perform their last Sacred Task, unable to recover from the aftereffects known as the Taint.

Such was the fate of a Member of the Order of the Coppice. In exchange for the great honor to serve society in their ordained capacity, they gave a little of their own mortality each time they took a life. They delivered death upon society's rejected masses while knowingly and willingly inviting death slowly upon themselves.

The gleaming white monorail maglev train whooshed through the archway cut into the prison's outer shell and, seconds later, slowed to a stop in front of the platform. The doors slinked open a few feet up the platform from Francesca. She waited a moment for the passengers to disembark before she boarded. Inside the train, she took a seat near a window, her mind occupied with the names on her list. Malina Maddox and Martin Aubrey would provide her with the locations of all four names and a good deal of background research, all of which would be helpful in her initial assessments.

The prison train moved almost imperceptibly, pushing back from the platform through the great curved maw and into the bright daylight. The rest of the ride, if she remained in her current seat, would be in reverse. The prison would grow smaller by the second as the train reached top speed, then around a wide curve and over a slight rise, it would disappear altogether.

Francesca's mind lingered on Hank. Sweet Hank.

* * *

Days later, Malina sent Francesca information on the first two of the four names.

Francesca caught Kyle Gardeaux in his office working late. Since the child theft scandal, he'd left his job with the state's Department of Child Residential Services and opened a private office, where he sold his services as a child welfare consultant to various educational institutions. Much like Gilda Elmyr, he'd sold out other key players in the scandal to keep himself out of prison. Unlike Gilda, he wasn't old enough and hadn't pilfered enough in bribes to retire.

Sitting on a comfortable chair in a darkened corner of his vast office, Francesca waited for him to come back from a quick meal out. He'd returned around midnight, and the rest of their time together went similarly to the night she spent with Gilda. Francesca judged him to be unrepentant, incorrigible, and defiant of the terrible impact his crimes had on the children affected. Not only had Gardeaux been unapologetic, he'd been convinced that his role in the scandal was minor, and he claimed that in the end, the kids were better off.

As chief psychologist for the department, Gardeaux's primary responsibility was creating environments in which the children in the state's orphanages could thrive and develop emotionally and intellectually. At some point, he discovered the misdeeds of Gilda Elmyr, among others, and demanded payment for his silence. Initially a passive participant in the scheme, over time, Gardeaux began working with the Order directly by helping them develop questionnaires to determine which children at the orphanages were the best potential candidates to be future Members.

Francesca waited to make her presence known until Gardeaux had drank from the water bottle that sat to the right of his keyboard. Gardeaux was obsessive about his health: he spent hours in the gym each day, gobbled down health shakes and supplements, and pounded water as regularly as an atomic clock—making the bottle an easy choice to administer the Solution.

Miles Armistead, the second name on the list, was a different story. During her observations, she realized that this man had indeed tried to repent. The substantial amount of money he'd made during the child theft scheme was gone, donated to juvenile welfare charities all over the East Coast. Files from the investigation into his involvement made it clear that he helped the police as much as he was able, and he did not ask for immunity; in fact, he insisted on some form of punishment. He'd been placed on long-term home confinement, which, given his age, would probably be a life sentence. The man was far from perfect, but it had been enough for Francesca to spare him the Sacred Task.

"Judge who they are," her mentor had said. "Not who they were."

10

The Zealot

"What has been is what will be, and what has been done is what will be done, and there is nothing new under the sun."

Reggie Toppin groaned inwardly, not daring to make the sound loud enough for the man to hear him. He wondered if the man would consider dispensing with all the scripture. The situation was terrible enough without the constant preaching.

"Ecclesiastes 1:9," the man said somewhere behind Reggie. It was hard to tell where exactly in the huge room. High ceilings and smooth surfaces made the space feel like a huge echo chamber. The harsh walls combined with the constant low thrum bleeding through the walls made Reggie feel like he was in the hull of tanker ship.

The man continued, "You see, the Lord has given us everything we need. Technology and its application in our society is us, mere humans, telling God the Father that we know better. That somehow we can do better than the one who created the vast universe. It's not only foolhardy, it's disrespectful, it's blasphemous, it's … it's … it's just wrong."

Reggie didn't know the bible; he knew code, he knew

programming—Python 3020, Canin, R—and religion was something he'd purposely avoided his entire life. But even he knew the man's interpretation of Ecclesiastes 1:9 was way off the rails.

He kept his thoughts to himself. A subtle sideways glance to the guy next to him was enough for him to express how big an idiot he thought the man was.

Reggie told himself to just keep going. Keep going, and it'll all be over soon.

A gust from a fan off to the side made him shiver; goose bumps rose across his bare chest and down his naked legs. His fingers kept working, cranking out code on the screen ahead of him. The sound of the clattering keys filled the empty silence during breaks in the sermon. He lifted his right hand off the keyboard momentarily, flexing and stretching his cramping fingers. He made a tight fist, squeezing for a few seconds, then straightening his fingers. The pain dissipated slightly. In a moment, he'd do the same with his left hand, never taking both hands off the keyboard at once, as that would only invite the man's wrath.

"I've known those who've loved technology," the man continued preaching. "I've known those who were addicted to it. Hard to escape it in today's world. We make our livings with it, we socialize with it, we complete every daily, mundane task with it, and in doing so, we do not serve the Lord. We do not obey his commandments. Like a loving father, he tries again and again to tell us how we're hurting him. But we don't listen. We don't hear him."

Reggie straightened his right arm. As he did, the elbow popped uncomfortably. He tried to rotate it, but the restraints strapping his forearm to the chair prevented much range of motion. His ass and legs were numb, had been for at least a day, but he did his best to flex his thighs and glutes to get some circulation down to his lower extremities. He rolled his shoulders, being careful not to rub the wounds on his upper back against the hard plastic chair.

His stomach rumbled. He was starving. The liquid diet the man had them on was keeping him alive, but he never felt sated. He'd been hungry every second of however many days he'd been held prisoner.

"So the Lord, our merciful Father, he seeks to teach the world a lesson." Reggie had heard this one twice already. "In his boundless wisdom, the Lord sought"—the man paused—"Wesley, why have you stopped working?"

Reggie noticed it too, had hoped that if he typed harder, the man wouldn't hear the silent keyboard over his own.

"I just need to stretch," the guy named Wesley said.

Reggie risked a quick glance at his fellow captive. Wesley had both hands off the keyboard, straightening his arms and twisting his upper body inside the cordage binding him to the chair. His naked skin reddened and chaffed beneath the ropes and cables.

"Just a few seconds." Wesley continued twisting. "I can't do this twenty-four hours a day, man. No one can. If you could even just let me walk around for five minutes, I would feel better. I could work faster."

"Shut up, man," Reggie murmured. Complaining and begging got the last guy killed, strangled to death in the spot where Wesley now sat. Reggie forced to watch and listen to the gagging and the gurgling, the purple and red splotches forming like storm clouds on the skin, then the blood bursting inside his eyes, flooding his corneas. Reggie had vomited his liquid diet all over himself, the salty mixture still on him like a crusty bib.

Footsteps behind him, the man walked closer to them, his feet dragging on the smooth floor.

"I've told you before," he whispered, loud enough so they could hear over the ambient noise of the room, "you can get up and stretch and do whatever you want when you finish." The man gripped the top of the guy's seat-back and leaned over his head, close enough to kiss him.

Reggie's heart was a rabbit inside his chest, threatening to break his ribs from within. His insides twisted and knotted. Suddenly, he had to pee.

The man's long sandy hair came loose from behind his ear, swinging down against his stubbly cheek. His eyes were a deep gray-blue, and when they looked at Reggie, they sent ice down his spine.

The man hovered over his prisoner, his nose brushing the guy's curly blond mop of hair.

"I'm sorry," the guy whimpered, "I just can't … I just need some rest. I'm in so much pain. Please."

The man straightened. "Rest? You have all the Z you want; I put it in your food. You have everything you need. If you worked a little harder, maybe you'd finish your job, and I could free you. Have you thought of that?"

"I know. I know," Wesley whimpered. "I just don't think we can do it. The AI is too fast, too smart. Every time we gain a little ground …"

"That's enough," the man said. He walked away for a moment, and Wesley began sobbing uncontrollably.

Footsteps again. He was coming back.

A crash of plastic and metal. The man had Wesley's head

pinned against the keyboard with one hand. In the other, he held an object resembling a screwdriver. But it wasn't a screwdriver. Reggie knew exactly what it was, a soldering iron and the tip glowed red-hot.

Wesley couldn't struggle. His arms and torso strapped, tied, and duct-taped to the chair. His naked skin stretched taught against his bindings as they dug in against the force of the man's pressure.

He was helpless. "No no no no no no. Please, I'm done complaining." The words rattled from his mouth. "I can do it. I can do it. I promise I'll be good." His eyes spewed tears. Snot bubbled and oozed from his nostrils.

"What you need is a little more incentive." The man's eyes were wide with rage and his teeth bared. "If your freedom from this chair isn't enough to motivate you. Maybe freedom from pain will be."

His raised hand swung downward, plunging the soldering iron into the Wesley's back. Screams filled the huge room, Wesley's face twisted in pain and desperation. The hot metal sizzled as it cooked flesh and sent streams of gray smoke into the air. The smell was horrifying, like a grotesque barbecue.

Reggie's stomach flipped inside him.

The man jerked the weapon free. A line of fluid clung to the iron, briefly linking torturer and the tortured.

Again, he jabbed it into flesh. More smoke. More sizzling. More screams that rattled Reggie's eardrums.

The captor extricated the iron free once more and moved to jam it into his prisoner one more time.

Reggie turned away. He squeezed his eyes shut tight and prayed for free hands just to cover his ears. Just to block out the terror a few feet away. Tears leaked from his own eyes, washing down his cheeks.

Something warm trickled down Reggie's legs.

11

Josiah

Eleven Years Ago

Josiah Palmero woke to a gentle rubbing on his chest. He let out a quiet moan and rolled away from his mom, who was seated on the edge of the bed.

"No, no, Josie, you've overslept," she said, her voice a soft tenor. "The rooster's crowing, and there is much work to do."

She patted his shoulder, and he rolled to his back and cracked an eyelid. Her smile shined through the half-light of the early morning spilling in through the open blinds of his window. Josie stretched his lanky eight-year-old body and let out another groan, this lament louder and more prolonged than the last.

"We don't have roosters, Mama. And if we did, they wouldn't even be up this early."

That got a chuckle out of his mom just like it did every Sunday morning.

"Wendy?" His dad's voice shouted from down the hall. "Now, please."

"Coming," she said softly. She patted him lightly again, then tussled his hair before standing to leave. From the doorway, she said, "Come on, Josie. We're leaving in five minutes, and you still need to get some food in you. You know your dad likes to be early."

He knew this. She didn't have to tell him. If there was one thing you could say about Kirk Palmero, it would be that he was on time for everything, and he made sure anyone traveling with him adhered to that standard as well.

Josie turned the knob of the lantern on his bedside table, turning it from barely a flicker to a bright, hissing orb that bathed his room in yellowish-red light. He slid out from under the covers and set his bare feet down on the cold wooden floor. Through the window came the first sounds of morning down on the street seven stories below. He stood and smoothed his pants with both hands. Sleeping in his church clothes gave him a few precious minutes more of sleep, but he always ran the risk of wrinkling them to the point they'd fail his father's morning inspection. He examined them in the lantern light for a moment and felt satisfied they looked all right to him. The stiff khaki cotton had made it through the night only slightly ruffled. His shirt, on the other hand, was hopeless, looking more like a crumpled map than his Sunday's best. He stepped to the closet, pulled a sweater off a hanger, and threw it on. Pushing his head through the neck hole, he searched for his shoes with his toe. He slid them on and jogged out the room and down the hall to the kitchen near the front of the apartment.

His mom waited near the corner of the living room, arms crossed over the front of her favorite purple dress. Seeing Josie, she extended a hand holding a napkin-wrapped parcel. He grabbed it, felt what was unmistakably a biscuit, and smiled his thanks. She smiled back, and without another word, they made their way through the front door of their home. They hurried down seven flights of stairs, and when they reached the bottom floor, Josie's mom threw open the heavy door that led outside onto the sidewalk.

They were greeted by Kirk Palmero's imposing form dressed in his best brown suit and narrow black tie. His dark hair parted neatly to the side. His eyes, full of impatience glowered back at Josie.

"Barely made it," Mr. Palmero said flatly. "Weren't for your mom, I'd have left you." With a meaty hand, he pointed down the sidewalk to Josie's left. "Let's go."

"Sorry, Dad," Josie said, unfolding the napkin to get at his breakfast.

Mr. Palmero grunted, not looking down at his son. After a few steps and with half the biscuit devoured, Josie felt his father give his shoulder an affectionate squeeze.

* * *

Sunday morning service at the First Church of God's Wheel was as it always was: long and boring. Josiah sat slumped in the pew between his mom and dad facing the minister, trying his best to look like he was listening. Only snippets of the sermon broke through his daydreaming. There was talk about their calling as Praeceptists, God's expectations of them, his chosen people, the sins of technology. The usual. Josie's mind was occupied with the coming afternoon when they would make their weekly trip to the grocery co-op, then the park. He loved the park. The park had a playground, and the playground had swings, slides, teeter-totters, and most importantly, other kids. Sam would probably be there. He was usually there on Sundays, but not always. He hoped Sam would be there.

"Amen," the pews around him bellowed, breaking his chain of thought. The minister had said something about bicycles, about their connection to the devil or something.

His mind wandered again. This time to the grocery co-op. He wondered if his mom would let him get those honey-flavored crackers, but he knew she probably wouldn't. Honey was too expensive, so, as she said all the time, "Anything with honey in it was also expensive." He'd pout, and she'd repeat the same old refrain, "Don't blame me. If you want to blame someone, blame the others." The *others* was the term used for people who didn't follow the religion. "The others ruined the earth, killed nearly all the bees. All because they couldn't bear to do without contrivances that only made things a little faster, a little easier. Now, they must suffer God's punishment. They're lucky all they lost was honey, so far."

"We eat honey too. Why is God punishing us along with them? Don't we follow the rules?" Josie had said the Sunday before.

"He punishes us along with them because we don't do enough to show them the way."

His mother and father got to their feet on either side of him, still facing the pulpit. Instinctively, Josie spread his hands just as his parents and the rest of the congregation spread theirs. The prayer spilled from his lips in a flat-sounding mumble while his dad's voice boomed out over the space in front of them.

"… the Lord provides and we thank thee. God the Father, the wheel in the soil, the blade of our bounty, we praise thee

...”

Josie knew the prayers, of course. He knew all of the ones they recited on Sundays. He wasn't sure what they meant or why he had to say them, but he could rattle them off if he had to.

” ... we shall prepare this world for you, for when, in peace, you come again to deliver us unto eternal paradise ...”

After the prayer would come the hugging, the part of the service Josie dreaded. Not that he hated hugs, he just didn't understand why he had to hug all these smelly, sweaty people.

“Amen.”

His dad leaned over to embrace his mom, squeezing Josie between them briefly until both bent down to hug him. Before he knew it, a large woman in a flowery dress seated ahead of them turned around and grabbed him by the shoulders. She pressed him against her squishy chest, filling his nostrils with the smell of body odor and hair spray, which was probably against the rules. After she released him, he sank back onto the pew, hoping to shrink to the point of invisibility.

* * *

With services over, he and his parents walked down the wide stairs outside the main doors of the church. While his dad spoke with another man in a suit, he and his mother kept walking toward the sidewalk. She waved to several other wives and mothers, spoke to a few more about the weather and some other things that Josie didn't pay attention to. He just stood there holding his mom's hand, patiently anticipating the honey crackers at the co-op.

During a brief silence, he looked up at his mom and said,

"Mom, when we're at the co-op today—"

"No co-op today, sweetie," she said.

"What?" he asked, confused.

"It's second Sunday. You know that." She smiled broadly at him because she knew he hated second Sundays.

Just then, he saw his dad approaching with a stack of folded pamphlets in one hand.

"We're taking the bus stop over on Ninth and Woodlawn." His dad handed his mom half the pamphlets. Josie saw the cross and circles on the back of the bottom one.

She frowned but took the offering. "The Bagleys usually take that spot. What happened to Metro Hospital—where we always stand? It's eight blocks from the apartment. Ninth and Woodlawn is a two hour walk home, at least."

"I don't know, Wendy," Josie's dad said with a clenched jaw. "They said we're doing the bus stop, so we're doing the bus stop."

Mr. Palmero stepped out in the direction of their spot for the day, ending the discussion. Mrs. Palmero pulled Josiah by the hand, and the two of them followed close behind his father. Forty-five minutes later, the three of them arrived at the spot they'd be standing in for most of the day—on the sidewalk behind a busy bus stop in the city's business district.

The bus stop itself was nothing more than a bright-blue awning held up by two posts on either end. One pole held what looked to Josie to be a map with dark lines drawn on it. Below the map was a long list with two columns, which, he figured, must have been the stops and their times. He didn't know much about the buses or the trains or even the cars on the road, having never been allowed to ride in them. He always found it amazing that people would rather cram into a box with so many other people when they could just walk everywhere, like he and his family did.

The bus stop was empty for the moment. His parents stood on either side of him, all three of their backs against the window of a clothing store. The mannequins behind the glass were all dressed in men's suits. As people passed on the sidewalk, Mr. and Mrs. Palmero would hold out a pamphlet and say something like, "Would you like to serve the Lord our Father?" or "Technology is the path of the wicked," or "Wouldn't you like to know your place in Heaven is secured?" Some people would hold out a hand and give a simple "No, thanks," while others would smile and shake their head, but most would simply pretend the Palmeros weren't there. They could have been ghosts.

Occasionally, maybe one out of a couple hundred people would stop and listen as Josie's mom or dad told them about the Lord's word, the evils of the contrivances of the devil, the honor to serve the lord through the old ways, and the benefit of adopting the Praeceptist way. Out of those that stopped to listen, only a handful would ever show up at the First Church of God's Wheel on some future Sunday.

"The Father makes things difficult," Josie's dad would tell him if he grumbled. "He makes things difficult to show us they're worth doing. The fast way, the easy way is never the right way, son."

The shadows receded as the sun climbed higher in the sky. When it was almost directly overhead and beating down on them, Josie's mom said, "Go stand under the bus stop, Josie, in the shade."

Under the awning, he felt a bit cooler, the heat on his shoulders and face fading. He leaned against the post opposite the one with the map and felt his stomach growl. The biscuit from earlier had been long digested and moved along inside him to make room for a lunch he wouldn't get. Their spot on this second Sunday was much too far from home to run back and grab a bite to eat, and there were no Praeceptist approved restaurants in the city, which meant he wouldn't be eating until they returned home later that night. Their duty was to give at least eight hours every second Sunday of the month toward *andragogation,* their word for trying to convert people. Members of their church were spread out all over the city handing out literature on Praeceptism, trying to convert *others.*

He and his parents usually stood outside the hospital that was just a few blocks away from home, which meant he could race home to eat lunch. How they got stuck at the bus stop, he had no idea. He just knew that he hated the bus stop. It was hot and too far from his house. He'd starve to death at the bus stop.

Whether it was the heat or his hunger or both that occupied his mind, he hadn't noticed the kid next to him until the boy nudged him. Josie looked over in shock; he wasn't used to strangers just elbowing him for no reason. Josie jerked away reflexively and spat, "Sorry." He stepped six feet away from the boy but kept his eye on him.

The kid didn't seem to have heard him. His face was only a few inches away from an object he held tight in both hands. The item was rectangular and thin, shiny black. The kid's thumbs jolted around the outer edges of the thing and his eyes darted impossibly fast over every inch of the device's face.

"Damn," the boy yelled at the object in his hands, startling

Josie for the second time in a minute. The kid had jet black hair, brown skin, and wore a sleeveless green T-shirt with numbers printed on the front and back.

Josie was mesmerized. This boy was his age or close to it and clearly on drugs of some sort. His mind had been totally melted by a deadly chemical or a pill he'd taken. The elders had warned Josie and his classmates about drugs and how to spot a user. The kid was obsessed with this object, which didn't appear to do anything at all. It was just a flat piece of glass and plastic. Josie figured the boy must think he was actually seeing something that wasn't there. The way his thumbs moved seemed like he was trying to touch and move invisible objects.

The kid looked right at him, and Josie froze, felt his eyes widen, and his heart start to thump uncontrollably. The strange boy squinted. "You fight?"

Josie twitched. The words were English but meant nothing to him. Fight? Did he fight? He had to get away from this crazy person before he got himself killed. Slowly, he lifted a foot and stepped away from the lunatic boy.

The boy closed the distance between them by half. "*Caverns of Carnage?*" the boy said as if this should mean something to Josie. "It's three, not *COC* four, but still pretty fun."

He held the thin object out, and Josie saw a kaleidoscope of color dancing across its surface, brighter and more vivid than anything he'd ever seen. There was a forest—trees swaying, vines twirling up their trunks, animals of all sorts weaving in and out of the shadows, monkeys leaping from limb to limb. At the bottom, two creatures stood facing each other. The one on the left was purple, had four short furry legs and two muscular arms. Armor plate covered most of its body, but the head was uncovered with flowing blue hair and a long snarling snout. The other figure was definitely human, wearing white pants and no shirt, dark skin with a red snake tattooed around his stomach and chest. He too had huge menacing arms. Both looked ready to murder each other.

Josie imagined this must be a television or a computer, which he knew plenty about. He'd even been up close to a few of them. The image looked so real, the person must be real, but what was the monster? Some animal he'd never read about?

The boy did something with his hands Josie wasn't ready for. He flipped the device on its side and opened it like a book. Suddenly the thing was in two pieces and he was handing one to Josiah.

"You be Klaatu and I'll be Ash," the boy said, indicating with an outstretched finger that the armored purple monster was Klaatu.

Before Josie knew what to do, the device was in his hands. He held it out flat like it was a sacred object to be handled with great care.

"You've played before right?" The kid gave Josie a sideways glance.

"Played?" It had never occurred to Josie that the device was part of a game. He stared at the image of the two apparent fighters facing each other. It looked so real to him he couldn't imagine how it could be a game. How could it not be real life?

"Yeah, look," the kid held up his device and stood next to Josie so he could see what he was doing. "Just move your left thumb to make him walk around and tap your right thumb to make him punch, kick, shoot blades—whatever."

The screen filled with a red number three, then a two, a one.

"Fight!" the device ordered, and at once, the fighter called Ash was high in the air, flying down toward Klaatu, colliding with Josie's fighter in a silver explosion of light. The device in Josie's hands shuttered, and he nearly dropped it to the ground. Ash bounded back to his corner, and Josie frantically moved his thumbs in random directions, rubbing the smooth glass under them. Klaatu juttered and twitched, ducked and jumped, spun in place, threw a punch at empty air, then slid toward Ash on two hind legs. The other limbs flashed fiery yellow, shooting flames at his enemy. The flames hit Ash and sent him flying, red fountains bursting from his midsection and head, smoke rising from his weakened body.

"Yeah," the boy cried out, "you're getting it. But you better watch out because I'm coming, and I'm bringing the thunder, son."

Josie licked his lips, eyes glued to the screen in front of him. He knew now the boy hadn't been on drugs, but he could definitely see how addictive something like this game could be. His heart raced. He wanted more.

Josie watched Ash right himself from the terrible blow dealt by Klaatu. He moved his fingers around on the glass, trying desperately to remember the last move. Did he do a circle with his left thumb and tap twice with his right? Or was it the other way around?

A flash of something flew in front of his face and smacked the gaming device out of his hands. It hit the concrete sidewalk with a sickening crunch, shattering the screen into an intricate spider web of broken glass. Behind the broken screen, Josie could see Klaatu in a fighter's stance, shoulders bobbing slightly, awaiting his master's next command.

Josie looked up. His father's face was inches away, angrier

than Josie had ever seen him. Another hand flew through the air, this time it connected with the side of Josie's face, twisting his head around, nearly sending him to the ground.

Icey needles coursed through Josie's cheek as he turned back to face his father.

"Home, boy. Now." His dad pointed a shaking finger in the general direction of their apartment.

Tears filled Josie's eyes. "I'm s-sorry. I ..."

"Quiet," Mr. Palmero shouted. "Go. Now."

The kid next to Josie didn't say anything. He just stared open-mouthed at the destroyed device at their feet, still holding the intact half in his hand.

Josie passed beside his dad, not daring to look him in the eye. Keeping his head down, he recognized his mother's shoes a few feet away. Black, flat-heeled slip-ons over white socks. A hand found his head and patted it gently.

"What the fuck just happened here?" A loud deep voice cried out near the bus stop. "What the fuck did you just do, motherfucker?"

Josie whipped around to see his dad chest to chest with a smaller, brown-skinned man. The man pointed at the game still at the other boy's feet.

"That was my kid's game. Cost me half a fucking paycheck." The man, although small, looked dangerous with thick arms and a sharp jaw.

Mr. Palmero raised his chin slightly. "Your son is better off without it. That ... game, whatever it is, is the devil's plaything. It's poisoning his ..."

The man swung his right fist at Mr. Palmero's head. The punch landed, and Josie's dad fell to the ground, not moving for several heartbeats.

Josie's mother wrapped her arms around Josie, gripping him tight, holding him back. He'd been trying to run to his dad and hadn't realized it.

"Dad," he screamed, trying to wrench himself from his mother's grip.

"Josie, no." Her arms coiled tighter.

The man straddled Mr. Palmero, muttered something, then dropped one knee onto his dad's chest. He then jacked back his right hand and slammed it into Mr. Palmero's face. A second later, the hand was in the air again, arm cocked. It flew down toward Josie's father in a blur. He couldn't see the punch land, but he heard it. A nauseating smack. The arm was up again, then down, and another smack of fist to face.

Josie could see his father's legs stretched out on the ground from beneath the other man. His toes pointed upward. The feet didn't move; they only shuttered a little each time the man punched his fist into Josie's dad's face.

Again and again it happened. Smack. Smack. Smack.

A shout from up the street, and seconds later, a police officer wrestled the attacker off Mr. Palmero and down to the ground. Josie could see his dad, finally free of the aggressor. Blood pooled in a wide circle around his head.

The arms around Josie loosened, and he slipped away, dashed across the twenty odd feet to his father, and slid on his knees to the man's side. Josie's dad, the pillar of the family, his hero, had been beaten unrecognizable. Red, purple, and blue mixed and swirled on his swollen face. His eyes swollen to the point that they were just slits. His mouth, agape, revealed dark gaps where teeth used to be. Lips puffed and split in several places.

Josie didn't know what to say or do. He just sobbed. As

the tears flowed like tiny rivers, the guilt for what he'd done inflated in him like a great balloon, consuming him.

He knew this could be only one thing—Lord the Father was showing him what happened when he disobeyed, even for a moment. God showed Josie what evils technology brought onto the world and what it did to the minds of people who let it control them.

Josie opened his watery eyes and looked down at his beaten father and knew, down in the deepest part of himself, that this would never happen again.

12

The Fourth Name

November 11, 2043—12:30 a.m.

Francesca opened the short metal gate and entered the narrow sloping front yard covered in deep green grass. At the top of the ridge sat the home of Yunni Tigunder, low and boxy, built in the style contemporary to the late twentieth century. Standing on the first of four huge natural stone slabs that created a walking path bisecting the lawn, she stood to take in the home. To her, it looked like several shoeboxes had been fitted together in seemingly random ways, then trimmed with dark lines over multiple tones of light grays. Glass streamed along the top edge of each box, spilling light from within and onto the neatly cut grass, but it was the enormous set of crimson-red double front doors that stood out as the dominant feature. To her left, at the top of the driveway, was a four-car garage with long glass doors for each bay, allowing all the world to see the luxury vehicles within.

It was a lot of house for a man who lived alone, had no kids, and no close relationships. He didn't even own a dog.

She felt fairly certain that Yunni's would be her last selection until returning to the Coppice. The third name on the list, Padmani Brar, had gone much the same as Kyle Gardeaux. Brar felt that her role in the scheme was actually helping the kids. They'd have ended up dead or in prison, she'd reasoned. She waxed poetic on the idea of her being a revolutionary and that sometimes people had to work around the law to do the right thing.

In the end, Padmani Brar begged for release from the pain the diluted Solution she'd ingested in her dinner caused her. Francesca did not grant her last wish. Brar died on her bathroom floor, cold and alone.

The night outside Yunni Tigunder's house was dark, but the street was well lit by quaintly curved lamps along the road. Nonetheless, Francesca was fairly certain she'd go unnoticed. She ascended the steps toward the front door, and after reaching the front porch, she lifted a finger and pressed the doorbell. A black circle above the button caught the light, a lens.

"Yeah?" The voice seemed to come from all around her, filling the air inside the recessed alcove.

Francesca didn't respond. She felt she understood the man well enough to know that he'd come to the door in spite of knowing who or what she was.

"What do you …" Tigunder's voice trailed off, no doubt having seen her on the camera feed.

Her hunches about the man were correct, less than half a minute after ringing the bell, the doors in front of Francesca flew open.

Yunni Tigunder was a tall, well-built man. He stood on the other side of the threshold, one hand on the door, mouth open in shock, horror, or fascination or a mix of all three.

Francesca's research had told her this man was intelligent, driven, and overconfident. This combination of personality traits is what gave Francesca her hunch that, upon seeing who was calling at his door, Yunni Tigunder wouldn't be able to help himself. For one, intellectual curiosity would light a spark, ambition would be the flame that drove his desire to acquaint himself with someone from the Order, and overconfidence would be the conflagration that would consume any notion that this death-bringer could be there for him—to end him.

It was this over confidence that tilted his smooth, pointed chin high as Francesca stepped past him into the foyer. It smelled clean and sterile with hints of wood polish. Passing within inches of the man, who did not move, she caught the scent of pomade, which accounted for his shiny black hair brushed straight back. He wore a white shirt unbuttoned to his chest and dark dress pants with no shoes.

Hands behind her back, Francesca stepped further into the home. A large great room to her left, a hallway to her right, the kitchen straight ahead with a glass containing amber liquid and one large ice cube on the breakfast table. Every surface was wood, polished stone, or granite.

"I'm Yunni," he said behind her. "But I'm guessing you already know that. Why else would you be here?"

Confidence.

"I'm told you have some information." She spoke without turning toward him, her gloved hands clasped tightly behind her back. "I need this information. Then we have other business."

"Business," he said. It wasn't a question. It was an understanding.

Yunni brushed past her toward the kitchen, not shying away from her like so many others, not giving her the wide berth she was used to.

Confidence.

"Would you like a drink?" He held a hand toward his own drink on the kitchen table, the glass sweating.

She eyed the glass for a moment, wondering. "I'm told you have files from the Department of Child Residential Services. Files that are sealed. I need you to unseal them and give them to me."

His eyebrows shot up. "That's a tall order. I mean, I could do it"—a smile began to stretch its way across his face—"but I would get in trouble."

"You're rather good at staying out of trouble." She matched his attempt at charisma with an equal amount of stoicism. "I need the names and whereabouts for every child adopted from the East Region Orphanage starting with the year 2025."

Yunni puffed his cheeks and blew out an exasperated breath, then sat down heavily at the table. "Like I said, I could get that for you. I still have access to all those files, but I might get in a lot of trouble."

Francesca entered the kitchen area, admiring the craftmanship of the cabinetry, the clean edges and tight joints. She ran a finger along the edge of the black granite countertop and inspected it. Clean. The kitchen was as spotless, as if it had never been used.

"But you'll do it," she said. "You'll do it because you like to make deals. And you know a person in my position, a person who does what I do, can offer unique opportunities for deals."

"Unique opportunities." He scratched at his chin, then reached for his glass and downed the remaining liquid. He cleared his throat and said, "Yes, I do like to make deals." He wiped moisture from his lips and sat down, rubbing his jaw. "Okay, come with me."

She followed him down the long hallway to an open door. Yunni hadn't asked what he'd get in return for sharing the information she requested. He probably didn't care. He was a loan shark, and his currency was information. Having a Member of the Order in your debt could be very valuable. He'd give her the information without too much haggling. Yunni's mistake, his grave mistake, was in assuming that Francesca was just another victim from which he'd extract an exorbitant payment.

They entered an office with a bulbous wooden desk in the middle of the room. Books lined the walls on shelves, and a picture window overlooked a manicured back lawn. Yunni sat at the desk and began working a touchpad and keyboard. Francesca stood off to the side, her full attention on Yunni.

"Those files are in a partition on the server that only a few of us have access to." He continued typing, and she watched as he opened and closed various windows. "The directors of each orphanage don't even have access to these. Once they enter the placement family's information, it uploads to the server via a one-way cloud feed, then self-deletes from their system. The archive is on a partitioned server physically separated from any other connections. As Department Head, I have access until my tenure is over, then someone else will have access to the fiber line that connects my office downtown to the server archive."

This made Francesca curious. "But we aren't in your office downtown."

"No," he said. "But I have remote access to that computer

from here. Not exactly legal," he turned in his chair to face her, "but neither is this. I assume." He gestured to the air between them.

Francesca nodded to the computer. "Please continue."

"Certainly," he said, spinning back to the computer. He leaned closer to the monitor, reading lines of text from what looked like a spreadsheet. "You said 2025 onward? How many years from there?"

"Better make it all of them between now and then just to be safe." Francesca removed the glove on her right hand and reached into her pocket.

"And you said East Region, right?" He filtered the data on his screen.

Francesca withdrew a vial of clear liquid and plunged her stained forefinger into it.

"I'm guessing you want everything about the kids and their adoptive families." He shook his head. "That's a lot of damn data. Hope you got some time on your hands. Where should I send it?"

Francesca told him the location of the secure cloud drive she'd arranged with Malina's help, then she replaced the vial of Sacred Oil into her pocket and withdrew another vial. This one was filled with the completely colorless, impossibly black Solution. After removing the lid, she dipped her oiled finger into it, coating it to the first knuckle.

"All right," Yunni said, still facing the computer screen. "It's uploading. I think we should talk about what comes next." He held a hand out toward the data still displayed on the monitor. "I mean, this won't be cheap, I'm afraid. But I'm sure we can work something out. I prefer to work on the barter system any—"

Yunni's face hit the keyboard with a clatter. His eyes locked open but lifeless, pressed against the keys. The dime-sized black dot on the back of his neck, the spot where Francesca touched him, shined for an instant in the bright overhead lights, then it faded. The Solution left behind a spot someone might mistake for a birthmark or an oddly placed tattoo.

Francesca wiped the tip of her right forefinger with a square cloth, rolled it into a tight ball, and placed it in a sealed plastic pouch in her pocket. She lifted the man into a seated position and rolled his chair back toward the picture window. He flopped to one side, mouth open, eyes still gaping into nothing. She bent over the desk and opened a browser window. After navigating to the digital cloud drive, what Malina referred to as a dead drop, she logged in. Her dashboard displayed one folder named for the current date. Its size read 3.5 terabytes. She clicked to open it. Inside the folder was no fewer than fourteen hundred files named with seemingly random jumbles of letters and numbers in no apparent order. The temptation to start searching was nearly overwhelming, but she had no clue where to begin, and she had much to do in the next few minutes.

She logged out of the dead drop and followed the instructions Malina had given her to cover her tracks, forever erasing any clues as to what happened on Yunni Tigunder's computer in the last hour. The file's upload to the dead drop would have pinged Malina, who would no doubt be checking the file for any corruptions. A part of Francesca chastised her decision not to wait to perform the Sacred Task until after Malina could check the file for safety and authenticity. On the other hand, the sealed file was not part of her duty. Her duty was to judge and select the man, or not, for the Sacred Task. Getting the sealed file that could possibly lead to her brother was a personal endeavor, which sullied the purity of her purpose at Yunni's house that night. She felt that waiting to check the file before the Task somehow crossed a line. Whereas asking him for the file, and his giving it willingly, then performing the Sacred Task when she had an opportunity to do so approached the line without actually violating it.

Crossing the office and entering the hallway, she felt the first chill shoot down her back. The Taint was on her. Her steps quickened, and upon entering the kitchen, her eyes shot to the clock on the stove: 1:06 a.m.

Heat crossed her forehead in several pulsating waves. Fog washed over her vision.

Summoning calm, she inhaled deeply and let it out. Another breath. Another. With each breath, she took a step toward the kitchen table. After a dozen deep breaths and a dozen long strides, she sat down in one of the chairs. Once seated, she leaned into the back of the chair, allowing the Taint to work its way through her while wondering what new pain she'd feel this time.

More chills, more heat.

A stabbing in her lower back made her wince. Her mind was in a dark haze, like she was blind drunk. Even with her eyes closed, the world spun, exacerbating a growing nausea.

When it finally ended, it was like the whole episode played in reverse. The last terrible sensation was the first to recede. The spinning world slowed until it spun no more. The knife in her kidney withdrew itself. Her head cleared, and she opened her eyes to see the fog lifting. The heat on her face and chest washed down to a bearable warmth, then disappeared altogether. Finally, the chills in her back and limbs faded until they weren't there at all. One last, long, deep breath in and out, and her body felt normal once more. Other than a lingering film of sweat that glued her clothes to her skin, she was back to her old self.

Francesca glanced at the clock: 1:14 a.m.

Eight minutes. Without a proper stopwatch, she couldn't be sure, but this episode felt a little longer than the ones before it. Certainly, if it was a full eight minutes, it would be around thirty seconds longer that the last Taint.

She pulled up her right sleeve and examined her stain, the purple-black mark that covered the killing hand and arm of every Member of the Order. The stain grew with each Sacred Task, illustrating the growing concentration of Solution in the Member's body. Francesca's stain completely enveloped her forefinger and thumb while only covering portions of her other three fingers. The stain reached toward her wrist with tendrils snaking up the back of her hand and palm. The longest dark tentacle nearly touched the small mound where her ulna bone joined the wrist.

"Every Member's path is their own," Rudolfo told her. She pondered on how many Sacred Tasks she would be able to perform before the Solution claimed her or until she chose to self-select.

13

Ambrosia

November 11, 2043—11:00 a.m.

"Tell me if I have this right."

From the corner of her eye, Malina could see Aubrey counting down on his fingers. She was trying to pay attention to a live broadcast playing on her watch.

"You think that the super sophisticated artificial intelligence that runs the Metro Traffic System, known the world over as one of the most advanced technologies to date, has been infiltrated. That bad actors are using it to cause chaos and murder innocent civilians."

She could feel him glaring at her from the other side of the elevator. "Shhh. I'm trying to listen to this."

"We'd like to inform the people of New Aberdeen that the Metropolitan Traffic System's artificial intelligence is currently undergoing a thorough testing process that will uncover any and all bugs in the system." Everyone in the city had been sent a notification, alerting them that the mayor and head of cyber infrastructure would be making statements. Onscreen, the mayor, a short woman with close-cropped silver hair, stood behind a dais speaking to the press pool. "Over the next twenty-four hours, the MTS will be shut down in various sectors of the city. If you find yourself in these areas, you must engage your car's autopilot and GPS or use manual control. Police officers will be stationed at all intersections in those sectors to direct the flow of traffic. Schedules for which sectors where the MTS will be shut down will be available on city hall's website. Every citizen has received a link to a recording of this announcement as well as the shutdown schedule."

"You really think that's possible?" said Aubrey.

Malina met Aubrey's eyes, which were full of incredulity.

"I mean, how?" said Aubrey. "The MTS AI has been operating for decades, and as far as I know, no one has ever even come close to hacking it."

Malina put a hand to her forehead and rubbed her temples. "It just seems really odd, what's been happening. The AI is the most advanced tech … probably in the world. It's virtually flawless, and by its very nature, it should be able to fend off any attack on its own." She threw her hands out to the side. "I get it. It's far-fetched, but …"

The elevator stopped. Malina looked up and saw the number "41" blinking.

"I don't know," she said, finishing her thought as the doors slid open. "Maybe I'm being paranoid."

Aubrey grinned at her. "That's okay. Paranoia can be a good thing. And it doesn't mean you're wrong. Come on, this is it." Aubrey stepped out and she followed. "Let's focus on the job at hand and figure out what happened to your friend Drillard. Someone else can stop the AI from driving people off bridges."

After leaving Champ's apartment, Malina had made short work of finding the true identifications of the two names Champ had given them, Elton and Ambrosia—two former members of her hacking group, the Colektive. Using Ted, a massively powerful processor of her own design, and access to the police database courtesy of Liz Reynolds, Malina found them in a little under three hours.

Elton, known to the real world as Reginald Toppin, still resided with his parents and, according to them, disappeared forty-eight hours ago. He'd left to go to work one morning and never came home. Elton worked at a local cybersecurity firm called Chimera Security, who said he'd never shown up the morning of his disappearance. The family filed a missing persons report shortly before speaking with Malina and Aubrey.

The two investigators now strode the brightly painted hallway of the forty-first floor of Wayne Tower, a midrange apartment building on Third Avenue on the north side of the city. Acer Sapindales, known as Ambrosia online, lived here alone, had no job in the physical world, and hadn't been heard from by anyone in four days. His family didn't think much of his going missing, which seemed to happen every few months. He'd go off the radar for a few weeks only to pop up again like nothing had happened.

Malina and Aubrey stopped in front of the door to apartment 41J. She knocked, and they stood waiting for signs of life within.

As the moments passed, Malina thought about the surreal collision of her two lives. One was her past, the pseudo legal world of gray-hat hacking while working with the Colektive. The other was her present, her real pursuit to do good and help others working with Martin Aubrey. For years in the Colektive, she'd struggled to come to terms with breaking the law in order to fix the world, hacking and cracking to reveal vulnerabilities to help prop up those in need or flat-out violating the law to steal from the wealthy and corrupt to give to the less fortunate. The line between right and wrong, in her mind, was hair thin, and every decision she made while traversing the cyber underworld was made as a give and take. Give enough to the right side to justify taking from the wrong side. It was like trying to zero out her moral scales.

Others in the Colektive didn't see it this way. Some stretched the line. Some stomped on it but left it intact. Others, like Ambrosia, pretended the line wasn't there at all.

After five minutes, Aubrey knocked again. Two more minutes passed with no response. He reached into a pocket and pulled out a device Malina had seen him use before. A small box connected to a round rubber pad capable of reading and reproducing fingerprints. With it, they could get past the thumb print lock on Ambrosia's door.

Something caught Malina's attention. About head height on the inside of the doorjamb, a penny-sized disk appeared to be scanning them with a green eye in its center.

"Shit," she said and pointed toward it. "A cerebral scanner. Shit." The only word that came to mind was hopeless. They were never getting past the door and into the apartment.

Cerebral signatures, or CS, had for years been used for a variety of security and identity purposes. As the mind processed external stimuli, billions of neurons fired along billions of neural pathways, forming billions of connections across the brain. While most human brains worked, in general, in the same way on the neural level, every human being was completely unique. A CS was an aggregate of all the specific pathways and signals fired in an individual's brain, creating a fingerprint, of sorts, for the brain. With hundreds of billions of possibilities for each brain to react and send electrical impulses, a unique identifier could be created for every human alive.

Most people didn't have their cerebral signatures registered due to the expense. Those that did could use them for all types of security and convenience. You could walk into your house, which would read your signature and automatically know what type of lighting, music, and temperature you desired. And in the case of Acer Sapindales or Ambrosia, his CS and only his could unlock the front door.

Malina sighed heavily.

Aubrey turned toward her with a look of obvious overconcern. "Why so glum?"

"Are you kidding?" She jutted both hands out toward the door. "You can't hack a CS. It's impossible. Only Ambrosia and his brain can get in there. Not surprised really."

Malina tapped her chin with a finger and began pacing the hallway. The only way through the door was with Ambrosia's CS. Maybe he had a significant other or a relative who also had their CS registered with his security system. They'd have to go back to their notes and find the most likely people it might be and try to convince them to come back here.

"Malina?"

"Hang on. I'm thinking." Ambrosia had no siblings, but maybe his mother or father would have access.

"I think I hear something," said Aubrey.

She halted her pacing and turned to see Aubrey with an ear pressed to the door. "Yeah, I think I hear someone inside calling for help. Don't you hear it?"

"What?" Malina was fifteen feet away and couldn't hear anything other than faint music from an apartment down the hall.

"Yeah, someone in there needs our help." Aubrey stepped back to the opposite wall, took two long strides to the door of 41J, raised a leg, and kicked it just above the knob. The door exploded inward, fragments of wood and metal flying with it. He ran inside the apartment, calling out.

"Hello? We're here to help!"

Malina didn't move. She stood in the hallway, aghast at what she'd just seen. Was he serious?

Not knowing what else to do she ran in after him.

"Martin, what the hell are you doing?"

Inside, she found the place to be a comfortably sized one bedroom, one bath apartment with a galley kitchen just off the front foyer. Aubrey ambled around the sparsely furnished living space, scanning the contents of a computer station that filled half the room. Opposite the desk, a large television hung on the wall with the only seating being a plush green bean bag.

He didn't look up from his visual survey. "False alarm. No one here. We might as well take a look around while we wait for the police."

"Police?"

"Yeah. His security system no doubt contacted them as soon as the door was breached."

"Should I be worried?" She genuinely didn't know if they were about to get arrested. She reminded herself that Aubrey used to be a cop, which made her feel better. He must know something she didn't.

"Nah, we're looking for a missing person, and I heard what I thought was a cry for help." Without touching anything, he bent low to inspect an area under the computer station. "Check the bedroom would you."

"What am I looking for?"

"I don't know," he said. "But you'll know it when you see it."

Shit.

She entered the bedroom, just off a short hall it shared with the bathroom. The bedroom was what she expected—a mattress on the floor with one blue sheet and one pillow, a closet full of gray and black shirts and sweatpants. No dresser. No nightstand. This room was rarely used. She assumed Ambrosia made enough money on the web to afford Zentransa, or a street knock-off. Either way, he wasn't sleeping much.

With little to search in the room itself, she moved to the closet. Pushing the clothes aside, coat hangers screeching on the metal bar, she saw two pairs of sneakers on the floor. She ran her hand on top of the shelf above the hanging clothes and found nothing but dust. She checked under the mattress and pillow. Nothing.

Feeling deflated, she left the bedroom. "Anything?" she called from the stunted hall.

"Maybe. I'm moving to the kitchen."

"Maybe is better than nothing," she replied. "Which is exactly what I have at the moment."

The last room to search was the bathroom. Opening the door, her feeling of defeat escalated. At first glance, a pedestal sink, toilet, and shower stall were all she found. No medicine cabinet behind the mirror, no shelves below the sink, no trash can. The toilet didn't even have a tank, just a pipe straight from the wall to the bowl.

"More nothing," she muttered.

She reached to flip the light switch off when she noticed something—a black object on the floor poking out from behind the toilet. She moved closer and knelt down to get a better look at it. It was a leather-backed book. A paper book, which was rare. It laid on its front cover between the bowl of the toilet and the shower stall. She pulled her phone from her pocket and used it to nudge the book from its hiding place.

She read the cover. Then, just to be sure, she read it again. It read: *Book of the Wheel.*

The golden letters were embossed in the soft leather cover. Below them, also in gold, was a symbol she had just recently learned about—a cross with three concentric circles centered around the cross's intersection. The Praeceptist cross.

A bookmark protruded from the top of the book. Pulling the sleeve of her hoodie down to cover her fingers, she turned to the marked page. A red circle had been drawn around a passage in the middle of the right-hand page. The page was titled The Book of Silliam.

Malina read the circled passage.

The wheel is the true symbol of our Lord God's gift to humans. God gave his children the intellect and abilities to do great things; the wheel being the first of such great things. But as with all things we humans create, it was equally great in its speeding along human advancement and terrible in the sins it enabled.

Genesis 11:6 tells us: "And the Lord said, 'Behold, they are one people, and they have all one language, and this is only the beginning of what they will do. And nothing that they propose to do will now be impossible for them.'" Others heed these words as a celebration of human potential, whereas Praeceptists see it for its true meaning: a warning.

Again, this brings us back to the wheel, whose symbolism can be found throughout the pages of Praeceptist texts and on the walls of our houses of worship. Think of the wheel's application as an instrument of convenience when attached to a lowly handcart. The farmer, the merchant, and the conveyer use the cart for simple yet great purposes. Its intent is to ease the movement of objects, while its fundamental end is to propagate life in the field or put coin in one's purse. Conversely, think of the wheel attached to a chariot. With increased speed, better mobility, and offensive superiority, it becomes an instrument of destruction. The simple wheel possesses all of these attributes, but its fundamental purpose has shifted dramatically: the wheel on the chariot is created to spread death.

"What do you have there?"

Malina twitched in surprise, Aubrey's question breaking through her focus on the strange book.

"Just this." She held up the book for him to see, careful not to get her prints on it.

He squinted. "What is that? A Praeceptist bible?"

She shrugged and examined the book's cover once more. "I guess so." She stood and approached Aubrey, who was standing in the bathroom's doorway. "Martin, if he was reading this, maybe he's not with Drillard at all. Maybe he gave up his old way of life to be a Praeceptist."

Aubrey raised his eyebrows. "You think the hardcore hacker found religion?"

"I don't know," she said, looking at her shoes for a moment.

She still held *The Book of the Wheel*. "But we should check it out either way. Ambrosia and Drillard were the best hackers out of all of us in the Colektive. If either of them wanted to do some major hack, working together might make logical sense, but they were always at loggerheads with each other. I just don't see them teaming up IRL."

"IRL?"

Malina smiled like she was looking at a toddler and fluttered her eyelids. "In real life, normie."

"Oh," he said wryly, "well, I found something too." Aubrey jerked his head toward the living room of the apartment and marched in that direction.

At the computer workstation in the room's far corner, with a gloved hand, he picked up a dwindled stack of square, yellow sticky notes. She squinted at the top square; it was, blank but as Aubrey tilted the stack in the light, she could see the indentations of past writing. The last square had been written on and then removed, but a trace of what was written had been pressed into the one below it. He pulled out his phone and tapped the screen to ignite the flashlight. Bright white light shined over the yellow square of paper, and when Aubrey held it at the right angle, she could nearly make out the letters.

"Can you read it?" he asked.

She grasped the corner of the sticky note pad with her sleeve and adjusted the angle of it against the light. Block lettering appeared, the tiny shadows betraying the shapes on the paper.

"Josiah Palmero, Ninth and First," she read aloud. "Any idea who he is? And what's at Ninth and First? That's way uptown and pretty residential."

"I don't know who he is." Aubrey extinguished the flashlight on his phone. "But it's not a very common name, and it looks like we have our next lead."

Malina pulled out her phone, and after a moment of scrolling and typing, said, "Huh, bet you can't guess what's at Ninth Street and First Avenue?" Aubrey gave her a quizzical look, and she continued. "A Praeceptist church. You think that's a coincidence?" She laced her voice with sarcasm.

Aubrey smiled. "Good detective work, Sherlock. No, I don't think it's a coincidence. Plenty of people find Jesus, Buddha, and a thousand other prophets and messiahs as a reason to turn their life around."

She cocked her head askew. "Maybe he just went to check it out. And the Praeceptists don't use technology, which could be why he's off the grid."

"Maybe," Aubrey said, scratching his chin. "But Drillard is dead, murdered. And Ambrosia is missing for the moment." He shook his head and looked around at the apartment. "Doesn't look like he cared to take much with him. He could have been here five minutes ago. Not to mention he locked the place up like he was coming back." He scowled at the floor. "Too many coincidences. We need to go to that church and ask some questions about this Josiah Palmero person."

She nodded her tentative agreement, then a photograph on the desk drew her attention.

"Who is that?"

She pointed at a small black-and-white picture of Ambrosia and a young woman embracing, both smiling broadly. His messy light-colored hair hung down over his forehead while a close-cropped dark beard stood out in sharp contrast. The girl's black hair was in a tight bun on the crown of her head. The photo looked like the type taken at an old-timey photo booth.

Aubrey held out his phone and snapped a picture of Ambrosia and the woman. Malina watched as he then ran the image of the woman through the police department's facial recognition database. A few seconds passed, and the name Trina Yuan appeared next to the picture with "99.97% Match" next to it. Below the name, it showed her birth date, April 4, 2017. The next line shocked Malina as she read it: the date of Trina's death—January 18, 2043.

"She's dead. Poor guy. That might be a reason someone like him would turn to religion." Malina's eyes lingered on the picture of Ambrosia and Trina. She wondered how long had they been together? Possibly since the Colektive was active? He'd never mentioned being with anyone in any conversations online, but that had been years ago.

Something crashed next to her. Glass broke, metal shrieked, and suddenly, a weight came down upon her. She was on the floor, Aubrey on top of her. A second crash, more like a crunch this time. Hollow sounds of bricks cracking and tumbling.

14

Overdrive

Aubrey lifted his head. Malina was under him, lying on her side. His eyes locked on the thing across the apartment. The object that had burst through the window two feet from them in a spray of glass and metal.

Malina twisted below him to see it too. "What the fuck?" she said between panting breaths.

The projectile now lay in a heap of rubble where the kitchen used to be. It was a twisted white-and-red rectangular mass the size of a refrigerator. A metallic whirring filled the space while wisps of black smoke rose from the wreckage. An intermittent red light flashed against the ceiling.

Aubrey got to his feet and helped Malina to hers. They walked cautiously toward the thing, the shrill buzzing growing more erratic, clanging loudly every few seconds until, with a final screeching *clunk*, it went silent. As they neared the object, Malina reached out and brushed away debris from a panel to reveal a number—MGH 528963.

"MGH. Metro General Hospital." He let out a groan. "It's a medical drone."

Medical drones were designed to carry injured people from traumatic accident scenes. This accounted for its size. Surveying the lifesaving flying machine turned potential killer, Aubrey noticed the front struts had been shorn off from the body of the drone when it entered the building. The rear struts were mostly intact, but the rotors had come loose and flew like shrapnel around the apartment. One lay near the hallway silently spinning in its frame. The other was a wad of crumpled metal at Aubrey's feet, attached to the rear strut by a single blue wire.

"Two rogue drones in one day." Malina wiped dust from her shoulders and pushed the hair from her face. "What was that you were saying about coincidences?"

Aubrey exhaled heavily. She was right, of course. Coincidences be damned, something was very wrong. Unsure what to do, he surveyed the apartment one more time, spinning slowly in place. It was then he noticed the red flashing again. It was coming not from the drone, as he thought a moment ago, but from the hallway. The fire alarm had been tripped, and the fire department had most likely been dispatched.

"Did we get everything we need here?" His eyes searched the living room, then settled on the gaping hole the window used to occupy. The wind buffeted him through it, bringing with it the crisp chill of air from hundreds of feet above the ground.

"I think so," Malina said behind him.

A pop and he turned. Sparks danced over a control box attached to the drone's exterior.

"Okay, let's get downstairs and wait for the fire department. We can explain everything when the cops get here." As Aubrey made for the door, an acrid stench reached him. Something inside the drone or in the kitchen was heating up. He heard Malina's footsteps close behind.

"Where are the cops? I figured since we broke ... I mean, since we entered the apartment, that they would have shown up by now."

Aubrey stopped in the hallway, using a hand to shield his eyes from the strobe lights blaring overhead. A few of Ambrosia's neighbors began to file out of their apartments, looking confused. An elderly man passed Aubrey and Malina, but not before sneaking a peek inside Ambrosia's door.

"What the hell you been up to?" He was hunched over, leaning on a cane. "Dumbass kids."

Aubrey turned back to Malina. "Good point. Cops should have been here by now." He jerked his head toward the elevator, and the two of them strode quickly toward it.

They rode the elevator down with half a dozen residents of the forty-first floor. More people joined them as the lift descended, making for a crowded ride to the lobby of the building.

Aubrey followed behind Malina as she pushed her way through a set of wide double doors. Head down and lost in thought, puzzling over the connections between Ambrosia, Drillard, the Praeceptists, and the rogue drones, he only looked up when the cool air outside hit his face.

The scene that met him forced him to do a double take.

The street was clear. No vehicles.

From where he stood, he saw cars on the cross streets stopped where they met the long avenue in front of the apartment building. Stepping out into the avenue, he peered left. About five blocks away, three lanes of traffic stood unmoving, lined up on the left side of the road like they were at the starting gate of a road race. To the right, a mirror image on the opposite side of the street in the oncoming three lanes. In both directions, the lines of cars stretched into the distance, all the vehicles standing stock still. The cross streets were the same, the cars were abreast of the avenue where Aubrey stood, but no cars moved further in it to cross or turn onto it. Drivers and passengers were dark shapes behind the windows, heads shifting and turning, most likely curious about the sudden hold up.

The Metropolitan Traffic System usually cleared traffic from the roadways for emergency vehicles, but usually it made the cars and trucks pull to the side. Only a couple of lanes would be open for first responders. Aubrey didn't see the crashed drone as a serious enough situation to warrant a complete clearance of the avenue.

"Coincidence?" Malina shouted from the sidewalk.

Aubrey eyed her with a hard look from the middle of the road. "I think we need—"

Tires squealed, cutting his words short. He spun on the spot. A red sports car on a cross street catty-corner from the building spun its wheels, white smoke belching from under its front tires. It burst from its spot, its electric motor whining in a high-pitched fury. It bolted straight at Aubrey.

Aubrey stood transfixed, not believing what he was seeing. He watched the car barrel toward him like he was a matador awaiting the sharp horns of a bull.

"Martin!" Malina screamed behind him. "Move now!"

Her cry broke the trance, and he pivoted, sprinting back toward the building. "Inside," he shouted, pointing toward the doors. He was ten feet from her, twenty from the building. The car's engine screaming. It was close. "Now!"

She turned to obey but hesitated to stretch out a shaking hand, urging him to move faster. He was with her in two more steps, his arm around her shoulders pushing her ahead of himself. Three feet from the double doors, he saw it in the glass. The speeding car filled the reflective surface.

Too close. They wouldn't make it inside.

He planted his right foot, sticking it like a cleat on turf, and darted to the left. With his right arm cupped around Malina's torso, he forced them both through the air with the car missing his feet by inches. The wind whooshed past him, then a loud boom reverberated as the vehicle plowed into the glass doors and windows. He raised an arm to cover himself and his partner. Shards and pellets rained down on them like a seconds-long hail storm, but they were otherwise unharmed.

Aubrey pushed himself up and helped Malina to her feet. He brushed the glass from her hair and visually checked her. "You okay?"

"Yeah," Malina said, looking up at him, a tired look in her eyes.

Through the car's shattered front window, he could see the driver coughing and pushing back against the plethora of air bags. She appeared okay.

"What the hell is going on, Martin? It's like the damn AI is trying to ..." Her gaze shifted to something over his shoulder and her eyes widened to saucers. "Shit!"

She grabbed Aubrey by the lapels and yanked him toward her. Feeling her intent, he pushed his feet to follow her momentum, not chancing a look to see what was coming. They darted along the building's front facade, Aubrey nearly carrying Malina bodily along with him.

The impact came a heartbeat later. An intense crunching

behind them as something cratered the block wall of the building. Aubrey stopped and turned back. A black SUV with a badly crumpled front quarter smoked from under its hood, resting inside the huge dent in the wall where he and Malina stood two seconds ago.

The roar of a motor and the squeak of a strained suspension caught his ear. Glancing left, he saw it, a cement truck fifty feet away hurtled in a beeline straight at them. Its tall, angular front cab containing its panicked driver, who waved his arms as if trying to move the two of them with telekinesis. Aubrey reached out, took Malina by the upper arm and pulled her back in the direction of the crashed vehicles. Two long steps, then he used the SUV's deflated front tire as a step to launch him and Malina onto its hood. They scrambled onto its roof, then jumped in tandem onto the trunk of the red car. As one, they leapt to the ground just as the huge truck collided with the building. Its force bulldozed the SUV and the smaller car, threatening to roll Aubrey and Malina under the latter. Stumbling and staggering on broken glass and debris, they managed to maneuver out of the path of the wave of wreckage. The rear fender of the red car slid and stopped feet from them.

Panting, Aubrey put a hand on Malina's back. "Inside. Let's get inside."

"How?" she said, waving a hand at the building's front entrance.

She was right. The door and the adjacent windows were all blocked by the three vehicles that had just tried to kill them.

"Across the street then." He pointed to a Chinese restaurant across from the apartment building. She nodded and they jogged toward it. A moment later, he threw the door open just as tires squealed nearby, seeming to come from every direction. Aubrey and Malina dashed into the restaurant. A bell jingled over the door. The place was nearly empty. The hostess standing behind the podium gawked at them with stunned eyes.

"Move! To the back. Go!" They both shouted and waved at the hostess and the handful of patrons seated inside. "Now! Move!" As one, they ran, dodging tables and chairs, Aubrey taking up the rear. Just beyond the kitchen pass-through, the group of a dozen or so people took shelter in a short hallway near the restrooms. At the cusp of the hall, he turned, bracing for the imminent collision.

No crash came. A gray sedan and a red pickup truck were stopped in the middle of the road outside, angled across two lanes. A white van sat with its front wheels just over the lip of the curb but wasn't moving. A fourth vehicle, a blue station wagon, had crested the curb and creeped toward the front door, barely moving, a slight decline of the sidewalk coupled with gravity as its only propulsion. It coasted to a stop, the corner of its front bumper lightly thumping the door to the restaurant. A quiet tinkle rang from the bell.

15

The First Church of God's Wheel

"What is happening?" The captor spoke through clenched teeth, his voice a harsh growl.

"I don't know what happened. I thought we had it, then …" Reggie lifted his hands slightly and bowed his head to the man's hovering form. "I don't know. We just lost it. Something is working against us." Through the corner of his eye, he saw the man examining the large monitor ahead of them on the wall. It was divided into four windows, each showing a different camera feed from Third Avenue just outside Wayne Tower. The four vehicles Reggie had just commanded to ram the two people on the street were stalled. One second, they were under his control; the next second, they weren't.

"No," the man said. "Not someone." A sneer crossed his face, on the edge of becoming a smile by the looks of it. A pause stretched out while Reggie's captor stared blankly ahead at the screen. "Get it back." He spoke calmly, in a near whisper. "Regain control. We must have control." The kidnapper stepped away from the workstation. When he did, Reggie could see the two empty chairs and blank monitors before them both.

The guy just couldn't keep his mouth shut, and now it was all up to Reggie. All up to Reggie. He thought about that fact for a moment. Could he use that?

"I could use some help." Reggie croaked the words, his emboldened spirit not quite manifesting in his voice yet. The man's footsteps halted, and Reggie continued, not yet brave enough to actually turn and look at the man. "When there were three of us, it"—his neck quivered—"it was going faster. Now that it's just me, I … it's just a lot harder and slower."

A quiet chuckle issued from the man's throat, then a loud sigh of relief.

Hands on Reggie's naked shoulders surprised him, making him flinch. They squeezed his muscles, kneaded them. Jets of pain exploded down his atrophied back, reaching for his numb buttocks. Reggie arched his spine reflexively and stifled a shout of protest.

"A generous person will prosper; whoever refreshes others will be refreshed." The man laughed in Reggie's ear. "You want some company? I'll get you some friends, Reginald." His lips touched the rim of Reggie's right ear. "Just get us back in control of the AI and follow those two." His outstretched hand pointed at the man and woman on the screen as they exited the restaurant. A green polygon outlined their faces, yellow dots floated in places to mark definable features for the facial recognition program to track.

The captor slapped Reggie's shoulder and sent him reeling sideways, almost toppling over.

The man walked away, the sounds of his steps receding into the distance.

Reggie hung his head, a knot forming in his throat. What did he just do? He'd condemned someone else to this hell. He'd sealed another person's fate to die like the other two. To die like Reggie certainly would.

He couldn't fool himself any longer.

He'd be the next one to die as soon as his usefulness had run out.

* * *

"Damn it!" Malina screamed at no one in particular, her fists clenched in tight balls. "What the hell is going on?"

Aubrey was bent double, resting his hands on his knees, breathing hard. They stood outside the Chinese restaurant, watching traffic calmly resume around them. The cars glided silently past with confused drivers and passengers craning their necks at the scenes on either side of the avenue. Medical drones hovered overhead and scanned those affected by the chaos. Aubrey shut his eyes against the bright green light as the eye of a drone analyzed him for injuries.

"I don't know," he said. "But did you notice they weren't going for anyone else?" He waved a hand toward some pedestrians gawking at them.

"Yeah, they were definitely after us." Her head snapped in every direction; every noise seemed to startle her. "Why did they stop? The cars outside the restaurant. What happened there?"

Aubrey was thinking about that too. Four vehicles plowed toward them that would have crushed the glass front of the restaurant and could have done a lot of damage to the building and to them. But they stopped on their own. He shook his head. "I don't know."

She scoffed. "Martin, I don't think the MTS AI is in control anymore. It's clear there is a human behind the wheel of that thing, and they want us dead." The peal of a siren in the distance made her flinch. "We need to get out of here. I don't feel safe out in the open."

Aubrey nodded. "I know a place."

* * *

Aubrey and Malina jogged the thirteen blocks to their destination. Along the way, Malina had asked the same question several times: "Why didn't we take your car?"

To which Aubrey would reply the same way each time. "After all that back there, you want to get inside a car?"

The pair were hypervigilant as they went, watching every car that seemed to drive a little too fast. Eying drones that flew overhead.

Aubrey called Deputy Inspector Liz Reynolds while they ran, informing her of what happened in and outside Ambrosia's apartment. He would come to the station later to give a statement, but he had to make a stop first. She encouraged him to wait for a uniformed officer and a marked car before leaving the location, but he merely said he'd try. It depended on what he and Malina discovered, he'd told Liz. If they needed to move on a lead, they would.

"Should be up here, corner of Ninth Street and First Avenue," he said panting when the two of them rounded a corner.

They'd entered a heavy residential area of the city. Apartment buildings lined the avenues running north and south, with five-story brownstone homes filling the streets east and west. On the corner ahead of them, a squat three-story church stood with wide wooden doors angled toward the intersection. Above the doors, in silver scrawl, were the words "The First Church of God's Wheel." Atop a low steeple sat a tall cross with three concentric circles around its center.

They crossed the street using the underpass tunnel and, after emerging, jogged to the steps of the Praeceptist sanctuary.

Inside the foyer, the air was cool and held the familiar scent of a house of worship—polished wood, burning candles, and aged books. He could tell right away, just from the smell, this church still used paper hymnals and prayer books, unlike most places of worship that had long since moved to tablets and touchscreens on pews.

The entryway was barren save for a donation box on a thin stand in the corner. It was a simple box with a slot for paper bills.

Malina saw it too. "Who uses paper money nowadays?"

Aubrey shrugged. "People who don't use technology." He pointed his chin at the tall brass doors on the other side of the foyer. "Through there."

They pushed open the large doors and entered a smallish sanctuary. The room was wide but short with long rows of wooden pews on either side of a central aisle. Aubrey noticed the pews were highly polished with some type of oil, which contributed to the scent inside the sanctuary. In the end of each pew was carved the Praeceptist cross. The rest of the room was unadorned except for two oil paintings of Jesus on either side. The altar, directly ahead of them and at the end of the center aisle, was a simple long white table with a thick top and robust square legs. Next to it was a pulpit bearing the Praeceptist cross and two wooden chairs behind it.

Doors on either side of the back wall, behind the altar, led off the sanctuary. Aubrey gestured to the door on the right and started walking toward it. As they passed the row of pews closest to the altar, the door on the left opened, and a silver-haired, bespectacled man stepped out, carrying a tall stack of blue hardback books. Apparently surprised by the visitors in the sanctuary, he stopped abruptly, which sent the top four books tumbling to the floor.

Aubrey scurried toward him. "Let me give you a hand, sir." He bent down and retrieved the books from the carpeted floor. "Where should I put them?"

The older gentleman didn't reply. He turned and stepped up onto the raised platform and set the rest of the books on the altar. "What can I do for you folks?" the man said, sorting the books into smaller stacks.

Aubrey glanced down at the four he still held. They were thin prayer books. The Praeceptist cross embossed on the front with the words "Missal of Our Lord and Provider." Aubrey said, "We're private investigators," feeling it was best to get right to the point. "We're looking for someone."

The old man audibly inhaled and exhaled before responding, his face seeming to relax a little. "Yes, of course," he said and shuffled to Aubrey, extending a hand to him and then to Malina. "I'm Reverend Buddy Yates, and this," he extended his hands upward and to the sides, "is my congregation. My flock is always willing to help those in need." His soft eyes peered at Aubrey over gold-rimmed glasses, and his lips formed a gentle smile. He wore a red tie over a denim long-sleeve shirt worn thin at the elbows and beginning to tatter around the collar. "Let's talk in my office."

They followed the slightly hunched reverend through the side door he emerged from moments before. They continued down a long hallway lined with wood paneling, linoleum tiles underfoot, and dull overhead lights. His office was a tiny hovel off the hallway dominated by a large desk covered in stacks of papers, ledgers, and pencils. A bookshelf covered an entire wall. After a quick scan, Aubrey saw that the books were all old and religious in nature. What surprised him were copies of the Koran, Talmud, and Bhagavad Gita alongside the King James Bible. Most of the others had the Praeceptist cross on their spines.

"Let me get you something to sit on," the reverend said, disappearing down the hall and returning a moment later with two wooden chairs.

Reverend Yates flopped down into a rickety chair that creaked in protest as he leaned back. Aubrey and Malina took their seats and introduced themselves.

"You'll have to forgive my cold greeting in the sanctuary," the reverend said. "Our faith is not without its controversy, and from time to time, we get journalists and writers looking to get an inside peek at how we conduct ourselves and our belief systems. The problem is we're just not that exciting. More often than not, after we give them a look at what we do and what we think, they realize there is no real story here. Just people worshiping the Lord in their own way." He steepled his hands in front of his face as he spoke.

A sound from the corner of the room caught Aubrey's ear. Somehow he missed seeing a small table behind the open door. On it sat an ancient beige computer monitor, its enormous bulk leaving little room for much else on the tabletop. The rear of the thing jutted out twelve inches, and the bezel around the curved fourteen-inch screen was three inches thick. He figured it must weigh thirty pounds. The sound he heard was a cooling fan, which came from the computer tower on the floor below the table. Thick cables ran from it and up to the monitor and to a keyboard leaning against the table legs.

"You have a computer?" Malina asked.

The reverend giggled quietly, a high-pitch undulating sound that surprised Aubrey. "Yes," he said looking at the antique beast of a machine, "a point of contention among our congregants. But as you can see, it's so old that you can hardly call it a computer at all. More like a glorified abacus." He gave another soprano chortle.

Aubrey squinted at the man. "I thought your whole belief system was about not using technology."

The reverend's eyebrows shot up, creasing his forehead. "Did you see the lights in the hallway? Did you notice the semicomfortable heat inside the building? Did you detect that I am well over eighty years old?" A pause. "Our abstinence from technology only goes so far, Mr. Aubrey. It's silly not to use any technology. What is a fire in a hearth or clothing or medicine? These are technologies if one uses a straightforward definition of the word as we do. Our faith is about focus. Focus your energy and mind and heart on the Creator, Our Lord the Father. When technology or any of life's extraneous adornments comes to dominate your focus, we see it as a hindrance to faith, and we shun it."

"Still, why the computer?" Malina asked.

"Alas, some things these days can only be done by computer and the internet." He pointed a finger toward the ceiling. "The power bill for instance. They used to let us pay by mail or in person, but ten years ago, they changed their policies. We procured this monstrosity"—he laughed in something near a squeal—"when it became necessary. We kept it simple so as not to be a temptation." He spread his hands wide. "But let's get to the matter for which you entered our humble church today. What is it I can do for you?"

They explained the recent death of Drillard and the missing Ambrosia and Elton. They showed him pictures of the two missing men, and after studying them for a moment, he said he'd never seen either of them.

"What do they have to do with my church, Mr. Aubrey?" the reverend asked politely.

"We found this at Mr. Sapindales's apartment." Aubrey placed his phone on the desk so Reverend Yates could see the picture of the Praeceptist book Malina discovered next to the toilet.

"Yes. *Book of the Wheel* is a popular text amongst our more fundamentalist members." The reverend pointed to the bookshelf, and Aubrey followed his finger. On the far left of the second shelf was a replica of the book they'd found at Ambrosia's apartment.

"Fundamentalist members?" Malina asked.

"Yes, those members of the congregation that believe that even our limited use of technology is too much. They match the assumption you expressed earlier and think that all technology should be forbidden. The more radical ones think we should actively seek to stop the use of technology even among nonmembers of the Praeceptist movement." He leaned forward, adjusting his glasses as he examined the image on Aubrey's phone. "But I struggle to understand how this man came to own this book. I'd say you would be unlikely to find it in the homes of most of our members."

"You're sure Mr. Sapindales wasn't a member here? Even very recently? Maybe you missed him." Aubrey pressed the faith leader.

"We are a small flock. I know everyone who comes and goes here."

Aubrey picked up his phone from the desk and typed a note. After a moment, he asked, "What about Josiah Palmero? Do you know him?"

The old reverend's eyes closed to slits, and his face went slack. A coldness crossed his visage, and he steepled his fingers once again. "I do. Josiah is a good boy."

"Have you seen him lately?" Malina asked.

Reverend Yates closed his eyes and kneaded his forehead with both hands. After a moment, he looked up at them, his former jovial countenance had vanished. "No. He hasn't been a regular attendee for some time."

Malina and Aubrey exchanged a glance. Aubrey asked, "Why is that? Why hasn't he been coming around lately?"

The reverend sat back, and his face turned to stone. "I don't discuss the personal matters of our congregants with outsiders. If the boy is missing"—his eyes fell for a moment—"it must be for a good reason. But I'm confident Josiah will rediscover the righteous path."

Aubrey picked up on the reverend's choice of words. "What do you mean by 'rediscover the righteous path'? Was he on the righteous path before he left?"

Reverend Yates's hands fell to the desk. "I'm afraid that's all I can do for you today. I have a worship service to prepare for." He stood and raised a hand toward the door. "I'll show you out."

"Please, sir, just one more minute," Aubrey protested.

"When was the last time you saw Josiah Palmero?" He pleaded his case as the older man shuffled them out of his office. In the hallway, a short brunette young woman in a long denim skirt stood aside as they passed, averting her eyes from the group.

"Excuse us, Samantha," the reverend said. "These folks were just leaving."

Aubrey and Malina continued with their questions until it became clear that Reverend Yates would not yield, and they resigned themselves to leaving the church in silence.

Outside on the corner, Aubrey kicked the base of a streetlamp. "Damn it. I thought we were getting somewhere."

"Well, it's obvious Palmero is persona non grata at the"—she pointed up at the sign over the front entrance—"First Church of …" She paused. "Uh, Aubrey? Turn around."

He turned to see a woman rushing toward them from the church, bounding down the front steps. She clutched her elbows against the chill air, her denim skirt flapping in the stiff wind. It was Samantha, the woman from the hallway. She stopped in front of them, her gaze bouncing between them, appearing unsure of herself.

After a moment, Aubrey broke the silence. "Ma'am … um, Samantha, right? Do you need help?"

Her head dropped, and she scraped the concrete sidewalk with her toe. "You're looking for Josiah?"

Aubrey locked eyes with Malina. "Yes. Yes we are. Do you know where to find him?"

"No," she said, raising her head to stare at him. "I don't know where to find him. Is he in trouble?"

Samantha had a kind face, and her concern appeared genuine.

Aubrey frowned and said, "We don't know. We just have some questions for him. Do you know why he left the church?"

"He didn't leave." Her words shot from her mouth like darts. "He had … some different ideas, that's all. About how we should worship God and they"—she threw an arm back toward the church doors—"thought he was wrong or something. So he stopped coming I guess." She clutched her elbows again, the ends of her sweater's sleeves in her fists.

"What kind of ideas did he have?" Malina asked.

"He looked up to Reverend Yates like a father. Josiah's daddy died years ago, and the reverend kind of adopted him and then just dropped him when Josiah started trying to spread the Word."

"The Word?" Aubrey pressed.

"The Lord's message." She shrugged deeply, and her head remained cocked to one side.

Aubrey shifted on his feet. He wanted to seem less stiff, to open her up a little more. "What kind of Word was Josiah preaching?"

"Listen, I'm only telling you this because—I mean, if he's in trouble or missing or something. I just want to help you find him. So he'll come back."

Malina touched the young lady's shoulder. "We'll find him, and if he wants to come back, we'll bring him. How did you know Josiah? Was he a friend or … something more?"

At this, Samantha scowled and jerked her shoulder away from Malina's hand. "That's none of your business." Samantha bent her head low again and muttered, "I gotta go. I shouldn't be talking to you."

"Wait, please." Aubrey raised his hands in supplication but

was careful not to touch her. "We just want to get Josiah some help, if he needs it."

Samantha was half-turned back toward the church but moved no further.

"What was the Word Josiah was preaching? What were his ideas?" Aubrey had a feeling where this was going, but he needed to make sure.

"Samantha!" A voice cried from the direction of the church. All of them looked up to see Reverend Buddy Yates standing on the top step, his hands firmly planted on his hips, his face twisted in a furious glower.

Samantha whipped around to face the reverend, then back to Aubrey, and extended an arm as if to shake hands. He followed suit, and as he gripped her outstretched hand, he felt an object in her palm. It was a thin paper cylinder about the size of a fat cigar. The woman pulled away and jogged back to the church, the object was now in Aubrey's hand. He slid it into his pocket and motioned to Malina.

"Let's get going."

16

Josiah

Four Years Ago

"And God the Father gave Adam and his bride, Eve, a garden. This garden was filled with every conceivable item they might desire." The youth pastor sat on a wooden milk crate speaking to the circle of teenagers. "He gave them everything they needed, right there." The young man's upper lip bore a barely visible mustache, and his short brown hair was parted down the middle. He pointed at the center of the circle with both hands. Everyone stared at the spot, apparently imagining the Garden of Eden right there in front of them.

Josiah Palmero saw nothing but worn-out mauve carpeting.

"All of you know this story," the youth pastor, Steven, said smiling. "I won't beat that dead horse too much longer, I promise."

Almost everyone laughed at his joke.

Josiah didn't find it all that funny.

"All they had to do was not eat from one tree. They could have everything they'd ever want for all eternity, and all they had to do was obey one rule. Does anyone want to tell me what happened next?"

Hands shot up around the circle. Steven pointed at a girl to his left, a girl about Josiah's age with blonde hair and dark eyes. Sheila Napkist.

"Satan tempted them, and they ate from the tree, so God punished them." The words came out of her mouth rapid-fire, like she was afraid someone else might steal the answer right from her lips.

Steven smiled again. Nodding, he said, "That's right." He pointed at Sheila, then the rest of them. "And all they had to do was obey one rule. How many rules have people broken since?"

Murmurs around Josiah as the young church members guessed at what he knew was an unguessable number.

"Thousands?" Steven shrugged. "Millions? Billions? Trillions? Does it matter how many it is?"

Cries of "No" rang out around the room.

"Whether it's one or one billion, we disobeyed His command." More dramatic nodding from Steven. "And we are being punished." He let that sink in for a moment. "Aren't we?"

"Yes," rang out from the small group this time.

"How are we punished?" Steven asked.

"Disease."

"War."

"Violence."

"Crime."

"Natural disasters."

"Poverty."

Answers to Steven's question shot from kids on either side of Josiah. They came so quick he could barely put eyes on who was speaking before the next person belted out their response. The youth pastor made another one of his overlong nods and looked around the circle, meeting the eyes of everyone there.

"What does our faith say about that? What does our faith, as observant, full-hearted Praeceptists tell us about the punishment Lord the Father is dishing out as we speak?" Steven leaned in toward the circle, resting his elbows on his knees.

No one answered for a few seconds, and Steven let the silence stew in the room.

"It says that technology is the great sin." Josiah's own words almost caught him by surprise. He glanced around at the others. Their faces urged him to say more, and Steven remained silent. "It says that if we obey God's laws, and if we get others to follow his laws as well, then we'll be rewarded with his love." He cleared a frog from his throat. "And we'll be welcomed into his heavenly kingdom."

Steven pointed a finger at Josiah. "That's right, Josiah. You see, guys—"

"But that's not enough," Josiah said, once again catching himself off guard.

Steven and the others turned to him.

The things he wanted to say out loud he'd only ever thought inside his own head. But the thoughts squirmed inside him like some baby lizard trying to break out of its shell. It had been living in him ever since his dad had failed to come home that night three weeks ago. That night when some stranger knocked on their door. A stranger with the news about his dad.

"It's not enough." The water in his eyes threatened to crest over his bottom eyelid and he looked at the floor, hoping no one could see him crying. "God punishes us every day. Every day people are dying and suffering." His squeezed his fists until the knuckles turned white. "Our own people, even though we obey the rules, His rules. God kills us right along with the others because ... because those people out there"—he shot a hand toward the door of the classroom—"can't see the truth that's right in front of their faces." His breath came in quick shots. He could feel the sobs about to erupt.

Somewhere to Josiah's left, Steven cleared his throat. "That's right. That's right, Josiah." He spoke softly, as though anything louder than a whisper might cause Josiah to crumble and turn to dust.

Steven knew about Josiah's dad. Everyone knew. Everyone knew about the crane at the docks, the one operated by a robot or computer or whatever. The crane that quit working properly and swung wildly one direction when it should have gone the other. They knew about how Josiah's dad was about to descend into a large container vessel to scrape detritus from its inner walls when the crane's cable swung right at him, catching him in the shoulder and neck. They knew that his spine snapped like a twig and that he was dead before he fell from the ship. They knew he dangled in midair since his body was still harnessed to the safety cable. They knew he hung there for fifteen minutes until a crew could detach his harness and lower him to the deck.

Steve whispered, "That's why we have to—"

"Have to do what?" Josiah barked. Trying to hold back the tears was fruitless. They came as freely as the rage boiling over inside him. "What do we have to do? Go around and stand on street corners handing out fliers, hoping that one person in ten thousand will actually read the stupid thing? And then feel lucky when one in a hundred thousand might come to the sanctuary one Sunday?"

"Well, Josiah …" Steven started to say something.

"It's not enough, Pastor Steven." Josiah stood. "What we do is so"—he paused to search for the right word—"passive. And weak. We're waiting for people to come to us. We're waiting for them to wake up and see." He threw his hands out to the side, still staring at the floor. "When we should … we should …"

"What should we do, Josiah?" Steven asked after a moment of silence.

Everything hit Josiah at once—all the eyes in the room on him, the tear stains on the front of his shirt, his trembling hands, the look of real concern on the Pastor Steve's face. He'd never been one to speak in a crowd, never one to raise his hand in class. He kept to himself whenever possible. Sweat dripped down his back, and his legs started to wobble. Gravity seemed to pull him down to sit.

"What should we do, Josie?" A girl with short brown hair leaned toward him. Billie something.

Josiah swiped a hand across his eyes and dried them on his jeans. He sniffled loudly, not caring anymore if they all knew he'd been crying. "We should wake them all up."

* * *

The early evening air was warm and heavy with humidity. Josiah thought he could smell the briny water of the bay just a dozen blocks north of the church. He threw his head back and let his eyes become unfocused as he took in the freshly darkened sky overhead. No stars could be found in the night sky above the city, but he knew they were up there somewhere, and that was a comfort to him. God's great works were all around them, even beyond their own senses.

A soft click, a hum, and a second sun flamed to life twenty feet above him. The street light illuminated the entire street corner and then some, bathing the ground and buildings in an unearthly blue-white light. He slammed his eyes shut to protect them. The great sin of technology was just above him. Man's arrogant attempt to simulate one of God's most precious creations—the sun. The hubris of it astounded him.

"Hey, Josie," a girl's voice said behind him.

He turned to find Billie, hands clasped in front of her, shuffling her feet nervously.

"I'm sorry. Is it okay to call you Josie?" Billie pushed a length of hair behind her ear. "I thought I heard your mom and dad call you that and"—she shrugged one shoulder—"I thought it was cute."

He suddenly felt queasy and physically uncomfortable, but he welcomed anything other than pain and despair.

He tried to smile. "It's fine. I don't care what people call me."

Billie's brow furrowed and her feet stopped fidgeting. "You should. You should care what people call you." She fixed her hair again. "What you said in there about waking all of them up"—she pointed her chin toward the heart of the city—"you're right. I think I've been thinking it for a long time too. I just didn't realize how I felt until tonight, until you said what you said."

Josiah's gaze fell to the ground, which he scraped lightly with the toe of his boot. "I don't know what I was talking about."

"Maybe you should write it down." Billie took a step closer, narrowing the gap between them.

Now he stared at Billie's feet, wondering how close she'd come to him. "I'm not a writer. People don't care about what I have to say."

"Well, I care. And I think other people will care too."

17

Josiah

Six Months Ago

"Josiah? Josiah, are you listening?"

He wasn't listening. Josiah barely registered that Reverend Yates was speaking to him. Instead, he stared down the darkened hallway, wondering who else was in his apartment loitering in the family room. Drinking up all the coffee, no doubt.

"Josiah." The reverend's harsh whisper cut through his thoughts, but he refused to reply. Hands on his shoulders finally brought his eyes up to the man trying to counsel him. "Did you hear what I said?" Reverend Yates's features were mostly hidden in the darkness, but his tone of voice conveyed urgency.

"No."

"We can bring her to the hospital," the reverend said. "It's permitted in order to save a life. Furthermore, if she's not too far gone by now, Nurse Mock tells me they have medicines that don't violate our way of life. She may not need their machines at all."

"No, Reverend, you misunderstand." Josiah looked into the man's eyes, level with his own. "I heard you the first time. My mother is not going to the hospital."

"Josiah, since your father died, the community has done its best to look after you and your mom." Reverend Yates gesticulated with his hands. "You, certainly, have done more than your fair share to take care of yourself and your mother, especially these past few months. These dark days have weighed heavily on all of us."

"Reverend…" Josiah interjected, but the man carried on regardless.

"I've been praying, we all have, and I think Lord the Father is telling us to try something else." The reverend's hands came together.

"I've been praying too, Reverend." Josiah lifted his hands and sandwiched the reverend's between them. "I know what the Lord wants of me. This is a test of my faith, and I will not fail him."

"She's still young, son, not yet sixty." Reverend Yates pulled his hands free from Josiah's. "She could be a grandmother to your children someday. I'm told this type of cancer is very curable nowadays." His hand gestured back to the cracked doorway of Josiah's mother's bedroom. The reverend whispered, "She will most likely die, my son. If we don't …"

"His plan is His plan. Whether we understand it or not." Josiah eyed the half-open door just behind Reverend Yates. "My mother is at peace with this, as am I. If my father were here, I'm confident he would be as well."

"Son …" The reverend placed a hand to his own forehead.

"Reverend," Josiah said, slightly louder than the reverend, "Lord the Father wants to see if I'll turn from him to save someone precious to me. I shall not do that, Reverend." Josiah rested his hands softly on the reverend's shoulders. "And if he should deem it necessary to bring my mother to her heavenly home, to sit at His feet, then he must need me to have more time to do His good work."

The reverend opened his mouth to say something but stopped himself, instead giving Josiah a gentle smile and a tiny nod before leaving him for the front room.

* * *

Josiah turned the knob down on the lantern to darken the room a bit. He wasn't afraid of what he'd see on the bed. The sight of his mother's ill form didn't bother him in the slightest. He simply detested the red-yellow glow cast by the lantern's gas-powered light. The small bed where his mother lay had a twin on the opposite side of the room against the wall. It was empty, once belonging to his father, but it was still made as if the man might turn in for the night at any minute. The pillow was nicely fluffed with squared corners. The sheets folded over the top edge of the comforter, just how he'd liked it.

Josiah sat in the chair next to his mother's bed. He rested one hand on the blanket that covered her. Her breath rasped through her mouth and nose, catching every few seconds with a wet clicking sound in her throat.

For five months, he'd spent most of his days in this exact position, waiting on his mother between her naps, her body growing sicker by the day, her mind fading with it. She hadn't walked in weeks, hadn't eaten in days. All she did for the better part of the day was sleep. When she was awake, she drifted in and out of coherence—one minute speaking clearly with Josiah and the next asking for her long dead husband. It had gotten to the point that when she was awake, Josiah secretly wished for her to fall back asleep.

His mother jerked her arms up to her chest, balling up the edge of the blanket in her hands. She rocked her head left and right, muttering unintelligibly. Josiah noticed one foot had come uncovered, and he stood to pull the quilt back over it. Standing at the foot of the bed, he took in the sight of his dying mother, trying in his mind to transpose the younger, healthier version he'd known for so long over the ghostly form laying in front of him. His fear was that he may never be able to recall her face, her smile from a time before she fell ill. Their religion prohibited cameras, and they were too poor for a portrait painter. He might forever remember his mother as she was at the moment—skeletal, scabbed, balding, her body beaten down by disease.

"Josiah!" she exclaimed in a weak but excited voice.

He rushed to her side and bent close, but she was nearly shouting.

"Josiah! We'll name him Josiah, after my father."

The memory of his birth. Strange to him because he'd never heard his parents speak of it. It had only occurred to him at that moment that he'd never heard the story of his own birth.

Her eyes went wide, staring into oblivion above her. "He's perfect, just perfect. I love him already, Kirk."

Josiah held her hand, which was still tight to her chest and tangled in the blankets. The thumb of her left hand hooked around his forefinger. Probably just a reflex, he figured, but he could pretend she meant to do it.

"I know that when we came here, I thought it would be a girl. I'd always pictured us with a girl."

For the first time since she'd fallen ill, Josiah felt hot tears pool in his eyes. Since that day five months ago when she'd uncharacteristically fallen in the kitchen, since she'd started to lose weight and strength, since she'd started to forget, he hadn't cried once. The Lord provided. That's what their faith taught them. Whatever they needed, He provided. Which meant, whatever this was, Josiah needed it. So he accepted it.

For the first time, he allowed himself to miss her, to miss the woman who'd always been there. To mourn the loss of the woman who taught him how to be. To mourn the loss His mortal world would now feel with her absence. To lament the long years he'd have to wait until he could see her again.

Tears ran in lines down both cheeks. He squeezed his eyes shut, felt his lip curl and begin to quiver.

"Mom," he whispered. "Can you hear me?"

"But when I saw him, I knew. I just knew. It had to be him."

He opened his still wet eyes.

"This is what Lord the Father has given us." Her voice softened.

Josiah blinked and leaned in closer.

"Kirk, I've always known he made me barren for a reason. He gives us only what we need. He made me unable to bear children so that we could find Josiah, so that he could be delivered to us. It must be him, Kirk, the one they call Hank. Baby Hank will be our Josiah."

18

Hank

November 11, 2043—11:00 a.m.

Francesca inspected the clock in the library's high corner above the second-floor stacks: 11:00 a.m. She'd been sifting through Tigunder's data for six hours. Using a tablet Malina loaned her, she'd accessed the digital dead drop via the tablet's secure connection and sat in a quiet corner of the Metropolitan Public Library tucked between rows of reference books. The books themselves were most likely digitized, but libraries had an affinity for physical books, which Francesca could appreciate.

Not being particularly tech savvy, it had taken Francesca some time to figure out the most efficient way possible to search each file, which ranged from three-hundred to a thousand lines of data. Once she discovered how to search and filter the data properly, she'd begun making better time. In six hours, she'd gone through 942 files with no luck yet of finding her brother, and her hope had begun to dim. The only oddity she'd found thus far had been the adoptions of three children by a private entity rather than an individual or a couple looking to grow their family. The entity, known as Wohlfühlwelt, held no other description in the files, only an address somewhere in a largely unpopulated area in upstate Maryland. She knew of one other entity, and only one, that adopted groups of children—the Order of the Coppice. She decided to log the oddity away in her memory for later investigation. Time was of the essence and she was running short of it.

The possibility that her search was in vain began to press down on her like a lead weight. There was no guarantee the data was complete. There was also no guarantee her brother Hank was anywhere in the data, as he may have never been adopted and therefore released into society when he turned eighteen. Even if she did find him and his adoptive family's information, there was every possibility that they were gone, out of the city or off the grid somewhere.

Francesca allowed herself a moment to breathe. She closed her eyes, the tablet screen's bright blue light burning through her eyelids. The library's scent—old books and musty carpet—and its sounds—shuffling feet, whispered conversations, and the quiet tapping of keyboards—filled her head, and she allowed it to consume her, refresh her senses, bring her back to the present moment. Seconds later, her brief meditation provided her with the clarity of mind she needed to press on in the futile-seeming task.

Forty-eight minutes later, she came across yet another file with a random assortment of letters, numbers, and symbols as its title; this one read WIEM%4849FEOON. She assumed someone, Tigunder most likely, had a cipher that could sort out the randomness into a discernible system, but she had no idea what they could possibly mean. Inside

WIEM%4849FEOON, she quickly saw that the dates for adoptions were from the year she left the orphanage, when she left Hank behind to start her life in the Order. Going through the motions of her search routine, she was only slightly more hopeful than she'd been in the previous 1,112 files. Minutes passed, and her hope began to wane once again.

Then a window appeared in the middle of her screen.

Found 1 match for "Henry James Green."

Reflexively, she jerked back, thinking, at first, that she'd done something wrong, corrupted the data. She read the alert again.

Found 1 match for "Henry James Green."

Her breath was trapped in her chest, refusing to leave, and she heard her heart thumping inside her ears. She raised a quivering finger and tapped the notification. The box disappeared, and the page shifted to reveal highlighted rows of data.

Green, Henry James. Male birth. Birth parents: Rodney Oscar Green—deceased, Henrietta Carla Ballentine-Green—deceased. Siblings: (1) female birth, Francesca Deborah Green. Current status for Henry Green: Adopted, May 16, 2025, into custody of Kirk Adam Palmero and Wendy Dale Newman Palmero (married).

Francesca read the lines a second time. Then a third and a fourth. She touched the screen where his full name filled the data cell, wishing it were an instant connection to him, wishing it could transport her to the only family she had left—if she still had him left.

The intense elation that surged through her chilled as dread and anxiety mixed with her happiness to create a nauseating emotional cocktail. Here he was, in this tiny line of information on her screen.

Hank had been alone at the orphanage for a month before he was adopted by Kirk and Wendy Palmero. There was no way he'd remember her, she'd already come to terms with that fact, but the Palmeros could have told him he was adopted and that he had a sister. Maybe he'd always been curious to know her. Maybe he'd dreamed about her, what she looked like, what she was up to, the same way Francesca dreamed about him.

Hope. Hope was all she had. Hope that he wouldn't turn her away. Hope that he would believe her. Hope that above all else, he met her with anything other than indifference. Fear, confusion, anger—she could accept and deal with any of those reactions from her brother. Not indifference. Not the great sin of not feeling—she couldn't tolerate that. If her brother felt nothing for her, if he brushed off her existence, if he disregarded the intense connection she'd felt with him for nineteen years, it would turn her to chalk.

19

Acer Sapindales

Two Weeks Ago

"It was the first of the Lord's gifts that was perverted, twisted, and corrupted by men," Josiah read aloud from the booklet, its pages filled with his own tight, leaning script. "That gift, of course, was intelligence. The ability to see the world around us and see what could be. The instincts to not only know when a problem existed but to also see a way to fix it."

Murmurs of agreement echoed around the circle.

Josiah continued reading. "For thousands of years, the blade has been the instrument of the warrior. Whether it be affixed to the end of a shaft or the metal itself is elongated into a sword, hardened and hammered flat and honed to a fine edge, it has been used to kill countless people on this planet." He raised a finger. "But for thousands of years before that, it was the instrument of the farmer. God the Father gave us the blade not to spill blood but to turn soil. Man wasn't satisfied with what the Lord gave him, so he sought more—more food, more gold, more power—and they fashioned a gift meant to propagate life into one whose sole purpose is to take life."

Josiah lifted his head and inhaled deeply, his gaze arcing over the people seated on the grass. Most of them held a copy of the booklet Josiah read from, but their eyes were on him, hanging on every word he said. The group was an even dozen made up, in large part, by members of his church. They'd come to hear him talk. Half of them had been coming for weeks by the time the numbers began to increase.

There was only one face he didn't recognize. A youngish man with shabby clothes and unkempt hair and stubbly face that made him look totally out of place next to the clean-cut group of young Praeceptist men and women.

"And so it is with everything," Josiah said, no longer reading from the booklet. "The Lord gives us a gift, and we take it and make it into something so far beyond what he intended that it ceases to be a gift. And those perversions that we create turn into addictions that we can't wean ourselves off. Imagine the others turning off their electricity for even a few days. Even a few hours."

"Chaos." A teenage girl spoke while staring at him over the rims of thick glasses. "There'd be chaos."

The discussion continued for half an hour, centering on the ways in which man had squandered God's gifts, thereby turning its collective back on the Creator's love.

"Praeceptism tells us all this, what we've been discussing." Josiah wanted to wrap up the meeting with the right message. It encouraged him to see the nods all around the circle. "But there's something missing, isn't there?" The affirmations continued. "What's missing is what to do about it. Praeceptists—and I count myself among them of course—are passive proselytizers, which means we put ourselves out there and hope the converted come to us. We put our hooks in the water, like good little fishermen, hoping a big one is going to swim by and snatch it up." Images of Josiah's parents handing out countless pamphlets on every second Sunday filled his brain. "And every now and then, a fish does come by, and we land ourselves a nice little catch. Most of the time, however, we come up dry. We go home hungry."

He paused and looked at the sky, closed his eyes briefly hoping the right words would come to him. All he wanted was for these people to feel what he felt, to understand the world needed fixing and to know that they were the ones to do it.

"And why do we come up dry?" He paused but the group knew to wait for him. The answer would come. "Is it because we fish with the wrong bait? Maybe we fish in the wrong spot, or maybe we fish for the wrong people." He shook his head and the circle mimicked him. "No. It's not for any of those reasons. The real question is: Why are we fishing at all? One hook and one line at a time waiting for the fish to come to us." Josiah leaned forward and pressed a finger into the grass. "We have to go to them, we have to go to the people, but not with one line and one hook. We should go to them with great nets, opened wide"—he spread his arms and bent his head to the heavens—"enveloping the world in His love."

"And if that doesn't work?" asked a young man across the circle from Josiah.

Josiah frowned. "In the old days, some fishermen would drop a stick of dynamite in the water and scoop out whatever came up."

Stunned faces greeted him around the circle, but no one protested or even hinted at disagreement. One face, the stranger, smiled wickedly.

* * *

The meeting concluded, and the group dispersed, most heading home, others walking toward the Praeceptist church several blocks away. Josiah stayed behind, as per usual, to answer questions and to provide comfort or guidance if needed. One girl, in her late teens, spoke with him for several minutes about her parents and their reluctance to actively spread the good word.

"One way or another, all God's children will find the righteous path," he told her. "We'll shoulder the burden for now, and when the time comes, we'll welcome the reformed and converted."

"But you said we have to go to them," she replied, "to make them see."

"I did. And we will."

The stranger stood behind the girl, ten feet away, hands in his pockets. The stranger's eyes were locked on Josiah, a strange smile frozen across his face.

Josiah forced himself to turn his attention back to the girl, who looked to be growing confused. "Let's catch up later and talk more about that. As the group has more of these talks, we'll begin discussing in detail about how we're going to go about casting our net." He cupped the girl's shoulders and smiled warmly at her.

She returned the kind expression and said goodbye.

When she was gone, Josiah turned to the man who still stared at him with wide eyes and that odd smile. The man's straw-colored hair hadn't seen a comb or a shower in quite a while, and his beard hadn't been trimmed in days by the look of it. To Josiah, this man looked to be in desperate need of …

direction.

"The way you talk is inspiring," the man said, shaking Josiah's hand. "Profound, exciting, eye-opening. It's"—his eyes searched the air while his hand stroked his chin—"everything I've been looking for. And I didn't even know I was looking for it."

"I'm Josiah."

The man hadn't let go of his hand. He seemed to be unaware of anything that wasn't directly in front of his eyes, which must have been why they were held open so wide. "I know." The hungry grin spread across the stranger's face once more. "I know. I came to find you."

Josiah reminded himself to ask the question of how the man came to know who he was. "And you are?"

"Acer. Acer Sapindales." The man shrugged, dropping Josiah's hand at the same time. "People call me Ambrosia, but that was from a former life."

* * *

The two men sat in the shade of a large tree talking for hours. Acer had many questions about Praeceptism but many more about Josiah's interpretation of the church's doctrine. Josiah did his best to answer the questions, but he wasn't sure how much sank in for Acer as he bounced excitedly from one question to the next, barely taking a breath.

"What's in the next life? What do Praeceptists believe will happen to the rest of mankind? Will there be a great awakening? A time when Praeceptism will come to be the dominant religion? What kinds of prophecies do you guys believe in? What is going to happen in the next hundred years? When will God judge the others?"

Josiah, in his turn, had many questions for Acer. It turned out they'd both had dark times in their respective pasts. Josiah shared the loss of his parents and the recent knowledge of his adoption, and Acer told him about his beloved girlfriend, Trina, who had died less than a year before.

"She drowned." Acer pushed the hair out of his face only to have it fall back a second later. "Crazy to think that could happen in this day and age, but it did. In the river. We'd been out drinking with friends and decided to drop a little *pastee*, just a couple of hits each to keep us going. We were crossing the bridge on foot, on the pedestrian skyway, and I look back"—he gestured in the air, and his eyes seemed to dim—"and the lights of the city were behind, and she looked so ... radiant. I told her I wanted to take her picture. So she ... she jumped up onto the railing and spread her arms out wide and ..." Acer paused, eyes closed.

Josiah waited for him to finish. He knew that reliving the tragedy must be painful.

"And she slipped." Acer wiped tears from the corners of his eyes. "The water was cold, the current was fierce, and it was dark. They didn't find her for a while, and by then, there was nothing they could do." Acer's face went slack. "All the tech in the world at these hospitals, and there was nothing they could do for her. Nothing." He looked into Josiah's eyes. "I'd devoted my life to using technology. I'd been a fighter for good causes, thinking there was nothing we, as a species, couldn't do with sufficient technology. Then Trina died and I did a lot of thinking and ... a lot of drinking." He took a deep breath and continued. "That was a dark time for me. At one point, I thought there was no way out of the darkness, there was no light left in the world. When I was at my worst, I met a guy who handed me a pamphlet with that cross on it." He pointed to the wooden cross hanging from Josiah's neck. "We started talking, and he told me I should find you." He gripped Josiah's forearm, as if to emphasize the statement.

Josiah had the feeling that no matter how much he learned about this man, Acer, he'd never really know him. One thing was certain: there was a great deal of pain in his eyes backed by even more passion. Acer had a deep sense of purpose, although it wasn't clear to Josiah what that purpose was.

"I think we're kindred spirits, Josiah." Acer gazed off into the distance. "We come from different worlds, but God has put us here together as partners."

"Partners?" Josiah had an uneasy feeling about the word.

"We're going to do profound things together. I know it."

* * *

Two weeks after their first meeting, Josiah returned home one night to find a note on his apartment floor. Apparently, the note had been slid under the door while Josiah was out. He walked into the kitchen and set his grocery bags down on the counter. A second later, he picked up the folded piece of paper and opened it. It was from Acer Sapindales. All that was written on it was a location and a time with the word *tonight* at the bottom just above Acer's blocky signature.

Josiah and Acer had met more than a dozen times since their first meeting at the park. Sometimes, Acer would wait for Josiah outside the church after services had concluded, then walk home with Josiah. He attended all of Josiah's group meetings inside and outside the church, always staying after to discuss different ideas he'd had since the last time they'd seen each other. In the last week, however, Acer would show up unannounced to Josiah's apartment at all times of the day and night.

Since his mother's passing, Josiah had lived alone, and not having any close friends of his own, he'd begun to delight in Acer's pop-ins. Some days, Acer would come full of questions about Praeceptism, God, and Josiah's view on world issues like hunger, poverty, and disease. Josiah would usually refer back to his fundamental belief: humankind had to atone for abandoning God, and until they did, tragedy would continue to plague His children.

"Is that why he took your parents?" Acer asked one evening. "Because they had to atone?"

Josiah had contemplated this question himself many times since his mother died. "I tend to think that I am the one who is meant to atone. Their deaths don't affect them as much as it affects me. Parents die; that's what they do. People have kids, they raise them, then they die to make room for those kids to grow up. When the parents die, I think, is up to the children. At some point in my life, I was deeply entwined in sin, and therefore, I was punished."

"What was your sin?"

"Was? I think the word *is* would be more appropriate. What *is* my sin? And the answer: I don't actually know, but I hope my work in the future will lead to my atonement."

Acer and Josiah would often discuss atonement. On that, their minds were one—atonement of God's children meant salvation for the world. What form and what steps needed to be taken to begin the process of atonement was a constant disagreement, but they both felt that each step had to be big, had to hit people hard in order to wake them up.

And it would have to hurt. Suffering was the only way to start a true rebirth.

Josiah read the note one more time. It would take him a while to reach the location Acer specified in the far northern reaches of the city, two hours at least. Glancing at the clock on the wall, he realized if he didn't leave right then, he'd be late. He grabbed his coat from the back of his father's favorite chair and threw it on.

* * *

A little over two hours later, Josiah stood in a dark corner of a park on the edge of a parking lot. Neither of which he'd ever been to. Behind him, the waters of the Chesapeake lapped lazily against a rocky shoreline. His breath came out in white puffs, and the cold penetrated his wool coat, another relic of his father's, which he pulled tight around himself. The fast walk to the meeting location had warmed him considerably, but now he'd been waiting for half an hour, and the cold had slipped through his patchy coat.

Lights lined the shore of the bay, but the park was scarcely lit, and the nearest light to him came from the strangely shaped building at the other end of the parking lot. Without his watch, he had no idea of the time. All he knew was Acer was very late. After several minutes, he decided to abandon the meetup, assuming Acer had gotten delayed and they'd end up meeting the next day more than likely anyway. He stepped onto the sidewalk that skirted the parking lot and had gone around ten paces when a pair of headlights pulled into the entrance of the lot, fifty yards ahead of him.

The vehicle sped toward him, looming larger as it approached until he realized it was a long white van with a high back. The van appeared to be aiming for him, and in shock, he took several steps back onto the grass. At the last second, the vehicle turned sharply exposing its broadside to him, the tires barking against the curb. The passenger side window rolled down, and from within the dark interior, a familiar voice called out to him.

"Sorry, I'm late, Josiah."

He took a few steps forward onto the sidewalk. "Acer?"

"Yeah," Acer said, still unseen from inside the van. "Hop in. We're not going far."

"Why are you driving that thing? And what makes you think I would step foot in it?" The offense was beyond the pale for Josiah. He knew that Acer, in spite of all their discussions, hadn't completely given up technology yet. Josiah accepted that it would be some time before his new friend converted totally to the Praeceptist way of life. But for Acer to invite Josiah into the electric monstrosity was inconceivably insulting.

"I know, I'm so sorry. You're right," Acer said, his voice sounding sincere. "Just meet me over there by that building."

Josiah pointed toward the odd building by the water. "That one?"

"Yeah, I have to unload some stuff anyway, so take your time." Acer and the van sped across the parking lot toward the building.

Confusion flooded Josiah. What was he doing here? Did he even really know Acer? In the two weeks they'd come to know each other, Josiah felt he understood the man and considered him a friend, a good friend. He did, however, have to remind himself that it had only been two weeks since they'd met.

In spite of his misgivings, he found himself walking toward the building and the van that had reversed into the grass along the side of it.

A lifetime in the Praeceptist Church had taught Josiah many important lessons. Chief among them was patience. It was with great reserves of this virtue that he tempered his anxiety and fear and anger, breathing deeply with each step, forcing himself to trust his friend. Whatever was in store for him at the end of the sidewalk, he had to have faith in Acer and, most importantly, Lord the Father. God sent him Acer just as he sent Josiah to his would-be mother that day in the orphanage. God had a plan for him. In this, Josiah had undying faith.

Before he knew it, before he could contemplate turning back, Josiah found himself mere feet from the front of the van. The rear doors were open wide, standing out against the gloomy sky like the wings of an enormous carrion beetle. He stopped. Shuffling sounds behind the van reached him, clanks of metal, huffing breaths of someone lifting something heavy, a thudding impact of an object in the wet grass.

Josiah's guts twisted into a knot. He shifted his feet.

A face shot out from behind the edge of the van's rear. Josiah nearly jumped in shock. He almost didn't recognize Acer, who wore a baseball cap and dark clothing.

"Don't be scared, it's just me." Acer's crooked smile was somehow comforting to Josiah. "Come on back. I need a hand."

Curiosity pushed him around the van to meet Acer. His friend had just pulled a large plastic trunk from the darkened cargo area. Two more lay on the ground, along with a six-foot-tall, wheeled hand truck.

"What is all this, Acer? What are we doing here?" Josiah gestured toward the boxes and the van itself. He peered inside the cargo bay, which looked empty except for a lump of blankets behind the driver's seat.

Acer began stacking the boxes. "I'll explain, but we need to get inside first."

"Inside where?" For the first time, Josiah examined the building up close. It was made up of three parts—the round front section was two or three stories high, the second section was tall and rectangular with strange protuberances weaving in and out of it, the last section was a long and low one-story structure that seemed to stretch all the way down to the river.

Acer didn't answer his question but slid the hand truck under the boxes and tilted them back. He beckoned Josiah to follow as he sped off into the grass toward the long low section. After a few seconds, Josiah saw their destination—a gray door in the side of the building. At the door, Acer propped the cases up and placed his hand on a square panel. The door lock clicked and opened inward with a pop.

A moment later, they were in a long, brightly lit hallway. Tubes of white light blared overhead, and huge pipes like none Josiah had ever seen ran along the wall opposite the door they'd just entered through. The black pipes were at least a foot in diameter, and he counted three mounted to the wall and two bolted to the floor. Josiah knew the office buildings must be down the hall to the left, although it was too dark in that direction to see anything. To his right, the hallway stretched into the distance and appeared to curve downward, but again, it was too dark to determine if that was true.

"Acer…"

"I promise I'll explain in a minute." Acer interrupted Josiah and stepped away from the hand truck and toward his friend. Acer placed both hands on Josiah's shoulders. "Just have faith, brother. Faith."

If Acer intended to put Josiah at ease, it worked. With that one gesture, he felt the fear and anxiety rush away only to be replaced by guilt. Guilt for not trusting his friend. Guilt for not trusting the Lord's plan.

Josiah closed his eyes and bowed his head solemnly. "Of course. Of course I have faith in you, brother."

Acer turned away and, after closing the exit door, leaned the hand truck back on its two wheels and led the way down the hall, away from the office building, down, it seemed, into the earth itself.

"So, do you work here?" Josiah couldn't help himself from asking questions, as the walk was long and he was still a little tense. Some talking would help ease the moment.

"No." Acer panted under the strain of the hand truck but refused to let Josiah help him. "But I know everything there is to know about this place."

"How did you get through that door if you don't work here?" Josiah felt a twinge of fear returning but tried to breathe away the rising trepidation. They had just broken the law.

"I told you about my past life."

Josiah remembered it well. Acer had mentioned it many times during their long hours of conversations. "Yes, you worked on computers."

Acer smiled wryly at him. "Yeah, something like that. More like I worked with them. Anyway, I was very, very good at it. This place was part of a project I was working on with a few people. So I've researched it quite a bit." He gave Josiah another sideways grin. "Don't worry. I'll tell you what we're doing here."

The hall continued its downward slope, and Josiah felt sure they must be underground a fair distance. After a few minutes, the floor leveled off, and they came to a pair of doors. Through the doors, they crossed a short stretch of hallway and came to another set of doors.

"Almost there," Acer said raising his eyebrows at Josiah. He backed into the doors, kicking them open with a raised foot. They entered a huge room, stretching perpendicular to the hallway they just left, with a high ceiling and filled with tall shelving units set up like bookshelves at a library.

"It's an old server room." Acer walked briskly toward the center aisle between the units, as if he'd been there many times.

Josiah followed him and noticed the shelves were made of metal and all of them were empty. Rows and rows of them, taller than he stood, like square skeletons of some past life. "Server room?" Josiah had heard the term but had never learned anything about them.

Acer stopped at the end of the aisle near the far wall. He let the hand truck stand up on its own and turned to Josiah. "Basically like a big brain for a really big computer."

Josiah turned in place, gazing at the empty shelves. "Looks like the brain is gone."

Acer laughed. "Yes, it is. Long gone. But it'll be full of brains again soon. Big ones."

Josiah looked at his friend. "I think now is the time to tell me what we're doing."

The smile never left Acer's face. "This is where we make a stand, brother. This is where we stage the Great Awakening.

This is where it all starts." He held his arms wide. "Right here."

Now, Josiah was the one smiling. "Tell me more, brother."

20

Rock Bottom

Two Weeks Ago

Acer stumbled forward through the crowd, elbowing his way past the thick tide of pedestrians who bumped, shoved, and, more than once, cursed him for the mortal sin of walking against the flow of foot traffic. His drunken body bounced against the bodies in the crowd like a ping pong ball against so many metal pegs in one of those carnival games.

"Fuckin' sheep," he shouted at the throng of people once he'd broken free of the small herd. They paid no attention to him; however, not a single person turned to reply.

It was another moment before he realized he was still standing in the middle of the sidewalk; the crowd of sheep had disappeared into another, larger herd. He shook his head numbly, neck hunched and attempted to blink away the feeling that the world was spinning around him.

"Fuckin' sheep."

A gust of wind billowed his jacket, and nearly knocked him over when a voice in his head told him he should either keep walking or succumb to the immense amount of alcohol in his system and lay down right there on the sidewalk.

He chose to keep moving. He didn't have a destination in mind as the act of walking consumed most of his available cerebral bandwidth. He didn't know what day it was or what time it was, only that it was daytime, probably late morning. The bar where he'd spent the last several hours closed at 7 a.m. and he'd been walking for quite a while, nursing the bottle in his pocket. So, late morning felt about right.

His phone was gone or he'd check it to be sure. He couldn't remember that happening either. Maybe he left it in the bathroom. Maybe someone stole it. He didn't care either way. He felt better without it. Lighter. Untethered.

This was his life now. In the long dark months since Trina's death, he'd spent almost every night in a drunken haze. He'd drink at a bar until it closed, then buy a bottle of something cheap and wander the city. Sometimes he managed to find his way home though most of the time he didn't—instead finding a park bench or a wide set of stairs to sleep it off.

After Trina died, Acer thought he could get through it on his own. He worked harder than ever, developing new cracking tools better than anything he'd seen before. He contemplated getting the Colektive back together. But the more he worked the more he felt like he was indirectly adding poison to a pool from which all people drank.

Technology failed to save Trina. The drones responsible for finding her in the river that night couldn't do it in time. She drowned the same way an Egyptian would have four thousand years ago. Technology hadn't improved on the fragility of the human body in all that time.

His devotion to technology, his faith in it had created a false veil of safety. He drank the waters from the poisoned pool and it clouded his mind. For a long time, he'd dedicated his life to pumping toxic waste into that pool by using high technology to solve what he saw as the world's problem. The whole time, however, he'd been an enabler, a supporter, a pusher of the poison.

In the end, Trina's life force left her body and there was no way to bring it back.

While he walked, he scanned the crowds around him. Every person he saw, every man, woman, and child, every age, every occupation, every strata of society was represented on the street. And all of them, every last one of them was plugged into the poison. Every one of them had a direct line to the poisoned pool through an attachment on their ears, a device in their pocket, a watch on their wrists, or glasses on their face. Humankind drank readily, willingly, passionately from the poisoned pool and they had no idea. They had no idea what it was doing to them and to the people around them.

A woman passed him, an earpiece blinking in her ear. He imagined the device exploding, cratering the side of her head like a pumpkin dropped from a second floor window. The thought sent a wave of exhilaration through his muddled, drunken brain.

A solid mass slammed into Acer's shoulder. He looked up from his slumped stance, saw the pole that had assaulted him, and decided it made for a nice resting spot for the moment. He leaned into it, chest first, searching haphazardly with his hands for something to hold onto. Failing to find anything suitable, he adjusted his feet so that his body weight pressed into the pole and to stay upright required little to no effort.

He had no idea how much time had passed when he opened his eyes to find a man, about his age dressed in a shirt and tie, staring back at Acer.

"I said, 'are you looking for answers?'" The man had a polite smile.

Acer ignored the question as he focused on testing his legs and torso to see if they could hold him up. Pushing himself away from the pole a few inches, he found that he was able to stand under his own power. Additionally, the world no longer spun around him.

"You look like you could use some answers."

"Answers to what? What are you talking about?" Acer swayed on the spot, holding the pole for support. The man held out one hand to steady him. The other lifted something into Acer's field of vision.

Acer's brain took a moment to focus his eyes on the object, when he finally saw it he laughed. It was a paper pamphlet, actual paper. And it looked handmade. Maybe handwritten or at least printed with a manual press.

The front of the pamphlet bore a cross with three circles around its intersection.

* * *

Hours later and with a splitting headache, Acer peeled his eyes open, grateful to be in his own home. The man he'd met on the street, the Praeceptist, had graciously helped him find his way to the apartment. While Acer couldn't remember the man's name, as much of the night and morning was a blur, he did remember their conversation.

While leaning on the man for stability, Acer told him about Trina, about his own work in the past, and his thoughts on technology and how it was poisoning society. To his surprise, the man had a sympathetic ear, and more importantly knew some people that Acer might have a lot in common with. The man told him there was one person especially he should speak to. He gave Acer an address and a name.

"Shit," Acer said aloud jolting upright on the couch.

The sudden movement sent his mind tumbling like it was in a paint shaker and he sat for a moment to gain his bearings again. When it was safe to stand he strode to the cluttered desk across the living room. He knew it was there, somewhere on the desk. The name. He wrote on something. His hands brushed garbage, food containers, dirty cups of coffee out of the way. Something foul smelling spilled to the floor.

From behind a framed picture of him and Trina peeked a sticky notepad. He pushed the frame aside and saw it. On the top square of paper he had written *Josiah Palmero, 9th and 1st.*

21

The Book of Josiah

Reggie squeezed his eyes shut, attempting to recover from the fugue state that had settled over him. For what felt like an hour, his kidnapper had pressed him hard, giving instructions that made no sense. Reggie issued commands to the AI to re-route sewers and storm drains all over the city. The man, despite his murderous sociopathic behavior, was purposeful in everything he had demanded thus far. Changing where storm water runoff and sewage travelled under the city didn't seem to have a purpose Reggie could see but, perhaps, he was simply too tired, too stressed, and too frightened to figure it out.

His vision had begun to blur. Despite all the Zentransa his captor pumped into him via a liquid diet, exhaustion and delirium clung to him like a wet towel. Most likely, it was a product of his body locked in a seated position for consecutive days without a break. He had no real idea how long it had been.

It had all started with the worm. The man didn't say where he'd gotten it. Then the Trojan horse coupled with a sophisticated root kit to invade the AI's back brain. Once they had control, it was easy enough to execute commands however they saw fit, but the AI was defending itself and squashed nearly every attempt they threw at it. They'd have control for a moment, maybe fifteen minutes or a half hour, but they'd always lose it. The worm remained in place. The AI either didn't know it was there or didn't know how to get rid of it, so it meant they could keep creating new versions of the Trojan horse and an updated root kit to regain control. The real enemy for Reggie, besides the maniac with the soldering iron, was time. He didn't know how much longer he could last in his current state.

The only glimpse of the outside world were the camera feeds he'd watched as he directed the cars to attack those poor people. He didn't want to kill anybody, but he also didn't want to die in this shithole.

Wherever he was.

The cool temperatures with no apparent air-conditioning and the constant thrum in the floor and in the walls made him think they were somewhere near the water. Or under it. A chill shot up from his stomach and settled in his chest.

A sound made him sit up straight. He refocused his eyes on the monitor but turned his head a small degree to listen. A squelch of rubber on smooth concrete, metal clanging on the floor, a quiet groan. He knew what the sounds meant and closed his eyes. Shame settled over him like a thick film. He had made this happen.

The man approached the workstation and grabbed the back of the chair next to Reggie and rolled it away. Sounds of movement, plastic snapping, the creaking of the chair followed by some grunting, and after few minutes the man returned. He rolled the chair in next to Reggie. In it sat a new prisoner.

The guy's head hung low, groggily swinging side to side. The bindings pressed into his muscular arms, causing creasing in the ebony skin. His bulky shoulders towered over the chair's back, and as his unconscious form slumped forward, the straps cut deep into his bare chest and abs. His bald head glistened with beads of sweat.

Reggie's stomach rolled over. His throat tightened.

What had he done?

"You see, Reginald?" his captor said, out of breath. "You ask and I deliver. I brought you a friend. And quite a big one too!" He paused to catch his breath. "I could barely get him down here. Anyway, he'll be awake in a half-hour or so, and you two can join forces to accomplish your mission."

The sob came without warning. It left Reggie's throat like a tiny eruption, and no amount of willpower could stop the flow of tears that came next. His body convulsed with dejected regret. His breaths came in short gulps interspersed with moans and wails. The moisture falling to his chest caused him to sprout goosebumps. All hope had left him. He'd die right there in that chair tied up and stripped like an animal. And now another person would die, and it would be Reggie's fault.

Fire flared in his back, and his body reflexively lurched forward. Pain. Ungodly intense and acute pain erupted between his shoulder blades. Sharp and white hot. His nerves cried out. His head swam, and a croak issued from somewhere in his guts. His jaw locked in a semipermanent state of shock.

As quickly as it came, it was gone. The stabbing pain and heat replaced with a dull soreness that throbbed and crept into his muscle tissue.

Suddenly, he was jerked backward. The chair he was bound to tilted on its two rear wheels, almost falling over, as it was dragged back away from the computer workstation. After a few feet, the chair was released and fell to all four wheels. Reggie looked up.

The man—his prison guard and warden wrapped into one—stood in front of him. A look of profound consternation was plastered to his face. His hair was pulled into a ponytail, and he wore a black sweater. He held a blue five-gallon bucket in one hand and cocked his head to the side. He held the pose for a second, then he stepped to within a foot of Reggie, lifted the bucket over his head, and dumped its contents.

The rush of cold was so shocking that his breath caught in his chest and refused to escape. Every inch of his skin seemed to contract painfully, and he immediately began to shiver violently. Cubes of ice collected in his lap, over his crotch. Water dripped from every part of him.

With a stuttering gasp, he was finally able to breathe again with labored inhalations. He shook against his bindings, and they cut into him deeper than before, pinching and rubbing in new places.

"Reginald," the man said, bending over with his hands on his knees. "Don't lose focus now. We're so close to the end, and I have a few ideas that I think might make for a delicious conclusion to our little adventure."

A moment passed. Reggie could breathe normally again, and warmth began to spread from within him. He still shivered, and his teeth chattered beyond his control, but he could think relatively straight. His chair tipped suddenly, and he was dragged back to the workstation.

"Now where are we on the tunnel?" his captor asked, pushing Reggie's chair in close so he could reach his keyboard.

"I th-think we're there." Reggie's jaw quivered. Both from cold and fear.

He reached forward with trembling fingers and typed a command. On one large monitor, the screen filled with a video feed that showed eight lanes of cars, four flowing in one direction, four going the other. The white tiled walls of the transit tunnel rose up from the roadbed to a curved roof, from which lights shined down on the silent cars moving at a steady clip.

"Brakes." The man's voice was quiet, barely above a whisper.

Reggie's fingers flew like disembodied tentacles across the keyboard, issuing commands to the infiltrated AI's back brain. On the big screen, Reggie watched all eight lanes of traffic slow to a crawl and stop.

The man drew an audible breath, and without expelling it said, in a pinched voice, "You know what to do next."

Once again, Reggie's chin met his chest, his stubble rubbing the skin there as he swung his head in a shallow arc side to side.

"Please, no. Don't make me do it." Another whimper slithered its way up Reggie's esophagus as he spoke. "There's s-so many of them. So many will …" his voice trailed off.

A painful impact on the side of his head made him straighten.

"Reginald, some of them will make it out." He raised his hands as if confused. "I mean, yes, many of them will perish, but we have to show the world what happens when God's word is defiled. Do you understand?"

Reggie's whole body vibrated with fear and woe and pain.

"Now type the fucking command, or the soldering iron comes out to play again."

Reggie barely registered pressing the keys to execute the command. He couldn't watch what happened next, and luckily, the camera feed did not include audio.

"Yes," the man whispered next to him. "This is it." His words grew louder as he spoke. "This is it, people. This is the Lord, Our God, the Father's work. This is his reckoning. We are the tools with which he reaps the sinners from the world." His voice was impossible to tune out. His words echoing off the smooth walls. "Your distractions now become your undoing. That which chained you to Lucifer's will shall be shattered by the Father's merciful hand." The kidnapper's hand came down hard onto the table with a deafening smack.

"Wha-what the? Where am I?" The new captor stirred and mumbled past a swollen tongue.

"Oh," the captor said, "you're just in time to see our deeds come to fruition. I mean, the bridge was impressive, and that pileup with the garbage truck was something, but this"—he spread his hands wide at the video feed—"this is art."

Reggie cracked an eyelid and glanced toward the other captive. The kidnapper bent low, almost cheek to cheek with the huge black man, and pointed at the screen.

"Watch, Anton. Watch as they're cleansed."

The prisoner turned a bleary eye toward the man, blinking long and slow. "H-how do you know my name?" Anton's words came out like warm taffy. "Nobody knows my real … Wait a second. What's going on here?" He flexed against the straps and zip ties for a second, then looked up at the monitor on the wall, seeing the action for the first time. "What are you watching? What movie is this?" He paused. His eyes went wide for a moment. His head swayed drunkenly. "Hey, where's that water comin' from? What are they doin' just sittin' there? They're all gonna drown. Hey! Hey, get outta there, man. You're all gonna die." His speech continued to stumble clumsily out of his mouth. "You don't wanna die, do you?" His chin fell back to his chest, and he began chuckling quietly. "What kinda stupid movie is this?"

Reggie shut his eyes again. He squeezed them as tight as he could, as if blocking out his vision would keep the images from forming in his head. But he couldn't stop them. He knew what was happening in that tunnel and couldn't help but picture it. Water creeping in from near the roadbed. Slowly, at first, then exponentially faster as the AI-controlled water expulsion pumps stopped then reversed their flows, quickly ramping up to full power. The people in the cars would try to escape, but they'd quickly discover their doors would not unlock. The water from the Susquehanna River flowing over the tunnel would fill the tunnel and leach into their cars, eventually expelling all the air inside. Lungs would gulp their watery poison. Brains would black out. Hearts would stop.

So many would die.

* * *

Aubrey unraveled the rolled booklet that Samantha had given him and spread it out on the table so they both could see. Malina sat across from him in the diner booth, leaning over the table to peer at the thin book.

It was comprised of a sheaf of white paper, the kind commonly used in older printers or copiers. The sheaf had been bound with thread in the middle and folded in half, making the book close to fifty pages altogether. The outside cover was nothing more than a thicker and somewhat darker page. On the front, in handwritten black script were the words *The Book of Josiah*. At the bottom, the author had written his name *Josiah Palmero*.

"The Book of Josiah? A little ostentatious," Malina said.

Aubrey turned the pamphlet over. A hand-drawn bust of a young man occupied two-thirds of the back cover. Done in pencil with what must have been great care, the face was soft, not quite pudgy but not hard or edged like a world-weary man. Feathery wisps of hair covered his forehead above squinted eyes and a small nose. Below the portrait, an inscription written in a hand far different than that of the rest of the book read, *The air in my lungs, the fire in my star, the salt in my tears; my Josiah.*

"Wow." Malina tilted her head and eyed the drawing and the handwritten note. She read it out loud and let out a low whistle. "Poor Samantha was sorely smitten with old J.P. Well, let's hear the word according to the prophet Josiah."

Aubrey flipped to a random page. Tight, stilted cursive writing filled every square millimeter. From the middle of the left-hand page, Aubrey read aloud the beginning of a paragraph: "A servant of the Lord, Our God, the Father, can only be so without distraction. Preaching the love of God and his infallible word with your mouth while Satan pulls your ear and your mind to an electronic device is, in and of itself, a fallacy. For it is the dark one who has given the world his most destructive weapon. That which pulls God's children into a world not their own. A world awash with filth, pornography, homosexuality, hedonism, dark thoughts, and dark deeds. The corrupted lizard crawls between the toes of man, seemingly harmless while his scales debone the flesh and flay God's children."

"That got dark pretty quick." Malina huffed a derisive laugh.

Aubrey chose another page and began again. "His calling is clear. To worship. To serve. To love Him above all else, and He will grant His children everlasting life in His loving grace. We are sheep to His shepherd, and we are meant to watch His signs and listen to His words, else we be led to slaughter. As the shepherd provides all for his flock, He provides all for His children. Yet, we gallivant under the guise of knowing what is best for ourselves. Meanwhile, the Lord, in all His glorious wisdom, tries time and again to pour His love and lessons upon us while we turn a deaf ear to Him."

He flipped to a page toward the end of the booklet. "His words are simple: I will provide. Ye shall not want. The Bible tells us, 'understand this, that in the last days, there will come times of difficulty. For people will be lovers of self, lovers of money, proud, arrogant, abusive, disobedient to their parents, ungrateful, unholy, heartless, unappeasable, slanderous, without self-control, brutal, not loving good, treacherous, reckless, swollen with conceit, lovers of pleasure rather than lovers of God, having the appearance of godliness, but denying its power. Avoid such people.'

"We must heed these words handed to us by Lord the Father, but as children must always do, we must anticipate the conclusion of the lesson and proact his commandment. To take literal the command, 'Avoid such people,' is not enough. To serve the Lord, Our Father, Maker of Heaven and Hell, Outcaster of the Evil One, Smiter of Unbelievers, we must not simply avoid the 'ungrateful, unholy, heartless, slanderous.' We must eliminate all that makes them so. We must cleanse the world of unearthly, ungodly things, the technologies brought to the world by the Evil One. The cleansing will cause pain. It will cause suffering. But through suffering, through pain, His children will grow.

"Once cleansed, a righteous earth can begin anew, and only then can we properly sing and praise His infinite goodness and love."

"Pretty intense stuff," Malina said, leaning against the padded seat back. "Not quite 'the streets will flow with the blood of the nonbelievers,' but it's getting there."

"Yeah. I'd say there's enough here to say Josiah's beliefs could be classified as extreme."

Aubrey rolled the booklet as tight as it was when Samantha gave it to him. His fists clenched around it reflexively, and he stared out the window, trying to digest this new discovery. The diner faced the Chesapeake waterfront and was aptly named the Seaview Diner. He watched the water churn under a fitful sky, washing against the large rocks that sat a hundred feet from where he sat.

"Thoughts?" he asked.

Malina was quiet for a moment, playing with her cup of coffee, turning it in its saucer. "If I had to guess, I'd say Josiah is an extremist. Maybe too much for the Praeceptists. He's out to 'cleanse' the world." She shrugged and raised her hands off the table. "Sounds pretty extreme."

"Capable of driving dozens of cars off a bridge?" He sipped his coffee.

She audibly sighed. "Maybe. Not skilled enough. I know that. He'd obviously need help."

"What about the hackers? If he connected with Ambrosia, we have to assume he could have gotten to Drillard and Elton."

"True. Could be Josiah finds Ambrosia or Drillard and befriends them, then forces them to crack the city's AI. And begin the cleansing." She cocked her head and raised an eyebrow. "Which, the irony there is pretty glaring. Using the most advanced artificial intelligence in the world to try to destroy technology. Little hypocritical."

Aubrey shrugged. "Is it? What is a bullet other than a tool to achieve peace and establish safety? But its purpose is to kill. Little ironies like that abound in the world. Doesn't change the fact that he's a very dangerous lunatic." He folded his arms and sighed. "So what do we do next?"

"We call Liz and tell her they need to look for this guy," said Malina.

He nodded.

"And we sit back and wait." She threw up her hands.

He shook his head. "Afraid not."

"I thought you might say that." Malina pointed an accusing finger at him. "You know, I told you a long time ago that I am not a field agent."

He remembered her saying it, but he also remembered how capable and shrewd she became in a real crisis, especially a fight. "You seem to handle yourself pretty well. And you don't seem to mind it so much when we do have to get our hands dirty." He leaned in. "We need to call Liz. But we also need to start looking for this guy ourselves. The police have their hands full directing traffic and dealing with rogue drones all over the city. We can't be sure they'll find him in time."

* * *

"'Find him,' he says. 'Just look wherever you would go,' he

says. 'How many places could he hide?' he says." Malina typed furiously on the portable keyboard while she muttered to herself. Her large tablet propped against her bag in front of her, a minuscule blue skull pulsated in the corner, indicating she was connected to Ted, her powerful processor tucked away at her home. She could see Aubrey outside the window talking on his phone. As if sensing her watching him, he turned and gave her a thumbs-up. She felt like showing him a finger too, just not the thumb.

She waved back to him halfheartedly, then got back to work. "Yeah," she said to herself, "I mean how many places could there be to hide in a city with a population in the millions, thirteen miles long and nine miles wide. No big deal." Her grumblings caught the attention of the waitress walking by with a full pot of coffee in her hand.

"Getcha anything, hon?" She wiped some unseen filth onto the front of her apron.

"More coffee, please."

The waitress filled her cup and left Malina to continue her search for a needle in a gigantic haystack.

Where would she go? The question sounded ridiculous to her. Where would she go if she were waging a cyber war against an artificial intelligence more sophisticated and complex than anything else before it? Aubrey might as well have asked her how she would fly to Venus.

She rested her forehead against the heel of her hand.

Hopeless. She couldn't fathom the place where Josiah might be. After the attacks at Ambrosia's building and the run to the Praeceptist church, her body and her brain didn't have the processing power for any more problem solving.

She didn't have the power.

Her head shot up. She felt her eyes go wide.

Power.

The question came back to her. Where would she go if she were waging a cyber war against an AI? First and foremost, she'd need power. The type of processors and gear she'd need would require a lot of energy. She could get the energy she'd need almost anywhere in the city, but that kind of huge draw would get noticed. It might raise red flags. Where would she go to get plenty of power but also hide its use?

She bounced this question around in her brain for several minutes, but again, nothing came to her. The answer wouldn't come no matter how much she willed it. There was nowhere in the city where a huge draw of power wouldn't get noticed.

She stared out at the water. Aubrey crossed her field of vision with his phone pressed to one ear, walking on the rocks like some kid, stepping from one peak to the next while he talked to Liz, running down their findings for her on the Drillard case.

Her gaze ventured back out to the expanse of the Chesapeake's north end. Its muddy-brown water undulating from one shore to the next. Waves crested with white tips in long, broken, jagged lines. There was no waterline on the rocks, which meant the tide was coming in. Soon the bay would be only a dozen feet from the edge of the city's man-made boundary. This end of New Aberdeen had been built on top of the old US Army Proving Grounds, just a few miles south of the mouth of the Susquehanna River, one of several rivers dumping fresh, silty water into the bay. The rivers fed the bay, but it was the ward of the Atlantic Ocean, and it rose and fell at the whim of its master. Just as sure as the sun would rise the next day, the tide she watched eke its way up the rocky shore would move back out hours later. In and out, never stopping.

The seed of an idea itched at the back of her brain, but she couldn't see it clearly enough to elucidate it further.

Her vision lost focus as she stared out at the bay, at the brackish waters that never stopped moving.

There was something there. What was she missing?

The water seemed to put her in a kind of trance, like a hypnotist's metronome. No patterns but always moving. Always there. As reliable as the sun.

In the distance, two long fishing boats crossed paths with red and green lights near the waterline, winking at her between waves. Atop each cab, white lights were visible in the dully sunlit day. Her angle to the vessels was such that they converged in line with one another. Slowly, they came together, the furthest disappearing briefly behind the nearest. As the boats became one in her line of sight, the white lights hovering above them did as well. Two bright globes became one, then two again. The trawlers grew further apart by the second, and as she watched them go, it hit her.

Like a kick to the head, the answer came to her.

Malina bolted from the booth and dashed through the empty diner. She threw open the door, ran outside, and skirted the corner of the building at a sprint. Sliding to a stop at the edge of the rock pile, she found Aubrey, still on the phone, perched on top of a turkey-sized boulder. He caught sight of her and raised his chin, pulling the phone away from his ear. The look on her face must have shocked him.

The wind buffeted her, blowing the hood off her head, and she had to shout to be heard. "I know where he is."

* * *

Tears rolled from the corners of Reggie's eyes, down the bridge of his nose, and into his bare lap. His abdomen distending with each stuttering breath.

His new partner sat beside him, a few feet away, snoring loudly in a drug-induced stupor. Somewhere behind him, his kidnapper read scripture in a near whisper, while every few moments, he'd scream a few words before returning to a low murmur.

"Lord's forgiveness … His wisdom and mercy … you have been judged."

Moments passed until Reggie was startled by the sound of heavy panting in his ear.

"Are we ready to move on to the next cleansing?"

Reggie could only muster a slow nod.

"Good!" the kidnapper shouted. "It's fitting isn't it, that first, the bridge and tunnel cleansed the city with water. Next, we shall cleanse with fire, and soon, as the final stitch in our beautiful tapestry of God's vengeance, we will use the air itself."

For a fleeting second, as Reggie heard the man's declaration, he pictured the sewers and storm drains he had been forced to hack. His captor's endgame blinked in and out of clarity in his mind like a firefly on a summer night. The answer was there; then, a moment later, it was completely forgotten.

22

The River

Nelson Sistrook, Operations Specialist for PenzoTec, Inc., sat at his workstation monitoring the carefully orchestrated mixing, blending, synthesizing, and processing inside the numerous tanks, vats, and tubs inside the cavernous chemical manufacturing plant on the other side of his office wall.

Nelson's office was no more than a windowless, glorified closet adjacent to the main catwalk that stretched across the vast facility that housed the plant.

Located ten miles northwest from the heart of New Aberdeen, PenzoTec produced industrial chemicals for use in the fabrication of metal alloys and carbon-fiber polymers. The vast majority of raw materials they used and finished products they made were toxic and highly hazardous to human workers necessitating a largely robotic workforce and computer-controlled systems.

Nelson's job was to keep an eye on the program, dubbed Eagle by him and his co-workers, that watched the operations programs. His task was to ensure that Eagle didn't fail. It never did. In three years at his desk, five days a week, he had touched the keyboard of his workstation a total of four times to interrupt or alter a command given by Eagle. In each case, after a review protocol conducted by his superiors, Nelson had been found to be in the wrong. After his last mistake, almost a year ago, Nelson was ordered to call his direct supervisor before doing anything to contradict Eagle.

Nelson hated his supervisor. He would rather take a swim in one of the processing tanks than call him.

Such was his thinking when, at 7:30 p.m., one hour before the end of his shift, Nelson read a notification from Eagle in the status updates queue. The notification was curious. It said that Eagle had scheduled a cleaning of two large storage tanks—one contained bromine monochloride and the other held with potassium fluoride. Each tank held 500,000 gallons of material, and were cleaned, when empty, about twice a year.

Nelson knew Eagle would schedule cleanings like this, although this one seemed a bit premature. In fact, a quick glance at the readouts on the monitor told him that both tanks were nearly full and would, therefore, need to be drained before the cleaning. Moving closer to the screen and its list of status updates, Nelson read the notification from Eagle one more time. In three hours, the tanks would empty into the facility's subterranean storage cells, then the highly toxic materials would be piped to permanent storage cells fifty miles upstate in a containment facility deep underground.

Draining close to full tanks was odd. Nelson couldn't remember it ever being done while he was on shift. Storing and then piping the hazardous raw materials via the underground transfer lines was also odd. The lines were rarely used, maybe once or twice a year, and then only for moving highly volatile substances meant for permanent containment or destruction.

Nelson reached for the phone seated in its cradle on the desk. He pulled it free and dialed the first three numbers of his supervisor's extension. His finger hovered over the last digit and, suddenly, his brain was flooded with the memory of the dressing down he received nearly one year ago the last time he went against Eagle.

He replaced the phone in its cradle and went back to watching the monitor. After a few minutes, the notification for the draining of the bromine monochloride and potassium fluoride tanks was pushed down toward the bottom of the queue of status updates and, after a few more minutes, it fell off the screen entirely.

* * *

2:00 p.m.
Aubrey and Malina ran from the diner toward the nearest avenue a quarter mile away. Chances of getting a hired car in the next sixty seconds were greater there. As they jogged, Aubrey relayed Malina's theory to Liz.

"Listen, I can't pull every cop and send them there," Liz said in his ear. "Most of the force is out directing traffic or dealing with accidents in the shutdown areas, so they're dispersed anyway. I'll get a team over there as soon as I can." She paused on the line. "Martin, don't go crazy. Just go scope it out and wait for us."

"Roger that," he said, between breaths.

In the hired car, they headed north, and Malina explained her hunch.

"They're going to need tons of power. I mean, I leave Ted at home because, as a processor, it requires so much power that batteries or wireless power just doesn't cut it." She stopped to catch her breath.

"How much would they need?" He watched the cars around them. Ready to bolt from the self-driven cab if necessary.

She shook her head. "I can't even begin to imagine what they'd need to crack the AI brain, but"—she shrugged—"I mean, we're talking megawatts, maybe a gigawatt. Let's just say a lot." She let out a sigh. "Anyway, the city is built on renewable energy. Wind, solar, geothermal, hydro. Redundancies to prevent brownouts and blackouts. Because we use renewables, the grid keeps a close eye on power consumption. If someone draws too much out of the ordinary, it throws up red flags. So how do you get the power you need without drawing attention?"

Aubrey waited for the answer while Malina pressed her fingers to her temples, clearly thinking about something. She shook her head and continued. "You go to the source."

She threw her hands out in front of her like knives. "No one would notice a spike of consumption at the source. It would just be chalked up to a decrease in production, which wouldn't be a drop in the bucket compared to what the plant is producing."

A drone buzzed overhead, and Aubrey twisted to look out the window. It continued on its way, but he couldn't help but think it was flying a little lower than usual. "And you think they're at the hydro plant? What about the other ones? The solar, wind, geothermal," he said without taking his eyes off the drone fading into the near distance.

The Susquehanna River Hydroelectric Power Plant used a submerged string of self-contained turbine generators.

Dozens of generators stretched for more than a mile upriver, taking advantage of the Susquehanna's ever-present current. Underwater cables linked the generators which, together, fed a power station onshore near the river's mouth, on the northern edge of New Aberdeen. A large section of the power plant, which housed the transformers, was located underwater to use the bay's natural waters to cool the station.

She continued, "A lot of reasons. There is no single source for solar, the panels are too dispersed, wind is way outside the city, but the biggest reason is that all of them are maintained and operated by people. Too many people at those stations to see Josiah and what he's up to. The river's hydro plant is the only one that is largely unmanned. Drones patrol the river turbine generators under the water and perform maintenance. Also, the powerhouse and transformers only require one or two people at a time to check on them."

He squinted, a question on his mind that he wasn't sure he wanted the answer to. He asked it anyway. "How do you know all this?"

She scooted back in her seat, and now it was her turn to gaze out the window. "The Colektive may have explored the idea of hacking the grid."

"The power grid?" His face hardened. "That sounds like some black-hat cracker stuff. Not gray hat. Not exactly helping your fellow humans."

Malina's face turned toward the floorboard. "It's not something I'm proud of. It was Ambrosia's idea actually. He and Drillard thought we should just do a little research. Just in case."

Aubrey limited his judgment to a raised eyebrow and decided not to pry further. The buzzing in his coat pocket would have prevented it anyway. The call was from Liz Reynolds.

"Hey, Liz. We're still—"

"Where are you?" she said, cutting him off. "Are you in a car?"

"Yeah, why?"

"Get out," she said. "Stop the car and get out now."

* * *

Reggie's tightly clenched fists shook over the keyboard.

The man breathed in his ear. "Do it, Reginald." The kidnapper inhaled harshly. "The cleansing waits for no man. No matter how pathetic he may be."

A pregnant pause was penetrated only by whimpers from his cocaptive, the well-built black man now sharing his fate. The scent of seared flesh still clung to the inside of Reggie's nostrils—the result of the new man's refusal to work. His back stood flayed in long streaks after the kidnapper had to resort to drastic measures to elicit his compliance.

"Finish the line of code, Reginald, or you will find yourself floating in the wake of Drillard."

"Fuck you!" The words came out as an angry sob. Spittle and mucus flew from his lips. "I'm done. No more."

His captor straightened, and Reggie could feel his eyes on him. "Oh, Elton, our brave little warrior."

Reggie froze. That name. His handle, but he'd only ever used that name for a short time and only online. How'd this man know that name? For a moment, his confusion masked his fear, and he turned to the kidnapper, whose face bore a twisted smile.

"Oh, yes, I know who you are, Reginald or Reggie or Elton—whatever you want to be called." The man placed a hand on the head of the second captive. "I know who you both are and what you're capable of."

Reggie's eyes fell to the other prisoner, his wounds still oozing fluid down the tight dark skin of his arched back.

"Reginald, you'll know Anton by another name. Won't he, Champ?"

* * *

Aubrey glanced at Malina, and her expression reflected his own confusion.

"Liz, what's going on?"

Frantic noise broke through the phone.

"We're still on our way to the power plant."

Reynolds yelled something inaudible to someone on her end of the call. "Martin, just listen to me and get out of the fucking car. Now. Something is happening. Cars are—" The line went dead.

He pulled the phone from his ear, staring at it, stuck momentarily in a state of indecision.

"Marty? What's happening?" Malina's voice tremored as she spoke.

He shook his head. "I'm not sure, but we need to get out of this car."

"What do you mean?"

Without answering her, Aubrey reached out for the emergency stop button on the car's front center console, a requirement for all self-driving cars in the city. Before he could press it, however, the car braked on its own. Confused, he looked around at the other cars on the road. All traffic had halted. By the looks of it, confused drivers were quickly becoming panicked. He watched the occupant of the car ahead of them try to exit via the driver's side, then the passenger side door. Both doors appeared to be locked.

"We're locked in," Malina said, reading Aubrey's mind. Beside him, she worked her door's latch, but it swung limply in her hand. "What the hell?"

"This is Josiah," he said. "It has to be."

"What do you think he's doing?"

"I don't know, but we need to get out." As he spoke, Aubrey noticed a red warning light on the self-piloted car's dash. It was a square icon, depicting the vehicle's main battery. Next to it blinked a red thermometer symbol with an exclamation mark superimposed over of it. A low tone sounded in the car each time it blinked.

"What is that?" Malina asked.

"I think the car is overheating," he said.

He scanned the lanes around them again, trying to read the faces of other drivers and passengers. Two men and two women sat in the car to their left. All of them were trying to get out of the sedan—pulling on latches, pushing flat hands against windows trying to force the glass down. In the front passenger seat, a man pulled at his collar then removed his coat. The driver banged her elbow against her window, but it didn't break.

Aubrey found similar scenes playing out in every car around them.

Panic was growing. So was the heat.

"You feel that?" he asked, turning toward Malina. "It's getting hot in here."

"Yeah, I feel it too." She stretched out a hand and held it in front of an open air vent in the backside of the front seat. "Not from the air-conditioning though."

For two seconds, Aubrey examined the interior of the car, searching for the source of the sudden heat. His eyes caught the blinking battery warning light again. Dread washed over him.

He knew most electric vehicle main batteries were mounted underneath the car. He reached down and felt the floorboard with his palm, then snapped it back after half a beat.

"Jesus. The batteries are overheating."

The air inside the cab had grown stifling, and a sharp, acrid smell filled the air.

"Martin, look."

He followed her outstretched finger and saw the floorboard's beige carpeting had begun to turn a darker shade. Initially, he'd thought it was a stain left by a previous passenger of the car for hire. But as he watched it, he could see the stain spreading and deepening in hue. The carpet fibers were beginning to melt.

"Can it catch fire?" she asked.

There hadn't been a battery caused fire in an electric vehicle for decades, but he also knew that a battery was just a box of chemicals, so he assumed it was still possible.

"I don't intend to find out."

Reaching inside his coat, he removed his pistol from its holster and gripped the barrel in the tight fist of his left hand. With his right hand, he firmly cupped the gun by the other end of the receiver. Using the firearm like a miniature battering ram, he slammed the tip of it into the bottom corner of the car door's window. The glass shattered into a million tiny pieces that pattered down onto his arms and hands.

Aubrey clambered out first, then reached back inside to help Malina. As he did, dark smoke rose from the floor, swirling above the carpet, quickly filling the cab. He pulled her through the open window and set her on her feet in the small gap between the two vehicles.

He glanced inside the other vehicle and watched as the man and woman in the front of the car each banged their fists and elbows against their windows. The passengers in the backseat had situated themselves so they could both kick the rear driver's side window at the same time.

Thunks and thuds were all they produced inside the sedan. The glass wouldn't give.

The man in the front seat nearest Aubrey caught sight of him and stared for a moment breathing heavily, wearing a haggard, resigned expression. The man pressed his hands together in front of his chest and mouthed the word, "Please."

"The rear window," Aubrey yelled through the glass, pointing in that direction. "Get them to back away."

The man said something to the people in the back of the car, and they moved as far as they could from the rear window.

Moving toward the trunk of the sedan, he reached up with his pistol-turned-hammer in both hands and brought it down, barrel first, into the lower quarter of the glass. Its entirety broke as one, disintegrating into clear pebbles that rained onto the rear dashboard.

The trapped passengers climbed one by one through the small space Aubrey created while he and Malina assisted each of them in turn. The sharp odor of charred plastic was strong in the air and grew more powerful by the second. When the last person, the driver, slid off the trunk, she was followed by a thick black plume.

Aubrey's mind and body were now on full alert, his blood charged with an energy he only felt in times when instant action was needed.

"We have to help these people get out," he said to the small rescued group standing around him. Three of the four passengers had pulled out their phones, preparing to make calls or send text messages. Heat bloomed around Aubrey's neck, and he slapped a device out of the hands of the man across from him. The man ogled in disbelief as it clattered to the pavement.

"Did you hear me?" He pointed a rigid finger to the side. "These people are in the same boat you were in a few seconds ago. And we have to help them."

"With what?" the woman from the driver's seat said. Hers wasn't a defiant tone. It was a sincere question—she wanted to help.

"There," Malina said, pointing across the road at a storefront with a red awning and a sign above it that read "Gary's Hardware and Paint."

"Good," Aubrey said. "Hammers, pipes, anything hard and heavy. Three of you work your way down the street. We'll work our way up the street. Get as many people out as you can."

The others bolted to the hardware store, and Aubrey and Malina set out up the street to the next car in their lane, a dump truck full of construction debris. The driver was already climbing out with a tire iron in his hand. He was short but strongly built and wore a white-pocketed T-shirt.

"Here," he said, tossing the tire iron in a high arc toward Aubrey, who caught it in one hand then passed it to Malina.

The truck driver reached back in his cab and pulled out a small sledge hammer. "You two get those lanes, I'll get this one."

Without another word, Aubrey peeled off with Malina behind him. He proceeded to the outside lane, and she took the one just inside it.

The first car he approached was a small sports car. He busted the front driver's window with his pistol barrel, and the driver, a young Asian woman in a purple sweater, leapt out with uncanny agility.

Aubrey turned toward the next car while shouting over his shoulder, "Start helping." But he needn't tell the woman, she was already running ahead of Aubrey to the next vehicle—a large church van full of people.

Aubrey stopped at the window of a blue four-door with two passengers. He smashed the window and lifted an elderly woman and a man of similar age from the car. As soon as their feet hit the pavement, he sprinted up the street past the van, where the young woman had broken its large side window with a fire extinguisher she'd procured from somewhere, maybe a nearby shop.

Three steps from a hulking silver SUV, the first car caught fire. The whoosh of air and crackling expansion of glass and plastic and metal could be heard over the chaos building around him. The flare came from an inner lane of the road two or three car lengths back the way he'd come. His first hope was that Malina wasn't near it, and his second was that the people inside had gotten out.

He paused only briefly to watch the flames consume the vehicle, tongues of fire filling windows devoid of glass, blue-black smoke rising like a pillar into the clear sky.

Busting the windows of the SUV, he didn't wait to help the passengers out but darted ahead to the next car. He felt intense heat nearby along with loud cracking and popping of burning metal and plastic. Another car was on fire somewhere close, but he had no time to check it out. Only time to focus on the next car, the next rescue. Before he reached it however, someone was already there, beating the window with a metal coat rack. After several glancing blows, the tall thin man was able to destroy the glass, allowing the passengers to escape.

For one second, Aubrey swiveled his head left and right to survey the street. What he saw surprised him—dozens of people had emerged from the shops, businesses, and apartments along the street. They flooded the lanes of traffic to extricate people trapped in their cars. And for the most part, the people that were rescued turned to lend a hand as soon as they were free. The numbers of rescuers and rescued grew exponentially as he watched.

A pickup truck to his left went up in flames, it's driver barely escaping before the inferno consumed it. Another conflagration erupted back near he and Malina's cab. More fires bloomed by the minute up and down the row of vehicles. Smoke reached toward the sky in spots along the road, most of the sources of which were out of sight.

He felt a hand around his bicep and turned to find Malina, her face and hands smeared with soot.

"Damn it, Malina, are you okay?"

"Yes, forget about it. Martin, we have to go. We have to stop this now." She breathed rapidly, physically spent but her eyes set with purpose.

"These people need us." He gestured to the street.

"They have enough help right now."

He looked and realized she was right—rescuers were every-where now.

"We have to stop Josiah now. He could murder hundreds, maybe thousands before this is over."

"You're right. Let's go."

Together, they ran across the street to the opposite sidewalk and turned left along the waterfront and toward the mouth of the Susquehanna River Power Station. Toward Josiah.

* * *

"Reggie, look. Look at what you've accomplished."

Reggie's entire body had gone as limp as a rag doll—his bindings the only thing keeping him upright. His muscles were deflated, his bones melted, his tissues liquefied. Tears remained in their home behind his eyes, refusing to budge.

So many dead and dying. By his hand. If he could will himself to die, to join them, he would. But this man would force Reggie to stay alive to imagine the heat from the flames, the smell of the charred flesh, the screams of the dying.

"Reginald, please, witness the purge we've wrought. This is a gift. A gift to the Almighty above."

Reggie had finished the final line of code that brought on this terror. Now, cars all over the city were catching fire, burning alive their trapped passengers.

"We're sterilizing the world, Reginald. You should be proud of what you've accomplished. Look at Anton. He appreciates the significance of what we've done here."

Reggie summoned the energy to lift his head slightly and take in the other prisoner. Anton, or Champ as Reggie had known him in the Colektive, viewed the monitors with wide eyes, his chest barely moving with each breath, and sweat pouring from his bald scalp. Appreciative wasn't the word Reggie would have used to describe Champ's current state. Stunned disbelief was more like it. The man was catatonic. It was likely that he was simply unable to grasp the terrible sins that had been committed.

"Let's check on the private dick and his little bitch," the man said with venom in his voice. A brief moment of silence was broken by the thick slap of a hand on flesh. "Anton! Find the two of them, now. Reginald is obviously incapable."

Clicks and taps as commands were input and executed. His fingers moved slowly from key to key, but he obeyed the kidnapper's orders. Anton's deep voice was robotic when he spoke. "There. There they are."

"Look at that," their captor said with surprise.

Reggie raised his head an inch, just enough to catch a glimpse of the monitor showing a river of traffic in total anarchy. Columns of smoke rose from the roadbed as cars everywhere burned to the ground. People raced in every direction into and out of the lanes of cars. Among the chaos, two figures raced along a sidewalk. A man and a woman. The detective and his partner. The same couple he tried to murder earlier in the day outside Ambrosia's apartment.

"Here they come. On their way to us no doubt. Lord the Father does respect tenacity. As do I, but wicked is their path, and there is much work left for us to do. We've purged only a tiny percent of the city." Another wet slap of a hand smacking skin. "Anton, do what you must, but do not let them reach us."

23

Familial Fate

Francesca stood outside the First Church of God's Wheel glaring up at the cross and its circles. Kirk and Wendy Palmero, Hank's adoptive parents, were both dead, but they'd been lifelong members of this church. Their lives were a complete mystery to her. Having no connection with technology of nearly any kind, they were among the very few people of the time that had almost no record of their lives online. The only mention she could find of Kirk and Wendy was a mention of their names in an online newspaper nearly fifteen years ago. Kirk Palmero had been severely beaten by a man at a bus stop. The article mentioned the two had a child but did not mention the child's name per the Palmero's wishes. That incident and their deaths were the only evidence she could find of their existence at all. Although the church did not post any news about the passing of its members, the city had an obligation to record the deaths of its citizens.

Inside, the church looked like most houses of worship—rows of pews facing a raised platform atop which sat an altar and a dais. She stood at the back, near the doors, and looked around the empty sanctuary. Prayer books had been placed every few feet on the seats of the pews that were lit by the sun's rays piercing high overhead windows. Someone stood up from behind the altar. They had been busy doing something on the floor out of sight. He was an older man with hair close to white and gold wire frame glasses. Francesca didn't move or say anything. She watched as the man read silently from a slip of paper on the altar with head down and gesturing with his hands to the empty seats. He was rehearsing, she realized. A service would begin soon, and he was going over his lines. He flipped several sheets of paper, never looking up as he memorized his sermon, accentuating the words in his head with occasional thrusts of his hands toward the invisible listeners or to the heavens. Only when he was nearly finished, raising his palms up to the sky, did he lift his head and catch sight of Francesca.

"Hello," he said, lowering his hands to the altar. With a grin, he said, "You caught me practicing. A rare sight."

"I apologize." Francesca spoke softly as she stepped toward the altar. "I didn't want to interrupt." If the man knew who she was or what she was a part of, he gave no indication. There was no fear or trepidation in his eyes, but there was something. Confusion. Maybe even a little amusement.

"No matter if you did, my dear. I'm at a point where improvement in my public speaking prowess is on a downward trend, I'm afraid. There's just no hope at my age." He broke out in a warm smile and watched her walk toward him with welcoming eyes. "You definitely aren't a member of the media dressed like that."

"Were you expecting the media?"

"No. Never mind. Which means you must be looking

for someone." The preacher bent his head back to the altar, rearranging his papers. Francesca couldn't help but think his attitude had chilled.

"How did you know?" She was now at the end of the aisle near the foot of the raised portion of the floor.

"Never mind. What can I do for you?"

"Kirk and Wendy Palmero. Did you know them?"

His head remained still, facing the surface of the altar, but she could clearly see his eyes and mouth, both wide with shock.

"Are you with the police?" he asked, his eyes still on the papers.

"No. Are they looking for information on the Palmeros?" She stepped onto the raised platform but no further. Any closer and she feared he might bolt, refusing to speak to her.

"No. Never mind. Why do you want to know about them?" It was like an unseen weight prevented the man from looking up.

"Sir, I'd very much like to know if they had a child. Specifically, a son." She cleared her throat, and feeling it might add some urgency to her request, she added, "An adopted son."

He looked up at her. His wide eyes had narrowed to slits. "How did you know that they adopted that boy? No one outside this community should know that, and even then ..."

Francesca stepped around the corner of the altar, a few steps from the preacher and faced him directly. "That boy is my brother. I'd like to find him."

The preacher's face softened considerably, and he spoke in a quiet, concerned voice. "Dear, I believe your brother may be in trouble."

24

Pain and Growth

November 8, 2043

Acer's plan was incredible. He'd given Josiah the fundamentals of it before running back out to the van to grab one last thing. They were going to strip away the object of the city's technological lust, the people's most coveted narcotic—the artificial intelligence, the brain that controlled all the automobile traffic and most of everything else. Before Acer explained it to him, Josiah had no idea just how deep the addiction to technology had gone for the people of the city. He'd never realized just how much control they'd handed over to this soulless robot. He and Acer were about to force the entire city to kick their addiction cold turkey. The process, he knew, would be painful. Painful but necessary. Like removing a diseased tooth without pain killers, it would be miserable at first, but they'd feel better afterward.

Alone in the huge dark room, Josiah couldn't believe he was underwater. According to Acer, this entire section of the building was submerged in the icy waters of the Chesapeake. Something about facilitating the transmission of power, but

Josiah didn't care about the details. To him, this building was just another example of humankind's hubris. Building a structure underwater when Lord the Father had provided them with an earthly paradise on which to live and thrive.

Next to him stood the stack of black plastic boxes Acer had brought with him. "Gear," he called the items in the cases. The fact that they would, in the process of starting the great awakening, use high technology and, in turn, violate the core tenets of Praeceptist beliefs tore at Josiah's conscience. At first, it forced him to balk at Acer's plan.

But Acer asked Josiah a simple question so he could see the wisdom in the approach. "Would you kill a man to protect the ones you love?"

Of course he would, he'd told Acer. Then he understood. Killing is against God's law, but is all killing bad? What if it brings about a righteous end, like protecting His precious children from evil doers? And what better righteous end than the great awakening?

The space by the wall was occupied by a few long tables and some rolling office chairs. This had clearly been a workspace of one kind at some point, but Acer assured him that no one would be coming down to this room. His research on the building and its workers had been extensive.

Acer had placed an electric lantern on one of the tables, its light flickering subtly off the greenish bricks in the wall. Somewhere in the dark, water dripped, slow and steady. In the quiet stillness of the hardened space, the tiny splash echoed like an ominous metronome.

A click and a creaking door announced Acer's return. The hand truck's wheels rubbed against the damp floor, filling the room with shrill squelches.

Acer entered the reach of the lantern, pushing the hand truck in front of him. At first, the object, the remaining piece of gear he'd retrieved from the van looked like an overfilled garbage bag: wide, bulging at odd angles, and filling the lower half of the hand truck while extending well beyond its upright rails.

On closer inspection, Josiah realized that it wasn't a garbage bag but a dark-blue blanket or a canvas tarp wrapped around a bulky object. Both had been securely strapped to the hand truck. He could only guess that this was some piece of necessary equipment.

"What is that thing?" Josiah asked, curious what all this technology was supposed to do.

"Later," Acer said without looking back. "Want to help get this stuff set up?"

Half an hour later, the crates were unloaded, and the computers were nearly ready. Josiah had learned more about the machines in thirty minutes than he had bothered to know in nearly two decades. And it was all fairly easy to understand, at least how they went together. Where cables were needed to go from one piece of equipment to another, the ends were usually shaped so they could only go into one receiving port. Most everything, he noticed, did not require wires or cables at all to function. The monitors unfolded like a huge pamphlet and were held to the wall by super adhesive putty. The room provided them with the power they needed through special connections to the station itself, which Acer didn't bother to explain. They even had food and water to last up to a week.

"All set," Acer said, stepping back from the newly assembled workstations.

Josiah nodded and moved to stand next to his friend. "Looks

good. I think." He laughed, having caught himself approving of it while remaining totally ignorant of how any of it worked. "Acer, I'm afraid from here on in—"

A sound cut him off.

He swung around toward the room's interior. The noise had come from somewhere in the dark, near the first row of server racks. A low moan. "What was that?"

Acer didn't seem to notice. "What were you saying about here on in?" He still faced the workstation like an appraiser.

"Um ... right." Josiah shook off the distraction and rotated slowly to face Acer. "From here on in, I won't be of much help. I know you have experience with ... hacking or whatever you call it ..."

"Hacking is the correct term. Or cracking, if you prefer." Acer stood with his hands on his hips, looking solemn, speaking softly.

Josiah continued his train of thought. "I don't have any experience with any of this. I don't know exactly what you have planned, but I won't be able to help with any of the technical aspects."

"I won't be working with any of this," Acer said, waving a hand over the array of equipment. "I know I have to go through some official rituals and what not, but I consider myself a believer. I'm a Praeceptist, brother. I will not be using any technology whatsoever from this moment forward."

This took Josiah by surprise. Although he regretted the need to use technology to bring about the great awakening, in the short time since he'd seen Acer's van, he'd come to accept it as necessary to their plan. Now, with Acer's pledge, he couldn't see any possible alternative.

"I don't understand, Acer. How are we going to shut down

the artificial intelligence without you using your equipment?" Josiah took a step back, suddenly realizing what Acer must intend. "You're bringing someone else in on the plan, aren't you? An outsider? How could you betray my trust like that? How could you not tell me? How do I know I can trust them?" Josiah fired the questions off without taking a breath.

Acer stepped forward and grasped a rattled Josiah by the upper arms. "Calm down, please, Josiah. Just take a breath. It's part of the plan. It's part of His plan. Believe me when I say, I don't trust anyone other than you and me."

Josiah stopped backing away and allowed himself a second to breathe. "Okay. Okay. I just need you to explain it to me. The details. What are we going to do, and how are we going to do it?"

Acer closed his eyes and bowed his head. "You know what we're trying to do. You know what we want to change." Josiah was well aware these weren't questions. It was his, Josiah's, teaching and insights that inspired Acer in the first place. "But the great awakening isn't about us, you and me. It's about them"—he threw an arm up and out—"saving them. From themselves. Delivering them a world that Lord the Father can bless with His love."

Josiah nodded vigorously. "Yes. Yes, of course. Please just—"

"Let me show you how we're going to strip the city of its most sinful vice without sullying ourselves in the process." Acer's face was asking permission.

"Yes, Acer, please show me."

Acer walked toward the aisle that split the columns of old server racks and disappeared into the shadows before returning, pulling the hand truck backward into the light.

The oddly shaped load was still strapped to it. He set it down with a metallic clank. Acer worked the straps on the backside of the hand truck, twisting and then unwinding the ratcheting connectors. The top strap fell loose, but despite this, the blue tarp stayed in place. A second later, the middle strap came free. This time, the bulk under the tarp moved. Something blunt and heavy fell from the load on the opposite side, out of Josiah's line of sight, but as the object shifted, the tarp revealed something pale between its folds.

The last strap, securing the lower third of the load, tumbled loose to the floor. A meaty smack echoed as the tarp unraveled fully and the object unfolded, then rolled from the hand truck. Seconds passed as Josiah attempted to process what he was seeing, hoping that his eyes were playing cruel tricks on him. But he knew they weren't.

On the cold, hard floor, between him and his friend Acer, lay an unconscious man. Hands bound with plastic ties, mouth covered in black tape, naked except for a pair of white underwear.

Josiah's feet moved without his noticing, backing away from the horrific scene. Words wouldn't come, yet he had no idea what they should be if he could manage to create them. He just kept stepping backward.

Acer broke the silence. "Goddamnit," he shouted, his voice reverberating in the dark. He threw the end of one of the straps he'd been holding to the ground. "Look, I know this is … is unorthodox and maybe … probably not what you were expecting."

"Unorthodox?" The word seemed so out of place in the circumstances. "What did you do, Acer? Why is he here?"

"He's going to do the work we can't do." He took two paces

toward Josiah. "He'll be our instrument of righteousness. A tool for us to wield just as the Lord wields us."

His back almost to the wall, Josiah said, "You kidnapped him. How did you expect to force him to work for us?"

Acer continued toward him, his eyes coldly focused on Josiah's. "We'll persuade him."

"You'll hurt him."

He shook his head. "I don't want it to come to that, but if it's necessary, yes we will."

"What about after?" Josiah's back touched to damp wall. "What about when all this is over? He'll tell the police what we did. We'll get arrested. Go to prison. Our lives will be over ... forever."

Acer stopped moving. A smile, the same kind that he wore when they first met, took shape on his face. He laughed pitifully. "Josiah, your words are what brought us here. Bringing the Lord's will to the people. Being active proselytizers. Using dynamite in a lake of fish. Remember?" He stretched an arm at the unconscious man. "He's a fish. They're all fish." He threw a hand skyward then slammed it, palm flat, against his chest with a hollow thud. "We're the dynamite."

Josiah slid along the wall sideways a half step toward the door. "You're talking about ... killing? Murder?" Another half-step. "When did we talking about killing? They were metaphors, you fool." Fear mixed with anger, filled Josiah with waves of emotion he hadn't known since he'd watched his father beaten to a pulp. "When did I ever mention murder?"

Acer gave a quick glance in the general direction of the exit. "What did you think was going to happen when we attacked the AI? We can't take it all down at once; it's too powerful with too many built-in defenses. We have to find weaknesses first, then start slowly ramping up. We'll hit the traffic control system, then the drones, then the tunnels, then"—he shrugged—"who knows what else. The city will be ours." He continued closing the gap between them. "But no matter which part of the AI we attack and take out, there will be consequences. People will get hurt. People will probably die."

"No."

"With pain comes growth." Acer increased his pace.

"No."

"I'm afraid so, brother."

Behind Acer, the bound man moaned, louder and deeper than before. Acer glanced in that direction for a split second. Josiah bolted toward the door. His feet slammed the concrete floor, the slaps bouncing off every flat surface around him, pummeling his ear drums. Ahead, jets of light shined through the windows in the exit doors. He pushed his body harder, commanded his legs to run faster. He passed the last row of server racks two dozen feet from the exit.

A rush of something to his left, then an impact in his side. He collided with the wall, felt his ribs crack and his head slam against concrete. On the floor, a hand clamped around his neck. It tightened. Tighter. His lungs screamed. Lights danced in his eyes.

His hands clawed and scratched of instinctively, like a dying animal.

Like a dying man.

Moments passed and Josiah's struggles weakened. A minute more and they stopped altogether.

Josiah Palmero's hands fell to his side and would not move

again.

25

Colektive Doom

Three Years Ago

Malina moved from the kitchen to the living room, sinking deep into the soft folds of the sofa. She lifted the cup of hot tea to her lips and blew across its surface for a moment before taking a sip. Bully, Anton's dog, approached her happily, his fluffy tail curled and wagging as he nuzzled her leg. She gave him a soft pat on the head then gently scratched him behind the ear as she stared out the window across the living room, puzzling over the request made of her the night before.

Anton, or Champ as the online world knew him and as she often called him, emerged shirtless from the hallway, his skin still glistening from his shower. Malina greeted him with a smile, which he returned, then resumed her train of thought. The request had come from Ambrosia, the unofficial leader of their gang of do-gooders, the Colektive. She rarely questioned tasks assigned to her, but then she was rarely blinded to their purpose as she was now.

"What are you thinking about, Mal?" Champ dropped into a chair across from her attracting the attention of Bully who quickly sought out his master.

"You know what I'm thinking about," she said, only slightly averting her gaze from the window.

Champ leaned forward to get nose to nose with Bully and tussled the dog's ears to his delight. "Ambrosia's ask? What is there to think about? This is what we do."

"I don't know if it is." She shook her head and set her tea down on the coffee table. "We go after industries, companies, and individuals who are hurting people. We take down the ones that treat the world like they're entitled to it, everyone else be damned. But we never, never do anything that might inadvertently harm innocent people."

Champ lounged back in the chair and let Bully jump into his lap. "Don't you trust him?"

"Do I trust Ambrosia?" She felt her eyebrows rise of their accord. "Do you?"

He shrugged. "He's a bit extreme, I guess. A bit erratic, but…" He glared off into space before continuing. "No, I guess I don't trust him. But who trusts anybody these days?"

"I trust you." She folded her arms. "And I assume you trust me."

"Of course," he said, nodding. "What exactly worries you about what he's asking you to do?"

Malina had thought about nothing else since the request came through in the Colektive's encrypted message board. Why was it such a problem for her? The answer she came back to time and again was the same: harming innocent people. What he asked her to do might get good people hurt.

Ambrosia contacted her the night before and told her to hack Datasine Security Sytems, a cybersecurity firm. He had asked her to find root access codes for one of their most popular security suites called Jericho. Specifically, he wanted superadmin permissions so he could navigate the system freely. Superadmin permissions in a security system like Jericho would allow him to toggle firewalls and gateways on and off. Once he had penetrated Jericho, he could manipulate the target entity's internal systems at will.

Malina had done similar jobs for Ambrosia in the past. In fact, her specialty tended to be finding needles in cyber haystacks for the Colektive. She hacked Datasine twice in the past six months alone for root access codes for security suites other than Jericho. The job itself didn't bother Malina so much as who she suspected the target entity to be. Jericho was primarily sold to hospitals.

"What if he wants to infiltrate a hospital and muck with their control systems?" She got up from the couch and began to pace. "He could literally shut down an ICU ward if he wanted. He could change someone's medication or switch off a breathing machine."

"You think he'd do that?" Champ reached for her tea. "And why would he do that?"

She had thought about this question also. There was only one reason she could come up that made sense.

"If there was someone admitted to the hospital that he wanted to..." She stopped pacing, wondering if saying it out loud made her sound crazy. "...murder."

"Jesus, Malina," Champ said with a furrowed brow. "Ambrosia is a little out there. I'll give you that. But he's not a killer."

Malina returned to pacing and began chewing the end of her thumbnail. "I'm just going to tell him no. I'll tell him I don't feel comfortable doing it and he'll just have to find someone else."

A few minutes later, she posted a direct message to Ambrosia on the Colektive message board. He did not reply. He did not ask her to reconsider.

For three days, Malina checked the headlines for the deaths of prominent people who may have died while in a hospital. Sincerely hoping she was wrong about her hunch, she also hoped that Ambrosia was unable to find anyone else to do the job for him.

On the third day since refusing Ambrosia's request, Malina was sitting with her tablet when she saw a headline on the FMM News website that read "Woods Family Blames Hospital for Patriarch's Untimely Death." Her breath caught as she tapped the link to the article.

The article explained that Xavier Woods, Founder and CEO of Xircon Conductors, Inc., had died while in the hospital for routine heart valve replacement surgery. He was sent to a recovery ward where he was supposed to stay for only a few hours before being sent home with his family. While in recovery, he was given a dose of tridoxycycline, an antibiotic. He suffered an allergic reaction to the medication and died from anaphylaxis.

Malina scanned the article further and discovered that the family of Mr. Woods was suing the hospital for malpractice while the hospital administrators were beginning an investigation into the man's death. The nurse on duty claimed she received orders from the hospital's central computer to administer the antibiotic. Orders such as these can only be given by an attending physician, so she didn't question it. Antibiotics are given routinely after surgeries, but Woods's allergy to tridoxycycline was documented in his chart. The hospital claims the central computer should have prevented the order being given and said this kind of thing has never happened.

Malina's hands shook so badly she had to set the tablet on the coffee table. Champ entered the room from the kitchen and sat next to her, placing a hand on her shoulder.

"What's wrong?" he asked.

"He did it." Her eyes unfocused. Her limbs felt numb. "I was right. I was right and he fucking did it."

"Who did what?" Champ spoke slowly, as if frightened of upsetting her further. "What happened, Mal?"

She didn't speak. Instead, she lifted a shaky finger to point at the tablet lying on the table.

After a moment, Champ said, "I don't get it. What does—" He paused. "Oh, shit. You think this is Ambrosia? Why? This could have been anything."

Malina closed her eyes, shaking her head. "It was him. Think about that name: Xavier Woods."

Champ dropped the tablet on the table with a clatter. "Oh my god, you're right. Woods was on our 'shit list.'"

The Colektive had a collection of names of individuals they deemed high value targets. These were people directly involved in acts that were especially heinous and unforgiveable, acts that contributed to major negative impacts on the health and safety of people or the environment. Xavier Woods wasn't the worst person on the list, but he was on it and had been for quite a few years.

The Colektive would work to take down a name on their "shit list" only when solid evidence presented itself. But murdering an individual from the list was never discussed. They'd expose them and allow the authorities to do the rest.

Malina allowed herself to calm down for several minutes then she jumped online and went directly to the Colektive message board. Expecting to find the password and PIN prompt, she instead saw an error message across her screen. "This site cannot be reached. Server IP address could not be found."

"Let me try," Champ said after reading the over her shoulder.

He tried his own tablet only to receive the same error. He stood and walked across the room to his laptop on the corner desk.

"No luck here either," he said.

Malina tried her phone then pulled her own laptop out of her bag and booted it up. The error was there on both devices. She used Champ's network to log into her home computer through which she accessed a VPN then the internet. At the message board web address, she received the same error notice.

"It's gone." She dropped her laptop to the floor. "He killed it; I know he did. I refused the job and he killed the site."

The message board the Colektive communicated through was only known to them and it was the only way in which they communicated. Other than Champ, Malina had no idea who the other members were in real life. Without the website, the Colektive was essentially dead.

For several weeks, Malina checked the Colektive's webpage every day. She wasn't sure why she wanted it to reappear because she had no desire to work with Ambrosia anymore if her theory was true. Maybe she wanted to ask him directly. Maybe she wanted to confront him. Maybe she wanted to tell the others and stage a coup against him if he really did have a hand in killing Woods.

In the end, it didn't matter. The webpage was never active after she refused the Jericho job and the Colektive was effectively dead.

231

26

Waste Deep

Zed Thomas adjusted the light attached to his hardhat to make it cast a wider cone in the space in front of him. The high-powered beam sliced through the air in the dark access tunnel. Motion activated tube lighting would usually light the way as he paced deeper into the cramped corridor but the part of the city's AI that managed the entire network of sewage and storm runoff pipes, which included ancillary systems like maintenance corridor lighting, had apparently gone haywire along with just about everything else in the city.

It was the sporadic breakdown of the sewer's maintenance and monitoring systems throughout the city's public works control rooms that brought Zed to the access tunnel. The human operators responsible for monitoring the sewage and storm water runoff network had lost connection with the system. They had no visibility into the functions of the hundreds of AI controlled valves, pumps, vents, and gates that fed and directed wastewater in the vast web of pipes deep beneath the city.

His boots squeaked on the damp concrete floor, the sound

echoing in the stillness. The corridor was so narrow his tool bag scraped the wall with every other step and if he wasn't careful, his opposite shoulder collided with fixtures protruding from the wall.

The access tunnel sat parallel with the five mile long central trunk of the system that ran north and south, bisecting the city into two sectors. Zed was tasked with inspecting the eastern sector's secondary and tertiary pipes which crossed over the access tunnel intermittently to dump into the central trunk. At each intersection, a maintenance terminal was located on the tunnel wall.

So far, twenty-seven of the maintenance terminals he checked showed things were operating normally. He even visually inspected and manually function tested a number of valves and pumps and they too seemed to be fine. Maybe the other inspectors were finding abnormalities in different areas of the system, but from what he could see, with the exception of the lights in the tunnel, the sewer was operating the same way it always did, flawlessly.

The only hitch in the system, at the moment, was visibility. Human controllers weren't able to see what the AI controlled components down in the pipes were doing. Everyone in Public Works had total faith in the AI, normally, and would overlook the lack of oversight for a time, but the accidents involving the Metro Traffic System gave some people, including Zed, pause.

Zed glanced at the tablet strapped to his wrist. The display showed a map of the pipe network with his location as a blinking red arrow. He could see that the central trunk's core maintenance terminal was about a hundred feet ahead. Several minutes later, he reached it. Like the others but twice as large, the core terminal for the central trunk was a single monitor set flush with the wall. He tapped the edge of the monitor and it blinked to life forcing him to cast his eyes downward and allow them to adjust to the sudden brightness.

A few seconds later, he stared at the screen and its many icons. He selected a diagnostic tool and ran it, then several more, testing various valve gates and servos integral to the central trunk's functions. Each test gave him a green checkmark in the status window indicating all operations were normal.

Satisfied that the overall health of the system was good, he reached for his radio to call the control room and report that all was normal. He brought the lipstick sized communicator to his lips and was about to press the transmit button when he froze. In the bottom corner of the screen, a small window showed the environmental readings from within the central trunk.

The hand gripping the communicator fell to his side as he leaned closer to the screen. He blinked his eyes several times to be sure of what he was seeing.

The levels inside of the twelve feet diameter central trunk usually hovered around twenty to thirty percent, but a major storm could dump vast amounts of water into tertiary runoff pipes and bring it close to fifty percent. It could, however, handle much more than that and was capable of moving millions of gallons of waste and storm water if needed.

What surprised Zed wasn't how high the waste level was inside the trunk, but how low. The readout showed the current level at around 0.001%—less than a quarter of an inch of liquid wastewater. Barely a trickle. Zed knew this was impossible considering that even on a light day, there would be two to three feet of wastewater flowing through the central trunk. Plus, all the wet weather the city had recently should double that amount at least.

Under the waste level readout was a meter showing the gas content of the trunk. All of the potentially toxic gases were there in extremely high concentrations—hydrogen sulfide, ammonia, methane, carbon dioxide, sulfur dioxide, and nitrous oxide—each well over 1,500 parts per million. At those concentrations, a person entering the sewer main would immediately lose consciousness and quickly asphyxiate and die.

Vents in the sewer system moved the toxic gases to processing facilities where the impurities were burned off or filtered out, lest they get too high and leach into the ground or, god forbid, into the air above ground. The AI controlled systems, it seemed, had emptied the central trunk of all wastewater, but did not remove the toxic fumes created by the waste.

As a final check, of both the system and his own sanity, he tapped an icon on the maintenance terminal's screen to pull up a video feed from one of the many infrared cameras mounted to the ceiling inside the central trunk. A window appeared showing the view from the camera, which displayed everything in easily discernible gray tones. A hairline of silvery thread snaked down the middle of the camera feed; the wastewater at the bottom of the central trunk was barely visible.

"What the hell is going on?" Zed whispered to himself.

The trunk was truly empty of fluid ... and full of deadly gases.

27

Power

"You know, I was just thinking …" Aubrey spoke between breaths as they ran along the wide sidewalk, an iron fence and rock piles beyond to their right. The rocks sloped dozens of feet until they disappeared into the edge of the Chesapeake. "If we have to get our hands dirty at the power station, if the police don't show up in time, there's no sense in you being there."

This part of the bay had been largely reclaimed during New Aberdeen's founding and subsequent development. The power station was almost a straight shot west from their position.

Malina shot him a look; she was clearly insulted. "Are you kidding? Do you know how to shut down whatever programs they've used against the AI?"

"Do you?" He had to shout over a fierce breeze cutting across the water.

"I have a better shot at it than you do, Martin. Would you even know where to begin?" Now she too was shouting, and her pace seemed to quicken.

"Look, I'm just trying to—"

"I know what you're trying to do." Malina threw up a hand effectively ending the discussion.

Aubrey let it go. He knew she could handle herself as well as anyone despite her size. She fought like a tiger when she had to. He pushed the rising tide of guilt aside and focused on the task at hand.

"Is that it up ahead?" He pointed in the near distance where a short round building, maybe three stories high, stood next to a much taller rectangular structure. The larger building was run through with a series of winding pipes and ducts. Massive vents, fifty feet wide, covered one entire face of it.

"Yeah. Those are offices for the handful of people that work there," Malina said. "And that's where the actual power plant submerges down into the river." She pointed to the rear of the buildings, where a narrow one-story structure snaked its way into the water, where the mud-brown Susquehanna met the dark brine of the Chesapeake. "It goes for another fifty feet into the water." She paused. "Back in the day, it was to keep all the servers cool year-round. But they don't use servers anymore, so now it's mostly empty. And that's where I'd be."

"Why there and not in the offices?"

"Too hard to hide in the office building."

Between them and the squat office tower was a large open green space circumvented by the concrete path that skirted the shoreline. They cut across the vast green lawn, making a beeline for the buildings. On a summer day, the park was usually crowded by sun bathers, dog walkers, and frisbee throwers, but with winter digging its teeth into the city, Aubrey and Malina were alone.

Her phone rang, and she reached inside her pocket.

"Now's not a good time," Aubrey said over his shoulder.

She slowed to answer the call. "It's Francesca. Maybe she can help us," Malina panted. She spoke into her phone, "Hey, we don't have much time ... What? How did you know we were looking for—"

Aubrey lifted a clenched fist, signaling to Malina to freeze.

She stopped. The silence of the park enabled Aubrey's ear to catch a familiar sound not far away. A high-pitched hum. The sound of tiny rotors slicing the air. Normally, the sound of a drone wouldn't make him think twice, but nothing about their current situation was normal. He pivoted slowly, scanning the sky high and low, trying to pinpoint the sound's origin.

"Francesca, I have to go," she said into her phone. "What is it?" Her face had turned grave.

"Drone."

Her head snapped in either direction, searching the skies with Aubrey.

He squinted. He thought he could make out a dark speck between the buildings a quarter mile away. Which way was it moving, and wasn't it too far away for him to hear?

The buzzing was louder now, getting closer. It seemed to be coming from all around them, but he couldn't see anything. The park gave them a perfect view for 360 degrees, but there was nothing in sight. He'd checked every direction ... except one.

His neck craned and his eyes shot skyward. Four drones ranging in size from a toaster to a hot water heater were clustered together in a tight formation barreling down toward them from above. A hundred feet over them. About to dive bomb them.

"Run," Aubrey shouted, propelling Malina ahead of him.

They ran. Aubrey pivoted on his toes, nearly slipping by the sheer force of his own movement.

Five long strides, and he stretched out a hand to keep Malina in front of him. He pumped his legs like he was on the last lap of a death race.

He glanced over his shoulder and saw the two largest drones skim the grass and dirt, their bulk making their course correction cumbersome. The smaller drones, however, were nimbler and turned at something close to ninety degrees. The two big ones still flew low to the ground, which gave Aubrey an idea.

Concrete benches lined the wide walking path. He found the nearest one and directed Malina toward it.

"Jump!"

First Malina, then Aubrey leapt over the bench.

"Duck!"

He bent low and pulled her back toward the bench as close as he could to the thick seat. A crash rocked the bench. Bits of debris and shrapnel pelted them. A blur of motion and the buzzing was right on top of them, then more sounds of impact.

In front of them, against the fence, lay two-thirds of the biggest drone and a tangled mess of metal, which could only be the second-largest flier. They had slammed into the back of the bench and pinwheeled over it, not able to climb high enough in time. Just beyond the thin smoke issuing from the downed robots, he saw the smaller drones banking in a wide circle to the right, quickly making their way back toward their prey.

"Run. Keep going." Malina was already on her feet, headed toward the power station. Aubrey got up and was quickly on her heels.

The buzzing was gaining on them. He knew they only had seconds before they were hit. He reached under his coat and drew his pistol. He slid to a stop and turned while leveling the gun to take aim. He sighted down the barrel at the closest of the two. It was about three feet long and a foot tall and could do the most damage. He'd only get one shot at either of them, so best to choose the one that could do the most damage. He drew a bead on its center mass, the guts of the thing most likely inside a black plastic heart hanging between the four large rotors.

He eased pressure on the trigger, half a heartbeat away from sending the firing pin home and blasting off the one opportunity he'd have to down the flying beast.

Suddenly, the machine banked hard to his right, flew for twenty feet then slammed into a light post. It ricocheted off the post at an odd angle straight into the ground, lodging itself in the soil.

Aubrey turned his pistol on the toaster, but before he could rest his finger on the trigger, it too instantly changed course. It turned hard to his left, and out toward the bay it flew low. After a few seconds, it found a wave that brought it down like a shark swallowing a seal.

By the lamppost, the drone's remaining rotors spun against the grass harmlessly, filling the air with the eerie sound of their dying momentum.

"Did you shoot them down?" Malina asked from several feet behind him.

"No, I never got a shot off." He still held his pistol at the ready, as if the drones would resurrect themselves from the dead at any moment and strike while he and Malina had their guard down.

"Then what the hell happened?" She stood beside him, looking as confused as he felt.

"No idea."

"Was it just a warning?" she asked.

"No. No, he's tried to kill us before and came damn close." He shook his head and holstered his pistol. "I don't have a clue what happened, but I do know it proves we're on the right track." Aubrey turned and pointed at the power station. "He's definitely in there. Let's go get him."

* * *

"What did you do?" The man kicked Anton in the back, sending him flying face first into the edge of the table. Blood spurted from his lips and nose. "You motherfucker!" He kicked again but his angle was off and Anton's chair simply spun. As it did, Reggie saw him grinning through crimson-coated teeth.

"I'm not killing for you again, you piece of shit." More blood oozed from his nostrils and ran down to his naked chest.

Reggie bent his tired neck up to see the monitor. The man and the woman were running across the park again. Behind them lay three mangled drones and one in the sea.

"Consider yourself a dead man, Champ." The man leaned over, his hands on his knees, and spoke in a whisper. "You'll be a floating buffet for the Chesapeake fauna tonight. A guy your size will feed a lot of fishies. And I think I'll leave you only half dead when I dump your body. I want you to feel what it's like to get eaten alive."

The kidnapper straightened and kicked like a jackrabbit,

hitting Champ squarely in the sternum. Champ doubled over in pain, gasping.

Their captor stepped to Champ's workstation. He brought his hands up in prayer.

"Father, I do what I must to bring about a righteous end."

He bent over and placed his fingers on the keyboard. His hands worked in a blur over the keys. Reggie watched the code the man created fill a portion of the wall-mounted monitor. He read it, astonished at the man's expertise. He'd imagined their captor was just a religious nut, some whacko using them to stage his own jihad. But the commands he created and the programming language he used were just as sophisticated and advanced as any Reggie had ever seen. This man, their captor, knew exactly what he was doing and had obviously spent years developing his craft.

"Why did you make us do it?" Reggie coughed the question. "Why make us? Why torture us when you … when you could have done it yourself the whole time."

The man didn't move and didn't respond.

"You killed three people and you could have been doing this yourself all along." Reggie found some strength from somewhere to press the man. Perhaps Champ's defiance inspired him. "You're as good as us. You don't need us. Why'd you do it?"

The man stood up tall and straight, his head tilted back slightly.

"What Lord the Father wants of me, He shall get." The man stepped closer to Reggie, the angle of his glare growing steeper. "He wanted me to keep my soul clean. Now, it seems, he wants me to sacrifice my soul for him. And that, I am more than happy to do." He stared for a second more, then turned back to the keyboard.

Onscreen, a list appeared, showing rows and rows of what Reggie knew to be vehicles and registration numbers. Listed were all the cars, trucks, boats, and aerial craft in the area. The man punched a command into the computer, and a search window appeared in the corner of the screen. He keyed in his query and pressed Return.

One result flashed on the screen.

"Oh, that'll work," he said. "That'll work just fine."

Reggie read the vehicle type and immediately understood what the man was going to do. "God, no."

* * *

Lieutenant Commander John Rickard of the US Coast Guard piloted the Airbus MH-95 Porpoise in a tight circle 550 feet above a fishing trawler below. Two miles off the northern end of New Aberdeen, Rickard watched with a leisurely eye as the captain of the trawler and four crewmen knelt handcuffed on the bow of the boat under the watchful eye of a petty officer and her rifle. Clad in the standard blue-and-black camouflage working uniform, she rose and fell with the ship as it rode the swells of the bay.

"Shouldn't local PD have jurisdiction?" Rickard's copilot, Lieutenant Charles Whitney, chirped in the ear of his helmet.

Without looking away from the scene below, Rickard said, "Usually, they would. But CO says they have their hands full today with something, so we got tagged, and now we're it."

Rickard's hands barely touched the controls. He held them close enough to feel the vibration of the rotor powered by the twin hydrogen engines, but the real control came from the onboard computer, which he'd already programmed.

"Ever flown over the city?" Whitney asked.

"Couple of times." Rickard kept his eyes on the vessel in the water below. After a moment, two seamen and another petty officer emerged from a cabin amidship. Between them, they carried four large duffel bags and three rigid green cases.

"It's creepy how the chopper just gives up control. Flying blind, man. That's crazy shit."

"Afraid of losing control, are you?" The second petty officer unzipped a bag and dumped its contents—large blue bricks of powder wrapped in shimmering clear wrapping. "Whoa, that's a lot of drugs."

"Oh yeah? Let me see." Rickard felt Whitney lean his way and instinctively lifted an elbow to keep him at bay.

"Don't worry. You'll get a good look. Just let me—"

Movement in the MH-95 made him pause. The chopper shuddered as if it had just hit turbulence. The control stick battered the palm of his right hand, and the throttle controls shifted violently up. The helicopter banked hard to the right.

"What the hell is happening?" Whitney shouted.

The engines screamed as RPMs soared above the redline. The nose of the aircraft dipped and the chopper shot forward. The mouth of the Susquehanna was dead ahead two miles out.

* * *

Aubrey and Malina leapt from the curb of the walkway onto the paved surface of the empty parking lot a hundred feet away from the front entry of the office building. They ran hard, as Aubrey expected more attacks until they could get inside.

"How do we get in?" he said.

Malina pointed to the long, low section that stretched into the water. "A maintenance door, side entrance. Keypad and biometric entry." She spoke quick and choppy, her breath surely failing her after all the hard running. "Only one door. Any other way in is too slow."

"Sounds good." He looked around. "And no cavalry here yet. I think we'll be forgiven if we have to kick our way in."

"That's … what … I was thinking."

They rounded the office building, the partially submerged section of the structure just thirty yards ahead. Then he heard it. The fast, steady thrumming of long blades cutting the air. The sound of a helicopter. Over his heavy breathing and talking with Malina, he'd missed it. And now, it was close. The noise grew louder with every heartbeat. It wasn't hard to spot the chopper. It looked like an orange-and-white bird of prey rapidly growing to the size of a house as it screeched toward them from over the bay, ready to pluck them from the world like two helpless field mice.

It was too close. The water was too far away even now. They'd never make it. He could almost feel the wind generated by its powerful rotor.

The building was their only hope.

He pointed at the door and Malina got the hint. The pair of them sprinted toward the gray door, staying close to the structure. The noise of the chopper's engines screamed.

"Down," Malina cried.

She threw herself onto the ground, and Aubrey crashed on top of her, doing his best to wedge the both of them into the corner where building met concrete.

The screeching assaulted them, the wind buffeted their backs, but the crash never came. Aubrey glanced up to see the orange bottom of the helicopter as it banked toward the water in a tight turn.

"What happened?" Malina shouted from under him.

"He must have had a bad angle on us." Aubrey's eyes followed the helicopter as it arced away from them. "He's repositioning. He's going to take another shot at us."

"What do we do?"

Aubrey helped her up off the ground.

"We get inside."

The thudding of the chopper blades faded slightly as it banked out over the bay a thousand meters away. Aubrey and Malina rounded the curvature of the main building and came abreast with the tall equipment tower, the louvers of its vented side spilling hot moist air on them as they passed.

"Right there," Malina shouted. There was no need to point. Aubrey saw the only door in the side of the long, low structure. Light gray against the seafoam green of the concrete walls.

As they neared the entry, the helicopter's roar leveled off for a heartbeat before slowly beginning to increase. A quick peek told Aubrey all he needed to know. The chopper was coming around for another pass and wasn't likely to miss its mark this time. His eyes lingered on the airship for a second longer, and as it turned hard to starboard, its side parallel with the water twenty-five feet below, two figures fell from its open rear hatch. They landed feet first and disappeared briefly before their heads popped through the surface a second later.

"What now?" Aubrey slid to a stop on the gravel outside the windowless maintenance door. Aubrey examined it from top to bottom. The door was featureless. On the wall next to it was mounted a card reader and below that a handprint scanner. No knob or handle. No hinges, which meant the door must open into the building. "Malina, what now?"

The two of them stood facing the door like a couple of dumbstruck birds on the outside of a high-rise building, trying to figure out how to get through the invisible barrier to where the humans hid all the food.

The roar behind them increased steadily louder. It was too damn close.

"Don't you have your thing? Your fingerprint scanner thing?" She beat the empty air with her hands searching for the words.

"No and there's no time anyway. If you have no ideas, we have to force our way through, which I don't think we can, or go through the front entrance."

In high-pressure situations like these, Aubrey rarely let the intensity of the moment overcome him. Charging down a corridor, not knowing if a shooter was behind the next corner was unnerving, but not knowing, not seeing his potential end coming helped him cope. He was able to confront almost any situation as long as he knew there was probably a way out of it, and if not, he wouldn't see his imminent death right in front of him. But in this moment, he could see the end coming. It was like standing in a train tunnel and watching the locomotive barrel toward you. The blades thrummed behind them. Judging by the sound, he guessed they had thirty seconds before impact. He grabbed Malina's hand and turned to pull her back toward the front of the main building, but she resisted.

"Malina. We have to try the front."

She stood blank-faced staring at the door and said, "There

has to be something." She looked off to her right where the grass sloped to the edge of the rock pile and beyond to the bay. She sidestepped in front of the print reader and brought her hands to either side of it, cupping the device. Other than looking intently at the flat face of the reader, she did nothing else.

Aubrey leaned in close to her, thinking she must be in shock. He needed to talk some sense into her. Slowly and in a voice as close to normal that he could manage, he said, "Malina, we need to go. We cannot get in this way. We need to go right now."

She closed her eyes, and her chest rose as she drew a deep breath. The thrumming of the helicopter's rotor was almost deafening. Aubrey looked back. The black nose cone of the chopper gleamed in the sunlight, barely ten feet off the ground. He could clearly discern the outlines of the stubby antennae and the wipers on the windshields.

They had seconds.

"Just a second." She squeezed her eyes tighter. He could see the creases extending to her temples.

"Malina"—he gripped the crook of her elbow—"now. We have to run now."

"When I say"—she bobbed her head subtly, as if counting down—"run toward the water."

The wind picked up dramatically. Aubrey couldn't hear himself think over the cacophony of the rotor blades. He didn't dare look back.

Her eyes burst open. "Now!"

She reached back and grabbed his hand to pull him, but he was already in midstride. They sprinted, motivated by the fear of being eviscerated by the chopper's rotor blades and incinerated by an exploding hydrogen cell.

He kept his eyes on the edge of the water, telling himself to just get there. Get to the water. But it was too far—by a long shot. They'd never make it.

The air hit him first. The rush of it along the exterior of the building, blasting his bare neck, sand and other detritus flying past him.

Another step. "Get down!"

They threw themselves flat to the ground, downslope from the maintenance door just on the edge of the rocks. Screeches from a banshee scorned filled the air. An enormous, heart-stopping impact shook the ground under him, followed shortly by an intense heat crossing his back. Debris thudded into the wet ground around them. Small bits of something hard and hot landed on Aubrey, and he shook them off. He lifted his head and turned to look back. The angle of the ground was such that the impact's epicenter was out of his line of sight. They'd been protected from the blast by the slope.

He rolled on his side to face Malina. He was speechless. This was her plan, but she had no time to tell him. And now the helicopter was out of commission.

She opened her eyes, still on her stomach, and shrugged. "Now, let's see if we got a two-for-one deal."

"What?" Aubrey was still stunned by all that had transpired in the last few seconds.

She got to her feet, and as Aubrey did the same, he spun around to see what she meant by a two-for-one deal. Over the crest of the soft rise in the ground, the helicopter's hulk lay in a tangled aggregation partially masked by white-and-gray smoke billowing from somewhere inside the orange shell. The tail section had doubled over the fuselage, which appeared to have impacted the building at a low angle. Debris lay everywhere—orange, white, and black hunks of plastic and metal, charred wreckage, some of which still smoldered.

"We got lucky," Malina said, jogging forward up the low hill. Aubrey didn't respond, and she proceeded. "Look. No fire. The onboard suppression system doused the flames. Pretty impressive when you think about it, but that tech has come a long way in the last couple of decades."

Examining the crash site, he could see she was right. The white smoke rising from the chopper wasn't smoke at all; it was the fire suppressant, most likely nitro-halon gas. And there were no flames at all.

"Holy shit, you're right." He ran ahead. The twisted mass that used to be the Coast Guard helicopter was lying partly in a small crater in the ground and partly against the building. Bright-white artificial light shined through the haze of smoke and gas. For a moment, he thought the light must be from some onboard emergency system, but as he got closer and could see more clearly into the chopper, he realized the source of the light. It came from inside the building.

"There's our two-for-one." Malina stood next to him peering through the smoke and gas. "Took down the chopper and made a door." She smiled widely and held out a hand as if she were the host of a game show revealing a prize to a contestant.

He smiled back. "Brilliant move, partner."

28

Ambrosia

Climbing through the wreckage had consumed more time than Aubrey had hoped, but after shedding their overcoats, they were able to twist, squeeze, and shimmy their bodies through the maze of hot, jagged metal and into the power station. Standing up with only a few lacerations on his arms and a slow trickle of blood from his scalp, Aubrey was dusting himself off when the much nimbler Malina shot upright beside him.

The air inside the building was warm and thick, filling his lungs with its weight. He drew his pistol and surveyed the interior of the building. Opposite the cratered wall ran five enormous black pipes at least as wide as his forearm was long—three mounted to the wall and two on the floor.

"What are those?" said Aubrey.

"Twelve-inch electrical conduit lines feeding the grid." She pointed to their right. "This way."

The pair strode down the hallway with the conduit trunks to their left. Every hundred feet or so, an LCD panel stood on a pedestal displaying data and other information on the functioning of the conduit lines or some other unseen mechanism. The floor curved gently down, and after a few moments, he glanced back only to see he'd lost sight of their entry point.

Malina slowed and said, "We must be below the waterline now."

Ahead, the floor continued sloping down for another thirty feet then leveled off. The conduit lines followed the contours of the structure, diving and curving with the floors and walls.

Where the floor leveled, a set of beige double doors with narrow window slits came into view. A wide freestanding metal cabinet stood beside the left-hand door. They approached them with caution. There had been no other doors, rooms, or pathways off the main corridor.

They each stood to the side of a window peeking through to the space beyond. On the other side, the lights were dim, and Aubrey could just make out a short corridor that extended another thirty feet to a matching set of doors at its other end. To the sides of the corridor, he could barely trace the outline of a pair of doors. Malina spun slowly and pressed her back to the door.

"What's beyond those other doors at the end of the hall?" Aubrey held his pistol pointed toward the floor and moved away from the glass as she did.

She pressed the heels of both hands to her forehead. "Mostly just empty space. I told you this power plant was built before the city was even an idea. It was used to power the Army Proving Grounds nearby, and this whole place was filled with a ton of old tech." She shook her head. "In there, they used to house enormous server stacks, transformers, and other equipment, like the pump house, to keep the structure dry." She shrugged. "Once they started building the city, they converted the power plant to the latest technology and got rid of all the old servers and stuff."

"Do you remember the layout?" He peeked through the window again, hoping his eyes would make out more than they just had a moment ago. They didn't.

"Vaguely," she replied.

"And these two doors in the hall on the left and right? Where do they go?" He gestured with his pistol in either direction, keeping its barrel oriented toward the glass in the door.

"Just storage I think."

"Okay. Well he's not behind us." Aubrey turned the latch. "So he has to be in front of us."

He nodded to Malina to step back. She did so and he raised the pistol, pointing it at the joint between the doors. He pushed inward as he held the latch down, and for a second, he thought it was locked, but after a slight nudge with his shoulder, the door moved away from its frame. As it opened, Aubrey heard and felt the pressurized seal give way—a sucking and whooshing sound as wind blew past him.

Keeping the door between him and unseen and uncleared areas of the hall, he kept his gun aimed into the ever-growing gap until he had it all the way open.

No one in the hallway.

Suddenly, he was freezing and could have sworn he heard water running.

"Oh shit." Beside him, Malina stared open-mouthed at the floor.

"What?" He looked down as he said the words and knew immediately why she'd cursed. Aubrey had been so keyed up entering the hallway and clearing it of potential assailants that he hadn't noticed the quarter inch of water that had come rushing out.

"I'm guessing there isn't supposed to be water on the floor," he said.

"No." She shook her head slowly. "It's pressurized beyond this point to help keep it dry in case there's a breach. Judging by how difficult the door was to open, I'd say pressurization is still intact. That means some seal or valve or the pump itself has been compromised in there." She directed her eyes at the room beyond the second set of doors.

Aubrey swept the water with his foot to confirm its depth. "Could the chopper crash have caused this?"

She pursed her lips. "Not likely. I think we're too far away and too far under the waterline for the impact to reach down here."

"Then this has to be Josiah." Aubrey held the door open with his back as Malina stepped through. "Flood the place and hope no one can come looking for evidence until it's safe. Make your escape and go on the run. How long until the whole place is underwater?"

She shrugged. "No idea. Depends on how bad the leak is in there, why it's leaking, where it's leaking."

After verifying the two small rooms off the hallway were clear, Aubrey moved to the next set of double doors with Malina close behind him. Peering through the narrow pane of glass, Aubrey took in the space beyond. It was darker than the hallway he stood in, but several flickering lights from a far corner gave him the impression of a large open room wider than it was deep.

"Seems like the building broadens here," he whispered.

"It does. The corridor we came down is really just a glorified tunnel." She scratched her head and said in a low voice, "There should be one large, wide room on the other side. Most of the old equipment used to be in there. Some of it may still be. That way to the left were rows of huge server stacks. At the other end of the room was a workstation." Raising her head, she eyed Aubrey. Even in the dark, he saw focus etched into her face like the look of a desert fox who'd spotted a tiny mouse out in the open. "Like I said, most of it should be empty space."

"Sounds like your research into this place was pretty comprehensive," Aubrey said. "Seems like the Colektive's plan to hack the grid went beyond the idea phase."

Malina didn't respond.

Aubrey nodded and squinted through the darkness into the room beyond the doors. Scanning left and right, it was too dark to make out the edges of the space. He shut his eyes and tried to imagine what it must look like based on Malina's recollection. He visualized his next steps, his next moves, where Josiah must be inside there. His best guess was at the far end past the old servers at the workstation.

He crouched below the bottom edge of the window and beckoned Malina to join him. He tapped the side of his pistol twice and a narrow beam shot from a flashlight under the barrel. "Okay, here's what we're going to do."

A slam made him jump.

"Help," came a weak voice from the other side of the door. It was a man whimpering. "Please."

Aubrey shot to his feet, careful not to move in front of the glass. He flicked off the gun's flashlight and turned his head just enough to catch sight of a pale form pressed against the window. It was a wet dripping hand, rivulets running down the glass. Dark smudges on the palm and fingers, not enough light to tell what, but Aubrey's first thought was that it must be blood.

He raised the pistol and pointed it at the glass without uncovering the light. A visual check to Malina who mouthed, "Wait."

He waited. One second. Then two. On ten, the person on the other side said, "Please. I know you're over there." A hacking cough. "We're gonna die in here … it's … it's flooding. He flooded it, then he left us. Please help." The voice pleaded. "For the love of god." More coughing came, then a long groan of frustration. "I'm gonna freeze to death in here, and I can't pull the door open against the w-water. Please, you have to help us."

"Us?" Malina whispered. An incredulous look spread across her face.

Aubrey uncovered the flashlight and shined it through the window slit. From the pale hand trailed a skinny arm with milk-white flesh covered in goose pimples. The face that greeted him as Aubrey moved to his right was drawn, tired, and gray with the red splotches covering its cheeks. A quick scan with his light, and Aubrey saw the man was nude. He also confirmed that the water was high, already almost to the man's knees.

Aubrey grasped the handle, put his shoulder against the door, and pushed. It wouldn't budge.

"You'll have to pull while I push," he yelled through the glass. The man nodded and appeared to brace one foot against the opposite door.

Together, they pushed and pulled until a crack emerged. Water rushed him, nearly taking out his footing. Malina pressed her back against the wall and gasped at the chill. Aubrey felt it too. The water was frigid, pins and needles stinging his lower legs.

He held the door open six inches for a moment and allowed the water to flood the room. He hoped to avoid a deluge that might bring them both down, soaking them and further complicating things.

"The other doors," he nodded toward the set at the other end of the hallway. "Open them."

"Are you sure? Won't it flood the rest of the building?" she said, looking hesitantly down at the quickly rising pool.

"Those doors open in, toward us. If this room fills up, we'll never be able to get them open."

Malina nodded and began wading through the ice-cold water to the other end of the hallway.

The weight against the door lessened as water poured through and began to equalize the two rooms. As soon as he saw Malina opening her exit, he added pressure with his shoulder, and the gap in the door grew along with the speed of the deluge filling the hall.

Soon, Aubrey was freezing, teeth chattering in his skull, water almost to his knees. When the door was open a foot, the thin man snaked through the gap, falling as he did so. He splashed for a moment, flailing in a near panic before he stood, white and scrawny, and collapsed against the bulkhead. He hugged himself tight. His breath came in quick bursts, his ribs stretching colorless skin that was stark against the low light of the corridor. His long, light-colored hair had plastered to his cheeks and neck.

Aubrey held his door open while he watched Malina jam the exit ajar then wade quickly to the man.

"Who else is in there?" She stood in front of his hunched form with her arms outstretched but not touching him. Her hands hovered over his shoulders as if touching him would make him shatter like an egg hitting the floor. "Are you sure your kidnapper isn't—"

"No one in-in there," he said with his eyes down. His teeth chattered wildly. "He's gone. Ha-has been for a day at least."

"You said 'us,'" Malina tilted her head. "You said, 'help us.'"

"Dead." His voice was like a hammer hitting a nail. "He killed them. Left me for dead. That maniac psycho piece of sh-shit." Saliva dribbled from his trembling purple lips. "Get me out of here, please. I'm f-f-fucking freezing."

Aubrey examined the man while Malina plied him for more information.

"Who did this to you?"

His porcelain skin had a softness to it, almost puffy with lack of wear. Although he was thin, his skin was flabby, his breasts sagged, and his arms appeared to have never held anything close to a toned appearance in their existence. No scars from what Aubrey could see, nearly no imperfections at all. He could have been a specimen, forever preserved in suspended animation and only recently extricated.

"I don't know who he was," the man said. "Some nutjob. He tortured us. Made us … made us do th-things for him." Tremors seized his entire body, but Aubrey was unsure whether it was from the cold, fear, anger, or all three.

"Was his name Josiah?" Malina asked.

Aubrey thought he saw the man's eye tic at the mention of the name.

"I don't know who he was."

"Did he talk about religion ever? Did he say he did it for

religious reasons?" Malina leaned in closer.

The man glanced up at her with eyes like saucers. His head twitched. "Yeah. All the time. Always."

Malina and Aubrey nodded to one another as the water reached Aubrey's thighs and his shivering became more pronounced. He had to act quickly.

"I'm going in."

Malina shot him a look, but before she could say anything, he held up a flat hand, "Just get him out of here, I'm going to take a look around inside for a few minutes." When her look of concern didn't fade, he said, "Just a few minutes, I promise. And don't worry, I'm an excellent swimmer."

She bent to lift the freed captive to his feet. Aubrey reached under his coat and detached the pistol's holster from its straps. He then pushed the door wider and jammed the nylon composite holster in the jamb over the top hinge.

"Wait," Aubrey said, turning to Malina and the man wading up the corridor. "What's your name?"

With his arm over Malina's shoulders, he craned to face Aubrey. "Acer. But everyone knows me as Ambrosia."

"Jesus," Malina said. "Ambrosia, it's me Malina—I mean Malrey. From the Colektive."

With a frozen face, Ambrosia said, "Oh my god, Malrey. I can't believe it's you. Can we get out of here now?"

"Yes, of course, let's go." She placed a hand on his back, and they left through the propped door at the end of the hallway.

29

In the Dark

"Damn it," Francesca growled as Malina killed the call. She looked at the device. The display on the phone had blinked back to the idle screen. "Damn it."

For the first time in years, she felt her emotions overtaking her. She'd found him. She'd found Hank. He was within reach, but something was wrong. Why were Aubrey and Malina looking for him? Reverend Yates told her all he knew—Aubrey and Malina came looking for a man named Josiah Palmero, born Hank Green, her brother. Yates explained that Josiah had grown more and more extreme over the years, especially since his mother, Wendy, died not long ago. He'd been leading groups of young people in discussions about the need for Praeceptists to become more active in converting nonbelievers to their way of thinking. Yates said there were rumors that Josiah suggested violent means to "wake up" the people of other faiths.

Francesca had never heard of the other person Aubrey and Malina had been looking for, Acer Sapindales. She didn't care who he was unless he was trying to hurt Hank or put him in a position to be hurt.

"Damn it," she shouted again. Passersby gave her sideways glances.

Francesca had pushed her assignment from the Member Principal to extremes to achieve her personal goal of finding Hank. Now, the assignment was over, and she was expected to return to the prison. But Hank was clearly in some kind of trouble. Worse yet, he could be in danger, but she had no idea from what.

The anger, confusion, and fear swirled inside her to create a toxic mix that would drive her to make unwise decisions if she weren't very careful. She squeezed her eyes shut, inhaled deeply, and held it. Only when her body screamed for oxygen did she release the breath and take another, repeating the exercise several times until her mind felt clearer.

She mentally divided her concerns down to one priority: find Hank. How? She'd first have to find Martin Aubrey and Malina Maddox. She'd tried that and failed. What next? Answer: find someone who can get her to Martin Aubrey and Malina Maddox.

After a moment, the answer came to her—the phone. Malina gave her the phone along with the tablet to help Francesca in the search for Hank. She told Francesca that the phone had several contacts saved on it who could help Francesca if she needed it when Malina wasn't around.

She extracted the phone from her pocket and tapped the contacts list. There were about a dozen names on it, most she didn't recognize, but there was one she did. Liz Reynolds was a high-ranking officer in the city's police department. She tapped the name and held the phone to her ear. The line rang three times before Reynolds picked up.

"Reynolds."

"Detective Reynolds, my name is Francesca. I'm a friend of Martin Aubrey, and I need to find him." Francesca felt it was best to get to the point quickly.

A pause, then Reynolds said, "Francesca? The Ta … from the Order?"

"Yes, that's me, Detective."

"You were with Martin and Malina at the prison. During the riots."

Francesca realized how insulated she was from the affairs of the rest of society. Of course, Aubrey and Malina would have had to give detailed accounts of what happened during the riots, and they would have mentioned her and Rudolfo. As a member of law enforcement, Liz Reynolds would have no doubt heard the stories if she hadn't taken their statements personally.

"Yes, I was with them." Francesca didn't have time to embellish. "Can you help me find them? It's very important."

Two minutes later, she slid the phone back into her pocket. Liz had explained that Aubrey and Malina were in fact looking for Josiah Palmero and thought they'd found him. Along with her two friends, a good portion of the police department was busy searching for him too. Yates was right, Hank was in trouble. Liz, Aubrey, and Malina suspected he was the one causing the mayhem throughout the city, and if she was honest with herself, their case against him seemed logical.

Reynolds told her that Aubrey and Malina thought there was a chance Hank would be at the hydroelectric power station. Guilty or not, Hank was the only family she had, and she would help him if she could. The phone's map told her the power station was a short car ride from her location near the church, but Reynolds had explained the dangerous car malfunctions occurring throughout the city. She would never find a hired car. She had to go by foot. If she ran, she could be there in an hour, maybe less.

* * *

Aubrey double-tapped the button on the side of the pistol's flashlight to widen the beam. With two hands on the weapon, he held it forward of center mass, pivoting his body and the gun as one when he turned.

The room he entered was cavernous, larger than he'd expected based on Malina's description. It was a single room, no divisions as such just like she'd told him, but the frames for the old server stacks were almost eight feet high, with standing room between them and the ceiling. Their breadth and depth was such that they segmented the space like stacks at a library, at least ten rows, two abreast with a wide center aisle.

Down one side of the room to Aubrey's immediate left was a pathway between the wall and the frames. Shining his flashlight beam down the wall, he saw what looked to be the end of the room in the form of a pale, seafoam green concrete wall seventy-five to ninety feet away. Immediately in front of him, across from the double doors where he stood, were four bulbous square shapes, as tall as he was and twice as wide. He figured them to be the antiquated equipment Malina spoke of.

With a painful shock, the water reached his groin. A moment ago, his legs lost all feeling, and he had the luxury of forgetting just how cold the water was. He was reminded with electric pins firing into his midsection, accelerating his muscle spasms and intensifying his chattering teeth.

"Hello," he shouted into the darkness. He waited and heard nothing but a steady stream of water entering from somewhere across the room.

A splash near the far wall.

"Hello," he shouted again. "Anyone there?"

Without waiting for a reply, he moved further into the room. He calculated that at the water's current flow rate, he had ten minutes before he was submerged. Another five or ten minutes for the room to fill. But he'd only need five minutes to get to the far wall, verify no one was left alive and get out.

All that assumed he didn't get hypothermia and pass out first.

Another splash from the same general vicinity as the last. And something else. It was hard to tell over the noise of the water and the vastness of the room, but it sounded like a muffled grinding of some kind.

He waded along the wall, checking each walkway between the old server frames with his pistol's light as he passed. He moved as fast as his legs would allow him without compromising his balance. Three rows of servers in, and he pressed his back against the cold wall, leaning his weight on it to steady himself. In this way, he slid sideways down the length of the room.

Just past row six, he shouted once more. "Hello? I'm here to help."

Another splash, and the same strange noise, but it was clearer now that he drew closer. He knew in an instant what it must be, and it sent a jolt down his nerves.

It was a voice. Shouting through a cloth or a gag.

He abandoned caution and half ran, half swam toward the end of the line of tall frames.

"Hang in there. I'm coming!"

The muffled cries grew louder, but when he rounded the corner of the tenth and last server stack frame, he saw nothing, no one. He whipped his light in a sweeping arc, the circle of light passing over a couple of keyboards floating near the wall to his left, a set of large monitors hanging on the same wall, the tops of chairs bobbing up and down with the rise of the dark water, and some books floating here and there.

His breath caught.

A face in the water. It barely broke the surface. The eyes were wide, staring up at the ceiling, black tape wrapped around the mouth. The person was halfway across the room, about twenty feet away.

Aubrey threw himself forward, splashing, running, swimming to reach the face that now issued a blood-chilling choked scream. The edges of the oval of water that surrounded the nose and eyes began to crest and close. The face would be fully submerged in seconds.

He lunged the last few feet, thrust his hands under the water and grabbed for the person's armpits. His fingers crashed into metal and after a second of blind fumbling, he realized it was the back of a chair. Confusion, then immediate understanding hit him.

The person was bound to the chair.

Through the water, he caught sight of the steel surface of a long table against the wall. Half a foot of water lapped across its surface. Without thinking, he dropped into the water next to the chair and spun it so its back faced the edge of the table. He pushed the chair until it slammed into the table, gripped both sides of the seat's frame, and lifted the chair in one fluid motion.

The chair, the person tied to it, and Aubrey's torso broke the surface in a burst of spray. While lifting, he flung his weight forward, and the chair's back ground the table's edge for a split second before its angle flattened, and it slid forward onto the flat tabletop. Aubrey whipped out his pistol and shined the light on the figure now coughing and sputtering water from their lungs.

His heart sank. He knew the man. "Champ?"

Champ's eyes widened, but he was still gagged. He was also zip-tied and duct-taped to the chair, and like Ambrosia, he was nude. Unlike Ambrosia, this man bore the marks of extensive abuse and torture. His arms and legs were lined with ligature marks and deep bruising. His biceps and shoulders showed wounds similar to those of Drillard, puckered and small round punctures.

Aubrey tore away the tape around Champ's mouth.

A coughing fit seized him. When he could speak, he said, "Martin, please get me out of this thing."

Aubrey drew a small pocketknife from his pants pocket and started cutting the man's bindings. "What the hell happened? How did you get here?" He worked the blade through the zip ties first, then the tape around the man's midsection and thighs.

"I'm not sure. I was drugged for most of the time." Champ rubbed his freed wrists gingerly. "Some guy, youngish, white. Crazy about his religion. Forced us … he forced us … to …" Champ's voice broke.

"It's okay. There wasn't anything you could do." Aubrey bent close to Champ's face. "Listen, there will be plenty of time for unnecessary guilt trips. But right now, we need to get you out of these bindings and then get the hell out of here."

When Aubrey cut through the last binding, he helped Champ to a seated position on the edge of the table. When he touched the man's back, he winced shrilly. It was then Aubrey noticed the extent of his torture. Long gouges had been cut along either side of his spine. The volcano like puncture wounds seemed to be every few inches between his shoulders and his waist. Dried blood and puss caked the unaffected areas.

Aubrey swallowed his revulsion. "Can you walk?"

Champ shrugged. "Yeah, I think so. Still a little woozy." He stretched out each leg, and they visibly shook.

Already nearly frozen, Aubrey looked down. The water now touched his ribs.

"We need to get out of here right now." He examined the space, taking in the area in more detail than he did a moment ago. The water covered everything. The only thing visible now were the tops of the old server stacks, a few feet of which still protruded over the water's surface.

"Is anyone else down here?"

"No." Champ rubbed his upper arms. He was shivering violently. "No one a-alive anyway."

Aubrey had more questions, but there would be a time for that later. "Okay, let's go." He pulled Champ's arm over his shoulder and helped him slide off the table into the nearly chest-high water. "We may have to swim for it soon."

They walked in tandem through the quickly filling room, random items floating around them occasionally bumping into their sides—books, papers, boxes, plastic bags. They were near the center row of server stacks when Aubrey asked,

"Where is the water coming from?"

"That was one of the f-few things he did on his own."

"Who? Josiah Palmero? He was the one that kidnapped you." Aubrey said the last sentence as more of a statement than a question.

Champ's chills forced his words out in chopped syllables. "D-don't know who he was."

"Religious, baby-faced guy. An extremist. Sound like him?"

Champ sputtered breath from his lungs. "Sounds right. Not … n-not sure about baby-faced part, but th-the rest is true." A harsh shiver overtook Champ for a second, then he continued, "B-b-but I watched him work the computer, and I think he … he shut down the pumps and forced the safeguard system to rupture a seal around the main power trunk. That's when I knew where we were. I'd had a hunch be-f-fore, but that confirmed it for me."

"How'd you know where you were just from seeing him shut down the pumps?"

The sound of the water filling the room seemed like was coming from somewhere to their left. He fished out his pistol with one hand and traced the beam of light along the ceiling. An enormous pipe, easily six feet across, ran across the room and into the wall to the right.

Champ saw it too. "That's the main power trunk. Splits into smaller conduit lines in the next couple of rooms. The seal is over there on the other side of that … wall." Champ gestured with his chin. "How'd I know where I was? Long story. I just knew."

That last comment poked annoyingly at Aubrey. Something about it stuck him like a needle, something he should pay attention to, but the cold slowed his mind while also stiffening his muscles and limbs. Plus there was the real possibility that he could be swallowed up by the infiltrating Chesapeake Bay.

Champ winced as he caught sight of something floating nearby. Aubrey saw it too, off to their right just several feet away. He shined his light in that direction and saw the marred back of a white corpse bobbing in the darkness. The body was nude and emaciated. Lines of ribs were clearly visible between small red craters similar to Champ's and Drillard's.

"Another captive?" Aubrey asked, shifting his weight and urging Champ to keep moving. The man slumped, pulling Aubrey down briefly before he could correct their fall. Champ's eyes had closed, and his head fell to one side. Shock had clearly begun to sink into the poor man. Aubrey knew he had to keep him talking, keep him occupied and moving, or he'd be dead weight.

"Hey, Champ, stay with me. Talk to me, did you know that guy?"

His eyes fluttered open, and he nodded weakly. "Yeah, he was ... he was the other prisoner."

"Do you know who he was?" Aubrey asked.

They were approaching the last row of server stacks. The icy embrace of the water gripping tightly around his chest. His feet were boulders. He wasn't so much walking as he was bounding through the water, attempting to spring off his back foot to propel the two of them forward. Champ came closer and closer to floating horizontal with each step of progress.

"Before all this, did ... did you know him?" said Aubrey.

After a fit of intense chills, Champ nodded again. "I ... I don't know. The ... the guy called him Elton once. I worked with somebody by th-that name. Guy k-k-killed him before he ran off." Champ's body shook more intensely. Aubrey could hear him sobbing for several seconds. "Just me after … after that."

Another needle of recognition jabbed Aubrey's brain. "Wai- w-wait"—his lips were hardened rawhide, refusing to form words, icy tentacles reached up his shoulders and neck—"you were th-the only survivor?"

A white flash in the dark and an object floated into view. It was a long white, cigar-shaped mass with one end pointed at Aubrey and Champ. Holding his pistol at eye level above the waterline, Aubrey examined the large object and realized it was white plastic tarp wrapped around something. Then some hidden force in the water, perhaps a by-product of the two men moving or something else entirely unseen, turned the object. The tip of a brown shoe peeked out of the plastic wrapping, corking up and down. Another corpse.

On instinct, Aubrey reached out and took hold of the toe of the shoe and pulled it toward them. He stuck the pistol in the crook of his neck and held it there with his chin, the light still playing on the body in the water. He pulled out his pocket knife and needing both hands to do the work, he let go of Champ. Pinching the plastic with his left hand, Aubrey cut a slit a foot long then tore at the sheeting from both sides of the cut.

The smell kicked him like a Clydesdale. Clearly, several days of decay had been enveloped in the wrapping waiting to escape. When he could breathe again, he peered closer at the body. The chest and neck were exposed. The victim wore a blue cotton shirt with white buttons, navy-blue suspenders, and a white undershirt. Bruising across the Adam's apple told Aubrey the cause of death—strangulation, most likely by hand.

The body was chin level now, half in and half out of the water like a canoe taking on ballast. Aubrey pushed down on the corpse's shoulder to get a better angle. Over the hump of the belly of the dead man he could see the exit, yellow ambient light pouring through the open door, so much brighter now that he'd been in near darkness for several minutes.

A glint of gold caught his eye. He pulled at a thin chain around the neck until a pendant slid from under the white T-shirt. The small object shined brightly in the beam from his flashlight. It was a cross. Around the center wound three concentric circles.

It was a Praeceptist cross.

Yanking back the white sheeting to reveal the face, a white-hot flame lit inside him. Although distended from bloating and decay, the soft, schoolboy face of Josiah Palmero was easy to make out. It was nearly identical to the girl's drawing of him on the back of *The Book of Josiah*.

Josiah, dead for days, down in the bowels of the power station, wasn't alive for the car fires on the street that day, nor the tunnel, nor the drones, not even the bridge.

Malina was in danger.

"Move. Now." He hefted Champ's bulk forward. "We have to get out of here. Malina's in trouble."

Ahead of them, the square of dim light from the door, his and Champ's means of escape, their path to dry land and warm air, started shrinking. It became a thin rectangle, then a sliver, a hair, then the light vanished entirely.

30

No Escape

"Get on top of that server stack." Aubrey pointed behind them. Reacting to Champ's sudden look of trepidation, he said, "I'll come back for you, don't worry. I just have to see if that door is shut, and you need to get out of this water right now."

He pushed the body of Josiah Palmero aside and flung himself forward, hoping to catch the door before it sealed home while knowing it was probably already too late. He reached out clawing at the water, urging himself forward. He dove under the surface, contracting and kicking his legs furiously, stroking his arms in long arcs through cold blackness.

Seconds later, the middle finger of his right hand collided with the wall. Were they not so numb already, he'd have felt the sharp jab of pain shoot through his hand and up his arm.

He pressed his left hand flat, feeling the wall for any indication of how close he was to the door. With his right hand, he pulled the pistol free and activated the light. The cylinder of bright white shot through the water like a hot poker. He swung the beam to his left, and in the narrow circle of light, he saw the set of double doors. He swam toward them. Seconds later, he gripped the silver handle on the door nearest him, turned it, and pulled. With the water level on both sides of the door somewhat equal, it came away from the frame easily, but only an inch. Something blocked it, or rather, something held it closed, he could barely get his fingers through the gap.

Aubrey sprung off the floor, broke the surface, and took a deep breath. A second later, he dove again.

He tried the left-hand door. As he yanked on it, the other door, still open slightly, pulled shut. Something had been tied tightly to both of them. Holding the gap open as wide as he could manage, he chased the narrow crack with his light beam, searching for the impediment. He found it quickly. Stretched between the doors was a flat, three-inch wide yellow nylon strap, the kind used to tow a car, seemingly threaded through the push bar of each door and behind the center divider, which acted like a pulley.

His first thought was the knife. Keeping his left hand on the door, he tucked the pistol under his chin to hold it, then fished out the knife from his front pocket. He stuck the pistol in his armpit to steady it and the light on the gap. Opening the blade with his teeth, he pushed it through the tight gap and watched helplessly as the tip of the knife swung several inches short of the strap.

He pocketed the knife and leveled his pistol at the gap. He tried to steady himself, but the burning in his lungs was getting the better of him, drawing his focus, reducing his discipline to fire a well-aimed shot. The spear of light jutting out from the end of the pistol wobbled and shook. He gravely needed a breath of air.

Maybe it was his desperation to be on the other side of that door, or maybe the lack of oxygen to his brain impeded his decision-making, but as the circle of white light landed on the centerline of the strap, he took the shot. The weapon bucked in his hands like he knew it would, but the surprise to his muscles in their frozen state shocked him. Burrows of pain flew up his arm into his chest. The water turned white with tiny air bubbles, which floated quickly away in a plume like a mini explosion. Without waiting for the cloud to clear completely, he jerked the handle toward him.

No change. The gap was the same size. He'd missed the strap.

His lungs would wait no longer. His mind foggy, Aubrey surged upward, feet catapulting off the floor, his head broke the surface of the rising water that, as he settled, he realized was nearly to his chin. A bite of air, and he readied himself to plunge down once more, this time to take a more carefully aimed shot.

He threw his head back with his mouth open wide, sucking in a great gasp, then he saw her, floating on her back, chin toward the ceiling. Malina, eyes closed, lips parted, floated unconscious with her face just above the surface. Fear twisted a knife inside him, cringing his stomach and chest.

Forgetting his immediate needs, Aubrey plunged into the water, driving his body toward Malina like he was shot from a cannon. He gripped her shoulder and braced her back with his free hand, simultaneously pressing his cheek to hers, listening, feeling for signs of life. Her head rolled toward him and warm breath bathed his ear.

Relief gushed inside him fighting back the acidic fear about to consume him.

"Thank god," he whispered.

Scooping an arm under her and around her chest, he paddled backward, back toward the first server stack. He was relieved to see Champ crouched on the top of the nearest, its top still a foot out of the water.

He pumped his stiff legs, unsure how fast he propelled himself, if at all. Finally, somewhere overhead, Champ shouted, "Where did she come from?"

"Take 'er," Aubrey hissed through an unmoving jaw.

With one arm atop the rack and one under Malina, he and Champ hoisted her out of the water and onto her back. He crawled up alongside her, and his body instantly contracted in on itself of its own accord. Reflexively, he tensed his arm and leg muscles to increase blood flow while he rocked to his side to examine Malina. She still looked alive. Her mouth hung open, and the curve of her bottom lip gave him reassurance somehow, as if a dead person couldn't possibly do that.

Aubrey lifted himself to an elbow, then his knees when a spasm in his midsection caused him to double over in violent tremors. After regaining control of himself once again, he placed two fingers on Malina's neck. There was a pulse—not strong, but it was there—beating gently against the pads of his fingers.

He and Champ carefully rolled her head side to side for a quick examination and found, on her left temple, a long purple bruise.

"Malina," he said, careful not to shine his light directly in her eyes but enough so he could see her clearly. "Malina, can you hear me?"

Her eyelids fluttered momentarily, and her mouth closed and opened like a fish out of water. Comfortable with his assessment that she was just knocked out and at worse had a concussion, Aubrey focused his attention back on their imminent demise if he didn't act quickly.

He peered in the direction of the door. "The exit is strapped shut."

"It was him." Champ sat with his knees to his chest and hugged his legs.

Aubrey hadn't thought about *him* since realizing they would be trapped in a room quickly filling with water, then seeing his partner and dear friend nearly dead. But the *him* that started all this, the *him* that kidnapped Champ, Drillard, and two others, the *him* that killed countless people in the city, the *him* that the police and Aubrey were chasing was not Josiah Palmero.

It was the man Aubrey himself had just helped get to safety—Acer Sapindales, also known as Ambrosia.

He wasn't sure what Ambrosia's motives were yet, but he knew how he'd done it. He kidnapped and tortured his old friends from the cyber underworld, members of the Colektive, friends he'd never met in person but knew only from online exploits, and forced them to crack the city's AI, then used the system to wreak absolute havoc on the population.

"Yeah," Aubrey said. "It was *him*."

Ninety seconds later, Aubrey pulled himself out of the freezing water onto the edge of the tenth server rack near the workstation where he found Champ. He needed cordage, a rope, something he could stretch from the first rack to the doors. He might need Champ's help pulling the doors against the enormous weight of the water, now that it would be higher on their side, and he'd have to pull them both across that distance anyway. Champ told him to look where Aubrey rescued him for the cordage he needed, and he hopped from rack to rack to reach it.

He clenched and unclenched the muscles in his arms, leg, and core, trying to circulate warm blood through his body. In his fist, he held the end of an orange extension cord he estimated to be about fifty feet long. He coiled the cord hand over hand then slung it over his shoulders. On his feet, he again used the ten metal cabinets like stepping stones across a fast-moving stream. The water lapped at the top edges of the steel, giving the three of them only another minute or two before their island was swamped by the frigid waters.

When he landed on Malina and Champ's stack, he shined his light down on his partner. She was still out, and something in the way she breathed, quick inhalations followed by long exhalations, told him he had to hurry. Malina was fading fast. He dared not think about the effect of being dragged through near freezing water for a second time would have on her.

He dropped the extension cord, doubled it over, and tied a knot to create a large loop that he handed to Champ.

"This goes over you and Malina," Aubrey said. "If you feel me tug twice, that means I need you to pull it in toward you. I might need help getting the door open." He waited for Champ to acknowledge. Once he did, Aubrey continued, "If you feel four tugs—four—Champ, you hear me?"

Champ nodded.

"If you feel four tugs, get ready to slide into the water because I'm going to pull you and Malina to the door."

Champ repeated the instructions but kept looking at Malina as if trying to remember something.

"What? What is it, Champ? We don't have much time."

"Nothing. I just … I hope she's okay."

Aubrey paused, wishing the same. "She will be, if we hurry." He tied the other end of the extension cord around his own waist, concentrating with every ounce of cognition to make his wooden fingers tie the knot properly.

"Malcolm Reynolds."

Aubrey didn't look up from the knot taking shape, the link that would connect this lifeline to Malina ... and Champ. "What?"

"Her name. That's what *Malrey* means. She called it a clumsy portmanteau of the name Malcolm Reynolds. He was some character on a TV show from thirty or forty years ago."

"Sounds good," Aubrey said, only just registering Champ's words. "When you feel me tug four times—that's four times, Champ—you grab Malina under her armpits, scoot to the edge of the stack, and slide in. I'll wait fifteen seconds and pull you both toward me. Got it?"

"Got it," Champ said. His eyes told Aubrey he'd do whatever he had to do to get their mutual friend to safety.

Aubrey did an about-face and threw the coil of cord ahead and to the left. Watching it fall into the water and feeling confident it wouldn't tangle in its current state, he bent at the waist, thrust his arms forward, and dove straight into the inky, bitter blackness. It enveloped him as his hands pierced its surface. He kept the lifeless image of Malina at the front of his mind, using it as a beacon to keep him focused and sharp as far as he was able.

He reached the door quicker than the last time, thanks to the momentum after the headfirst dive. Pistol in hand, he squared himself with the center post dividing the two sides of the doorframe. Being a right-handed shooter, he pulled the left door as far out as he could and shined the light through the narrow slit. The strap was there, but it looked different now. A rough notch, frayed all to hell, stretched a half-inch from the bottom edge. His first shot hadn't missed, it had been just a bit low. Remembering his mistake from last time, he let himself float to the surface, took a deep breath, and plunged again, using his outstretched arms like wings, flapping in reverse to push his body down.

Once again, he stared down the strap, one foot away, taunting him. And once again, with one hand holding the door open and one hand holding the pistol, the light beam that was his de facto aiming mechanism bounced and swayed as he moved around with the motions of the water and the energy generated by his own body. He couldn't trust himself to take the shot. Even with all the bullets in the world, he just didn't have the time. Malina didn't have the time.

His body's own buoyancy was the problem. He'd filled his lungs with so much air that he couldn't keep himself level long enough to take a well-aimed shot.

He planted his right foot on the other door and jerked hard on the left. He then jammed the tip of his left foot into the gap as low and far in as he could until it was good and stuck.

Now, he had an anchor, and the gap would stay open. With two hands on the pistol, he steadied himself. He centered the circle of white light on the strap, just above the notch he'd already made. He figured he'd need two shots but didn't know if he had time for the water to clear of air and gas after the first shot to get a good aim on the second. He'd have to guess.

He pulled the trigger. The recoil threw the pistol back, his wrists absorbing most of the shock. No change in the pressure of the door against his foot.

He closed his eyes, tried to remember the exact position of his hands, fingers, wrists, and arms from the first shot.

He fired the pistol.

Nothing happened. Everything felt the same. He opened his eyes and the water was a circus of air bubbles dancing to the surface. The door and the gap weren't clearly visible. He pulled on the door.

It wouldn't move. He jammed the pistol into the waistband of his pants and repositioned his right foot. With both hands, he gripped the handle, planted both feet, arched his back, and yanked with the small amount of strength he had left. Lungs, arms, legs—all burning.

Five seconds of pulling, then ten seconds, and still nothing happened. He relaxed his legs a little, ready to give it one last jerk. A brief pause of two seconds, then with an explosion of force in his legs, he rammed his body outward.

With a bump and snap, the door flew toward him, and he was sucked into the corridor beyond with a deluge of water.

31

Reaching

For a moment, Aubrey thought he'd be swept away down the corridor, unable to return to rescue his friends. But he managed to hold on and brace the door long enough for the level inside the corridor to equalize with that of the server room. Soon, the rush of water slowed, then stopped.

Disoriented, he released the door and kicked his legs in the direction of the ceiling and air.

Breaking the surface, he was met with blunt force to the top of his head. Stars danced across his retinas, and warmth blossomed on his scalp. Confused, he dropped in the water and shined his light upward only to find the ceiling an inch or two above the water.

He chastised himself for not thinking of it before. The corridor's ceiling was much lower than that of the server room. He tilted his head back and floated up once more, slowly this time, using his hands against the ceiling to gauge the distance. When he felt his nose touch the hard concrete, he opened his mouth and sucked in all the air he could hold, then he pushed off and dove down and into the door into the server room. After making sure he had a clear line and no obstructions, he pulled on the extension cord to take up any slack and gave it four strong tugs.

Fifteen seconds. That's how much time he had before Champ slid into the water with Malina.

Aubrey needed more air. He started counting in his head as he floated to the surface. His head clear of the water, he continued counting to himself. At twelve seconds, he heard a splash from the direction of the server stack.

"Okay," Champ's voice called from the dark. "If you can hear me, we're ready. Both of us."

Aubrey started pulling on the cord and quickly realized he wasn't pulling them in, he was pulling himself out. He was three feet away from the wall when he discovered his mistake. He'd need to brace himself. He needed leverage.

Aubrey dropped the cord and swam down in through the double doors, spun around, and anchored one foot on the wall and one on the metal divider. He reeled in the slack and after a few seconds, it went taut, the weight of his partner and her friend bearing down on it.

Hand over hand, he heaved the line in. A moment passed with his arms desperately wanting to seize up and quit. A moment more and his lungs caught fire. His movements went sluggish, they became gelatin around him. The water grew darker.

In some corner of his drunken brain, he perceived that the cord was at a steep angle, indicating the two were quite near.

His hand slipped on the cord. Or did it? His hands were malfunctioning, a glitch in their circuitry, unable to close. He felt sure this time that his hand slid along the cord but couldn't grip it. The cord wriggled, went limp, fell from his hands. Shocked into clarity, he thrashed wildly for it, the bottom edge of his left hand struck something and he reached for it. It was the lifeline.

Not trusting his finger muscles to cooperate, he swirled his arms in a circle to wrap the cord around them, adjusted his grip, and with a sudden surge of lucidity and strength, he rocketed himself off the wall. The line came with him for five feet, he guessed, then stopped dead, the recoil pulling him back toward the door. He kicked his legs, but he was like a dying frog flapping pointlessly in the bottom of a pail—without air, without strength, without hope. All he had left was will. Will drove his legs to bend and straighten, bend and straighten—as long as he had synapses firing in his brain—bend and straighten.

It was working. Somewhere deep in his mind, he picked up on the fact that he was moving again. Moving fast. Something pressed against his face.

The floor? The ceiling?

No, too soft.

Was he flying? Did he get outside somehow?

No. Something had him. Someone had him.

He was jostled. He was twisted and rolled. Lights too bright glowed red through his eyelids. Crippling pain, too much to bear. Seconds ticked by, and the pain turned to tremors, then shivers. Sounds came to him—his own breathing, coughing, wheezing, and gurgling.

More sounds. Someone speaking.

"Martin?"

Someone he knew. Malina. His partner and friend.

"Martin? Answer me, Marty."

Tingling spread across his cheeks. Heat against his frozen

flesh. Hands on his face.

He broke an eyelid open, the light was too strong for both eyes. Through the blur, he made out Malina's soft face and short hair flattened to her scalp, her purplish lips and water dripping down her nose.

"Malrey, my hero." He grinned. She smiled back at him but shook her head in obviously feigned consternation. "You okay?"

"Fine." Her face went somber. "Alive. Thanks to you."

Moments later, he sat on the floor warming himself slowly. From the cabinet outside the short corridor, they'd found a package of large absorbent pads, the kind used to soak up industrial spills, still in their packaging. Though the cabinet itself was almost totally underwater, Champ had procured a dozen packages of the pads before meeting Aubrey and Malina beyond the steadily rising waterline in the hallway.

Aubrey sat with several absorbent pads wrapped around him. The cold in his torso and upper limbs faded quickly, fueled mostly by adrenaline and anger. As the cold dissipated, his senses came back to him, slowly at first, then in a downpour.

"We have to go." He tried to stand up, but Malina put a hand on his shoulder. "He's going to get away."

"He's gone," she said. "I already checked." Pointing down the hallway, she continued, "He must have crawled through the wreckage like we did. No idea where he went after that."

Aubrey exhaled with defeat. He peered at Champ sitting with his back to the wall and eyes closed. White cottony pads were wrapped around his waist and shoulders. The man looked exhausted but otherwise fine.

"What happened?" Aubrey asked Malina, who was standing

next to him. "What did he do to you?"

She blew out a breath and adjusted the pad over her shoulders. "We came out of the second set of doors, and he went for those cabinets. He found a key somewhere on top of them, which should have been a big freaking clue, but …" She groaned and sank down next to him. "Anyway, he threw on a set of coveralls, and right when I was about to ask him how he knew they were in there, he turned and took a swing at me."

Aubrey used his thumb and forefinger to gently pinched her chin. He turned her head sideways until he saw the deep purple mark on her temple. Fresh blood oozed from it, soaking her dark hair.

"Yeah, that was him, but he didn't get me with the first shot. We went back and forth for a minute before he got the better of me. Pretty sure it'll be a while before he sits comfortably." Her grin returned, this time filled with mirth.

"Then I guess he threw me in the water back there," she said, gesturing to the server room. "He locked the doors behind him. You found me. And I woke up while you were pulling us across. I freaked out for a minute, but Champ calmed me down. We got to the inner doors, found you, and between the two of us, we were able to swim the rest of the way with you." She turned toward her old hacker friend for a moment before facing Aubrey. "He's really beat up, but he pulled through when we needed him."

Aubrey closed his eyes. A tsunami of exhaustion hit him.

"When I went up there," Malina said, "I heard sirens. Paramedics are here, and cops are close."

"I can't believe that piece of shit got away with it." Aubrey could feel the desperate need for sleep flooding his core.

"There's no way we can catch him." His breathing was heavy; he couldn't fight the tired anymore.

"I'm sorry, partner. You may be right." Malina's hand patted his knee.

"Boss," he said.

"What?"

"I'm your boss. You called me partner." Aubrey chuckled quietly.

Malina joined in laughing with him, then still smiling, she said, "Fuck off, Martin."

They allowed the moment of levity to linger a while longer. Aubrey was relieved the three of them made it out with their lives, if not their pride, intact. His body felt like he'd been run through a juicer and then cobbled back together by a toddler. He wanted a hot drink, a warm bed, and many hours of sleep.

A fit of coughing caught him off guard. His body heaved with each rough exhalation. His pharynx and larynx rattled behind his tongue, and his chest burned with the effort. The spell passed, and after a couple of deep breaths, he opened his eyes. Malina still by his side, glaring at him with concern, to which he tried to reassure her with a complacent smile. It was just another day, nothing to worry about. Across from them, Champ seemed to be feeling marginally better—he no longer shivered violently, and his eyes appeared sharper, more alert, darting back toward the server room every few seconds, as if waiting for a monster to awaken and drag them all back to their watery doom.

Aubrey stretched his neck side to side as far as he was able and stared up the hallway back toward the chopper crash. It sloped steadily upward some fifty yards before it crested at something near water level, then less dramatically so back onto land.

Everything appeared unmolested—the twelve-inch conduit lines along the bulkhead, the maintenance pedestals with their touchscreen diagnostics panels. He concluded that Ambrosia made a clean getaway, and finding a guy like him with a good head start would be near on impossible.

He was about to ask Malina a question when something caught his eye.

"What is that?" He pointed at the nearest maintenance pedestal, twenty feet away. The thing in question wasn't the pedestal itself or the touchscreen unit; it was something protruding from the edge of the touchscreen—a small blue box no bigger than a tube of lipstick. He didn't recall seeing one like it on any of the other maintenance terminals.

Malina followed Aubrey's finger. "What? The terminal? I told you, they use them to check the conduit lines. They all do the same thing, but I guess when they built this place they figured—"

"No, not the terminal." He rose to his feet. The white pads fell to the floor, and a rush of air chilled him to his bones. He stalked shakily to the terminal, Malina close behind. "That." He pointed at the tiny box, which appeared completely innocuous.

Malina plucked the device from the side of the terminal and turned it over in her fingers. It was a blue rectangular block with no markings, and no breaks in the casing. It was clear something was encapsulated inside it. "If it weren't attached to a computer terminal, I'd say it was a hunk of worthless plastic. But I actually think it might be a—"

"Wireless C&C." Champ had sidled up beside them, two absorbent pads tied around his waist and one across his back.

He gingerly took the strange device from Malina to examine it. "Is that what you were thinking?"

"Yeah," she replied.

"Someone going to clue me in here?" Aubrey asked with a touch of impatience.

Malina explained. "It's a wireless command and control port. You use it to interface between a device you control and a piece of hardware that doesn't have a physical way to connect to it." She felt the edge of the terminal and underneath, searching for something. "These computers don't have a way to plug into them, and they're on a closed network. So this thing acts like a wireless version of a CAT30 line or an FNG 5 cable."

"Uh huh," Aubrey nodded. "And it wasn't here a few minutes ago, so …" Aubrey let the pause hang, allowing the two hackers to fill in the rest.

"Yes, it could have been Ambrosia, but it's possible we just missed it the first time, Marty. Maybe it's always been here."

Aubrey shook his head, but the effort made him dizzy, and he had to rest one hand on the terminal to hold himself up. "I would have seen it. It's identical to all the others, so it would have stood out just like it did when I saw it a minute ago."

"I can check," Champ said. He held out a hand toward Malina's bag laying against the wall. "May I?"

She planted a hand to her forehead. "The cops will be here any second," she protested. "We should just hand it over to them. We're overstepping again."

Aubrey and Champ exchanged a quick look. "Of course, we're overstepping, but we may not have time to wait for them to get here." He gave her a pleading look. "Let's just see why Ambrosia used this thing. Knowing what he did might give us a clue where he went. We'll turn it all over to them when they get here."

She bent her head to the ceiling and sighed slowly. "I'll get it." She went to her bag and removed a tablet. After wiping away most of the water, she allowed the biometric reader to scan her eye and roughly handed the device over to Champ.

He replaced the C&C port on the terminal's edge, sat down cross-legged, and quickly went to work on Malina's tablet, typing, scrolling, and tapping.

Aubrey took a peek after a moment and saw a black screen subdivided into quadrants, each with minuscule lines of green, orange, and white lines of code. He looked away, a headache taking up residence inside his skull. He stepped back to the wall, leaned against it, and allowed himself to slide to the floor. He sat there with his eyes closed for several minutes and began to wonder how long it might take to figure out what Ambrosia had done when Champ broke the silence.

"Damn sure was him," the hacker said.

Aubrey's eyes flew open. "Ambrosia?" He moved to sit next to Champ.

"Yes. He must have cracked this terminal after he locked us all in the server room." Champ squinted at the screen, reading the tiny lines of code. "Looks like he used this terminal to access the Trojan horse he used to infect the city's AI, then hacked the power station's internal server, through which he connected to the internet. Makes sense why he used this place as opposed to—"

"What did he do?" Aubrey cut him off.

"Oh, right, yeah." Champ continued reading. "He executed a few commands to infiltrate the AI's flight coordinator and rerouted a casualty evacuation drone to come here." Champ rubbed his chin. "But it only stayed for a few minutes, then disappeared."

"Shit," Aubrey and Malina said simultaneously.

"Ambrosia's in the goddamn drone," she said.

Aubrey rubbed his chin. "He won't get far. We can—"

"What the fuck?" Champ's eyes were saucers as he spoke. For a moment, he didn't move, then he slowly handed the tablet to Malina. "Look at that block of code."

Her eyes scanned the section where he pointed. She scrolled up and down with her finger several times. "What does the switch do?"

This piqued Aubrey's attention. "What switch?"

Champ ignored Aubrey's question and addressed Malina. "Right after I woke up in there," he nodded toward the server room, "when he made me start … working, I reviewed some of the stuff Elton, or Reggie, coded and the commands he executed. Most of it made sense, as far as how Ambrosia would use it to hurt people. But there was one thing I didn't understand. He made Reggie reroute a bunch of sewer pipes and storm drains and some other stuff I didn't fully get. Then, he made Reggie crack a chemical plant just outside the city. He installed a trojan horse in their operating system but didn't do anything with it."

"Oh, shit." Malina stared blankly at the tablet like she was staring through it. "Oh, shit," she repeated in a whisper.

Aubrey felt his face turn hot. "What, Malina? Tell me."

She turned slowly. "He's going to gas the city."

"What?"

"She's right," Champ said.

"How?"

Malina didn't answer him. Instead, she frantically scrolled

on the tablet, tapping here and there, speed reading the whole time. A few seconds passed and she said, "He's going to move chemicals from the plant into the sewers under the city. He's emptied the main sewer trunk underground and he's going to fill it with hazardous chemicals."

Aubrey could imagine the risk that dangerous chemicals posed for the population of a crowded city, but he didn't understand one thing. "The chemicals will be underground. How is that going to poison anyone? Maybe if he got it into the water supply, but that's still—"

"Not the chemicals themselves," Malina barked, still scrolling and reading lines of code on the tablet. "It'll be the fumes. He's programmed the valves and gates in thousands of storm drains to flow backwards, up toward the street. A liquid can't travel upward on its own, but a gas could. Once the chemicals are in the main sewer trunk in the center of the city, all the gases they produce will be vented through the pipes, up to the street, and out of the storm drains." She finally looked up from the tablet. "Sewer gases mixed with toxic fumes will rise like a cloud. He could suffocate anyone on street level in a couple of minutes."

A heat wave climbed up Aubrey's spine. "What was that you were saying about a switch?" He put a hand on Malina's forearm.

She turned. "It's what Champ showed me, just now. Ambrosia programmed a switch. A remote trigger set to initiate the command that will dump the chemicals into the sewer."

"What kind of switch is it?" Aubrey gestured to them to hurry with their responses. "A manual one, is it on a timer, is it a dead man switch? What is it?"

Champ pulled the tablet from Malina. "Based on what I'm seeing, it's on a timer. He probably did that in case he was killed. He's built in a countdown."

"How long do we have?" Malina's face was gray.

Champ shook his head, not looking up from the tablet. "Fifty-seven minutes."

"Where is the switch?" Aubrey asked Malina, tension squeezing his throat.

She looked at Champ, who said, "He probably has it on him. I would guess it's just an app on his phone or on a tablet."

Aubrey's mind raced. Catching Ambrosia quickly went from a selfish desire for him to an absolute necessity for the sake of his city.

He looked at Champ. "What did you mean when you said he disappeared? How could a drone just disappear? Can't you track it?"

Champ shrugged. "It's just gone. It's not on any UAV flight plans, and it's been disconnected from its parent control program and deleted from the drone databases." He waved a capitulating hand over the screen. "He covered his tracks really well."

Medical casualty evacuation drones were large and powerful enough to carry a full-grown adult from a trauma scene to a medical facility. Some could travel tens of miles or more when carrying a victim. They were also fast, which meant Ambrosia could be far away by now.

Champ said, "Let me check something else." He continued typing on the screen, occasionally stretching and cracking his neck. Finally, he held up the tablet and said, "Mal, make sure I did this right. My brain is still moving pretty slow."

She leaned in close, and after a moment of examining

Champ's work, she said, "Looks right to me."

Champ worked the tablet for a few more seconds, then said, "Okay, I got him. I know where he is."

Sounds reached them from up the main hallway, from the direction of the helicopter crater—hurried footsteps getting closer. Aubrey took off toward the newcomers. Malina called out to him, but he ignored her, his wet shoes squelching on the smooth floor as it rose gently in front of him. Slowly, the rate of rise decreased, and his line of sight crested the peak.

He slid to a stop; the soles of his shoes squeaked. There were half a dozen men and women rushing toward him. All wore the dark-blue uniform of paramedics and carried medical bags; two had lightweight stretchers tucked under their arms.

"Are you all right, sir?" A female medic shouted. "Any injured down there?"

"Yeah," Aubrey said quickly, "I'm fine. There's two more down here that need to get checked out. Where are the police?"

This question made the medical team slow to a walk, and the same woman replied to him. "They're on their way, sir. Is there any danger in us proceeding without them?"

"No. Come on down." He turned and jogged back the way he'd come.

While he ran, he pulled out his phone and dialed Liz Reynolds. As quick as he could, he explained the situation—the attacks at the power plant, their near drowning, Ambrosia's escape in the drone, and, finally, the coming chemical attack on the city's population.

When he paused to take a breath, Liz said, "Martin, I'm sending people there now and I'm dispatching aircraft to go after him as soon as we hang up, but, and I hate to say this, you might be in the best position to catch him in time to stop the attack. Find a way to get airborne and stop that asshole."

32

Flight

Less than fifty-seven minutes. Aubrey had to find an aircraft.

He thrust the phone into his pocket as a plan started to take shape in his mind. He just needed a few seconds alone with Malina to get it fleshed out. He quickened his pace and reached her thirty seconds ahead of the paramedics.

After quickly explaining his idea to her, he asked, "What do you think?"

"I think I've told you a million times I'm not a field agent." She sighed audibly. "But, I guess you can't do it without me."

"Can you duplicate his flight path? Can you follow him?" He shot a furtive glance at the paramedics closing in on them.

"I don't know …" She trailed off, her eyes moving to Champ.

Champ nodded subtly. "I think I could do that. But you'd need an aircraft to come close to catching up with him. I would just need the ID number off it and I could make it follow him."

"I can get that. Tee it up so all we have to do is enter the ID number, and Malina will do the rest." Aubrey felt a blanket thrown over his shoulders and a pair of hands helping him to the floor.

"Just take a seat, sir," a male voice said softly but with authority. "Let's take a look at you. You and your friends are in good hands now."

Sensors prodded him in several places, and something metal touched his forehead. There was a jab of something sharp in his arm, but he only took fleeting notice of the medical care being given to him. He focused instead on Champ working on the tablet. The paramedic knelt behind him, applying some device to his back, checking various readings through a window in the side of her bag. She draped a thin poncho over Champ a moment later, then took one arm and placed a patch on the inside of his elbow. All the while, every few seconds, she casually asked him to put the tablet down.

"Sir, I promise you, whatever it is, it can wait."

After a dozen requests, Champ acquiesced. "You're right, ma'am. So sorry. I'm all yours." To Aubrey, he gave a definitive nod.

"Sir?" One of the medics tending to Aubrey got his attention. "You've suffered fairly extreme hypothermic trauma. Frankly, I'm surprised you're not in shock right now. We need to get you to a hospital." Over a space blanket he outfitted Aubrey with a poncho like the one given to Champ.

Aubrey nodded as if he were accepting the unpleasant inevitability. "Can my friend walk me out?" He gestured to Malina who was in the middle of picking up the tablet and placing it in her bag.

"Sure." The medic helped Aubrey to his feet and radioed to someone outside, "Priority one, male, coming out."

The four of them, Aubrey, Malina, and the two medics, made their way up the long hallway and out of the building.

The burnt-out husk of the helicopter had been removed by a fire department recovery vehicle, which allowed them to easily step through the enormous hole the chopper left behind.

Outside, the day had stretched into early evening but was otherwise just as they'd left it—cold and windy. Aubrey had lost all track of time in the underwater bunker that was the power station, and he'd half expected it to be well into the night.

"This way, sir." The paramedic led Aubrey to an area in the grass fifty feet away. He then watched as the man pressed a spot on the shoulder of his uniform and verbally read aloud Aubrey's vitals, current condition, and a list of other instructions, which Aubrey assumed were meant to keep him stable on his way to the hospital.

From overhead, the familiar sound of rotors purring came as wind blasted him, lifting the edges of the poncho, and chilling his still wet hair. The casualty evac drone landed thirty feet in front of them. The white-and-red rectangular box had four rotors outstretched from each corner like the wings of a gargantuan beetle. It stood on four appendages of landing gear that were nothing more than squatty, duck-like feet. Its rear end separated from the rest of the flying machine, lowering to the ground by one hinge along its bottom edge to form a ramp. Across the top edge of the ramp read an aircraft ID number thirteen digits long—14G86202CVD19. Under the ID string, was printed "Reg. Med. Ctr., NA, MD." From the corner of his eye, he caught Malina snapping a picture of the ID number.

From the white interior, a gurney slid out on rails built into the inner bulkheads, and without a sound, it raised itself up off two silver bars to waist level, ready to receive its patient.

"See you soon," Aubrey said to Malina with a wink before stepping forward and lying down to allow himself to be strapped onto the gurney.

The inside of the drone was less like a tomb than he'd imagined. It was quite warm, but not too warm, and the thick patch applied by the medics to his arm seemed to be communicating with the drone's computer, as it would occasionally heat up or click. Lift-off was smooth, and as he felt momentum shift forward, a disembodied female voice checked in on him.

"Your pulse is a touch elevated, Mr. Aubrey. May I give you something to help you relax?" The voice came from somewhere by his head.

"No, thank you. No drugs." As much as he'd love for something to stop the body-wide ache he felt, he needed to remain sharp.

The most surprising thing about the interior of the flying ambulance was how nonclaustrophobic it felt. Although the ceiling was only a foot away, the soft blue interior lights were angled upward from the corners at such angles as to make it seem much more spacious. Additionally, as he examined the ceiling further, he noticed faint lines carved into the white surface. The patterns formed columns that tapered almost imperceptibly from head to foot, adding to the impression that there was much more room inside the drone.

"Can I play some music for you? I have a very comprehensive selection."

"No, thank you. Just silence for me." He looked at his watch and wondered how much longer it would take for Malina to take control or if he'd even notice when she did. The seconds passed, and the silence drummed on. The space inside the box filled with the white noise of the buzzing rotors emphasized by a soft but constant vibration. The intermittent hums, clicks, and hisses became a soothing pattern of mechanical operation.

"Apologies, Mr. Aubrey. Our destination has been altered. I'm very sorry for the delay, but I assure you your care will not be diminished in the least."

"No problem at all. I was expecting a course change. Thank you."

He surveyed the interior of the drone once more, trying to guess if there would be enough room for a second passenger.

The drone banked left. The straps around his midsection and upper chest pressed against his right side as his body tried to roll against the turn. The drone's flight controls were so smooth that, a minute later, Aubrey was caught by surprise when he felt a slight bump, a hum he forgot was there went silent, and the rear ramp hatch began to open. He hadn't realized they'd descended, much less landed.

Aubrey lifted his head as a setting sun peeked around the edges of the opening hatch. Soft yellow beamed into the drone as the ramp lowered completely, the light dimmed by the slight form of a person at its center. The figure stepped onto the ramp and approached Aubrey.

Eyes still adjusting to the sudden burst of sunlight, he squinted.

"Move over," Malina said heavily.

He huffed a stifled laugh and let his head fall to the gurney.

"I'm kind of strapped in here, Malrey."

"Please don't call me that." She stood at the end of the bed and started working the straps loose. "Okay, now scoot over."

He complied, moving to the edge as far as he could. "I thought that's what you wanted to be called from now on."

"That was a long time ago," she said, breathing hard as she slid in next to him. "And it was just a call sign. No one in the real world used it."

"Where are we?" Aubrey tried to guess by the scenery outside the drone, but the sun washed out any discernible landmarks.

"Roughly a two-minute run from the power plant. Near the river." She shifted her bag around to her front and pulled out a tablet. "Just far enough away so none of the medics would be able to catch up to me when they saw me climbing into a highjacked medevac drone. Most of them were down with Champ anyway."

She tapped on a command window filled with text, paused, and glanced around it toward the rear hatch. It began to close. "Good. Still working."

Seconds later, after Malina entered several more commands, the drone lifted off silently. Aubrey felt a gentle shift as the aircraft powered forward.

She reached into her bag and removed another object, handing it to Aubrey. It was his pistol. He took it and slid it into his waistband. He'd given the gun to Malina for safe keeping before he was put on the medevac drone. His fear was, at the time, that the paramedics wouldn't allow him onboard if he was armed.

"How much time left?" he asked.

She glanced at one corner of the tablet. "Forty-five minutes. No, forty-four and change."

"Where is he going?" Aubrey's left side pressed awkwardly against the bulkhead, the edge of the bed in the middle of his back with Malina firmly against his right side. A almost imperceptible change in g-force told him the aircraft was rapidly picking up speed.

"Flight path took him out of the city, headed west." She tapped the tablet screen several more times until a map appeared with a glowing red dot at its center. Surrounding the dot was a large network of roadways. The roads slowly shifted to the right as the dot moved west. "He hasn't programmed a flight plan, at least not with the coordinating program server, so he must be controlling it manually."

Aubrey grunted and gazed up at the strange contour lines on the ceiling. "So, all we can do is follow him and hope time doesn't run out."

"We're cruising at …" She minimized the window currently occupying the tablet's screen and pulled up another displaying several readouts. "One twenty-five and steadily accelerating. Oh, and I have a bot sending Liz updates on our location. She knows where we are along the way and she'll know when we touch down. Backup should be right on our heels."

Aubrey was amazed at the airspeed. He knew the medical evacuation drones were built for stability and swift travel, but it astounded him that he could barely feel the thing moving through the air. And it was so quiet. "I had no idea these things could go that fast."

"Oh yeah, they're built for speed, this one will hit one seventy-five top speed, but they rarely get a chance to run wide open in the city." She laid her tablet face down on her chest and clutched it. Eyes closed toward the ceiling, she said, "I just realized we're basically inside a flying coffin." She opened her mouth and inhaled several deep breaths, each one causing her arm and shoulder to increase their pressure against Aubrey.

"What do we do about the switch when we catch him? Can you disable it?" Aubrey wished he could face her directly to read her expression.

"Yes." Her reply came without hesitation.

"What makes you so confident?"

She stretched her neck to both sides. "A lot of reasons. First, he's not expecting us, so he probably hasn't beefed up security on the switch. Second, we'll have him, so we can use his retinas or prints to pass any biometric security. And lastly, we have me." She flashed Aubrey an over the top grin. "I'm pretty good at this hacker crap."

He returned the smile. "Yes, you are, Malrey." After a moment, he asked, "What kind of range do these things have?"

"This model has about fifty miles before it needs a recharge. Ambrosia is in a similar type."

"One hundred and seventy-five miles per hour. That's a fast coffin. And with a fifty-mile range, we've got"—he feigned glancing at his watch—"twenty minutes or so before this thing plummets to our mutual demise." This time, he took a deep breath and let it out. "At least I won't die alone."

"Less than twenty minutes. And there's two of us in here, which will surely drain power faster and further reduce that time. And you're not helping. Please, shut up." At a glance, she appeared calmer but had shut her eyes again and held tight to her tablet.

He smiled. "Sorry. That means that if he lands just before he runs out of power, less than twenty minutes from now, it gives us another twenty minutes, plus or minus, until the trigger switch goes off. How far behind are we?"

Without opening her eyes, she said, "He's going a good deal

slower, I guess, so he won't draw attention, and I don't think he knows we're after him because he hasn't sped up. We've gained a good bit of ground, but we're still about twelve miles behind him."

He did some quick math in his head. "Given he doesn't speed up and we pick up a little more ground by the time he lands, he'll have a two to four-minute head start on us before we touch down, which now gives us sixteen minutes to find him and stop the switch."

She grunted her confirmation. "We'll have to decelerate and find a place to land. Let's call it a five to seven minute head start. Truly, we'll have about thirteen minutes to catch him before the timer lapses and the switch goes off."

If Ambrosia picked his spot carefully, he could be long gone in five to seven minutes. He wouldn't stay where he landed; he'd just use it as a jumping-off point. A crowded place was the easiest to blend into, but where could he land a hijacked drone without attracting too much attention? If he chose the roof of a tall building, that might work, but a city or even a large town would have too many cameras and sensors for the landing to go unnoticed. Aubrey concluded that Ambrosia would have to park the drone somewhere secluded, then move on foot to someplace packed with people.

"Show me your map again." He rolled a few degrees toward her to better see the tablet, which she propped up on her midsection. The red dot crossed a jungle of gray 3D buildings cut through by streets and highways. "Zoom out. Let's try to predict where he might be going."

She made the map larger. The cities and towns stretched for miles in every direction.

"What are you thinking?" Malina glanced toward him, her

face lit by the soft glow of the tablet screen.

"Um"—he snapped his head back to the tablet—"I'm thinking he'd go someplace out of the way. Somewhere he could land with few people noticing and no security cameras. But he'd want to be able to get somewhere public in a hurry so he could disappear."

They both stared at the map on the tablet. Other than a seemingly never-ending network of roadways with blocks of buildings mixed in, there was the river snaking across the top edge of the screen and two large green splotches—one up near the river and one on the left side of the screen. As Aubrey watched, the second green splotch, which he now realized was a state park, inched closer to the center. Closer and closer to Ambrosia's drone. It became clear where Ambrosia was headed.

"What is that? Zoom in on that," he said, pointing at the green patch.

After Malina zoomed in, he read the name of the park: Rocks State Park.

"Hey, I've been there," Malina nearly shouted. "When I was younger, we went there a few times." She paused, rolled her head back, and stared blankly at the ceiling for five long seconds. "I know where he's going." She faced Aubrey with a furrowed brow. "I know where he's going to land."

33

Hank at Last

Francesca was greeted at the Susquehanna River Hydroelectric Power Plant by a barrage of flashing blue-and-red lights and the wailing of sirens from police cars just arriving at the scene. The parking lot was full of blue-and-white vehicles parked haphazardly, people in and out of uniform running around like ants on a dead bird. Overhead, drones of all shapes and sizes buzzed about.

She entered the parking lot from the south end, opposite the bay, and crossed the pavement in a beeline to the commotion on the side of the power station. White clouds of gas and gray smoke rose from wreckage of some kind, and nearby, a dozen officers and official looking men and women stood conversing. Even from a distance, they appeared to be consumed with a sense of urgency. One of them, a woman, pointed at the water, then back to the people around her. Francesca recognized her from the contact photo in her borrowed phone. It was Liz Reynolds.

Anyone in the lot who saw Francesca coming quickly found something to busy themselves with, avoided her eyes,

305

or pretended she wasn't there. Thus, she encountered no obstacles on her way to Liz Reynolds. Stepping onto the curb and into the grass, she was several strides away when a male uniformed officer standing next to Liz, spotted her. His face melted into a mix of dread and confusion. He tugged on Liz's sleeve and nodded toward Francesca. She and Liz locked eyes, and Francesca ceased her approach. She knew the effect she had on people was often disturbing, and she had no desire to interrupt or derail any of the police work occurring on the scene.

With a few unheard words, Liz dispersed the group around her and walked over to Francesca. Liz's face was serene, as if she met executioners on a daily basis. Francesca noticed a subtle hint of curiosity in her eyes.

"You must be Senior Inspector Liz Reynolds of the New Aberdeen Police Department."

To Francesca's surprise, Liz extended her hand in greeting, which she took with a firm grip in her gloved right hand. "I am," Liz said. "You're Francesca, I take it."

"I am."

Liz nodded, still looking Francesca over, like one would a museum display. "Aubrey and Malina aren't here. It's a long story, but they're tracking our man. We have aircraft and officers right behind them, and I'm about to leave myself to join them."

"Senior Inspector." A uniformed officer approached Liz, making erratic sideways glances toward Francesca. "The server room is almost drained. They've gone in to stop the inflow of water, and officers are beginning to search the room."

Liz nodded her thanks and the officer hurried away.

"Did you find Josiah Palmero?" Francesca's stomach knotted. She wanted to scream out for Hank, desperate to know if he was inside or hidden from view somewhere outside.

"Can you tell me why you're looking for him, Francesca?" Liz spoke quickly but not in a way that seemed rude or rushed.

The Member of the Order straightened to her full height, and with as much authority as she could summon, she said, "I'm on Order of the Coppice business." It was the first direct lie she had uttered in years, and it stung as a part of her became corrupt.

Liz did not press the issue or demand further explanation. "We have two victims, both male. Neither is Palmero, I'm afraid. One man is on his way to the hospital, where he'll be questioned after he's stabilized. The other is deceased. We believe both were victims of the kidnappers, likely forced to do the dirty work on the AI."

"Kidnappers?" Ice water trickled down Francesca's spine. One of two possibilities arose in her mind: Hank was kidnapped or he was one of the kidnappers. Her entire body turned to stone.

"Yes. At least one, possibly two kidnappers." Liz's face showed genuine concern, her head slightly bent, hands on her hips. "Apparently, the AI was being hacked from here, causing chaos and failures in all its systems. Someone had kept these men prisoner and forced them to take control of the AI and MTS."

"And you were all searching for Josiah too. Which means you think he may be …" Francesca couldn't bring herself to finish the sentence.

Liz did it for her. "We believe he may be involved in the kidnappings, yes. But"—Liz held up both hands in a heedful gesture—"nothing is clear at this point."

Francesca's insides went molten. She couldn't bear maintaining eye contact with Liz any longer and shifted her gaze to the bay. Her baby brother was likely a kidnapper and a torturer. Alternatively, he had been kidnapped and tortured.

Fifty yards away, a helicopter began touching down on a bald stretch of grass, its rotors beating the air furiously, drawing the attention of both women.

"Any chance there are more survivors?" Francesca shouted over the noise of the helicopter.

Liz raised her voice over the cacophony. "Listen, that's my ride. I need to go. All I can tell you is they're still searching inside. When all the water is gone, we'll be able to say definitively."

Only two possibilities presented themselves to Francesca—Josiah was either a dead victim or a living murderer.

"Senior Inspector?" A plain clothes officer called out to Liz from behind the wreckage nearby.

"Excuse me." Liz turned and walked briskly toward the other detective as the screaming of the helicopter rotors diminished somewhat.

Francesca considered which option she preferred. A living brother capable of terrible crimes, a person responsible for mass deaths, or a dead brother.

Her duty as a taker of life, as an executioner, gave her unique perspective. She understood the difficulties criminals had reforming their own minds. She knew that the likelihood a violent criminal turning over a new leaf, after committing such atrocities, was infinitesimally small. If Hank ended up at the Keep, he'd most likely end up dead in his sleep by the hand of a Member of the Order.

And yet, she couldn't help but hope. A living brother was hope. Criminal. Murderer. Kidnapper. It made little difference to her. If he had a pulse, she'd love him. Perhaps he'd love her back. Perhaps she was all he needed to seek self-reform.

"Francesca." The voice belonged to Liz Reynolds, now waving her over from nearby the wreckage. When Francesca stepped in front of her, Liz spoke in a slow voice. "What was Josiah to you, really? You said you're here on official business, but"—Liz scrutinized Francesca with an intense glare—"your connection with this man is clearly, profoundly personal."

Francesca thought of simply lying further, or she could remind Liz that she was a full Member of the Order of the Coppice and that she'd find out what she needed to know one way or another. She could show Liz the skin on her right hand and tell her that her status and purpose bought Francesca access to anything she wanted to know or see. But there was something in Liz's eyes. There was an honesty there, a sincere concern.

Francesca knew full well that the truth would get her everything she needed.

"He is my brother. We were separated when he was a baby. I was sent to the Order, and he was adopted." She drew a breath. "I did not know until very recently what happened to him after I left the orphanage."

"Hmm," Liz grunted, casting her eyes to the waiting helicopter. Then she straightened, appearing to steel herself against some unseen force. "Francesca, we found the man known as Josiah Palmero, your brother." She gave the smallest shake of her head. "I'm very sorry to tell you he is dead."

A sledge hammer hit Francesca in the chest. An invisible

wire tugged at her knees, threatening total collapse of her skeleton. Her eyes blurred. They caught sight of something on the water. A boat. Her brain wanted nothing more than to watch the boat go by. Just watch the boat so the sadness couldn't take hold. She watched it sail along, its occupants unaware of the events on the shore, unaware of the mayhem on the streets, unaware of Francesca's pain, her loss.

A gust of wind pulled at loose strands of her hair. Her braid was nearly dismantled from the run to the power plant and the rotor wash from the helicopter.

One moment with him would have been enough. Just one moment.

"Francesca?" Liz's voice cut into her thoughts. "I really have to go but … is there anything I can get for you?"

"I want to see him." The words left her mouth before the notion had time to circle her brain.

"I don't … I don't think that's a good idea," Liz stammered.

Francesca made eye contact with the senior inspector, conveying to her the need, the absolute need, to see her brother one time. She spent her life around death, facilitating it, hardening herself to it. This she said without words, and Liz seemed to understand.

"Okay." Liz held up her hands in a halting motion. "But you need to be aware that he … he doesn't look … normal. They pulled him from the water. You need to know that this won't be a pleasant sight."

Francesca nodded her understanding.

Liz walked her over to a spot near the wreckage of what Francesca could now see had been an aircraft of some kind. Two female paramedics stood on either side of a gurney. One of them blocked Francesca's view, but she could clearly see the bottom half of a black body bag. A third woman, dressed in a shirt and tie, appeared to be examining something on the other end of the stretcher out of view. As they approached, the woman in the tie had just finished zipping the head of the bag. The form of a body pressed through the material of the bag so it looked like the lid of an ancient Pharaoh's sarcophagus.

Francesca moved around to the head of the gurney. The paramedics, who had been securing the body for transport, stepped aside. The woman in the tie wore a badge on her chest that read "Medical Examiner." She looked up at Francesca and Liz, her eyes bouncing between them several times before she greeted Liz with a tilt of her head.

"May we?" Liz gestured to the seal on the bag.

The medical examiner said they could and reached out with gloved hands to open the seal. The face was grimly pale, puffy, with blue lips and sunken eyes, but through the years that aged him and the cruel mechanisms that had already begun to decay his flesh, she could see her Hank. Soft cheeks. Tow hair. This was her brother, of that she had no doubt.

"We ran his DNA. It's Josiah. I'm very sorry," Liz said. "Take as much time as you need with him. I've got to get on that chopper." She paused. "Are you going to be okay, Francesca?"

Francesca nodded to Liz and caressed Hank's cheek with the back of her bare left hand. It was cold as stone under her fingers.

As Liz started to walk away toward the helicopter, Francesca asked the medical examiner, "How did he die?" She wanted to understand his last moments; she knew so few moments from his life after all. She touched his hair, attempting to straighten it.

"It was most likely strangulation." The medical examiner removed one glove, her voice carrying loudly over the ambient noise of the chopper blades. "Bruising and ligature marks on the neck, but it happened too long ago to be certain without autopsy. He also could have been asphyxiated."

Liz stopped ten feet away. "I thought he drowned."

"No, Inspector," the woman said. "He didn't drown."

Francesca's eyes went to Liz, who glared hard at the medical examiner. "My people said they pulled him out of the water. Paramedics said—"

"I know." The medical examiner pulled off her second glove by the bottom edge. "They told me the same thing. But he didn't drown, and he's been dead for a minimum of three days."

34

King and Queen

Standing 190 feet above Deer Creek Valley, the King and Queen Seat rock formation jutted out of the forest like a tongue made of hard quartz and quartzite. It stood out against the backdrop of the forest not only for its color, a harsh gray nearing white, but for its shape. The soft round curves of the valley and the trees that lined it made the stone outcropping appear as if it were the hilt of a knife stabbed into the heart of the forested land.

Ambrosia's drone began its approach, and he could think of no better place to land than the King and Queen Seat, stretching one hundred feet long and twenty feet across at its widest. Especially as he eyed the dot on the map that represented his pursuers, who were just a few minutes behind him. He had learned he was being tailed only a moment before, and he now realized his chosen landing spot was yet another sign of provenance.

"Lord the Father provides," he whispered as he clutched the Praeceptist Bible against his chest with one hand while holding his phone in front of his face with the other.

On the screen, he watched the enemy dot gain slight ground as his own began to slow. He felt his body surge forward slightly which could only mean the craft was preparing to land. A swipe with his thumb revealed a viewpoint from an outside camera mounted to the drone's nose. On screen, the light-colored stone of the King and Queen Seat grew in size rapidly, and the aircraft tilted to one side then the other, stabilizing before touchdown.

Ambrosia rested his head on the gurney and pressed the phone flat against the bible on his chest. He'd shed the device and all other attachments to technology of any kind as soon as he was clear of his pursuers. The trigger switch on his phone would function without him. His magnum opus would play on whether he was around to hear it or not. He'd find out about the aftermath of the final cleansing tomorrow, relishing the terrible price he'd leveled on the city that had abandoned Lord the Father.

The two detectives in the fast approaching drone were nothing more than a thorn in his side. Constantly attempting to thwart the awakening he'd enacted, constantly one step behind. It was no matter to him. Once he'd abandoned the drone and disappeared into the forest, there'd be no way of finding him. The detectives would have to land far away because Ambrosia's aircraft would occupy the only suitable landing area, which only qualified as suitable by the loosest interpretation of the word. There was no room for two large medevac drones on the King and Queen Seat, and from anywhere else in the state park, it would be a difficult hike followed by a strenuous climb to the outcropping. By the time they made it up there, he'd be gone. He could then make his way to the nearest Praeceptist community and disappear among them.

"Blessed be His servants. And I am certainly blessed, for I am a true servant. Thank you, Father, for seeing me this far. It is a sign that my path is a righteous one. And I shall stay on this path until I am shown otherwise by you, Lord the Father."

Vibrations under him coursed through the gurney, more than he'd expected but nothing that alarmed him. A rumbling outside. A crunching sound, and he gripped the bible ever tighter. More vibrations came, intensified, lasting several seconds. His breath quickened, his heart pounded, then stillness. The drone settled and stopped moving.

"Welcome, citizen," a voice said near his head. "Medical personnel will now see to your care. Be well."

A slow whooshing sound came as the rear hatch lowered to form the ramp. One second later, the gurney slid of its own accord from the belly of the drone and down the ramp. Ambrosia sat up just as a rush of frigid air found him and sent chills down his arms. The lightweight coveralls he'd donned before leaving the power station weren't nearly adequate to keep the cold of the higher altitude at bay. Ahead of him, the rock formation ran like a crooked, pockmarked runway into a mass of thick green vegetation and trees. He jumped from the gurney and spun to look back where his drone touched down and beyond it to the end of the prominence and back again toward the forest. Satisfied that there was no other possibility for even a near-safe landing spot, he pocketed both the phone and the bible and jogged toward the forest. The boughs of the trees and the darkness they held within them called out to him. It was safety. It was freedom from capture. It was Lord the Father's embrace promising comfort and forgiveness.

His foot slipped on some scree, and he nearly tumbled into

a small crater. The sky darkened quickly, and the gray rock was slowly becoming difficult to navigate. He righted himself and jogged more slowly toward the trees, careful to place each step on solid rock. Fifteen feet from the trailhead, he heard the deep buzzing of a large drone enhanced by the wall of wooden trunks in front of him. Ambrosia did a 180, his heel grinding gravel underfoot. The detectives' drone hurdled toward the outcropping, angling itself as if to land, its nose slightly up as it decelerated to take up a hovering position twenty feet above his own drone.

The question of what the fuck were they doing entered his brain in a flash, and just as quickly, he understood the answer.

"Shit!" His hand went to his hip pocket, desperately searching for his phone.

* * *

"Malina." Aubrey's voice reverberated in the tiny robot cocoon. "There's nowhere to land. What the hell are you doing?" He watched her tap the screen of her tablet in what appeared to be a frantic attempt at something, but one look at her hardened face told him she was in control.

In a shockingly level voice she replied, "You'll have to trust me."

Her screen showed two views from cameras mounted to the outside of the drone. One on top and one on bottom, each able to give a 360-degree panoramic view. At the moment, Malina was focused on the view from the bottom camera pointing straight down. The top of Ambrosia's stolen medevac drone filled that section of the screen.

"Jesus, Malina, please tell me you're not trying to—"

"Not now," she spat.

Aubrey took a breath. If they didn't land on the outcropping like Ambrosia did, there was a good chance he'd get away. And Aubrey did trust Malina. He squinted at the scene and noticed a red dot on the roof of the drone beneath them. He also noticed Malina's thumb pressed against a small square in the bottom right corner of the tablet.

"Is that how you're—"

"Not now," she said, cutting him off again.

A readout on the camera feed displayed the distance to the top of the landed drone. Twenty feet. Sixteen. Eight.

A blur filled the screen. A jolt hit his back, and the sound of crunching metal filled the cabin. He was tossed into the ceiling, crushing into it with his shoulder. A shout of pain from Malina next to him. He reached out and found her, pulled her in close.

The drone steadied. Teetering to either side and back and forth like a drunken party-goer, but still aloft.

He took a breath. Steadied himself. They needed to land, obviously, and he needed to think. Could they even land now? Or was the drone damaged too badly? And what the hell had just happened?

A deafening collision slammed them from their precarious hover. Gravity shifted. They were pulled down by it, then up. Down, then up again.

The drone was in a tailspin, tumbling like a leaf on the wind.

* * *

Ambrosia had whipped out his phone and opened the command app just in time; the detectives' aircraft was only a few feet from landing squarely on top of his. With quick and careful action, he'd commanded his drone to buck upward, its front end lifting first like an angry bull while a trick of the wind caused it to twist at the same time. The front-left quarter panel and the rotor attached slammed into the bottom of the oncoming drone with just enough force to knock it off balance and send it flying.

The invading craft twisted and spun but, a moment later, recovered. He remembered that these drones had self-stabilizing technology, but he also remembered that they were limited in that capacity. They could only handle so much force and relied more on sensors and geotracking software to avoid collisions in the first place.

Ambrosia sent his drone high into the air, thirty feet above the other. Flipped it so it was nose down. Dead center onscreen was the front third of the detectives' drone. With a swipe of his thumb, Ambrosia increased the throttle to one hundred percent.

His craft collided with the other like a freight train smashing into a bread truck. The damage was instantly catastrophic as the carbon fiber, plastic, and metal splintered, peeled, and cracked into a dozen pieces. The two crafts became one mass of flying detritus, falling beyond the edge of the outcropping. Three seconds had passed when the sound of an explosive impact climbed the crosswinds to find him—the report of the drones meeting the rocky floor of the valley two hundred feet below.

With a deep breath of cold air, he pocketed his phone, now thinking that he may need it again before he was free. Turning toward the forest, he stepped onto the trail and disappeared into the dark shadows.

* * *

They plummeted in a tight death spiral that flattened Aubrey's guts and pinned him against the bulkhead. Malina pressed hard against him. His neck was locked in an impossible angle from the centrifugal force. Although he could not see clearly, he was vaguely aware of his own consciousness collapsing in on itself. The lights began to fade.

An explosion erupted somewhere in the near distance. Not them. Somehow he knew this as fact. The blast came from somewhere else.

Slow motion. The world slowed as they approached certain death. Everything slowed. The drone no longer spun so violently. The pressure in his head eased. The weight of Malina against him slackened.

It seemed it was no figment of his imagination or some cerebral trickery to soften the blow of his life cut short. The drone was actually slowing down. Another moment of sedated turbulent spinning and they hovered steadily. Soft purring was under him once again. His heart jackhammered audibly in his skull.

"Oh my god," Malina gasped and spied around the inside of the drone in disbelief. "I really thought that was it."

"Me too. What happened?"

"Stabilizers. The drone must have engaged the onboard safety measures and crash protocols." She shook her head appearing as bewildered as Aubrey felt. "We're lucky the valley is so deep, and that the drop off is so severe or the computer wouldn't have had time to counteract the spin."

Several deep breaths later, and Aubrey was able to tamp down the panic and quiet his mind. They'd been lucky too many times that day. They needed to put Ambrosia down and be done with all of it.

* * *

Ambrosia stopped. He twisted his head, searching for the noise that brought him up short. A distant hum didn't fit in with the auditory tapestry that surrounded him. Aircraft of all shapes and sizes were common everywhere and were usually just background noise to him, but considering the dogfight he'd just taken part in, he thought it was best to check it out.

He reversed course on the trail. After inspecting the spot where he'd entered the forest, he realized he hadn't covered nearly as much ground as he first thought. He'd made it maybe seventy yards into the woods when he heard the sound. The trail now rose and twisted to the left, where it flattened for several dozen feet before presenting the long and narrow King and Queen Seat.

Traveling up hill, he quickly winded himself. A life behind a computer afforded him the luxury of foregoing one dominated by the physical, but it came with a downside. He was terribly out of shape. Always had been.

A sustained gust of wind rustled the trees overhead. They bent and rubbed and scratched their neighbors in a harsh discordant mixture that drowned out the very sound that forced him to backtrack. The wind grew; it howled. It was a white noise that intensified to the point of deafening.

Fed up and unable to hear himself think, he stopped. "Probably nothing anyway," he shouted to himself over the din. "They're dead. I just need to get the fuck out of here."

Ready to resume his path off the mountain, an irregularity

got his attention. A rectangular shape hovered in the clouds. No, he realized, not in the clouds. Over the trees. No, he corrected himself again, not over. In. It was in the trees.

It came from the valley, and it crashed through the trees directly toward him.

He sprinted downhill, taking no care for a safe descent. Branches snapped over his shoulder. Scraping, bending, twisting wood. It was too close. He'd never make it away. He dove, face first, into the dirt, rocks, and roots, throwing his hands behind his head in one motion. His face grinded against the grit. His elbows grated on the rough ground. A gush of air over him. More crashing. Metal tearing. An impact beyond him down the trail.

He dared a peek at the scene ahead. The tail end of a drone faced him from a thicket of sapling sugar maples. One rotor burred in its housing, while the other three were silent, smashed, or missing. Smoke rose from the ground where the battery pack laid on moist vegetation. The aircraft lay at an angle with its nose about five degrees above the rear. Other than the rotors and ancillary lights on the shell, the rest of the drone looked to be in one piece.

As he pondered whether passengers on board could survive such a ferocious impact, several slams echoed from it. Then, a crack of light appeared along the top edge of the rear hatch. Then the sides. The drone was opening. The ramp was dropping.

He leapt to his feet. What could he do? Run? They were down the trail from him already, blocking most of it. Back up toward the rocks was out of the question, considering his wavering stamina.

The opening grew larger by the second. A soft whooshing

as the mechanism released and gravity took hold of the thick door.

He stood frozen with indecision for a moment before he noticed a form taking shape down the trail, just on the other side of the drone from him. A woman in a large-brimmed hat—a park ranger.

Was it a sign?

The ranger kept her distance from the drone, clearly not sure if it was safe. An idea came to him. On the ground nearby, he noticed a branch, three feet long, straight and as thick as his arm. It had fallen at his feet. It was delivered to him just as the ranger had been. The signs from Lord the Father were unmistakable.

He knew what he would do next as sure as he knew he served God.

* * *

Aubrey blinked back tears as the fire suppressing gases filled the compartment. He pushed against the gel-filled restraint bags that formed a soft, protective cocoon around him and Malina. The gel bags began to pull back of their own accord just seconds after impact, and bright white lights replaced the softer blues from a moment ago.

Malina coughed and gagged next to him. Her face, clear in the new light, turned red and splotchy and her spiked, mousy hair was pressed flat.

"Are you okay?" he wheezed.

She gave a thumbs-up with eyes squeezed tight.

"How much time do we have?" he said through a tight throat.

She didn't reply but held up both hands with her fingers spread wide.

"Ten minutes?"

She nodded.

"Can you open the hatch?" He twisted in place and kicked at the gel bags to free himself. He'd need to bolt as soon as the hatch opened wide enough. Malina continued coughing but gave another thumbs-up and pointed to the hatch, which had just begun to open.

"You stay here and make sure Liz knows where we landed." He shimmied down toward the growing opening in the drone's back end. "I'll get to Ambrosia and let you know when I have him."

She said nothing, just nodded her reply through fits of coughing while tapping on her tablet.

Either side of the interior of the drone was filled with the giant hot-dog-shaped gel bags slowly draining their contents somewhere unknown. Pressing his way through them, feet first, felt like sliding down the gullet of a giant worm.

Reaching the hatch, he could see it was stuck—only open about a foot. The whining sound of a straining actuator emanated from above him.

Time was quickly slipping away and, with it, their chances of stopping Ambrosia's attack. Without much room to sit up, he scooted as far down the bed as he could and folded his legs to his chest. One deep breath, and he kicked like a mule at the hatch. It gave, but only a little. He kicked again. Again. Each time gaining a few inches. With the fifth kick, the unseen impediment gave way, and the hatch slowly glided to the forest floor.

Emergency lights lit the ground. In the brisk night air, the dust clouds swirled in the light.

At the end of the gurney, Aubrey reached into his waistband and took out his pistol. He slid off the edge of the bed, ducking low to clear the end of the drone's patient bay. He blinked away lingering tears from the fire suppression system. He scanned the area just outside the drone, but the emergency lights were too bright to see beyond the stark white circle on the ground. He focused his attention on the sounds around him, trying to catch footfalls or movement in the forest.

Everything was quiet.

He stepped down onto the ramp, and branches crunched under it. The pistol came up automatically, following his eyes. His forefinger would remain straight and off the trigger until he found a target. His lungs were still tender from the gas, and he had to repeatedly suppress the urge to cough. Left and right, he panned across the ring of light, urging his eyes to see past the invisible barrier. The darkness at the edge of the light was a wall his brain couldn't penetrate. The night was still—the only sounds came from the drone's dying motors behind him and the breath in his throat clawing its way past raw tissue.

If he kept the drone behind him, it would be difficult for Ambrosia to get the jump on him … if he were still in the area. Most likely, he bolted down the trail away from his landing spot, which meant Aubrey needed to move quickly. Satisfied he and Malina were alone in the immediate area, he angled his head toward the interior of the drone.

"I'm going to follow the path down the hill. I think I can catch him if I hurry." His feet clanged on the metal ramp.

Between coughs, Malina replied, "I'm right behind you, just firing off a ping to Reynolds."

The soil beyond the ramp was a dark loam speckled with large gray rocks that reflected the exquisitely bright floodlights from atop the drone. He shielded the glare from the ground with his hand and the darkness beyond the sphere of light came into better focus. Each step he took from the drone was cautious, his eyes and ears sharp. Two steps more toward darkened ground, he vigilantly scanned the area around him with all his senses and the pistol.

Beyond the edge of light, thirty feet away, a shape materialized. Aubrey took two steps more and saw it was a person crumpled into an awkward fetal position with branches hiding the details of the body.

Was he lucky enough to have Ambrosia right here at his feet?

A low moan came from the body. "Help ..." a weak female voice whispered.

Aubrey ran to the body, keeping one eye on the injured person while scanning his surroundings. He activated the pistol's flashlight and passed the beam over the tightly packed trees flanking the path. He reached the woman's feet and whipped a long branch off her, uncovering most of her body. She wore dark-green pants and jacket, a uniform with gold and white patches on the shoulder. This woman was a park ranger.

"Are you okay?" In the light of his flashlight, he saw she was olive-skinned with straight black hair. He saw a shiny spot on her forehead—she was bleeding from a wound to her scalp. Something had fallen on her. She moaned again and Aubrey spoke louder this time. "Ma'am, I'm going get you some help."

He was turning back to the trail when a crunch in the dirt made him swing around back toward the downed drone.

A person stood in the harsh light silhouetted against the brightness. Malina.

He raised a hand to shield his eyes from the light. She was a dozen feet away. "I'm going down the trail. Call ahead and tell them a ranger is down. She's hurt pretty bad—" He stopped himself. The shape of Malina's shadow was off. It was too tall. Not Malina.

The shape pounded toward him, coming fast.

Aubrey raised his pistol. He fired wildly. Then a cold crack to his head, a blinding impact. He fell numbly, slowly to the ground. Lights played across his vision, but he cleaved to consciousness with every ounce of will he could summon. He was aware that he landed on his back, and he still held the pistol. Dazed and bewildered, he picked out the dark figure of a person against the light, his attacker, Ambrosia, and pulled the trigger. The blast reverberated off the tunnel of trees, filling the forest.

Aubrey's head cleared a bit, and he caught the snippets of someone groaning in pain nearby.

"You fucking shot me," Ambrosia whimpered from his left.

Aubrey tried to roll onto his side, and as he did, a wave of dizziness struck him. Through the fog of his mind, he sighted Ambrosia on his ass, pushing at the dirt with one foot, a hand pressed against the side of his belly, and a thick branch in his free hand. Fluid smeared across Aubrey's eyes as he tried to blink away the haze covering them. Ambrosia's backlit form disappeared in the cloud of light and shadow. Before losing him, Aubrey knew he was five feet away and getting to his feet.

Aubrey got to all fours; his eyes looked down the trail. Somewhere in his brain he picked out a vision of bouncing lights and shouting in the near distance, coming toward him. He lifted his pistol hand and brought it to bear on the spot he'd just seen Ambrosia.

"Nope." A hard smack met his gun hand, sending the pistol flying. "Not this time, detective." Another rap to the side of his head and cheek. Cold, electric pain shot through him as the ground rocketed into the other side of his head. Paralysis spread over him like a wet blanket, weighing him down, pressing him into the gravelly earth.

Shuffling sounds, then footsteps near his head. He could hardly see, but he could hear the soft grinding of shoes against the dry pebbles. Through blurry eyes, he picked out the drone's lights ahead of him. The ranger should still be at his feet.

"Lord the Father, make me your righteous instrument." Ambrosia spoke into the night.

Aubrey raised a feeble arm to deflect the blow he knew was coming. A rush of air. A crack and a thud followed by thick silence. Aubrey felt nothing. Had he been hit so hard that he was now completely numb? No, his head was still throbbing. His eyes burned. His hand ached. He lowered his trembling arm from over his head.

"Marty, are you dead?" It was Malina's voice coming from somewhere nearby.

Aubrey croaked his answer. "Almost." His head felt twisted like a tangled rubber band. "The switch." He could only whisper.

He made out the sound of grunting, cursing, more soil and gravel getting pushed around. Then, Malina said, "I'm working on it."

His eyes cracked open and he saw the bouncing lights were

there again, much closer now. Shouts of, "Police! Let me see your hands!"

Aubrey tried to raise a hand, to somehow signal to them that it was okay they were the good guys, but his strength failed. His hand fell limply into the dust.

Just then, another voice called out, "That's Maddox, and that's Aubrey. Let her work and get him some help."

The lights cutting through the night seemed to dim, slowly at first, then rapidly. They swirled like ropes tossed into a maelstrom, twisting and spiraling into oblivion.

* * *

Aubrey awoke with a spotty recollection of being handled and moved, of people talking loudly to him, of hands slapping his face.

When he opened his eyes, he was aware that he was still on his back, still on the trail near the wrecked medevac drone. His body felt like molasses, like his bones and muscles had been liquefied into the dense, sticky substance.

"Well, you're not dead. That's a good thing." It was Malina speaking from somewhere near his shoulder.

He rotated his head and saw, behind her, flashlight beams swinging through the air. He heard people shouting orders, communicators blaring, a helicopter and drones whirring just over the treetops.

"Are you sure about that?" Aubrey attempted to take a deep breath but couldn't feel his chest or diaphragm moving. This, oddly enough, did not bother him. "I feel pretty dead."

She laughed. "They gave you something to help with shock and pain. You probably feel pretty relaxed."

"You could say that." He could not be more relaxed. He didn't know the exact definition of relaxed, but something close to rubberized bones would probably be right.

Suddenly, he remembered the city, the chemical attack. "The trigger switch," he blurted out.

Malina's face came into view; her expression placid, satisfied. "Don't worry. We got to it in time. I disabled it." She looked exhausted but managed a smile. "Everything is fine now."

35

Frannie Green

Acer Sapindales blinked in and out of consciousness. One second, he was lying on his back inside a brightly lit room; the next, he was … nowhere. The span between his waking seconds didn't seem to exist at all, going by as if no time had passed.

He was … and then he wasn't. Then he was again.

Coming out of one dark spell, he caught the scent of earth, wood, dust. He felt cold, but not the kind of cold from being outside, the kind of cold only human-made machines could produce. He saw one enormous white light, a fixture that occupied the entire ceiling of the tiny room. A heavy awareness that he was alone settled over him. Then, as quickly as he reentered the waking world, he was gone.

When he came around once more, he took notice of small cabinets on the walls with medical equipment housed within. Tubes and wires ran from devices across the room into various parts of his body. Muffled voices reached him from outside the room. No part of the conversation was intelligible to him. A dull pain throbbed in his side. A black ring circled his field of vision. Its edges grew thicker in the outer limits of his peripheral vision. The ring's clear center rapidly decreased in size until he was out again.

He had no idea how much time had passed since he last opened his eyes, but without looking, he knew there was someone else in the room with him.

"Acer Sapindales." A woman's voice cut the silence. She sat very close.

Acer rolled his head to the side, and his body jerked at the sight of her. He squirmed on the bed; he had to get away. He tried to sit up, tried to roll over, tried anything to get away from this woman, but he couldn't. He was bound to the bed, noticing for the first time that he was strapped down across his chest, wrists, waist, and legs. He had been totally immobilized. Nonetheless, he fought against his restraints. He pushed, pulled, and twisted to no avail. They cut into his muscles. They rubbed and chaffed him and burned him. He didn't care, he had to get away from this woman.

His lungs began to rapidly fill and deflate. His heart thumped wildly. A squeal threatened to break loose from his voice box.

After a moment, he fell still. Too tired. Resigned.

Acer dared glimpse the woman again. She was a killer. A monster. An executioner.

As frightened as he was, he couldn't look away. She wore the black cloak all the Tappers wore. Her skin was pale white, her hair nearly so. One hand was stained inky black. A birthmark maybe, unless … unless the rumors were true.

"Acer Sapindales." Her voice was low but sharp.

"What? W-what do you want with me?" he stammered.

"My name is Francesca Deborah Green. I am a Member

of the Order of the Coppice." She didn't move. She didn't blink. If her lips hadn't parted, he'd say she was a statue with a built-in sound system. "Are you aware of what the Order does, Acer?"

"Of course," he said, his voice breaking, betraying his crippling fear.

"Good." Her head cocked to one side; the rest of her remained still. "You're in an ambulance. A road vehicle. No drones this time. The police outside allowed me a minute to sit with you."

"They're just … they're just gonna let you kill me? While they sit out there on their asses?" His eyes bounced around the ambulance to confirm her words but also to see if there was any source of video or audio he could plead into.

"There was no discussion of killing. I asked if I could be alone with you, and they said yes." For the first time, something other than her head moved. She lifted her hands and shrugged her shoulders. "I have certain leeway with law enforcement authorities."

His jaw trembled from the cold and the adrenaline pumping in his blood. "What do you want? You people aren't allowed out here in the real world."

She raised her eyebrows and scratched at her temple with the stained hand. She crossed her legs and set both hands on her knee. "That's not exactly true. I'm not sure why so many people assume that, but suffice it to say, it's a gray area." She stared at him with those eyes again, the color of ice, piercing right through him. "Either way, I'm not here on official Order business, Acer. My visit with you tonight is personal."

This took him aback. The fear and anxiety faded slightly, only to be replaced by confusion and curiosity. "How … could you possibly have personal business with me? Tonight?"

She didn't respond at first. She just used those cold eyes to slice through him. Finally, after a moment, she said, "Josiah Palmero."

He shook his head. "What about him?"

"He was my brother. I knew him as Hank."

The confusion and curiosity disappeared to give way to his old companions: fear and dread.

She knew. He knew she knew. But why hadn't she killed him yet?

"I only knew him for a year before I left him, but the memories of my brother have … been with me since and have been …" Her head cocked again, and her gaze drifted momentarily before she snapped back to him. "Well, that's not really for you to know. I want to ask you some questions about the last few days, and I want you to be truthful. If you are honest with me, I give you my word that everything you say stays between us."

This was literally a deal with the devil, but what other choice did Acer have. He believed the rumors now. She could kill him with a single touch from her poisoned fingers, and it wouldn't faze her in the slightest.

He whispered his agreement. "Okay."

The Tapper leaned back slightly. "I've only seen pieces of the overall puzzle, but from what I can gather, your friendship with my brother does not go back very far—a few weeks at most."

"That's true," he confirmed.

"Tragedy bonded you. The loss of his parents and the death of your girlfriend."

Acer closed his eyes. "Yes."

"Hank, or Josiah as you knew him, was a bit radical in his community. Just as you were in the Colektive. This also bonded you."

The mention of the Colektive would have shocked him, but he knew Malrey was with Aubrey, the detective.

"Yes." He swallowed a stubborn lump in his throat.

She leaned forward. "Given your background, the technical aspects of the plan to terrorize the city obviously fell to you. The philosophical aspects of it, however, could have been Josiah or you or both."

He didn't answer this time. Despite her word to the contrary, he wasn't about to confess his crimes just yet, if ever.

She moved closer, a foot away from him. "At some point, just before you two could get started with your grand plan, Hank, my brother, got cold feet." She slid forward on her seat, her face peering down at him. Her chest inches away from the edge of the gurney. "And, fearful that he might go to the police or angry that he turned his back on you"—a pause; Acer opened his eyes—"you killed him."

Acer's head twitched at the sound of it. His hair rustled against the harsh sheets on the gurney.

"Isn't that true?" she whispered.

He didn't say a word. Hot tears formed in the corners of his eyes, and his head continued to tremble. For a split second, he looked at her again. Those eyes, like barbed spears, tore at him. Then she placed the diseased right hand on the edge of the bed, so close he could see the individual white hairs on her knuckles that stood out against the polluted flesh.

The adulterated hand of death was a warning to him.

He croaked his answer. "Yes."

* * *

Outside the ambulance, blue lights flashed from two police cruisers on the edge of the parking lot for the Rocks State Park Visitor Center. Unlike the lot at the power plant Francesca had left not long ago, there were only a handful of first-response vehicles and fewer than a dozen cops and other personnel. Several yards away from the rear of Acer Sapindales's ambulance, Martin Aubrey and Malina Maddox casually leaned against the fender of an unmarked police car. Aubrey held a cooling pack to his head. Both had blankets across their shoulders.

Francesca approached her friends.

"Find out what you needed to know?" Aubrey asked, peering at her from beneath the ice pack.

"Yes." Francesca reached into her pocket and withdrew the phone and small tablet and handed them back to Malina. "I won't need these any longer. Thank you for lending them to me. And, when you see Liz Reynolds, thank her for me—for the ride here."

"No problem," Malina said, taking the devices from her. "Where do you go from here?"

"Back to the Coppice to resume my duties." Despite her sorrow over losing Hank, a part of her welcomed her life at the prison. Routine and normalcy would be good for her. She was also curious to see how her experiences over the past few days affected her role as a Member. She had no doubt it would alter her judgment and empathy. Just how she would be affected remained a question.

Before she left, Aubrey called out. When she turned, he stepped toward her.

"Francesca, I'm really sorry about your brother."

The telltale signs of her emotions pressing to overtake her spread over her body and mind like a forest fire. Her stomach twisted, throat tightened, skin prickled. She inhaled deeply and held her breath for a moment. Afterward, she felt well enough to respond to Aubrey.

"Me too."

Epilogue

The next morning, Malina woke with soreness all over. Her thighs, neck, and especially her back felt like she'd been hit by a train. She sat up on the couch in Aubrey's living room and gave herself a good long stretch. They'd left the scene at Rocks State Park so late at night that they decided it best if she just sleep at his place. He'd insisted that she take the bed, of course, but she declined just as fervently. She preferred sleeping on couches anyway, and between the two of them, Aubrey was much worse for wear from their adventures the day before. He needed the bed more than she did.

She'd slept in her clothes, removing only her hoodie before lying down. Throwing the blanket aside, she promptly snatched up the jacket as if she were vulnerable without it. She stood and parted the thick curtains over the window, allowing the sun to warm her while it bathed the apartment in the welcome light of late morning.

Five minutes later, she was leaving the kitchen with a fresh cup of coffee. The sounds of movement from Aubrey's room told her he must be up. She was making for his room when she collided with the corner of the dining table, spilling her coffee. She set her cup down, and she dashed into the kitchen to fetch a towel. After wiping up most of the spill, she picked up the loaner tablet she'd given Francesca. The dark liquid dripped from one corner into the soaked towel. She wiped the device dry as best she could and placed it on the counter, then she set about cleaning up the rest of her mess.

When all was set to rights, she threw the dirty towels into a laundry hamper and returned to the kitchen to freshen her depleted cup. While waiting for the cup to fill, the tablet on the counter caught her eye. A droplet of coffee rested comfortably in the center of the screen, and although the device was waterproof, the coffee would dry and become sticky, eventually crusting over. She had to clean it. After grabbing yet another towel from the drawer by the sink, she dabbed the tablet dry. As she did, the screen, sensing her touch, came to life. The odd thing was that she didn't remember the lock screen looking the way it did now. Malina inspected the tablet and was confused, at first, but then realized what she was seeing. The lock screen image had been replaced with a screenshot of typed notes from the document creator app. It wasn't notes, however. It was a message addressed to her from Francesca.

She started reading the note but only made it halfway through before the screen timed out, going blank. Frustrated, she tapped the screen and logged into the tablet, going right to the document creator app. The last document created popped on the screen—the message typed in neat paragraphs. The title, at the top of the page, was one word: "Malina." She read the note.

While searching for my brother, Hank, I came across some data that seemed out of the ordinary. Three names out of the many I searched stood out from the others, as they were not placed into a home with an individual or a family. Instead, they were placed with a private entity.

I found this odd because out of the thousands of names in the dataset, these three were the only three placed as such. Moreover, the only private entity I know of that accepts or, rather, takes children from orphanages is the Order of the Coppice. You'll notice in the data, which I've copied to this device for your reference, the Order does not appear at all. The names of children in the data are only of those placed with adopting families and this other private entity. To clarify, the three names I list below were all placed on the same day to this single private entity. This oddity does not occur elsewhere in the dataset.

I give this to you in the hopes that you and Martin may look into it. As the children were placed long ago, I suspect you will not find much. As I must commit myself to my duties as a Member of the Coppice, I cannot pursue this, so I pass it on to you. Whatever you decide to do with this information will be the right decision, of that I am certain.

You'll see, as I did, that the entity is only referred to as Wohlfühlwelt. You'll also see the three children, listed at the time of placement, as Chadwick Rosemont, age two; Geraldine Simms, age seven; and Namir Avrahim, age thirteen.

Your friend,

Francesca

* * *

Martin Aubrey stepped out of the shower and toweled off. He wiped the steam off the mirror and gave his reflection from the waist up a once-over. From the neck down, he looked like he always did, a man in his late thirties in decent shape with subtle hints of the years catching up to him. From the neck up, however, it was a different story. His eyes were bloodshot, with one surrounded by a deep purple bruise. The folds of his ears were caked with blood despite his scrubbing. The pièce de résistance was a gash running along the hairline across his forehead. It had been sutured and glued on the scene. Aubrey had insisted on not going to the hospital, but it still looked rough: deep red on the edges with violent purple-and-yellow bruising still spreading. The wound was the result of one of the blows from Acer "Ambrosia" Sapindales. Aubrey had never been hit with a tree limb before last night. He preferred never to be hit with one again.

Minutes later, after slipping on a T-shirt and jeans, he heard Malina working on her computer in the front room. The woman was a workaholic. After the events of the night before, Aubrey needed a long break, but she was already back at it.

When he entered the kitchen area, she didn't slow down. If anything, she sped up. Her eyes intently scanned the screen on the dining table in front of her, the keyboard clacked loudly as her fingers danced across it frantically. She didn't look up while he crossed to the coffee maker. He pulled down a mug from the cabinet, filled it, and leaned back against the edge of the counter, silently watching Malina blaze away on the computer. By the time his mug was half empty, she hadn't looked up or even noticed he was there. She had the look in her eyes of someone who had doggedly bit into something and refused to let it go.

Draining the last sip of coffee, he dropped the mug into the sink and walked toward his partner. He rested one hand on the back of her chair, the other on the table, and leaned over her shoulder.

"Whatcha got, Malrey?"

"Sit down. You're making me nervous," she said, still focused on the computer.

Aubrey sat down and watched her for a moment longer before pressing her. "I hope you're going to tell me what you're working on because it looks juicy."

At this, she stopped working and reached for her coffee, which she promptly guzzled. She set the cup down on the table, then rested her head in the palms of her hands.

"How do we keep finding this shit?"

Aubrey raised an eyebrow. "What shit have you found?"

She finally looked at him. "Francesca turned me onto it. Something she found in all the names she searched while looking for her brother." Malina took a deep breath and let it out heavily. "The names of three kids who were adopted on the same day twenty years ago by some company called Wohlfühlwelt. I looked it up—or I tried to. There isn't much out there. The only thing I could find was a mention of it in a local newspaper a couple of years before the kids were placed there. That's it. And when I say, 'I looked everywhere,' I looked *everywhere*." She gesticulated with her hands to emphasize her point. "There's nothing out there on Wohlfühlwelt except that article and the name of the company next to these kids in the dataset."

"What does the article say?" Aubrey's interest was genuine. Malina's passion for this fledgling investigation had already rubbed off on him.

She snapped her head to the thin monitor and pointed a finger at a window on the screen showing the newspaper article. "It says it's some kind of wellness center out in the woods near Jernigan, a tiny town in Western Maryland."

Aubrey's brow furrowed. "Why would a wellness center in the middle of nowhere adopt three kids?"

"I don't know, but that's only part of it." Her eyes went wide staring hard at the screen.

"What's the other part of it?"

"The kids they adopted are … gone." Her hand flew up in exasperation. "They're just gone. Again, I've searched everywhere I can think of, and there is no record of their lives after being adopted to Wohlfühlwelt. They're just gone. According to every official and unofficial record I can dig up, there is no evidence of their lives after leaving the orphanage. And after just a few quick searches about the town Jernigan, I found a lot of weird things that have happened out there."

Aubrey pursed his lips. When Malina turned to him

questioningly, he said, "And you think we should check it out?"

"I do."

"Okay," Aubrey said. "Okay, but can we eat breakfast first?"

BEFORE YOU GO

Just a couple of things before you move on.

Martin Aubrey and Malina Maddox are going to continue kicking ass in future thrillers! Stay up to date on new releases by joining Justin's mailing list. Just go to justinrishel.com to sign up.

Also, did you know that reviews are a book's lifeblood? Good reviews, middle-of-the-road reviews, and even bad reviews tell a potential reader whether or not that particular book is meant for them. How many products have you ordered or not ordered based on the number and quality of reviews? Probably a lot and the same goes for me!

Do your fellow readers a favor and leave a review for the books you read. Maybe start with this one? Wherever you like to find and discuss books would be a great place for leaving reviews.

You can leave a review for this book by returning to the book's product page. If you decide to write a few honest words on what you thought about *Hollow Resolve*, you would make this author's day.

About the Author

Justin is an author of thrillers, science fiction, and tech-nothrillers like the Martin Aubrey Series.

Before becoming a writer, Justin was a U.S. Marine, a high school history teacher, a woodworker, and a corporate schmuck. Born and raised in Long Beach, Mississippi, Justin now lives in Tennessee with his wife, three kids, and the family dog.

You can connect with me on:

- https://www.justinrishel.com
- https://www.twitter.com/jrishelauthor
- https://www.facebook.com/justinrishelauthor

Subscribe to my newsletter:

✉ https://mailchi.mp/8683b99bf2e0/rishelreadinggroup-signup